THE ADVENTURES OF
HUGH BARNABY
AND THE PLACE OF SHADOWS

Diane Bevan

The Adventures of Hugh Barnaby
and The Place of Shadows

THE ADVENTURES OF HUGH BARNABY AND THE PLACE OF SHADOWS
Copyright © MMXII by Diane Bevan
Diane Bevan has asserted herself as the author of
THE ADVENTURES OF HUGH BARNABY AND THE PLACE OF SHADOWS, an original work.

© ACASHIC™ INTELLECTUAL CAPITAL PTY LIMITED

Published and distributed by

ACASHIC INTELLECTUAL CAPITAL PTY LIMITED
PO Box 8030, Subiaco East
WA 6008, Australia
+618 9324 4455
mail@acashic.com acashic@gmail.com

Font size — 12pt, Liberation Serif Size — Royal
Editor in Chief: Michael Garcia

Creative Director & Cover Design: Evonne Hew

Production: Acashic Actuality

ISBN 978-1-105-76989-4
90000

9 781105 769894

AUTHOR'S DISCLAIMER

The Authors assert the following in regards to the book ("the Work") and the cover ("the Cover"):

Caution is advised when reading or using the Work. The Authors are not responsible for any damages sustained by the Reader ("the Reader") or User ("the User") of the Work, when reading or using the Work. The Authors shall not be responsible for any aspect that may result in claims of defamation and invasion of privacy. In all instances, and as far as is reasonably possible, the Authors have relied on third party representations and expertise.

It is assumed that a Reader and or User reads books front to back and therefore start at the front owing through the Disclaimer. This means that the Reader and or the User of the Work has entered into a "contract" with the Author that includes that the Reader and or User read and or used the contents and its information in the Work with full knowledge of and agreement with the Disclaimers.

Acting affirmatively or continuing to read and or use the Work is deemed by the Author that the Reader and or User accepts the terms and conditions of the Work and or its Disclaimers. If the Reader and or User of the Work refuse to accede to the terms of any of the Disclaimers contained herein, then it is agreed by the Reader and or User that the Reader and or User shall immediately return the Work. If the Reader and or User do not so act, the Author may argue that a "contract" was formed with the Reader and or User making the Reader and or User bound by the terms of the Disclaimers.

If the Disclaimers are defective in some way, or that the Disclaimers are defectively placed, the use of all Disclaimers will nevertheless in all instances still act as a claim to a defense.

If a claim, action, or proceeding is brought against the Authors, its licensees, or any seller of the Work, based on facts which, if true, would violate any of the warranties or representations in this Agreement, the Authors may defend the same through counsel it chooses and may settle the same in their sole discretion.

Contents

The World Of Tomorrows

Chapter One

There was nothing unusual about the Barnabys Newsagency from the outside at least. Each day seemed to glide into the next with nothing out of the ordinary happening, which was just the way Mr Barnaby liked it – nice and simple. If somebody had told him that his family was being watched from what was supposed to be the empty flat across the street, he would never have believed it. And when later that week a few very strange people came into the shop, he had no idea how his cosy life was about to change.

There were many who had often commented that the Barnaby children were as different as chalk and cheese. When Lucy, their eldest, had taken up singing and dancing classes, Mrs Barnaby had mentioned on several occasions that she wouldn't mind betting that her daughter would choose the stage for a career. 'After all, it runs in my family,' she'd said, and had chosen to ignore her husband's, 'That's pie-in-the-sky stuff, Margie.' Mr Barnaby expected Lucy to have more sense than choose to live out of a suitcase, traipsing from one draughty theatre to another. A secretary would be a good choice or, failing that, something practical at least. But then again, he reckoned their son was a bit of a dreamer as well. Of course he blamed his cousin, Winston, who was an archaeologist for that, filling Hugh's head with all sorts of romantic stories about his adventures to exotic lands. Well, he'd have to put more effort into his studies if he wanted to be an archaeologist.

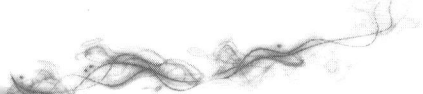

Not that his wife's snooty cousin Agnes would agree – as far as she was concerned, neither Lucy nor Hugh were anything like the Barnabys. 'Well let's face it, Jack, the boy takes after our side of the family,' she constantly reminded him. 'I mean to say, look at his blond curly hair for starters.' Then she'd fixed him with that steely blue-eyed stare of hers before adding, 'I'm sure he'll turn out to be just as intelligent as my darling son, Randall. He was an avid reader from an early age, just like Hugh.' Mr Barnaby had nearly choked on his cup of tea at hearing that. 'Oh?' he'd said, 'Randall liked reading comics and adventure books, did he?' Cousin Agnes had looked as if she was going to burst a blood vessel she was so angry, but managed to come back with, 'Of course, we all know where Lucy gets *her* talent from.' And then her eyes flittered over his black hair. 'And before you say anything, if I remember rightly, way back in the Lilly family there was a Countess who had dark hair.'

Hugh was lingering over making his bed, for the family were expecting a visit from great-aunt Beatrice. He was dreading it. Apart from the fact that she always made a point of tweaking his cheek or planting a sloppy wet kiss on his forehead, she made no bones about the fact that, 'Children should be seen and not heard.' As if she'd know, she'd never had any children. Anyway, the last time great-aunt Beatrice came to visit, she'd accused him of making her trip over and land on the settee. 'You know full well I don't like the soft cushions,' she'd grumbled. Considering he was nowhere near her at the time, he had no idea how she came to that conclusion. Lucy reckoned he willed it to happen when they were laughing about it later. And thinking of his sister, she had been conveniently invited out for the day with her best friend, Pamela and her family, to Windsor Castle and when he'd grumbled about it she'd said, 'I can't help it if it's Pamela's birthday, can I?' and to make matters worse, she said it with a smug grin. Although he hated to admit it, Hugh kind of liked Pamela; so did his friends Jamie and Will, even if she was a bossy-boots like his sister. Still, all girls were bossy as far as he was concerned.

Pamela's parents had bought her a new dress for her birthday and her mother had curled her long blond hair with rags. She had twin

brothers who were four years younger than her and could do no wrong as far as her mother was concerned.

Pamela had recently made up her mind to work in a clothes shop when she left school. Not that her parents would approve, they wanted her to be a school teacher like her cousin, Emily. Maybe she could talk Lucy into working in a clothes shop as well? Then perhaps one day they could buy a shop of their own. Yes, she liked that idea.

Lucy had already decided that she wasn't going to be a secretary, no matter what. She wouldn't mind becoming a hairdresser, and being as her grandparents had owned a ladies and gents hairdressers' before they retired, she knew that they would stick up for her if her father said, 'no'. At least she had an idea of what she wanted to be, unlike her brother. All he could come up with was finding a job one day where he could travel the world. She could see that happening like a hole in the head. Still, as their mother was quick to remind them, a lot could happen before they left school.

Hugh made his way slowly down the stairs to where he could hear the muffled voices of his parents and great-aunt Beatrice behind the living-room door. He stood for a while, his hand on the doorknob, trying to think up an excuse to escape the inevitable.

'Lucy not here did you say?' snapped great-aunt Beatrice. 'I seem to remember the last time I came to visit – she had been invited out somewhere then.'

'Well, it's her friend's birth...' Mrs Barnaby began, but she was cut off by great-aunt Beatrice, who had exploded into one of her tirades about, 'the rudeness of young folk these days.'

'Lucy's doing very well at school, and...'

'I suppose she still goes to dance classes? A sheer waste of time if you ask me, I don't hold with such frivolities. In my day...'

'Hugh was top of the class for reading, and geography,' butted in Mr Barnaby thinking that Hugh seemed to be pulling his socks up of late. He'd actually finished all his homework before Lucy. Wonders would never cease! 'As a matter of fact, he's upstairs,' he quickly added. 'I'll just go and fetch...'

'He is, is he? Well, I certainly hope you've got that boy under control since the last time I laid eyes on him. We can't have the family nonsense rearing its head again, I mean to say...' The ring of the telephone and his mother answering it blotted out most of her words. Hugh could just make out, 'making things happen just by...'

'I think you're exaggerating Aunt Beatrice,' he heard his father bluster.

'*Exaggerating*?' she squeaked. 'I think not! What about the time when you were, about eleven I think it was and...' Hugh heard his mother put the telephone down and mumble about putting the kettle on. He reluctantly opened the door.

'Ah, here you are, Hugh,' a relieved Mr Barnaby said, 'come and say hello to great-aunt Beatrice.'

Hugh entered the room to the strong smell of mothballs. Great-aunt Beatrice turned around and waved her walking stick at him.

'Come, boy,' she barked and he received the usual tweak of the cheek, but no wet kiss, thank goodness.

'Hello Aunt Beatrice. How are you?' That was met with a loud sniff.

'My, how you've grown since the last time I was here,' she remarked twisting him around. 'And looking more like your father every day, except for the hair of course,' she snorted over to Mrs Barnaby who had just returned with a cup of tea and slices of fruit cake. What was that supposed to mean she wondered?

Alone in his room after great-aunt Beatrice had left, Hugh decided that it was too late to call around for his friend, Jamie, so he decided to read his new book instead. Great-aunt Beatrice had met Jamie at a Christmas party once. She had also tweaked his cheek and had commented what a handsome lad he was, 'I was always one for dark hair and brown eyes – shows strength of character,' she'd smiled showing her yellow teeth. Jamie had gone beetroot red and mumbled, 'My great-grandmother was Spanish...I think.' Great-aunt Beatrice had raised an eyebrow at that.

Jamie's father and uncle owned a panel-beating shop called *Smart Brothers Panel & Paint* and they had just branched out into wrecking

cars and selling the spare parts. Jamie had no intention of working for them when he left school. He didn't have a clue what he wanted to be, but it certainly wasn't a panel-beater. His sister was four years older than him and wanted to become a nurse.

Hugh's other friend, Will Marshall, had moved with his family from Brighton when he was three years old. His father was an electrician. He had a little sister and an older brother who had managed to get an apprenticeship in carpentry. His mother worked in the local chemist.

Will had corn-coloured hair and an impish face with a smattering of freckles sprinkled over his nose. Great-aunt Beatrice had eyed him with suspicion, mentioning later that he was too forward for his own good. 'Why, he came straight over to me and shook my hand. What a nerve,' she'd said. 'I'd keep an eye on that one, he's got mischievous eyes.' At least he was spared the cheek-tweaking.

Great-aunt Beatrice was right about Will...in a way. He was always playing jokes and had great delight in ribbing Hugh and Jamie about a couple of girls at school who according to him, were always making eyes at them. 'Don't be daft,' Hugh had scoffed at him. 'And while we're on the subject of girls. What about Sarah Parsons? She likes you.' Will looked very uncomfortable and quickly changed the subject.

They all agreed on one thing though, they enjoyed sport. Hugh was a very fast runner and had been chosen to be in the school running team when going up against other schools. That was considered to be an honour, especially as most of the other runners in the team were older than him. Mr Barnaby was beaming from ear to ear when Hugh came home from school with the news. 'That's my boy,' he'd said. Mrs Barnaby got straight on the telephone and told his grandparents.

Jamie loved and was very good at, football. He had a secret ambition to play for Chelsea when he left school. Not that he could see his father agreeing to it, especially when he'd hinted at it once and had got a, 'You're joking, surely?' from him. 'There's nothing like an apprenticeship. After all, look at Will Marshall's brother, Steve, he's doing very well, and while we're on the subject, what's wrong with panel-beating?' 'Nothing,' Jamie replied. Mr Smart nodded in satisfaction, 'Well, that's settled then.' Jamie wondered what his father

would have said if he'd liked rugby, for he and his uncle often went to watch a game at the local rugby ground.

Will liked playing cricket more than anything else. Mr Marshall was also a keen cricketer in his spare time and was more than happy when Will became his school team's captain. He even promised to take him to Lords Cricket Ground if he brought home a good school report that year. 'I don't want any more, "Will's a good student – when he puts his mind to it." Understood?' he'd warned.

Across the street from the Newsagency, were a few shops and a small Trolleybus terminal. And just along the road from the terminal, there was a small enclosed park everyone called the "Rec". It had a couple of swings, a spider web, a broken-down slide, a see-saw which had one of the coils missing, and a round-about that needed oiling. The boys had since found somewhere else to hang out; an old overgrown orchard just a little way along from the newsagency. There were lots of trees to go scrumping for fruit and nuts, and also two nisson huts which had been used for storing ammunition during the war. Yes, the orchard was far more interesting than the crummy old "Rec".

One Saturday morning when they were collecting blackberries, they heard a, 'Wotcha fink yer doin,' coming from one of the huts. They swung around to see a tall thick-set man dressed in dirty overalls. He had come out of a hut and was now brandishing a lump of wood menacingly at them. A lady was washing clothes in an old iron bathtub. How long had they been living there?

'Go on git goin',' the man growled, 'or I'll clip yer ears fer yer.'

The boys took off as fast as they could only to return the next day on a dare from Will. He was more than curious about them. 'Let's see how far we can get before we're spotted by the squatters,' he'd said.

They'd crept into the orchard, made for the nearest bush to the huts, and hid behind it. There were several people sitting around a fire. A cooking-pot hung over it from three iron poles tied together at the top with wire.

Clothes were thrown over branches – drying. Children dressed in ragged clothes were kicking a small chewed ball about and two scruffy-looking dogs ran after it yelping excitedly.

The man, who had shouted at them the previous day, threw another log onto the fire. His black greasy hair was now slicked back showing a gold earring in his right ear. An elderly lady came out of a hut and shouted something at him in a foreign language. He spat on the ground and followed her inside but not before giving the ball an almighty kick. Horror-of-horrors; it rolled towards the bush where the boys were crouched behind. They were terrified. What should they do? To make matters worse, a little boy came running towards their hiding place followed by a barking dog. Jamie and Will held their breaths as the dog sniffed the ground around them. Would they be discovered? Hugh's eyes were firmly fixed on the ball and it suddenly rolled out of the bush and the dog grabbed it in his jaw to, 'Let go of it, Rufus – now!' from one of the children.

'Let's get out of here while we can,' Jamie had whispered.

Hugh hadn't mentioned anything to Will and Jamie on the way home, but he wondered whether it was him that had made the ball roll away. And then the grumpy face of great-aunt Beatrice popped into his mind. Had he made her trip over as well? He was now almost certain that he had. He didn't know why, but weird things had started to happen to him about a year ago. He'd gone to the school fete with his sister and Pamela. The girls had wandered off leaving him to wait for Jamie and Will by the pond where they had arranged to meet. Nearby, a crowd had gathered around a magician dressed as a clown. He'd thrown a coin into the air and it had miraculously found its way into Hugh's pocket.

'Now, if yer feel into yer pockets, one of yer will find me coin,' the clown had said.

'I've got it,' Hugh had called.

'Keep it, lad, it'll bring yer luck.'

That was fine, until the clown came up to him and stared into his eyes. 'Crikey,' he'd gasped, 'yer him...aren't yer?'

'What do you mean...?' Hugh started to say, but the clown had vanished. Hugh had searched everywhere for him and then decided

that the best bet would be to ask someone if they'd seen where he'd gone. Mrs Lovejoy, who was serving at the bring-and-buy stall, didn't know what he was talking about. 'Ask her ladyship over there,' she'd said, nodding over to the cake stall where a tall lady wearing a large-brimmed sunhat was busy setting out plates of sponges and cakes. He'd made his way over and...'There you are,' Jamie had said. 'We've been looking all over for you.'

'It looks as if Mrs Wiggleworth's cakes haven't improved since last year,' Will had commented, nodding to a plate of cakes that were burnt around the edges and had sunken in the middle.

When Hugh arrived home later that afternoon, he'd gone straight up to his room to look more closely at the coin. To his surprise, it had strange symbols etched on either side and thinking that it was probably foreign, he put it into a tin cash box his father had given him for his collection of stamps and old coins.

Following that, his mother had caught him talking to a little boy who apparently, only he could see. He'd had to think up a good story to explain why he was talking to a brick wall. How many other people could he see that nobody else could? He'd sort of mentioned it to his father once, but he'd got all shifty-eyed on him and changed the subject.

Looking back at those events brought his thoughts back to the squatters again. And then a very loud VROOM ph-phut V-VROOM had him run over to the window and peer out. An open-hooded sports car whizzed around the corner and screeched to a halt outside the Newsagency – steam billowing from the bonnet. Sssssss – BANG.

A red-haired man emerged from the steam, opened the boot and heaved out a container of water which he fed into the radiator. A golden Labrador jumped out and cocked its leg up against a lamppost. The man reached into the small back seat, pulled out a cane and with a loud sigh, leant against the car stroking his waxed moustache. He felt into his pocket, brought out a little gold box, opened it and let out a frustrated, 'Blast!' He then whistled to his dog, marched to the Newsagency, pushed the door open with his cane and entered. The dog trotted behind him sniffing the floor. Hugh turned his attention back to his book but put it down again, wondering why his scalp felt all tingly.

Meanwhile, Mrs Barnaby couldn't get over the cheek of the man bringing a dog into the shop, especially when there was a sign on the door reading "No Dogs Allowed". Well, she would soon see about that, and was about to tell him so when she noticed that the dog was not in the shop as she had first thought, but was sitting just outside the door.

'Good morn to you, Madam,' the man smiled hooking his cane onto the edge of the counter. 'Major Fitzgerald Osletwistle at your service, er – Mrs Barnaby, is it?'

'Yes it is, um…how can I…?'

'You don't mind, Fido, waiting outside the door do you? He won't frighten off your customers or anything?'

Before she had a chance to reply, he asked for an ounce of snuff. He then brought out his wallet and said, 'Sorry, I've only got a ten bob note.'

'That's okay,' said Mrs Barnaby taking the money from him. She went to give him his change and…

'What do you make of that, Jack?' she said, rushing over to the window. 'He's disappeared.'

'He probably zoomed off in that sports car of his,' he replied, not wanting to even think about the fact that he must have done so in a split second. And what about his dog – being in two places at once?He glanced out of the window and noticed the empty water container lying on its side. At least he wasn't completely bonkers.

Hobbies And Things

Chapter Two

It was Saturday morning, and Hugh met his friends outside the cinema for the "Saturday Morning Pictures Club". Lucy had gone off to dance practice and had arranged to meet Pamela later.

The boys paid the entrance fee, found seats near the front, and bought a bag of Maltesers from the usherette.

'Look who's sat behind us,' whispered Jamie to Will, 'your girlfriend.'

'Leave off,' he scowled back at him.

It was at that moment, Sarah Parsons tapped Will on the shoulder and said coyly, 'I didn't know you came to Saturday Morning Pictures.'

What rot, he thought and was about to tell her so when a tug on her hair had Sarah Parsons turn around in her seat and hiss, 'I'll get you later, Jeffrey Smidgen.'

'I'd like to see yer try,' he sneered back. Jeffrey Smidgen went to their school and was always picking fights with people.

'That's enough of that,' snapped the usherette, 'or I'll get yer thrown out.'

More sneers from Jeffrey.

'I'm warnin' yer,' she shouted wagging a finger in his face.

Jeffrey slunk down in his seat. There were sniggers around the cinema.

The lights went out and the *Pathe News* burst onto the screen followed by *The Cisco Kid*. Jamie's attention was on something else though. He nudged Hugh's arm and nodded to his right. At the end of the row, the children from the nisson huts were munching on popcorn. And sat the other side of them, was the man with the slicked-back hair. Feeling eyes on him, the man looked along the row and spotted the boys who were now pressed hard into their seats trying to look inconspicuous. His eyebrows drew together in a ferocious frown and then he leaned forward and smirked at them. The boys decided there and then to sit somewhere else, preferably as far away from him as possible. They stood up, but the usherette, who had an uncanny knack of appearing from nowhere, shone a torch in their faces and ordered them to sit down again. Hugh stole another look along the row of seats but there was no sign of the squatters.

'That's the last time I'll go to the "Laugh and Scratch",' said Will when they were waiting at the bus stop later. 'That man gave me the creeps. Anyway, what's he doing going to Saturday Morning Pictures? It's not for grownups. It's very peculiar if you ask me.'

'We can always go to the Dominion instead,' Hugh suggested thinking his friend was right; it was very, very, peculiar.

'They might turn up there.'

'Or Sarah Parsons,' Jamie nodded knowingly as he nudged Hugh. Will gave him the darkest of looks.

Back at the newsagency, Mrs Barnaby had just said goodbye to a customer, when the door opened and a tall man carrying a briefcase entered. He put it down on the counter and brought out a pencil and notepad. The Barnabys were mesmerized as they watched him stroll over to the card stand and check it for sturdiness. He then ran his fingers up and down the window-frames before putting an ear to the wood.

'You don't think we've got Deathwatch beetle, do you?' whispered Mrs Barnaby.

The man scribbled something in his notepad and continued on his tour of inspection, stopping in front of a wall. He tapped at it several times with a hammer that, according to Mr Barnaby, he'd miraculously

produced from thin air. He was just about to ask him what he thought he was doing, when the man came up to the counter.

'Good day to you sir, my name is Arnold Demdyke, representing the Swift and Artfawl Insurance Company.' He gave Mr Barnaby a cheesy smile. 'Would you be kind enough to tell me if you are satisfied with all your insurance needs?'

Mr Barnaby was taken aback for the minute – if this dodgy bloke thought he was going to change his insurance company to one by that name, he'd got another think coming. And what about his purple streaked hair, all sleeked back and tied with a velvet bow?

'We're quite satisfied with our insurance company, thank you,' was Mr Barnaby's curt reply.

'Point taken, sir, but here's my card in case you change your mind.'

He reluctantly took the business card giving it a cursory glance. 'I can assure you, I'm not…' but with a wave of his hand, the salesman picked up his briefcase, turned abruptly and left the shop.

'That soon got shot of him,' grumbled Mr Barnaby and was about to chuck the card into the waste paper bin, when he noticed that what he at first thought was blue writing, had changed to green. He turned it over to inspect the other side and turned it over again. Well, it certainly looked normal enough, until the card faded before his very eyes. Surely he'd imagined it? Of course he had. The door burst open and in came Lucy and Pamela.

'Dad, could I go with Pamela to ice skating?' a breathless Lucy asked.

'Of course you can...er...why are you looking at me like that?'

'Could you take us, please?'

'My Dad's car needs a new battery,' Pamela explained.

'Okay,' he replied before turning to Mrs Barnaby and saying, 'You'll have to hold the fort, Margie.'

They followed Mr Barnaby out to his car and soon they were on their way to the ice rink. They arrived there in good time and Mr Barnaby said he would return for them in two hours.

They entered the foyer, paid the entry fee and for the hire of the skating boots, and made their way to the rink. While they were tying their laces, Pamela looked up and said, 'isn't that Clara and Priscilla over there?'

Lucy groaned, if it wasn't enough that Clara Dingle lived next door to her, here she was at the ice rink. Unfortunately for the girls, Clara had noticed them as well and before they could make their escape, she came sauntering over to them. Behind her, her friend, Priscilla, was tottering on scuffed boots which were wobbling at the ankles.

'Fancy seeing you here,' Clara all but sneered. 'We belong to the Saturday Club and get to go on the Arosa Rink,' she bragged. 'Do you like my new skating boots?' she said making a point of looking down at their hired ones.

Priscilla tightened her laces again wondering if the lady had given her the wrong sized boots.

'By the way,' said Clara, 'did you know that squatters have moved into those nisson huts?'

'No I didn't,' Lucy replied. So that's where the boys have been disappearing to, she thought.

'Mama says we should keep well away from the likes of them,' snorted Clara.

She bent down and put on her sparkling white skates making it obvious that she had no intention of continuing with the conversation. That was typical of Clara – acting all snooty, just because her father was a bank manager. Meanwhile, Priscilla was trying to decide whether or not to change her boots.

Lucy and Pamela made their escape and stepped onto the ice rink. It was Lucy's third visit and she was beginning to get the hang of it – well, at least now she could stay on her feet. Pamela had been several times and was quite keen to become a member. Her parents had told her that she had to be absolutely sure she'd stick to it before they spent any money on skating gear.

They'd been on the rink for a while and were beginning to feel cold. So they bought some chips and a hot chocolate. Pamela suggested they go and take a peek at Clara and Priscilla.

At the Arosa Rink, skating classes were taking place and it was Clara's first lesson. Of course, Clara had conveniently forgotten to mention that. Priscilla had been going to classes for a while and was a really good skater. She was in the middle of practicing a figure eight followed by a little jump, when Clara went ploughing into her at an alarming speed. They landed on the ice with a resounding thud to screams of,' Why didn't you get out of my way,' from Clara.

'I thought you'd said you'd skated before, Clara Dingle,' barked the teacher. 'You'll have to join Mrs Smith's pre-beginners class over there,' she said pointing to where several girls were standing in a line looking petrified.

Clara clung on to the barrier for all she was worth as she made her way to the other class. Priscilla inwardly groaned, now she would have to put up with her sulking all the way home.

Lucy and Pamela decided to return to the main ice rink before they were spotted. They stepped onto the ice again and Lucy watched as Pamela glided backwards and spun around on one foot. She was thinking that her friend was far better at skating than she'd let on. And then an uneasy feeling come over her, she glanced up and noticed a man with dark slicked-back hair watching her. He wore an earring in his right ear. A little girl tugged at his sleeve and he led her onto the ice rink.

Lucy looked up at the clock and realized that they had ten minutes to return the boots and meet her father in the foyer. Somehow she was really glad that it was time to go.

Strange Folk Aplenty

Chapter Three

Later that afternoon, Mrs Barnaby was busy wiping the counter top, when the shop bell sounded almost as if giving a warning and their next-door neighbour strutted in for her husband's newspaper. 'For the financial section of course,' she constantly reminded them. According to Mr. Barnaby, Mrs Dingle resembled an over-stuffed chicken, poking her long nose into where it didn't belong. As usual, she headed straight for the magazines, picked up several and flicked through all of them from front to back. It's about time that woman bought one, he thought, but then again she'd have to prise open her purse first.

Mrs Dingle waddled over to the counter, stopping to inspect the new stationary which had just been delivered. She gave the price tags the once-over and tutted disapprovingly.

'Goodness me, Mrs Barnaby,' she said making a point of ignoring Mr Barnaby, 'what a dreadful din that ramshackle of a car made the other morning, you'd think the owner would've had it seen to.'

'What car was that, Mrs Dingle?' asked Mr Barnaby.

'The purple sports car, never seen such a gaudy colour. You must've noticed it surely.'

'Oh, that one – the old Alfa – worth a lot of money,' commented Mr Barnaby before he disappeared to the other side of the shop. Mrs Dingle snorted at his back and turned to Mrs Barnaby again.

'And…er…there was the other gentleman who came in later. I was cleaning my windows at the time. Of course, I only noticed him because…well, he did look a bit odd with his purple-streaked hair of all things. Moved into the neighbourhood have they?'

'I really couldn't say, Mrs Dingle,' Mrs Barnaby replied trying to sound disinterested.

'Well, between you me and the gatepost, they're up to no good, no good at all.'

'They seemed harmless enough.'

'You think so do you? I'd keep an eye open if I was you, something very odd is going on, mark my words. And while we're on the subject of strangers, did you know that squatters have moved into those nisson huts? I suppose you're going to tell me they're harmless as well.' And with that parting statement, she marched out of the shop.

Mr Barnaby peeped around the card stand when he heard the door slam. Good, that old sourpuss had gone. He fetched a broom and busied himself sweeping the floor while Mrs Barnaby returned to her cleaning. The bell chimed again.

An elegant lady stepped inside followed by a little tubby man whose eyes darted furtively around the shop as if he was looking for something in particular.

'Good morn…' the lady began.

The opening of a brown paper bag had her looking sharply at her companion as he licked his lips noisily before shoving a jam doughnut into his mouth.

'Good morning,' Mrs Barnaby smiled, 'How can I…?'

The little man burped loudly and wiped his sugary mouth with the back of his hand – a splodge of jam clung precariously to his chin.

'Well, *really*,' snapped the lady, her vivid blue eyes flashing angrily at him. She gave Mrs Barnaby an apologetic smile.

'We were wondering if there was anywhere we could stay for a few days?'

'There's only Mrs. Fairweather's at number six.' Mrs Barnaby offered, 'She does a bit of bed and breakfast from time to time.'

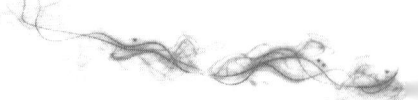

On the other side of the shop, Mr Barnaby had finished sweeping the floor and was busy tidying the magazines that Mrs Dingle had left in disarray, giving him a good opportunity to watch the couple from afar. But curiosity got the better of him, so he came over to the counter trying to appear as casual as he could.

'Will you be staying in the neighbourhood long?' he asked pleasantly.

'As long as our business takes,' the lady replied.

The little man burped again and was about to shove another doughnut into his mouth, when the lady gave his sleeve a sharp tug, 'Come on, Siras, we must be on our way.'

She gave the Barnabys a curt nod and with an abrupt, 'Good day to you,' they hurried out of the shop.

It was then that Mrs Barnaby realized the lady had dropped a small silver box, which she hurriedly picked up. She rushed out after them and peered up and down the street.

'You're never going to believe this, Jack,' she said, dashing back into the shop, 'but they've vanished.'

'What? Like that bloke in the sports car?' he chuckled. 'They probably hopped on a bus.'

Mrs Barnaby decided that there was no sense in arguing with him knowing how stubborn he could be. So she put the box under the counter for safekeeping, should they venture into the shop again.

'I don't know about you,' said Mr Barnaby, 'but I could do with a nice cup of tea and a large slice of chocolate cake.'

Meanwhile, the boys had arrived at Will's house where sandwiches and cakes had been left for them on the kitchen table. Mrs Marshall had taken his sister shopping. They were discussing the squatters when the door opened and Mr Marshall who had over-heard what they were saying, barged into the room.

'Did I hear you call those homeless people: squatters? Think yourselves lucky that you've all got a roof over your heads. And if I find out that you've been over the old orchard annoying them, William Marshall, you'll be grounded for a month.'

'But Dad, we were only...'

'And I'll be having a word with your parents as well,' Mr Marshall snapped at Hugh and Jamie. Satisfied that his message had got home, he about-turned and strode out of the room.

'You don't think your Dad will tell our parents...do you?' asked Jamie.

Will shook his head, 'Nah, he wouldn't do that...at least, I don't think he would.'

'Oh great,' murmured Hugh, knowing he would be in for a right bollocking if his father found out.

On the way home, Hugh was about to walk past the orchard, when an old van turned into the opening and stopped in front of him. His stomach did a dive when he saw who was inside the van – it was the creepy man and the foreign lady. To his astonishment, she wound the window down and said, 'It vill not be long now, zay are comink.'

The man grunted and shoved the van into gear and drove towards a hut without looking his way.

Hugh walked home thinking about what the lady had said. Who were coming? And what did it have to do with him? He decided not to mention anything to his parents, because then he'd have to tell them that he'd been spying on the squatters. He wouldn't mention the squatters to Lucy either. Knowing her and Pamela, they would probably nag him to death about it and want to tag along.

Very early on Monday morning, Mrs. Fairweather came into the Newsagency thanking the Barnabys for sending such a nice couple to her. 'What a lovely blue dress the lady had on. And don't you think the bloke was handsome? I've always liked tall men.'

'Handsome?' queried Mrs Barnaby.

'Ooh yes,' she cooed, 'with his dark hair and those gorgeous green eyes of his, and I reckon his suit would've set him back a tidy penny, don't you?'

Mrs Barnaby was stunned. She had thought the man very odd and certainly not tall and handsome...or was he? However, Mr Barnaby was beginning to think there was something very wrong with his eyesight.

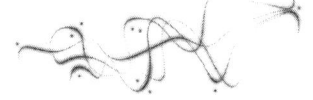

'And apart from that,' said Mrs Fairweather breaking into his thoughts, 'they paid a week in advance.'

'Unlike some people we have to deal with,' murmured Mr Barnaby as Mrs Dingle came to mind.

'Well, must go,' said Mrs Fairweather, and she dashed across the road to the greengrocers.

Mr Barnaby stood looking out of the window wondering about the strange people who had suddenly appeared in the neighbourhood. He felt very uneasy all of a sudden. He didn't have time to dwell on it though, because the shrill ring of the telephone had him run into the living-room to answer it.

It wasn't long before the shop door opened again, and an elderly lady walked in carrying a basket of pegs, lace, and bunches of heather.

'Vill you be kind enough to buy somezink from an old lady?' she said plonking the basket on the counter.

Feeling uncomfortable under the lady's gaze, Mrs Barnaby chose a bunch of heather. After all, she didn't want bad luck to befall her, did she?

'Would you also like to buy zee pegs, or what about zee lace?' she asked.

Mrs Barnaby found herself looking into the lady's large hypnotic eyes and before she knew it, she'd opened her purse again.

'I'll have the pegs and perhaps a lace handkerchief for my mother.'

'A vise choice,' nodded the lady as she handed over a bundle of pegs and a handkerchief.

For some reason, Mrs Barnaby's hand was shaking as she took the items from her. The old lady picked up her basket, nodded to Mrs Barnaby, and was just about to open the door, when Mr Barnaby came back into the shop. She turned and said, 'Take care of zee family,' and then she walked out.

Mr Barnaby stared after her in surprise. 'What was that about?'

'I don't know,' Mrs Barnaby replied. 'She must be one of the squatters.'

'Don't tell me you bought those pegs from her! And what's this you've bought?' he said picking up the bunch of heather. 'Afraid she'd put a curse on you?'

The door opened again and in walked Maud Underwood who owned the Inn not far from the Newsagency.

'Mornin' folks, I been burstin' to tell yer about these odd lookin' people that came into the pub last night.' She glanced around the shop. 'Mrs D's not hiding behind the magazine stand is she?'

Mr Barnaby grinned broadly until she launched into a description of the same couple who were staying at Mrs Fairweathers' place.

'I thought to meself, what's the likes of her doin' wiv a bloke like that? Right peculiar he was.'

'There's no accounting for taste,' commented Mrs Barnaby, who was getting more bemused by the minute.

'But wasn't he tall, dark, and handsome?' asked Mr Barnaby thinking back to Mrs Fairweather's description of him.

Maud shook her head, 'He was very short and to tell the truth, a bit uncouth.'

Now the Barnabys were more confused than ever. That's the very same man they remembered.

'But the strange thing is, they were askin' about Hugh.'

Mr Barnaby looked at Maud sharply. 'I hope you didn't give them any information.'

'Oh no, Mr Barnaby, mum's the word,' she replied, tapping the side of her nose.

'Well, he should know better than to talk to strangers,' thinking that a strong word to his son was in order.

'But that's not all.'

'What do you mean?'

'When I went to point them out to one of me customers, they... you're never going to believe this...but they faded away before me very eyes.'

Mr Barnaby was rapidly coming to the conclusion that they'd all landed on Mars. Surely Maud was mistaken. 'Are you sure?' he asked.

'That's exactly what me hubby said. But I know what I saw, Mr Barnaby.'

Mrs Barnaby threw her husband a smug look. 'So much for you saying they'd hopped on a bus, Jack.' And then the reality hit her like a ton of bricks – oh dear, what did it mean?

'Anyway, I've chatted long enough,' said Maud looking at her watch. 'Why don't yer drop in fer a drink some time? Have one on the house. Bye fer now.'

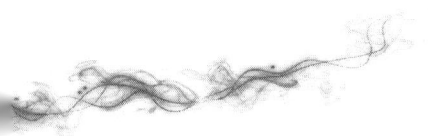

A Trick Of The Eye

Chapter Four

Mr Drummond had just reached the Newsagency and was about to open the door, when Maud Underwood came rushing out, 'Sorry, can't stop,' she said tugging at her tight red dress that had risen well above her knees, 'in a hurry.'

In Mr Drummond's opinion, Maud Underwood was trying unsuccessfully, to look younger than her years. He watched as she struggled to walk up the street on her stiletto heels. Why women chose to wear those ridiculous shoes he'd never know. Thank goodness the wife had more sense. He straightened his tie, entered the shop and marched up to the counter.

'I'll have the usual if you please. How are you both today?'

'Very well thank…'

'I'm convinced this hot weather plays tricks on one's mind,' he said, wiping the beads of sweat from his top lip.

'Why do you say that?' asked Mrs Barnaby.

'Well, there was this man…ah…ah…atishoo! Sorry, a touch of the old hay fever,' he sniffed, wiping his eyes. 'Now where was I?'

'About that man…'

'Ah yes,' a mop of the brow, 'he was standing by the kerb when out of the blue, an old stagecoach – you know, like they have in those ghastly Cowboy films with horses and reins and things…well…it drew up beside him.'

'What happened next?' gasped Mrs Barnaby ignoring her husband's snort of disbelief.

'He was about to open the carriage door, when a blue mist came swirling around him. But when I asked a passer-by what she thought about it, the lady looked at me as if I was batty.'

Oh really? You could've fooled me, thought Mr Barnaby.

'Why?' asked Mrs Barnaby.

'No sign of the mist at all.'

'Good grief.'

'But that wasn't the last of it. There was no stagecoach either, only a taxi he was climbing into.' He dabbed at his cheeks. 'I tell you, I'll be glad when this heatwave is over, especially as the lawn's got brown patches all over it. Not that I'm much of a gardener – leave all that nonsense to the green thumbs of this world.'

'We've had some strange goings on in here as well,' said Mrs Barnaby.

'Have you?' queried Mr Drummond leaning closer, so close in fact, that Mrs Barnaby could see the veins on his nose.

'It was only a salesman who overstayed his welcome,' Mr Barnaby quickly added.

'Must go,' said Mr Drummond who had suddenly lost interest in the conversation, 'I've chores to do for the wife.'

He went to hurry out of the shop, but turned around as if he'd remembered something important.

'Before I forget, I was passing by that old empty cottage opposite the Heath.'

'You mean the one next to the shop that's boarded up?'

'That's right – there was a foreign-looking chap walking around it writing things into a folder.'

'Perhaps it's up for sale,' commented Mr Barnaby.

'And about time too, I say.'

'Well, maybe whoever buys it will renovate it.'

'Hmm, as long as it's in keeping with the neighbourhood, I mean to say, we don't want any old job done on it do we? Oh, look at the time, the missus will give me a right ol' nagging when I get home.' And he rushed out the door.

'I can't imagine Mrs Drummond laying the law down, can you, Jack?'

Mr Barnaby raised his eyebrows at that.

The Rumble Of Wheels

Chapter Five

Jamie was on his way to call around for Hugh, when four large trucks carrying fairground equipment rumbled past him on the way to the Heath. He was so busy looking at them that he nearly collided with Mr Drummond who had just come out of the newsagency.

'Did you know it's nearly half past eight, Jamie?' he frowned. 'Shouldn't you be at school, boy?' and he marched towards his car without waiting for a reply.

Silly old coot, thought Jamie, we don't all get up at the crack of dawn.

The door opened again and Hugh came hurrying out to, 'It's about time you got yourself more organized in the mornings,' called Mr Barnaby from the shop doorway. 'That boy worries me,' he grumbled closing the door behind him.

It looks like the fair has arrived at last,' said Jamie.

'That reminds me, the other day I saw that foreign squatter-lady and get this; she told me someone was coming.'

'Why didn't you tell me before?'

'I forgot, anyway, what do you make of it?'

'Did she tell you who was coming?'

'That's the thing, she didn't.'

'How weird,' said Jamie, 'do you think she meant the fair?'

'But why would she tell me?'

Jamie shrugged, 'Who knows. C'mon we'd better hurry or we'll be late for school.'

They stood at the curb waiting for a lull in the traffic when a dog shot out from a garden in front of an oncoming car. Hugh stared in horror as the car was about to smash into the dog. For a split second it was as if time stood still, and the dog was suddenly plucked from the road by an invisible force. The car screeched to a halt, but the dog had vanished. The driver cursed and drove off.

'D-did you s-see that?' Jamie blustered.

'What?'

'Th-that dog – it sort of, was z-zapped from the road.'

'Don't talk rot,' scoffed Hugh. 'How could that happen?'

'It did,' Jamie insisted. 'I saw it.'

'Maybe you thought you saw it,' said Hugh. Jeepers, how *had* he saved the dog from being hit by the car? And how could he explain it to Jamie, when he didn't understand it himself?

'I saw it happen, I know I did.'

'Well, I didn't. And I wouldn't be telling anybody, they'll think you're loopy.'

On the way home from school that afternoon, Hugh and Jamie passed by the orchard but it looked deserted. They decided to creep up to the huts to see if anybody was about. They crouched down and made their way to the first hut and peered inside. The hut was empty, except for a couple of broken chairs. They stole a look inside the other one. That didn't look as if anybody had lived in it at all, which was strange because that was the hut that the old lady came out of.

'They didn't stay long, did they,' said Hugh after they'd come to the conclusion that they'd made a mistake about the other hut.

'Perhaps the Council found them a place to live.' And they walked away already talking about the weekend.

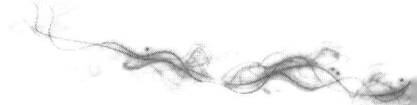

O n Saturday afternoon, Hugh and Lucy met up with their friends at the fair. There were already crowds of people about. They decided to go on the Ferris wheel because the queue wasn't as long as the others. When they handed the money to the attendant, his face lit up in surprise.

'Hello there, I remember yer from last year. I'm Charlie.'

'If it ain't the Barnyards and their stuck up mates,' said a voice from behind.

They turned around and came face to face with Jeffrey Smidgen and his friend, Godfrey Twigg, who were about to push their way to the front of the queue.

'Come on, lads, fair's fair,' said a man who stepped out in front of them barring the way. Godfrey's eyes were now fixed on the man's tattooed arms and bulging muscles. No way was he going to argue with the likes of him – neither was Jeffrey.

'We don't wanna go on yer crummy ol' ride anyway,' Jeffrey sneered. 'C'mon, Godfrey, let's go.'

'That soon got rid of them,' said Lucy to Pamela as they climbed into their seat.

The boys climbed into the carriage behind. As soon as the carriages were full, the music blared and the Ferris wheel started to move. The carriage, which the boys were sitting in, reached the top and they could just about make out the airport in the distance. Overhead, a raven circled. Round and round it flew. For some reason Hugh shivered, until he looked down at the people below. Wasn't that the squatter man? At the same time Will noticed him as well – he was standing by the swing boats.

'What are you looking at?' asked Jamie following his gaze. 'Jeepers, is that who I think it is?'

'Yeah, it looks like it.'

'But I thought they'd gone.'

'We'll check the man out when we get off,' said Hugh. 'He might be someone else.'

T he ride came to an end and one by one the carriages came to a halt and they climbed down. They couldn't see the man anywhere, much to their relief.

'What did you find so interesting?' asked Pamela.

'Nothing,' said Will, whose eyes she noticed, were shifting from side-to-side.

'Come on, tell us.'

'There's nothing to tell.'

'Look over there,' said Jamie quickly,' isn't that Nick Farrington?'

'Yeah, see ya girls,' said Hugh and the boys rushed away.

'They're up to something,' said Lucy. 'And I wonder why they never mentioned about the squatters – it's very suspicious if you ask me.'

Spying

Chapter Six

The the fair had been in town for almost two weeks, and Charlie and his sister, Rosa, had visited the newsagency nearly every day to buy a newspaper for their father. Hugh and Lucy had bumped into them a few times on their way home from school, and they'd walked along the road together. They found the gypsies easy to get along with and it didn't take long before they became friends. Mrs Barnaby had suggested to Lucy that they invite them for afternoon tea with their other friends. And so after school that Friday afternoon, Charlie and Rosa arrived at the newsagency. Mrs Barnaby took them through to the garden where Hugh and Lucy were laying the table. Soon they were joined by Jamie, Will, and Pamela.

Meanwhile, Mrs Dingle had just arrived home after gossiping with Mrs. Dotty who lived across the road from her. Mr Barnaby considered her to be almost as insufferable as his neighbour, if that was at all possible.

'Well, Cedric,' she said, 'as I was just saying to, Mildred, we've just got shot of those squatters, and now we have to put up with that ghastly fair. And if that wasn't enough to contend with, I've seen the Barnaby children walking along the road with the gypsies on more than one occasion.'

She glanced across at her husband expecting a reply, only to find him slumped in his old comfy armchair, mouth open, fast asleep – a newspaper draped over his lap. As if on cue a funny sound escaped his lips, somewhere between a pig snorting and a frog croaking. The newspaper slid to the floor.

'Oh...I'd get more sense out of a brick wall,' she snapped plumping up cushions on the settee, ' and why Cedric doesn't do something about that wind problem of his, it's disgusting,' she grumbled as the door burst open and in came a breathless Clara.

'Mama, did you know those gypsies are in next-door's garden?'

'What?' she gasped glaring over at her husband as if he was to blame. 'I'll be having a word with the Barnabys about that,' she spat. 'Not that I approve of spying on people.'

'I didn't *spy*, Mama, I heard them...you know...whispering.'

From his armchair, Mr Dingle had been listening to his wife's grumbles and now his daughter had got in on the act. Not approve of spying on people? What a load of hogwash! Gertrude spent most of her time sitting at the window stuffing her face with chocolate biscuits. What she finds so interesting, he'd never know. Better to keep his eyes well and truly closed, though. After all, he could never get a word in edgeways anyway. And if he did, he was usually wrong.

'Be that as it may, Clara, I don't want you going anywhere near those gypsy vagabonds and that includes hanging around that dreadful fair.'

'As if I would, Mama,' she replied having already made arrangements to go to the fair with Priscilla.

'Is that a new dress you've on, Mama?'

'This?' she asked, smiling at the compliment. 'It's just a little something I bought at the sales simply *ages* ago,' and she cast a sideways glance at her husband.

'It really suits you. Oh...um...Priscilla has asked me to go out with her tomorrow. Can I?'

'I did want you to do some shopping for me but – oh alright, after you've made your bed and tidied your room.'

The following day, Hugh and his friends had just come out of the fish and chip shop when they spied two girls walking towards them. One of them had squeezed her short dumpy body into a bright pink full-skirted dress puffed out by layers of brightly coloured net petticoats. A wide plastic belt had been pulled in at the waist as tight as the bulging flesh would allow it. Her dull brown hair was sticking out all over the place after a failed attempt at curling it. Podgy legs with dimpled knees were wobbling on her mother's red shoes that she'd smuggled out of the house. Were they handkerchiefs she'd stuffed around her ankles? How gross is that?

The auburn haired girl, who towered over her friend, was wearing a blue dress with a hooped skirt that billowed from her waist like an umbrella. On her feet she wore her prized possession – yellow shoes she'd bought from *Twinkle Toes*, a new shop that had just opened in town.

'Sorry luv, I've only one pair left and they're a half-size smaller,' the assistant had told her. Priscilla wanted the shoes more than anything in the world so she bought them anyway. So now, being forced to walk pigeon-toed, the shoes hurting like mad, she'd wished she'd worn her old white sandals. To make matters worse, look who was walking towards them.

'Well, if it isn't snooty, Clara, and prissy, Priscilla.'

'You don't have to be so rude, Jamie full-of-it, and you pronounce my name, Clahra, not Clairer,' she snapped, looking down her long nose and flaring large nostrils at him.

'Ooh, pardon me for speaking,' he smirked. 'Going to the fair, are you?'

'I would think that was painfully obvious, if you had half a brain.' That said, the girls pushed past them and raced on ahead.

'Remind me to ignore them in future,' mumbled Jamie.

The girls arrived at the fairground and made straight for the ghost train. The boys had intended to go on it as well until they saw Clara and Priscilla paying the attendant, so they decided to go on the bumper cars instead.

The girls climbed into the first carriage and strapped themselves in. 'Ouch!' Clara cried out when she felt a nudge in her back. She turned around and glared at the boy who was had just sat down with his girlfriend.

'Sorry,' he said, not sounding sorry at all. His girlfriend pushed her glasses up her nose and giggled as the train clunked forward and slowly began its journey.

The girls promptly closed their eyes, screaming as the train pushed its way through the swing doors. The cool air that greeted them was in complete contrast to the warm day outside. They opened their eyes and peered into the misty darkness as the train sped them further into its ghostly domain. Then suddenly out of the blackness, the walls became alive with images of skeletons, leering faces, and elf-like creatures. The girls clung to each other in fear. Did something soft and clammy touch them?

They journeyed further into the darkness, crashing through doors to icy corridors as they made their way to a large opening where they came to an abrupt halt. The train suddenly lurched forward and continued on its journey into the unknown, only this time it appeared to be climbing. Up and up it went and then went full speed downhill, splashing through water to the screams of the passengers.

They zoomed around corners and through tunnels where bats fluttered their wings as they sped by. The train crashed through yet another door where a massive cobweb and a giant spider with glowing eyes greeted them. Squeals and nervous laughter followed.

Clara gasped out loud when she felt something pull at her hair and, thinking that it was the boy who was sat behind her, she swung round ready to give him an earful.

'Do you mi…' she started to say, but instead of the boy and his girlfriend, a skeleton was sitting in the carriage with its head turned towards her.

'Priscilla,' squeaked Clara, 'l-look…'

But Priscilla was too busy pointing at a hideous green face that was floating towards them.

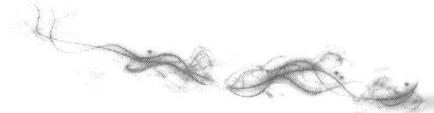

Loud screams from behind had Clara sneak a peak over her shoulder again. To her relief, the girl was clinging onto the boy's arm; her spectacles were now dangling off one ear.

'Clara,' called a voice.

'What do you want, Priscilla?'

'I don't want anything, why?'

'You just called my name.'

'I didn't.'

'Yes you did, you're trying to mess with my head.'

'I'M NOT,' shrieked Priscilla.

'Co-o-o-e-e-e Cla-a-a-r-a,' echoed the voice.

Clara's eyes darted frantically in every direction – there was nothing but the misty darkness. The voice called her name again, but this time with more urgency. She heard a fluttering sound overhead, and looked up to find an old hag flying about on a broomstick, hovering just above them as the train twisted its way down the track.

The witch threw her head back and cackled excitedly, spinning around and around, flying back and forth, back and forth.

'Welcome to my parlour,' she cackled and zoomed away.

'THAT WAS CLEVER,' yelled Clara to Priscilla over the rumble of the track as the train went crashing through the last door into the sunlight.

'What was?'

'You know, when the witch spoke to me.'

'What are you talking about?'

'I could've sworn that…oh, it doesn't matter.'

The train pulled up at the platform and they climbed out. They both agreed that it was the scariest ghost train they had ever been on.

'But it would've been better if we hadn't been by ourselves,' said Priscilla.

Clara felt her blood turn to ice. What did she say? What about the boy and girl who were sitting just behind them? And surely she had heard the screams of the other passengers? She glanced back at the empty carriages thinking that she'd give up on reading ghost stories in future.

'Let's go to the palm reader,' suggested Priscilla.

Clara gave her friend a frosty look. 'I don't want to have anything to do with common gypsy fortune-tellers.' In fact, she'd had enough of spooky things for a lifetime. And if Priscilla even so much as mentioned the word: ghost train, she'd never speak to her again...ever!

They headed for the candyfloss stall instead and were surprised to find Hugh and his friends waiting in line.

'Look who's joined the queue,' whispered Jamie.

Hugh turned around and locked eyes with Priscilla, who stood and stared back at him with her mouth open. She tried to look away but it was as if he had cast a spell on her.

'What are you looking so gormless about,' said Clara.

'Hugh's looking at me all funny, and he's wearing a black cloak.'

'What cloak? And he's not even looking this way.'

'But he definitely…'

'Oh, don't be ridiculous,' snapped Clara, and yanked Priscilla away without so much as a backward glance.

'Blimey, they soon took off in a hurry,' said Will.

Jamie looked at his watch and said his grandparents were expecting him, so he'd better be on his way.

When Hugh arrived home, he poured himself a glass of lemonade and sat down wondering why he felt as if something horrible was about to happen. And why did he get these feelings in the first place? It was a mystery to him. If only he'd been able to hear what great-aunt Beatrice was saying when she'd last visited. It was bad luck that the telephone rang when it did. The little he did hear made him wonder about his father's family. Did they have a dark secret? If so, what could it be?

Mr. Barnaby had never told his children about the: family peculiarity, as great-aunt Beatrice had called it. 'Delving into the unknown and talking to goodness knows who. What will people think?' she'd complained. He'd shrugged it off as ridiculous and just something that one of his relatives had drummed up to make an ordinary family seem more interesting. He didn't want to even consider the fact that it could be true even if a few strange things had happened to him. He'd so

far managed to avoid any more awkward questions from Hugh, and in any case, what would he tell him? Some things are best left alone.

Later that evening, Mrs Barnaby suggested that they take up Maud Underwood's invitation and go for a drink. Mr Barnaby readily agreed, for it was quite a while since they'd had an evening out together and, he had to admit, it was long overdue. The door was locked behind them and they made their way to the Jolly Bodger Inn with the intention that they would only be gone for an hour. They were totally unaware of peering eyes behind a net curtain.

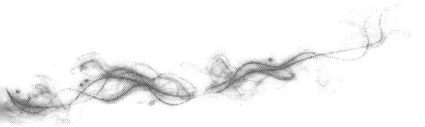

The Inn Of Intrigue

Chapter Seven

The Barnabys entered the busy Inn and managed to find a corner table with a good view of the entrance. Mrs Barnaby liked the Jolly Bodger with its low-slung ceilings and oak beams – it was cosy. She especially liked the fireplace decorated with copper pots, horseshoes and a brass bedpan.

Mr Barnaby went over to the bar, ducking to avoid a beam, and was warmly greeted by Maud Underwood.

'This is a surprise, what'll yer both have?'

'A pint of the best, and a sweet sherry for the wife please, Maud.' To say that he felt a little put out was an understatement. He reminded her that she had invited them over for a drink.

'Did I?'

'Don't you remember rushing into the shop? You know, to tell us about the strange people you'd served?'

'Oh dear, I can't say as I do.'

Mr. Barnaby was shocked. Had he dreamt it? He decided that he must have, at least he hoped so. He thanked her and carried the drinks over to Mrs Barnaby.

'You look as if you've lost a shilling and found a sixpence, Jack.'

Lost a shilling, he thought. I think I've lost more than that – my marbles!

'It's just that – oh…let's just enjoy the evening eh, luv?'Mrs Barnaby took a sip of her sweet sherry. He picked up his pint.

They were on their second round of drinks when the Drummonds entered the Inn. Mr Barnaby nudged his wife, nodding over in the direction of the newcomers. Unfortunately for them, they had been spotted and, having first bought their drinks and a packet of crisps, Mr Drummond made straight for their table. His wife hovered in the background.

'Good evening, mind if we join you?' he said, plonking himself next to Mr Barnaby before he had a chance to reply. Bang goes their quiet evening together, he was thinking. Mrs Drummond hung back until Mrs Barnaby patted the chair beside her. She cautiously sat down on the edge of the seat, as if ready to make a bolt for the door.

'We don't often see you in here,' boomed Mr Drummond. 'A special occasion, is it?'

'Well, not really, you see…'

'We come here quite a lot; it does one good to mix with the locals,' butted in Mr. Drummond. 'And, of course, the wife likes to dress up in her Sunday best,' he beamed.

Mr Barnaby's eyes flicked over her dowdy clothes and then to Mr Drummond's new blazer, complete with shiny gold buttons. Mrs Drummond took a nervous sip of her shandy.

'Mr. Drummond, when you …'

'Don't need to be so formal, old chap. We're not in your place of work now. Call me Berty, that's short for Bertrand, you know,' he winked. 'And call my better half, Gladys,' he nodded across to his wife who shifted in her seat.

Mr Barnaby smiled at Gladys Drummond who shoved a handful of crisps into her mouth. Crrr – unch!

'Mr – er – Berty, do you remember when you came into the shop and told us…?'

'You mean about the cottage?'

'No, you were telling…'

Crackle, crackle – Gladys Drummond had finished the last of her crisps and was now screwing the packet into a tight ball. Mr Drummond

gave her a withering look, and then a man sitting at the bar wearing a brown hat tilted to one side, caught his attention. Now, where had he seen him before? It wasn't in the Inn. Where was it? And what was it he had draped over the stool beside him? It was then that he remembered. Good heavens, wasn't he the chap he'd seen the other morning? He leant forward trying to make out if he was.

The man sat nursing a drink and munching on peanuts whilst chatting to Maud Underwood who was busy pulling pints. He suddenly looked at his watch, stood up and brushed peanut crumbs from his trousers.Mr Drummond took a large gulp of his brandy and dry, his eyes watering as the fiery liquid travelled down to his stomach. Golly, he wasn't the same chap at all. And what he at first thought was a purple cloak, turned out to be none other than a jacket, which the man put on before he went out the door.

Moments later, an old man came shuffling in carrying a large carrier bag. He was wearing a long black cloak over a dark green tunic, and on his feet he wore roped sandals. He looked around the Inn and then made for a table near the door, slowly eased his body onto a chair and sighed. He then took off his floppy blue hat to reveal silvery-white hair that, according to Mr Drummond, seemed to grow from short to long in the blink of an eye. And if that wasn't enough, a monocle with a white cord attached floated through the air and landed on his right eye.

Mr Drummond felt his mouth dry up. It has to be the inferior brandy he reasoned. It's far too strong – must make sure the publican's wife gave him the best stuff in future. With a shaky hand, he poured the rest of the dry ginger into his glass. That should do the trick. And then he saw something that made his hand shake even more – the old man clicked his fingers and a silver goblet appeared on the table in front of him.

'Well I be damned,' he blustered, and was about to point him out, when the man faded from view.

'What's wrong?' asked Mr Barnaby of the white face and wild eyes that stared back at him.

'What? Oh, er…nothing. A touch of indigestion,' he belched rubbing his chest.It's those juicy pork chops the wife gave him for dinner, he thought, too much fat often made his eyes play tricks on him.

After all, look what happened the other day? And then he turned his attention back to Mr Barnaby, deciding that he'd stick to lamb chops in future.

'Now about the cottage, it's about time someone bought it, a disgrace to the neighbourhood. And that brings me to…' And on and on he went.

Mr. Barnaby sat back in his chair and decided that the best bet would be to forget all about trying to make sense of anything. He glanced at Mrs Barnaby who was trying her hardest not to look bored, and then to Gladys Drummond, who was clutching her handbag close to her chest, staring into space. It was time to make their escape.

'Sorry to butt in, Mr. Drum…sorry, Berty, but time is marching on and we don't like leaving the kids too long on their own. It's been nice, must do it again some time…' and was amused to see the look of horror on his wife's face.

'Your kids, did you say? I'd forgotten about them. Well, of course, we decided against having any children didn't we, Gladys? Far too dangerous for youngsters when we lived in Africa – all those wild animals about, and that leads me to another…'

'We'll be seeing you then.'

The Barnabys hurriedly left the Inn before Mr Drummond could launch into another drawn-out story. They made their way home, glad to have had a change of scenery albeit not exactly what they had in mind. They didn't notice the raven circling overhead.

Mirrors Aplenty

Chapter Eight

The following Saturday proved to be bright and sunny, and the Barnabys had mysteriously forgotten all about the chain of events of the past few of weeks.

Hugh hurried to the fairground where he had arranged to meet his friends by the Hall of Mirrors.

'About time you showed up,' said a grumpy, Will.

'I had to run an errand for my Dad,' Hugh explained.

They paid the entry fee and went inside. After trying several mirrors without any luck, they were about to call it quits when Jamie touched one and it sprang open.

'At last,' he said.

They set off on their mission, but somehow Hugh got separated from them and the mirror slammed shut. No matter how hard he tried, it wouldn't budge. What should he do now? Go out the way they came in? But where was the opening? He was so engrossed in trying out every mirror that he had no idea he had company. A man and lady had entered.

'We're looking for our little girl and boy,' said the lady looking upset.

'They didn't happen to come in here?' asked the man hopefully.

Hugh shook his head. 'Not as far as I know.'

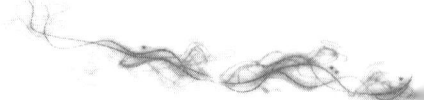

'This is *too* much, George,' grumbled the lady. 'Why you let them out of your sight, I'll never know.'

'I didn't, Peggy,' he protested.

'Well, come on, we'll have to go and look for them,' she snapped,' we don't want them to panic.'

It was at that moment the children came bursting in.

'Where have you been?'

The little girl pulled a face as if she was about to cry. 'S-sorry, Mummy, b-but we lost you in the crowd.'

The lady bent down and stroked her cheek. 'Never mind, you're here now. Let's see if we can find our way out of here, shall we? It'll be fun.'

The man grabbed hold of the little boy's hand to screams of protest. 'I'm not letting go of you, Johnnie, so you can pack that noise up,' he growled.

'I wan' ice cweam,' he wailed.

'As soon as we get out of here you can have your ice cream, so behave yourself.' And all Hugh could hear was, 'I don' wan' ice cweam, I wan' chips,' as they stepped out of sight.

'This is the way, young man,' said the lady, pointing to a mirror.

'Where are you, Hugh?' called Jamie.

'Coming,' he called back and rushed to follow the family. But when he reached the mirror, he reeled in shock to find a dark cobbled street awaited him. Gas lamps had cast eerie shadows of cloaked figures walking along the dimly lit pavement – but there were no people. Suddenly, a horse-drawn carriage appeared out of the darkness. It stopped in front of a rickety building. A coach driver stepped down and opened the carriage door. The family stepped out of the shadows, climbed aboard and the carriage took off.

'What's keeping you?' said Jamie who was now standing beside him.

Hugh's heart lurched. 'Sorry, but my shoe had come undone.'

Should he tell Jamie about the strange mirror and the vanishing family? He decided against it, Jamie would think he was nuts.

A mirror opened and Will peeped around it. 'C'mon,' he said impatiently.

They followed Will and he led them on a wild goose chase looking for the way out. It didn't matter which way they headed, they always arrived at dead ends, and every time they retraced their steps, the glass corridors seemed to grow longer and longer.

'I don't know about you,' said Will, 'but I'm sure there are more mirrors than before.'

'It's probably just seems that way,' Jamie answered looking round about him.

'At this rate, it'll be dinner-time before we make it outside.'

'More like bedtime,' muttered Hugh.

They retraced their steps once more and finally a mirror opened to the outside.

'That's the weirdest Hall of Mirrors I've ever been in,' said Jamie.

You don't know the half of it, thought Hugh, but all he said was, 'I'm thirsty. Let's buy a drink.'

They weaved their way around the stalls and bumped into Charlie who was on his way to the shooting range. Hugh thought it was a good opportunity to invite him and his sister, Rosa, to his birthday party the following week. Charlie had some good news for them too. His family had decided to stay put for a while and he and Rosa would be attending their school until the end of summer term. He explained that they would be staying at the Travellers yard not far from the Heath, where they often rested up for weeks at a time.

'Oh, oh, it looks like Nobby's waving to me,' said Charlie, 'I'll see yer later.' And he rushed off.

The boys decided to go to the dodgem cars, but Hugh had other things on his mind.

'You go on ahead, I just want to ask Charlie about something,' and he ran to catch up with him.

Jamie was instantly suspicious, 'I wonder what Hugh's up to,' he said.

Will shrugged, 'Search me, c'mon lets go to the dodgems.'

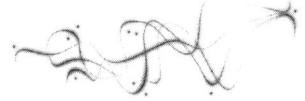

'Could I ask you something, Charlie?'

Charlie spun around in surprise. 'Sure, what's up?'

By the time Hugh had finished with his story, all Charlie could do was stare in amazement.

'What do you think?' Hugh asked.

'Well, I...'

''urry up, Charlie,' called Nobby impatiently. 'I ain't got all day.'

'Sorry, Hugh, I'd better go.'

Sinister eyes watched Hugh as he made his way to the dodgem cars.

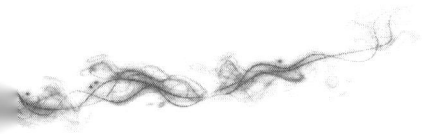

Rumours

Chapter Nine

The school was abuzz with the news that Romanies were going to attend until the end of term. Mrs Pertwee had let it be known that the students were under no circumstances whatsoever, to call the newcomers "gypsies". A hushed silence fell over the Assembly Hall as a tall, stern-looking woman stepped on to the stage.

'Good morning, students.'

'Good morning, Mrs Pertwee,' the students chorused.

'Charles and Rosa Romanski will be attending our happy school until the summer holidays. I want you to make them welcome, as I am sure I can rely upon you all to do so.'

The Headmistress glared around the hall, daring them to defy her wishes. She nodded over to the music teacher who was sitting hands poised above the piano, ready to begin playing the first hymn. As usual, Mrs Grimshaw, the Arts teacher, could be heard over everyone else, which made the students giggle as she constantly got the words wrong and never sang in tune.

After assembly was finished, the students made their way to their temporary classrooms, for the original buildings had been badly damaged during the war. Unfortunately, the restorations were still on the drawing board mainly because the re-building of houses was on top

of the Council's list. Many of the teachers were beginning to think that they would be, "stuck in those dreadful prefabs forever and a day."

In the meantime, Mrs Pertwee, having been given the unwelcome task of being in charge of both the Junior and Senior High schools, was finding it increasingly difficult to keep tabs on everything. And much to the teachers' disgust, she was constantly calling staff meetings over what they considered to be, absolutely nothing. To add insult to injury, pictures of birds had replaced classroom numbers. 'Just to add a little brightness in these difficult times,' she'd said.

Because Charlie was two years older than Lucy and Pamela who were thirteen, he was sent to another classroom. He walked between the buildings looking for a picture of a Magpie. A dark-haired boy caught up with him and told him that they would be sitting together in class.

Timmy Armstrong was known to be a bit of a prankster, as Charlie was about to find out. The girl who sat in front of them suddenly jumped up, stood on her chair and squealed just as their Form Master entered the classroom. He had a fleshy face, was completely bald, had no eyebrows or eyelashes and was very, very tall.

Mr Ramsbottom was instantly suspicious and looked straight over at Timmy and then back at Sally Prattle. 'What's going on?' he demanded.

'Th-there's a...er...m-mouse in m-my desk, sir,' she stammered.

'Get off the chair then, it won't bite you, girl,' he grumbled, peering at her with his pale grey eyes. The mouse jumped out of the desk and scurried out of the classroom.

Mr Ramsbottom tugged at his high starched collar cursing his wife for making him wear the pale blue shirt she had bought him for his birthday. But she had insisted it went very nicely with his dark blue suit. He glanced at a gold fob watch draped across his waistcoat, and took a step closer – squeak. Mr Ramsbottom looked down at his new leather shoes and mumbled a few choice words.

'GOOD MORNING, ONE AND ALL,' he boomed.

He squeaked and crunched his way over to the blackboard, brushed it clean and turned to face the class again. The students were sniggering behind their hands.

'Bring out your geography books,' he barked, and squeaked over to his desk.

'Maybe the mouse has come back,' grinned Timmy to Charlie.

'What did you say, Armstrong?'

'I didn't say anything, sir.'

'Hmm...May I remind you all, that this is a place of learning, so PAY ATTENTION,' he bellowed. He sat down, opened his desk top and brought out a large geography book.

Meanwhile, Timmy had scrunched a piece of blotting paper into a small ball and dipped it in the inkwell. He flicked the inky blob with his ruler and aimed it atMr Ramsbottom's shiny head. The blotting paper missed and...SPLAT – it landed on the wall behind him. Mr Ramsbottom looked up from the book and frowned.

'What was that?'

Silence from the students.

'I heard a noise,' he growled, 'now what was it?'

Mrs Pertwee swung the door open and came striding into the room. She quietly informed Mr Ramsbottom to come to her office after school.

Lucy and Pamela took Rosa to their classroom that had been named: "Woodpecker". And that just about summed up their Form Mistress, as far as Lucy was concerned. A snooty prefect named, Francis Goodfellow, showed Rosa to her seat next to Nicholas Farrington, who Priscilla had a crush on. The rest of the class scrambled to their desks and waited for the dreaded Miss Nelly to arrive.

Dudley Fipps, a pimply-faced boy and his friend, Rodney Higgins, had made paper planes and were throwing them about the classroom. Rodney, who lived with a foster family, was always getting into fights with Jeffrey Smidgen, who taunted him continually. Rodney had originally been evacuated out of London during the war and it was rumoured that his parents had emigrated to Australia without him. Lucy had a sneaky suspicion that it was Jeffrey who had started the rumour. It was a well known fact that he was miffed because Rodney was good-looking and a lot of the girls fancied him and not Jeffrey.

The door opened and in came Miss Nelly who instantly noticed the paper planes strewn about the floor. The fact that Jeffrey Smidgen and Godfrey Twigg had flicked bits of bubblegum at the ceiling went totally unnoticed.

'Pick that rubbish up,' Miss Nelly ordered. 'And if I see so much as a fleck left on the floor, every one of you will miss morning break and write an essay on the importance of good behaviour.'

In her opinion, all her students were an unruly bunch, always messing about and wasting her valuable time. Well, she soon put paid to their nonsense this morning.

'Now,' snapped Miss Nelly putting on her thick-rimmed reading glasses. 'I trust you have welcomed the new girl?' and instantly glared over at Clara who looked the other way.

'Now, bring out your math books and sharpen your pencils.'

The boys pushed open the door to the "Bluebird Room" and sat at their desks. Hugh and his friends really liked their Form Mistress and hoped that they wouldn't be lumbered with Miss Nelly the next term. After greeting her class, Mrs Burton handed out their maths test.

Mrs Burton, who was a lot younger than the other teachers, was dressed in the latest fashion. Miss Nelly had on several occasions complained that Mrs Burton should wear sensible clothing befitting a schoolteacher, 'After all, it only encourages the girls to dress inappropriately for their age. And as for those ghastly spiky heels! Need I say more?'

Hugh was checking an answer to a tricky algebra question when he felt his scalp crawl. Something made him look out of the window and what he saw made his stomach flip over. It was the same horse-drawn carriage that he'd seen in the Hall of Mirrors. Only this time, it had a huge black cat sitting in the back. It turned its head and grinned over at him. He rubbed his eyes and looked again; the only thing he saw was a raven flying past the window. He became acutely aware of his heart as it thumped in his chest. Was his imagination working overtime? He really hoped so.

'What's the matter, Hugh?' asked Mrs Burton. 'Are you okay?

'What? Oh – er, I was just trying to think of the answer to question nine, Mrs Burton.'

Mrs Burton looked down at the page and frowned, 'But you've already finished the test.'

Hugh went all red in the face and blustered, 'I know, but I was making sure.'

The dinner bell rang out, summoning the school to the Assembly Hall which doubled as a dining room. The folding tables and wooden benches were joined together in several rows. Mr Garbin, the school janitor had constantly complained to Mrs Pertwee about having to erect the tables every day, but it had fallen on deaf ears. He'd just finished his chore when Mr Ramsbottom and Mr Grimble, a really grumpy teacher, entered and took their place on the stage waiting for the students. That meant no talking.

Hugh and his friends found an empty table as far away from the stage as they could and Nicholas Farrington sat down with them. Dudley Fipps and Rodney Higgins joined their table and horror of horrors; it looked as if Clara and Priscilla were heading their way as well. Charlie and Timmy sat at the next table with some of their classmates.

'Oh no,' whispered Nicholas to Jamie, 'I thought I'd managed to dodge, Priscilla.' Jamie's face broke into a broad grin.

'Well, if it isn't, Hugh Barnaby, and those…those friends of his,' sniffed Clara as she came up to them, 'and look who's sitting at the next table.'

'Sit somewhere else then.'

'STOP TALKING, JAMIE SMART,' bellowed Mr Grimble. 'And Dingle, there's an empty seat over there.'

Priscilla was about to push in next to Nicholas, but much to her annoyance, Clara grabbed hold of her arm and dragged her away.

Meanwhile, Dudley had helped himself to an extra chicken drumstick making sure that the dinner ladies were looking the other way. That was typical of him – always stuffing his face with something. They cringed as he scoffed his food down and sat sucking at the bones making as much noise as possible.

'Give it a rest,' snapped Jamie.

'Are you gonna make me?' he sneered sticking his chin out.

'FIPPS,' barked Mr Ramsbottom, 'a word in your ear.'

Lunch was over at last, and the students headed for the playground. Will suggested that they catch up with some of their other classmates who were dying to find out more about Charlie and Rosa.

In the meantime, Clara and Priscilla were gossiping about the gypsies to anyone who would listen. So far it was only snobby Doris Parsonby, who called them "the intruders" and Doris's best friend, Primrose Femworth. Her father owned a large factory making tractors and farm machinery and was thought to be considerably wealthy. Doris Parsonby's father was a doctor who had a practice in Harley Street, or so she said.

Mrs Dingle had tried without success, to invite the Femworths over for dinner, but somehow, they never seemed to be available. 'Why can't you see more of Primrose, Clara?' she'd wailed, but only received a, 'Because she's so-o-o boring,' from her. Of course, Primrose had made it painfully obvious to everyone but Clara, that she had no interest in being friends with daggy Clara Dingle! Why Doris bothered with her was a complete mystery.

Last but not least was, Hortense Dagwater, whose father was an accountant and played golf with Mr Dingle. Clara and Priscilla had once been invited to spend a Saturday with Hortense at her uncle's farm in Sussex. It turned out to be a disastrous day for Clara who was very wary of animals, especially horses. And when Hortense told them that they were going to go horse-riding, Clara all but fainted. Priscilla took to it like a duck to water, which annoyed Clara no end. And to make matters worse, when she eventually managed to climb onto the horse, she slipped off the other side and nearly landed in horse dung. She refused point blank to go on again. And when Hortense suggested she ride the donkey instead – that was the last straw. Still, Hortense did invite them to super parties, so Clara decided she'd keep friends with her.

Hugh had been approached by several of his classmates asking if any of what Clara and Priscilla were saying could be true.

'What have they been saying, then?' asked Hugh.

'That they put curses on people.'

'Priscilla's been telling us stories about you as well,' said Terry Smith.

'Yeah get this, she was hinting that you can make things happen by just looking at her,' laughed Bobby Snook.

'What rot,' he replied, 'how am I supposed to do that?'

The next day, Miss Nelly instructed her class to bring out their history books and sharpen their pencils.

Clara lifted the top of her desk and blurted out, 'Someone's stolen my books, Miss Nelly,' looking straight over at Rosa.

Miss Nelly strode over to Clara and peered into her desk. 'What are these, then?' she glared. 'You obviously didn't look properly.'

'But I…'

'I want you to stay back after lunch and write a hundred lines. That will teach you to jump to conclusions, Clara Dingle.'

'But I didn't, Miss Nell…'

'I saw the look you gave the new girl.'

Clara slumped back in her seat with a face like thunder.

'That's enough from you, young lady.'

After what seemed to be the longest history lesson ever, the girls met up with the boys in the dining hall. Unfortunately, Miss Nelly and Mrs Grimshaw were on dinner duty and were considered to be worse than Mr Ramsbottom and Mr Grimble. Especially when they patrolled the rows of tables like sergeant majors making sure that all the students ate their meal in absolute silence and with: no messing about, thank you very much.

Priscilla had somehow managed to get herself wedged between Fitzroy Flatt, (who sniffed incessantly and followed her everywhere), and his friend, Gerard Little. Nicholas Farrington, who was sitting at the other end of the table, breathed a sigh of relief. Meanwhile, Clara made a beeline to sit across from Timmy Armstrong because she really liked him.

Timmy groaned, 'That's all I need.'

'Why, Timmy, I didn't see you for the minute,' Clara gushed, fluttering her short eyelashes at him.

Charlie nudged Timmy's foot under the table. 'Me finks yer've an admirer,' he whispered.

'We'll see about that,' Timmy whispered back. He had a little surprise for Clara Dingle that would soon wipe that soppy grin off her face and, luckily, would get her off his back.

Clara gave Timmy another flutter of the eyelashes, picked up her knife and fork and squealed.

'My lettuce hasn't been washed properly,' she shouted, pointing to a large fat snail that had eaten half of a lettuce leaf.

'There's no need to shout, you disruptive girl,' barked Mrs Grimshaw. 'I'll be sending you to Mrs Pertwee's office after dinner-break, of that much you can be absolutely sure.'

Clara had the distinct feeling that not only would she have to write a hundred lines but, in all probability, would be made to stand to attention outside Mrs Pertwee's office in full view of everyone. That was the usual punishment dished out by the Headmistress and was, for Clara, her worst nightmare. She was still thinking about it when Miss Nelly bent down and spoke in her ear.

'Now go and apologize to Mrs Sprightly and Mrs Potts,' she ordered, 'AT ONCE, Dingle.'

Alone in the classroom, Clara began writing the hundred lines, seething because she had to miss out on tennis which she particularly liked playing and was actually quite good at. 'You wait Hugh Barnaby; I'll get my own back on those gypsy friends of yours if that's the last thing I do,' she vowed.

Having completed the first fifty lines, she dipped her pen into the inkwell and was about to turn the page, when she felt a soft touch on her cheek. Clara was so startled that she almost flicked the ink all over the exercise book. It must be Miss Nelly, she thought, she had a habit of creeping up behind you. She looked over her shoulder, but the shadows caused by the sun shining through the windows, were her only companions. Had she imagined it? Fancy letting Priscilla talk her into going on that ghastly ghost train. She'd had scary dreams ever since.

Clara turned the page and was about to start writing the next fifty lines when to her surprise, they had already been written and, what's more, in her handwriting. 'I'm sure the page was blank. And I know I counted fifty lines,' she said to herself. She flicked back to the beginning and started to recount the lines, just to make sure. 'There's definitely a hundred. I must've made a mistake after all.' She quickly left the classroom and made her way to her appointment with Mrs Pertwee.

A black cat sat purring as it watched Clara walk towards the Headmistress's office.

Hugh and Lucy arrived home from school and after dinner, Mr Barnaby opened the door of the fridge and took out the ice cube tray. There were wooden sticks standing up from what looked very much like frozen orange juice. He handed them one each.

'Well, come on, don't keep me in suspense, what do you think? I was thinking of selling them in the shop.'

'They taste great, but they'd have to be a bit bigger, wouldn't they?' said Hugh, reaching for another.

'I've already thought of that. I've been to the shops and bought a couple of dozen metal tumblers.

'What would you call them?'

'What about, ice lolly?'

'I think that's a great name,' nodded Hugh, thinking that his father was full of surprises and couldn't wait to tell his friends.

Whispers

Chapter Ten

Several days later, nearly all the school had visited the newsagency to buy an ice-lolly and soon the word had spread. Mr Barnaby had journeyed far and wide to buy metal tumblers and was up half the night making ice lollies in different flavours. He was rewarded by the queue outside the shop the next day. His brother-in-law, Basil, had just given him an old bike and after much thought, decided that it would be a good idea to fasten an icebox on the front of the bike and offered him a job selling the ice lollies around the streets.

'Quite by chance,' said Mr Barnaby, 'I've met a, Mr Birdie, who owns a factory making toys and dartboards in town. Apparently, he has a vacant building he is willing to let. So if all goes well, I'll think about it seriously.'

And then he set about painting the icebox yellow with "Barnaby's Ice Lollies" written in bold red letters. And underneath he wrote, "To Refresh and Delight".

'Now I've finished that little chore, I'm off to get a licence.' Hugh volunteered to go with him.

They entered the Council Offices and followed an arrow pointing to where an Enquiry sign was dangling precariously over a desk on two pieces of frayed string. They stood for a while trying to get the

attention of a man who was doing absolutely nothing, as far as Mr Barnaby could make out.

'Good afternoon, my name is Mr Barnaby and I...' The man looked up and cast an irritated look in his direction.

'A good afternoon, you say? It's too hot for my liking.' He sighed heavily as if he carried the problems of the world on his shoulders, and came over to the counter.

'Er, Mr – I'm sorry, I didn't catch your name?' said Mr Barnaby.

'That's because I didn't give it to you,' he snorted. And then he turned and hurried through a doorway that had "Staff Roo" on it – the letter, "m", dangled on a rusty nail.

'I wonder what we have to do to get some service around here,' hissed Mr Barnaby. A lady carrying a tray of cakes came over to them. After finding out what he wanted, she nodded over to a doorway with "Licences" written on typing paper which had been stuck on the door with a piece of Sellotape.

'These council employees seem to do quite well for themselves,' commented Mr Barnaby, thinking that instead of gorging on cakes, they should smarten the place up and then just maybe, the service might improve. Staff Roo indeed! Several pairs of eyes peeped around corners at him.

They knocked on the door and entered. Sat at the desk behind a typewriter, a small elderly man wearing National Health spectacles was bashing away at the keys with two fingers. He ripped out the paper and rammed in another and bashed the keys again.

Mr Barnaby cleared his throat loudly. Were they expected to stand in front of the desk forever? The man continued typing.

Hugh nudged his father and nodded to a name-plaque that read, "Mr Cuthbert Pleasant".

As the minutes ticked by, Mr Barnaby decided that a little action was needed, so he tapped the top of the typewriter.

The man looked up. 'What do you want?'

'Good afternoon, Mr Pleasant, my name is Mr Barnaby and ...'

'AYEEE?' he said, cupping his hand around his ear.

'I wonder if...?'

'You'll have to speak louder. And for goodness sake, sit down. You're making the place look untidy.'

'I WONDER IF YOU COULD HELP ME,' yelled Mr Barnaby.

'WHAT?' Mr Pleasant felt inside his shirt and switched on his hearing aid. 'That's better, you were saying?'

Mr Barnaby launched into his story.

Mr Pleasant's eyebrows shot up in surprise. 'Well, I certainly won't be granting you a licence for that.'

'Oh dear, and I've got everything ready.'

'That was rather presumptuous on your part, I must say,' he snapped. 'First of all, you'll have to bring your bicycle contraption into the Transport Department for a thorough checking over.'

Had he agreed then? 'Shall I take that as a "yes"?' asked Mr Barnaby.

Mr Pleasant didn't reply but rummaged around in his filing cabinet, pulling out a yellow form. 'The licence you need is a C Licence,' he said, waving the piece of paper at him. 'Now, if you will fill in your details, and be quick about it!'

Mr Barnaby filled in the form as quickly as he could. Mr Pleasant scanned the page twice and then frowned.

'I see you're self-employed, Mr Barnaby. But what are you self-employed with? You must be more specific.'

Mr Barnaby counted to ten. 'My wife and I own a newsagency.'

'A *newsagency*?' he gasped as if Mr Barnaby had committed a terrible crime.Mr Barnaby nodded weakly.

Mr Pleasant frowned again. 'So you are responsible for selling those rubbishy newspapers we are inflicted with these days,' he tutted. 'Not a very good recommendation for your business venture.'

'Oh dear,' murmured Mr Barnaby who had a sinking feeling in his stomach. Had he change his mind?

Mr Pleasant grunted and suddenly found himself looking into – that boy's eyes…those large blue eyes…unusual eyes…spooky eyes… eyes which seemed to look into his very soul…telling him to…

'All right, but you will have to bring your other half in with you as she is part-owner of your business.'

Mr Barnaby was baffled. What a change in attitude. Mr Pleasant glanced at the licence form again and then back at Mr Barnaby who sat with his hands clenched. Would he come up with yet another obstacle? But Mr Pleasant calmly put the licence form down.

'I'll see you tomorrow,' he said. 'Now, seeing as you have interrupted a rather busy afternoon, I'll bid you farewell.' He reached into his pocket and switched off his hearing aid.

Mr Barnaby wondered what his wife would make of the not-so Mr Pleasant.

B ack at the school, Mrs Pertwee had called a meeting with Mr Ramsbottom, Miss Nelly, and Mrs Burton. Miss Nelly was the first to enter followed by Mrs Burton. Mrs Pertwee looked irritably at her watch and sat tapping her foot impatiently. The minutes ticked on. The door burst open and Mr Ramsbottom strode into the Staff Room looking thoroughly fed up, which didn't go unnoticed by the Headmistress.

'I won't keep you long, Mr Ramsbottom, as you are obviously anxious to get on your way.'

'I don't mind staying for a while,' he mumbled sheepishly and pulled at his stiff collar. That's the last time he was going to wear this shirt, no matter how much the wife nagged him to.

Mrs Pertwee pursed her lips at him and wrote something down on a notepad. An uncomfortable silence followed. Miss Nelly raised her hand.

'Yes?'

'I wonder if you've had any word from the Council about the renovations. After all, it has been ten years since the war and…'

'We are here to talk about other matters,' the Headmistress snapped, 'and NOT the school buildings.'

'But…'

'ENOUGH,' barked Mrs Pertwee.

Miss Nelly sat back abruptly in her chair and folded her arms across her chest in a huff.

'Now, about the Romanies,' said Mrs Pertwee giving her a sideways glance. 'How have they settled? No trouble from the students?'

'Nothing in my class, Mrs Pertwee,' commented Mr Ramsbottom, 'that young Charlie is quite a charmer and quite bright. He sat next to Timmy Armstrong.'

'That was brave,' laughed Mrs Burton.

Mrs Pertwee frowned.

'I think Charlie was a good influence on him. In fact, as far as I'm aware, Timmy hasn't indulged in any of his usual pranks. '

'That's a miracle in itself,' chuckled Mrs Burton again.

Mrs Pertwee sniffed.

'Charlie is especially good at geography,' he added. 'All that moving around makes one learn a lot about the world, I suppose.'

Mrs Pertwee and Miss Nelly exchanged glances.

'I'd hardly call traipsing around England in caravans learning a lot about the world,' grumbled the Headmistress.

Mr Ramsbottom grunted in reply.

Miss Nelly suddenly sat up straight in her chair deciding to enter into the conversation. 'Rosa Rromanski is *very* well behaved. Which is more than I can say for the usual troublemakers. I'm sure you know who I mean. And as for the Dingle girl…'

'She would try the patience of a Saint,' nodded Mrs Burton.

'Still, most of the students have ignored her innuendos.'

'Yep, that's what you get for ghost whispers,' said Mr Ramsbottom.

'Er – I think you mean Chinese Whispers,' offered Mrs Burton.

Mrs Pertwee glanced at her watch and called the meeting to a close.

Word Play

Chapter Eleven

Jamie opened the front door to Hugh and Will who had been invited to spend the afternoon with him. His parents had taken his sister and her friend to Windsor for the day. They were discussing what to do when the bell chimed. It turned out to be Lucy and Pamela. Before he could say anything, they followed him into the sitting room.

'Mum said we'd find you here,' said Lucy.

Hugh felt niggled to say the least. He was sure his sister and Pamela could have found something else to do. They were just being nosey, he was sure of it.

'What do you want?' he frowned.

'We were on our way to the fish and chip shop and wondered if you'd like some chips.'

Will's face lit up at the mention of chips. 'You bet,' he said.

'Okay, shan't be long.'

'Now you've done it,' Hugh grumbled, 'we'll be stuck with them all afternoon.'

The girls went on their way only to return fifteen minutes later armed with threepenny bags of chips. They sat down making it obvious that they had no intention of going – anywhere. Hugh raised his eyes to the ceiling and sighed.

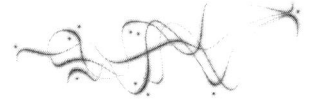

'Do you fancy playing a board game?' asked Jamie. Well, what else could they do now that they were lumbered with the girls?

'Okay,' said Pamela.

He went over to the sideboard and brought out a box. They were expecting it to be Monopoly, but it turned out to be something entirely different.

'What's that?' asked Will.

'It's a new game called, "Scrabble".' He explained that his sister had been given it for her birthday.

'It's about making up words, isn't it? My cousin's got one,' said Pamela.

'Do you know how to play?'

'Sort of, I've only played it once, though.'

'You can show us then,' and he pushed the box over to her.

'We're supposed to make up words from the letters dealt from this bag.' And then she had a quick look at the instructions. 'Each letter has points and whoever gets the most points, wins. I'll read them out to you.'

'I'll never remember all that,' said Hugh after Pamela had finished reading the list. Jamie opened a drawer and took out a notepad and pencils.

'Here, we'll jot them down,' he said ripping the pages from the notepad.

Pamela opened the board and explained that the first player must make a word of two or more letters, place them in the centre of the board, with either a line going straight up and down or across.

'It sounds very complicated,' said Will, his eyebrows puckering into a frown.

'Let's have a practice game first, until we get the hang of it,' suggested Lucy.

Pamela dealt out seven tiles from the stock and soon the game was well under way. The boys had great fun making up several words – bogies, poo, stink, fart, slime – to cries of, 'You're disgusting,' from the girls.

'Well, they're words,' grinned Hugh.

Lucy gave him the darkest of looks. It was then that the light suddenly came on.

'How did that happen?'

'I don't know,' said Jamie switching it off.

Pamela dished out the tiles again warning to boys to play the game properly. Lucy was about to make up the first word, when the door burst open. The curtains flapped against the windows, although the windows were closed tight and the room became icy cold.

They sat in stunned silence as the tiles took on a life of their own, moving around the board until they spelt out – S-E-N-T-I-N-E-L.

The tiles moved around the board again making a clicking sound as the letters formed another word – B-E-W-A-R-E.

'Blimey,' croaked Jamie. 'What does sentinel mean?'

'I d-don't know,' stammered Lucy. 'Have you got a dictionary?'

'I'll go and fetch it.'

'How on earth did the tiles move about like that?' said Pamela.

'Perhaps there's a magnet under the board and they're supposed to,' Hugh suggested hoping against hope that he was right. What other explanation could there be?

'My cousin's didn't do that,' Pamela commented.

Jamie returned armed with the dictionary and he flicked through the pages until he found the word, "sentinel". 'It says here, "a person or animal sent to guard a group".'

'Why would someone want to guard us?'

Jamie shrugged. 'I don't think it has anything to do with us, do you? After all, it's just a game.'

'Well, why did it spell out – "beware"?'

'Perhaps we're letting our imaginations work overtime.'

Jamie wasn't convinced. 'If you say so, Pamela,' he said.

Neither of them dared to mention about the door opening, the light that switched on, or the flapping curtains. Click. A key was inserted in a lock – the Smart family had returned.

Jamie said goodbye to his friends at the front door, having arranged to meet with them the following day at Will's house.

They made their way home glancing over their shoulders continuously. The sun began to sink into the horizon; the moon had

already begun its ascent into the early evening sky, creating eerie shadows in the twilight. A raven flew onto a tree branch and watched as they hurried along the street.

The following afternoon, they caught the bus to a large park where there were all sorts of things to do including two cricket pitches, a bowling green, four tennis courts and a putting green. The girls had brought their tennis rackets with them and with a, 'We'll see you later,' they rushed off.

'Have you thought any more about that Scrabble game?' Will asked, when the girls were out of earshot.

'Not a lot,' Jamie replied not letting on that he had thought of nothing but that. What *did* make the tiles move about the board?

'But do you think it's for real?'

'Do you?'

Will shrugged. Hugh didn't say a word.

They went over to the putting green but it was booked out, so they watched a game of cricket and then went over to the bandstand where an army band was playing. They stood listening to the music for a while and then strolled over to the tennis courts where the girls had just finished playing. Jamie mentioned that he wouldn't mind having a go at Scrabble again and would nick home and fetch the board while they made their way to Will's house.

'I must admit,' said Pamela, 'I'm curious to see if the same thing happens.'

There was one person who didn't want to put it to the test – Hugh. He'd had enough of creepy things, thank you very much.

They returned to Will's house where they went into the shed to wait for Jamie. It wasn't long before he turned up.

The board was opened and Lucy dished out the tiles. Pamela was about to make up a word when a blast of air caused by the opening of the shed door made them jump with fright.

'What's going on in there?' growled Will's father who immediately took in the startled and guilty expressions on their faces. What had they been up to?

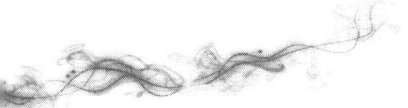

'Well, answer me,' he demanded and marched into the shed.

'We were playing Scrabble.'

'You could've played it indoors,' he frowned. 'Anyway, your dinner's ready, so I suggest you give it back to whoever it belongs to and come inside.'

When at school the following day, they told Charlie and Rosa about the Scrabble game. Charlie looked at them warily. 'Me Gran reckons there are poltergeists that roam the earth.'

'*What*?'

'They're mischievous spirits, accordin' to me Gran, that is,' Rosa explained.

'You don't think it was a polterwhatsit that moved the tiles around, do you?'

'Of course not,' said Will. 'That's daft.'

Charlie shrugged. 'Believe what yer like, but I wouldn't want to find out.'

The school bell rang and they made their way to their classrooms.

Miss Nelly came strutting through the door carrying a box.

'I suppose you're all wondering what I have in here?' she smirked placing it on a small table she'd borrowed from Mr Garbin, the school janitor. 'Gather round class, you're about to find out.'

She donned a pair of gloves, put her hand inside the box and pull out a dead bat. She noticed with satisfaction, the look of wariness on Jeffrey Smidgen's face and that Godfrey Twigg had turned white.

'Return to your seats,' she ordered. 'I told you I would bring in something special for biology, didn't I?'

The class kept quiet.

'We have been studying bats for some time and the fact that they are nocturnal mammals. Can anyone tell me how they catch their prey?'

One of the boys raised his hand.

'Yes Farrington?'

'Bats search out moths and other forms of prey by using a natural form of radar.' Miss Nelly was suitably impressed. At least someone

had paid attention. Priscilla looked over at Nicholas adoringly. He's so-o-o clever, she thought.

'Very good,' Miss Nelly nodded. 'I thought it was about time that you studied the anatomy of a real bat,' she smiled. 'You've learned about their habitat, now I'm expecting a detailed essay on the subject.'

The girls squirmed. Who wanted to know about bats anyway? They certainly didn't.

Miss Nelly eyed her class with satisfaction. Well, she'd certainly caught their attention this morning. 'Now, I want you to form groups of four, starting from the front row. You will then be able to acquaint yourself with this poor misjudged creature.'

She sat down at her desk and folded her arms across her chest, looking decidedly smug. That'll teach the Smidgen boy and that spoilt brat, Godfrey Twigg, a thing or two. No more would they take advantage of her good nature. After all, she'd made that mistake before only to find that they'd glued her chair to the floor. She'd put time and effort into their education and taught them a much-needed discipline – for their own good, she'd told their parents. And what a waste of time that had turned out to be!

The first to inspect the bat was Rosa and her group. Nicholas Farrington put on the gloves and was first to pick it up. He turned it this way and that, pulled at its wings and carefully put it down. Dudley Fipps snatched up the bat, flipped it over, gave it a brief look and plonked it down.

'Do you have to be so heavy-handed, Fipps?'

'Sorry, Miss,' he replied. That's what you think, you old dragon, he thought.

'Rosa Romanski, it's your turn,' she said, giving Dudley a glare of disapproval.

Rosa put on the gloves and picked up the bat by its feet. She inspected it as quickly as she could and returned it to the table.

Bradley Perciville raised his hand. 'Excuse me, Miss Nelly, but I'm allergic to animals.'

'It's hardly going to hurt you if it's dead...is it?'

Bradley looked into her unblinking eyes and said, 'I know, but...'

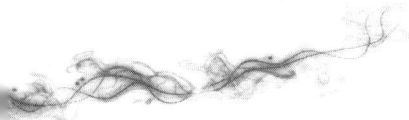

'Then do as you're told,' she snapped.

He immediately had a coughing fit, going all red in the face and gasping for breath.

'Stop making such a fuss,' hissed Miss Nelly.

'I can't breathe, Miss,' he croaked.

Miss Nelly wasn't at all convinced that his coughing fit was genuine, but just in case...'All right, I'll let you off this time, but I expect a note from your parents.'

Bradley gave another little cough, sat back in his chair and smiled triumphantly at her back.

The remainder of the class inspected the bat and all went well until it was the last group's turn. Rodney Higgins was the first of the group to inspect it. And then came, Jeffrey Smidgen, who dropped it immediately.

'What did you do that for, Smidgen?' growled Miss Nelly. 'You could've damaged it.'

'That filfy fing moved, Miss.'

'*Moved*? Why, that's ridiculous!'

Rodney Higgins smirked.

'I'll get yer later, Higgins,' Jeffrey sneered.

'As if I'm scared,' he sneered back.

'SMIDGEN – HIGGINS! Come and see me after class,' she ordered. 'Dingle, you're next. Give me a description of the bat, from top to bottom.'

Clara was about to protest, but the determined expression on the teacher's face had her donning the gloves and picking up the bat. She gingerly started to inspect it when it suddenly twitched, gave its body a shake and then to everybody's amazement, took off around the room dive-bombing the class.

The girls were too petrified to move. The boys were throwing pencils at it trying to scare it off.

Meanwhile, Miss Nelly had dived under her desk.

'What's that strange noise? It sounds like a wasp being zapped with a flyswatter,' whispered Pamela looking round about her.

'I think it might be, Miss Nelly,' Lucy grinned keeping a wary eye on the bat, which was now hanging upside down from the ceiling. And

then it took off again whizzing around the room until it found an open window where it flew to freedom.

Miss Nelly came out from her hiding place looking somewhat green in the face. 'I don't know what happened,' she croaked wiping her sweaty brow, 'I could've sworn the bat was dead.'

She then hurried out of the classroom, hand cupped over her mouth, leaving her astonished students thinking that if this was Miss Nelly's idea of "something special" – she had received a lot more than she bargained for.

A shadow leaning against a tree, laughed heartily. Yes, let the games begin.

The Message That Was

Chapter Twelve

The opening of the newsagency had been a welcomed addition to the neighbourhood. Mr Barnaby had decided several years previously to convert one of the two front rooms of their large detached house into a shop. People had often remarked how very forward-thinking it was of him. No more did they have to trudge into town in all weathers for their newspapers, magazines, greetings cards and the like.

'Cor, you're so lucky to have a place like this,' Jamie had said of the hall that was in their back garden.

The old building used to be hired out for parties before the war, but a bomb had been dropped nearby causing several houses and shops in the area to be damaged, including the hall. A part of the roof was missing and although there were a few holes in the floor, the building was quite safe. Restoring it was going to be one of Mr Barnaby's projects when he had saved up enough money.

Behind the hall was a surprisingly large garden where an old cherry tree stood proudly in the centre of the lawn. Mr Barnaby had worked hard to create the garden and didn't appreciate the fact that Mrs Barnaby's collection of gnomes, elves and fairy statues had almost taken over the flower beds.

'Where are you, Jack?' called Mrs Barnaby.

'Here,' he said, stepping out from behind the runner beans. Whatever was Margie carrying?

'Look what Mrs Winthrop gave me.'

'Mrs Winthrop?'

'You know, who moved here a couple of months ago from Canterbury.'

'What is it?' he asked giving the ornament the once-over.

'It's supposed to be a rare type of gnome.'

'That's not what I'd call it,' he scoffed. 'Where on earth did she get it from?'

'Apparently, she bought it at a jumble sale. But I think it resembles an old elf, don't you?'

'It looks more like a grotesque gargoyle that's fallen off some ancient ruin to me.'

'I think it's rather cute.'

'Do you? Well, I think Mrs Winthrop gave it away because her husband most probably told her to get shot of it,' he growled and set it down next to a hydrangea. With a bit of luck, that would bush out and cover it.

'He did want her to get rid of it, in a way. Mr Winthrop has been offered a job up North, so they'll be moving next week.'

'I hope she doesn't give you any more of her junk. She obviously knows a soft touch when she sees one,' he growled again.

Mrs Barnaby decided to get out of her husband's way – and quick.

Grumbling to her back as she disappeared into the house, he turned his attention to the raspberry bush which he had trained into an archway that acted as an entrance to where he grew his pride and joy – his fruit and vegetable patch.

One afternoon, Hugh decided to spend some time in the garden reading his mystery book. He made himself comfortable under the

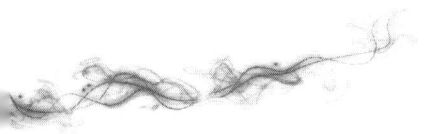

cherry tree and it didn't take long before he dozed off to sleep. He was woken by something tugging at his arm.

'Wake up, wake up,' said a voice.

He opened his eyes to his mother's new garden ornament; only it had grown in size. Was it a gnome? He wasn't sure but whatever it was, it was now standing with its hands on its hips smiling down at him.

'I thought yer'd never wake up, lazy bones,' the ornament said.

Hugh sat bolt upright. 'W-who are you?'

'Me? I'm Wallynus.'

'What do you want?'

'Is that how yer treat a friend who is here to help yer?'

Hugh was speechless. Help him? Help him with what? And why was he having a conversation with a garden gnome, or whatever it was supposed to be? He must be bonkers. And then he remembered the board game. Hadn't it spelled out the word "Beware"?

A pigeon landed on the ornament's head and proceeded to peck at a couple of grass seeds that had shot up from Mr Barnaby's lawnmower. With a few choice words aimed at it and the slapping of his hand, the pigeon took off. Splat!

'That's disgusting,' yelled Wallynus, 'I'll get yer next time, I can promise yer that much!' He angrily grabbed hold of a leaf and wiped the poo off. 'Come with me, lad,' he said.

Hugh found himself following Wallynus through the raspberry archway and along the gravel path to where they came to an old oak door.

'Where did the door come from?' gasped Hugh.

Wallynus didn't answer but tapped at the golden doorknocker. The door remained tightly shut. He banged on the door repeatedly until a piece of clay chipped off his finger.

'Oh blast,' he said, and shouted impatiently, 'For goodness sake open the door, Poz.'

With a rattle and a groan the knocker lifted up to reveal a mouth which was turned down at the corners in annoyance.

'About time yer showed up, I've bin waitin' so long, me hinges 'ave turned mouldy.'

'We had to make sure he was – yer know – the one.'

'Yeah, well, I 'ad to make sure this was the right place 'n' all.'

'Give him the message.'

'Er, excuse me,' said Hugh, 'I think you've made a mistake, you see…'

'MISTAKE?' the mouth bellowed. 'We don't make MISTAKES.'

The knocker slammed against the wood and the door shuddered in protest. Wallynus went in search of his missing finger-piece. Hugh shifted from one foot to the other wondering what to do. This was the most peculiar thing that had happened to him, he was sure no one would believe it in a million years. And then the knocker lifted again. Bushy eyebrows suddenly appeared on the door and underneath, a pair of owl-like eyes peered down at him.

'You're the Barnaby kid, aren't yer?'

Hugh went to speak but somehow he couldn't form the words, so he nodded his head instead.

'An' yer middle name's Stanton?'

'Yes but…'

'Yer the one all right, but let me tell yer this, lad, we've 'ad a terrible trouble findin'…'

'Oh, do spit out,' snapped Wallynus, 'without going around the houses to get there.' The owl eyes glared at Wallynus. 'Okay, keep yer hair on, that's if yer 'ad any hair,' he chuckled and then his eyes swivelled over to Hugh again.

'Listen ter me, lad, yer must be careful of the dark shadows. Keep…'

'Hugh, where are you?' called Mrs Barnaby. 'You'd better come in and wash your hands. I'm about to serve dinner.'

And when he didn't answer she knew exactly where she'd find him, under the cherry tree – reading.

She found him asleep, his book lying across his chest. 'Oh, there you are,' she said, giving him a nudge, 'too many late nights reading your books, my boy. Well, come on, if you don't want cold food.'

A drowsy Hugh followed his mother back to the house. But he did glance over at the latest addition to her garden ornaments.

The day was July the seventh, and was Hugh's twelfth birthday. It had been decided that the party be held in the back garden as it was a lovely afternoon. Mrs. Barnaby had placed a table adorned with a red and white checked tablecloth under the cherry tree and on it, their favourite foods.

Feeling eyes boring into him, Jamie glanced over his shoulder just in time to see Clara and Priscilla, (who were peeping over the fence at them), duck out of sight.

'Did you want something?' he called.

Not a sound came from the garden next door.

'C'mon, Clara, we know you're there.'

At that moment, a gust of wind came out of nowhere and the apples tumbled from the tree next door and onto the girls. They squealed and took off up the garden path.

'Serves you right,' called Will.

'I wonder where the wind came from. I mean, it wasn't windy here,' Pamela pointed out.

'Who knows,' said Will.

Lucy thought it was time to change the subject; things were getting too weird for words. 'If you were allowed one wish, what would you wish for?' she asked glancing over at her brother wondering why he looked guilty.

And then the boys came up with the most outlandish things they could think of. Jamie said he'd find a Genie's lamp so he could have as many wishes as he wanted. Will said he'd wish for a magic carpet and travel the world for free.

'Be careful what you wish for,' said a voice from above.

'Did you hear that?' gasped Hugh.

'Hear what?'

'I swear I heard a voice.'

At that moment, a raven flapped its wings and flew out of the cherry tree. The girls gasped with fright.

'It's only a crow,' scoffed Jamie.

'That's a raven, not a crow,' said Lucy.

'So? That doesn't explain why Hugh thought he heard someone talking.'

'Funny things can happen yer know,' said Charlie. 'Me gran hears voices; some people are just like that.'

He went on to explain that she could also read palms and immediately regretted it when he saw the look that passed between Lucy and Pamela.

'Do you think...?' Lucy began.

'Charlie,' said Rosa giving him a meaningful look 'weren't yer supposed to ask about the party?'

Charlie looked puzzled, 'What?'

'Yer know...the camp fire party.'

'Blimey! I did forget. Yer all invited to a Romany gathering.'

M rs Barnaby came into the garden armed with her Brownie Box camera. She took a few photographs promising to give them each a copy. No one noticed a shadow leaning against the cherry tree.

The Dreaming

Chapter Thirteen

The squawking of a raven greeted the stagecoach as it pulled up outside enormous wooden doors. The coach-driver jumped down and pulled at a skull dangling on the end of a rope. Four black horses snorted steam into the cold night air. A faceless being opened the doors to a place where shadows were in abundance and ghosts swept through lonely dark corridors. The carriage door opened and a cloaked man stepped down dragging a struggling hooded prisoner through the opening. The doors slammed shut and the raven flew away. The castle stood lonely and foreboding as it loomed hauntingly from the top of a black mountain casting a giant shadow over the surrounding area.

Hugh was jolted awake by the sound of flapping wings in the darkness. Thankfully, he was in his bedroom and there was no sign of the raven. Or was it there among the many shadows?

In another room, Lucy was lying half asleep when she noticed a movement at the end of her bed. She sat up with a start and – golly, was that a man and lady dressed in Victorian clothes looking down at her? She switched on her lamp, but there was no one there. Was it a trick of light?

Sunday morning had arrived, and Mr Barnaby intended to close the shop by midday. The bell chimed and the most beautiful lady he

had ever seen entered. She ran a delicate hand through long black hair whilst staring at Mr Barnaby with her big blue eyes. An odd little man stepped out from behind her.

'Good morn' to yous, Mr Barnaby,' he said. 'We came to thank yous and your good lady for telling us about Mrs. Fairweather's abode, very comfortable indeed.'

'Yes, we'll definitely recommend the place to our friends,' the lady nodded.

Before Mr Barnaby had a chance to ask her what she meant, she tugged at the man's arm and said, 'We must be on our way. We bid you good day, sir.'

Mrs Barnaby came into the shop and found her husband staring out of the window.

'What's up?' she asked.

'You'll never guess what happened. There…' He was about to launch into his story but the bell chimed again and a customer came in to ask if her magazine had arrived. Mrs Barnaby looked under the counter where she usually kept goods on order, and noticed a small silver box which she showed to Mr Barnaby.

'What's this?' she asked.

'I've never seen it before,' he replied.

'Perhaps one of the kids found it somewhere,' she said, and went back to searching for the magazine. She found it at the back of the shelf. The customer thanked her and left.

'Now what were you saying, Jack?'

'Do you remember recommending the Fairweather's place to a strange couple?'

'What do you mean – strange?' He launched into a vivid description of the beautiful lady and funny little man. Mrs Barnaby didn't remember them at all.

'But that's not all. As they left the shop, I swear I could see right through them, you know, like ghosts.'

Mrs. Barnaby looked at her husband as if he was mad. Surely he was joking? 'Go on with you, you're pulling my leg,' she grinned.

'Of course,' he laughed, having decided there and then to push the incident out of his mind – best forgotten.

Mrs Barnaby suddenly remembered the silver box. Now where had she put it? She looked everywhere, but the box was nowhere to be seen. The loud shrill of the telephone had her running to answer it. Her mother was on the line making arrangements to meet with them that afternoon.

The Barnaby family made their way to the river, turned right at the old bridge and followed the road until they came to a good picnic spot. They parked the car and set up their picnic table under a shady tree by the water's edge.

A short time later, Mrs Barnaby's parents arrived. Mr Barnaby suddenly came up with the idea that the river park would be a good place to sell his ice lollies. 'That's if I'm able to get someone to work over the weekends, of course.'

Squawk! Squawk! A raven flapped its wings and circled them.

'That frightened the life out of me,' gasped Grandfather Albert.

'Ooh, I don't like ravens,' said Grandmother Lily, 'they are a harbinger of doom.'

'That's superstitious nonsense,' her husband snorted.

'If you say so, anyway, it's gone now.'

'No it's not, it's over there.'

They glanced over to where he was pointing but instead of the raven, sat a black cat licking its paws.

'Some raven,' scoffed Grandmother Lily. 'You're not getting a migraine are you, dear?'

'No I'm not,' was his indignant reply, but something made him glance over at the bush again and to his surprise, two children were standing beside it. They gave him a friendly wave and then vanished in a puff of smoke. He certainly wasn't going to tell the family about that. After all's said and done, he didn't want them to think he'd gone senile, did he?

Unknown to him, his grandson had also seen the children disappear. Hugh instantly recognized them as the children from the Hall of Mirrors. Things were getting spookier and spookier. And then a word crept uninvited into his mind again, "Beware"! If Jamie ever suggested playing Scrabble again, he'd refuse point blank.

Mrs Barnaby brought out her camera and took several photographs before they returned home.

Lucy felt restless after the outing, so she took herself off to the front room next to the shop. It was more of a storeroom-cum-junk-room, but she loved rummaging around amongst the old things stored in there. Just inside the door, against the wall to the left of the room, stood a piano belonging to Mr Barnaby's father. He didn't have the heart to get rid of it for it was a memento of his parents who had died several years before. He had hoped that one of his children would show interest in learning the piano, but what with Lucy and her dancing, and Hugh – well....anyway, he was too interested in those books of his and hanging around with his friends.

Lucy went over to an old trunk and pulled out a feathered bower, a sequinned evening bag, and long satin gloves. She was about to try them on when she noticed an old leather photograph album at the bottom of the trunk. That was more than strange, because she'd never noticed it before. She picked it up and turned the pages until she came to a photograph that made her heart skip a beat. She rushed into the sitting-room and found her mother alone drinking a cup of tea.

'Who are these people, Mum?' she asked, pointing to the faded photograph.

'Goodness me, I'd forgotten all about that old album, here let me see,' she said taking it from her. 'Oh my goodness, that's your father's great-grandparents.'

'Do you know anything about them?'

Mrs Barnaby was very quiet for a minute. Should she tell her daughter? Why not? 'Well, there was a rumour that they could see things that others couldn't and were into all sorts of strange things. But as your father loves to remind me, people do like to exaggerate about their ancestors.'

Bubble, Bubble Toil And Trouble

Chapter Fourteen

In a dimly lit room within the walls of a castle, black flickering candles had been placed in a circle, creating eerie shadows on the crumbling walls. The lady in the long flowing blue dress had returned to the Realm of Shadows and was admiring her beautiful face in a mirror, knowing full well that it wouldn't be long before an old hag with cruel black eyes would be staring back at her. Her perfect nose would become long and crooked and her mouth would droop at the corners grotesquely. No longer would her black hair be long and glossy – but grey and wispy. And the thought that her tall slim body would no longer exist, but would be hunched over a crooked staff, was too awful to think about.

She was furious with herself for being in too much of a hurry to capture the boy. That episode in the Hall of Mirrors had been a disastrous mistake, especially when that friend of his called out and broke the spell. But since then she had consulted the oracle. It was time to lure children into her web, for she needed their energy to allow her to stay in the World of Tomorrows until she completed her task.

'Siras,' she called. 'Bring me my cauldron.'

Morag paced back and forth eager to begin casting the first of many spells. She had wasted enough time and precious energy toying with the mortals. After all, they were only a means to an end. Still, it wouldn't be long before they would fall under her spell, but she would

have to be very, very, careful not to be detected. Now, where was that servant of hers?

Siras heaved the cauldron into the centre of the room and set about lighting the wood. In no time at all the fire sprang to life and with a flick of Morag's wrist, he was zapped from the room on a thunderbolt.

The sorceress walked around the cauldron three times mumbling softly to herself. She reached into a bag, brought out a bunch of mistletoe, and was about to throw it into the cauldron when an angry cry rang out.

'STOP THAT AT ONCE!'

She turned around, hand in mid-air, and gave the intruder a withering look. An old man had entered the room carrying a staff in one hand and a basket of herbs in the other. His purple cloak brushed the floor as he shuffled over to Morag and peered at her through hooded lids, nostrils flaring.

'Who gave yer permission ter take me mistletoe?' he growled snatching it from her.

Morag looked at him with contempt. 'I wasn't aware that I needed *your* permission, Marius.'

'Well, it's extra special. I've spent many moons cultivatin' it, and I don't take too kindly ter yer usin' it afore it's ready.' By this time, the old wizard had gone red in the face, his saggy jowls flapping about his chin.

'How was I to know that?'

'If yer'd studied more when yer was younger, yer would've,' he grumbled, pointy eyebrows drawn together.

'Well I…'

'I told yer father that yer were too interested in flirtin' wiv them young warlocks, than ter concentrate on yer lessons.'

'But I…'

'Yer brother knew the importance of potionology,' he persisted.

With the mention of her brother, Morag all but exploded. 'DON'T MENTION HIM TO ME,' she bellowed. And then she lowered her voice dangerously. 'My magic is far greater than his could ever be,' she sneered.

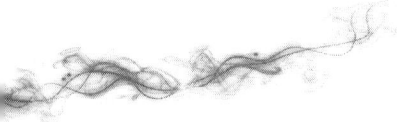

'That's a matter of opinion,' the old herb master replied. He wasn't the least bit afraid of this slip of a sorceress.

'And what about yer cousin?' he taunted. 'She 'ad a natural gift, an' more ter the point, she took note of *all* me lessons.'

'Pah! Look where that got her,' she flung back, 'she's disappeared.'

'Never yer mind about her, it's you we're talkin' about.'

'Humph! Considering the Lord of Thunder has chosen me to be by his side,' she hissed, 'I'd say my powers speak for themselves – don't you?'

He shrugged his shoulders indifferently. 'Anyway, I've brought this mistletoe from the old oak tree. Made a mess of me hands, pullin' it away from the trunk,' he moaned, and shoved it into her hand.

'I suppose this will have to do,' she said, turning her nose up.

The old wizard tugged angrily at his long beard. 'Yes, it certainly will,' he snapped. He reached into his basket and pulled out a bunch of sage. 'Yer'd better use this fresh bunch,' he snorted. 'Yours 'as wilted.' And with that parting statement, he shuffled out of the room, his staff tapping the ground angrily as his cloak brushed the floor.

The sorceress glared at her old tutor's back and furiously chucked the mistletoe into the cauldron. Yellow smoke spouted into the air. She then performed the cleansing ritual, waving the sage at the four corners of the room before taking hold of her broom. But the more she swept the floor, the more the dust reappeared. The herb master peeped from behind the door and chuckled as she angrily swept the floor again.

'That'll teach yer ter steal wot belongs ter me,' he muttered, waving his hand and conjuring up a silver broom. With a flick of a hemlock herb, the broom went whizzing into the room and swept around the cauldron leaving the floor sparkling clean.

Morag shrieked with delight, she was oh-so clever. No more would she have to do that menial task herself. 'How's that, Marius? I don't need your rotten old sage now,' she called.

The old herb master grinned from ear to ear. He could keep it all for himself and, more importantly, his special mistletoe. He had plans, important plans, when he found the missing mandrake of course.

A strong gust of wind howled around the sorceress as she circled the cauldron. She lifted the lid, gave it a stir, and threw in a bunch of rosemary, a dragon's tooth, an eagle's claw and two owl feathers. She then raised her hands to the ceiling chanting:

> Round the cauldron the circle doth grow
> This magic spell I do surely sew
> Energies will dance and create the fire
> Bringing to me all I desire

A circle of fire soared high into the air and Morag watched as it died down to an eerie glow. A haunting silence filled the room until terrifying creatures stepped from the walls. They bowed to the sorceress, joined hands and danced around the cauldron chanting, 'We are your servants o' the night, to do your bidding is our plight.'

Morag clicked her fingers producing a crystal-tipped wand made from the root of a maple tree and the blood of an owl. She passed it over the cauldron five times before calling upon her master.

A clap of thunder and lightning flashes lit the room. From the cauldron rose the dreaded Lord Drago, snakes slithering around his ankles. His black cloak embroidered with a serpent spun in silver thread, hung from his shoulders and onto the floor. Upon his head he wore a hat, a snake coiled in sleep. The snake suddenly reared its ugly head with its beady eyes fixed on the sorceress, before sliding down its master's body. Morag watched transfixed as all the snakes weaved their way around the room hissing at her cowering slaves, their tongues darting in and out hungrily.

The Lord of Thunder grinned maliciously as the sorceress welcomed him to her hall. The snakes slithered and slithered and slithered.

'So, Morag, are you ready to seal our pact?'

'Yes, my Lord.'

'And when you have completed your mission, you will be rewarded. You will stay forever beautiful. You will stay forever young.

Your powers will be less only than mine.' And then he gathered his snakes together in a whirlpool of dark energy and vanished in a swirl of black smoke. Morag was already plotting her next move.

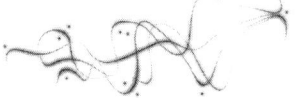

Spellbound

Chapter Fifteen

'To think that it had occurred right under our noses,' said Charlie's father, King Leo. He had just found out about Hugh's experience in the Hall of Mirrors. 'Are you sure he is the one, mother? I mean, he is rather young.'

'It is written in the stars, son.'

'So be it then. Isabella and I will call a meeting on the morrow, and shall send our messenger, Demdyke, forthwith.'

'Well, make sure he doesn't get lost, yer know as well as I do that his sense of direction is far from accurate.'

'I'll be sure and give him a compass if that makes you feel any better,' he grinned.

The very next day, the Romany Council transported to a meeting place known as the Place of Mysteries. They were astounded to hear the news.

'That must be why my silver goblet has turned black. A sure sign that something isn't right,' said Mervin, the chief of the clan from Glastonbury.

'And Augustus, my jackdaw, has been quieter than usual,' said Dumas whose family originally came from Europe.

'Of course, at the end of his thirteenth year, will end all opportunity in this decade for the boy to prove that he is worthy of the legacy,' said King Leo.

'But wasn't his father next in line?'

'Yes, but I'm afraid, Jack Barnaby, refused to accept his gift, so now it's up to his son.'

'Poor lad, I feel sorry for him,' said Demdyke, shaking his head.

'Fiddlesticks, where's your sense of adventure?' snorted the Major.

'I've had enough of so-called adventure for a lifetime, if you must know,' he shot back.

'We'll have to be on our guard at all times and you must report all signs and portents to me immediately. So until the next meeting, I'll bid you farewell.'

The Romany Council vanished into the night, leaving behind the silvery glow from the moon and an eerie mist covering the ground.

Queen Isabella instructed Demdyke to bring together the wizards, sorcerers and witches.

Many of the old ones came whizzing in on their broomsticks and joined the younger of the coven whom had already arrived by just a click of the fingers.

Old Mouldheels Pontefroy looked as disagreeable as ever. 'Getting us here at a moment's notice, I hope it's worth it,' he moaned. He was one of the founders of "The Book of Shadows", a sacred book of spells, curses, anti-curses and enchantments; in fact, all things magic. He plonked himself down next to an old sorceress and gave her a nudge, 'Shove over,' he grunted.

Agatha Hagswart gave him a steely glare and snapped, 'You don't have to be so rude, you grumpy old wizard.' Although she and her twin sister, Harriet, were wizened and bent over, they could cast spells as quick as a lightning flash.

'I think you've done very well to come here at all, Mouldheels,' said Audra Swithin, who was a beautiful young witch with long blond hair. She was excellent at reading the tealeaves and casting horoscopes.

'Humf, I'm glad someone appreciates the effort I've made.'

There came a flash of light, and Elspeth Lott, looking somewhat dishevelled, zoomed in on her broomstick with a bundle of scrolls tied to the handle. 'I hope I'm not late,' she said breathlessly.

'No more than usual,' grumbled Harriet.

'I was in the middle of giving a lecture at Salem's University of Spells and Potions, when I received word by way of, Professor Picksworth, that I was to return.' She had been a student of Old Mouldheels and had now taken over his role as the Oracle of Spells since his retirement.

'Don't say that pompous nincompoop is still knocking around,' snorted the old wizard.

'I don't hold with that lot in Salem,' sniffed Agatha, 'they've got some funny ideas.'

'No more than the coven from Pendle Hill,' said Harriet giving Old Mouldheels a sideways glance.

'And I suppose you haven't,' he retorted.

The oldest sorcerer, Chattox Cantonberry, who had a striking resemblance to Father Christmas, gave the grouchy wizard a nudge. 'Isn't this exciting to be called out of retirement?' he beamed, remembering with pride how he was able to go up against any evil spell that was sent his way.

'I wonder what this is about?' asked Nobab Wiggleslick, whose cheery round face had turned bright red with excitement. Although he was known for his healing potions, he was a dab hand at everything, even if he did say so himself.

'If everyone kept quiet we might be able to find out,' grumbled Harriet.

Queen Isabella explained that the heir to the legacy had been found, 'And when a spell had been cast to trap Hugh Barnaby in the Hall of Mirrors, we knew we had to take action.'

'Well, it looks as if we're back in business,' said Nobab rubbing his hands together.

'I think it's about time we used our magic again. After all, if yer don't use it yer lose it,' nodded Old Chattox knowingly.

'I was quite content as I was, as a matter of fact,' grumbled Mouldheels, who was now busy rubbing his knees. 'And if you ask me, I think we're wasting our time until we find out what he's up to.'

'What who's up to?' snapped Agatha. 'I haven't a clue who you're talking about.'

'Yes, I wish you'd stop talking in riddles,' hissed Harriet.

'The Lord of Thunder, of course. That's my opinion on the matter, anyway.'

'Well, we weren't asking for your opinion.'

'Anyway, I'm getting too old for this,' he grumbled again.

'Codswallop,' said Old Chattox, 'if you're too old, so am I, and I don't feel a day over twenty. I'm not bad for three centuries plus,' he grinned.

'Pity you didn't look it,' muttered Agatha.

Queen Isabella knew that the sisters would go on arguing for hours if she let them, so she called the meeting to a swift close.

The old ones climbed onto their broomsticks and flew away, leaving a trail of dust and fallen leaves behind them.

A gentle breeze blew the blades of grass, hiding all trace of the meeting from prying eyes. An old man stood looking out of a broken window. A ghostly white falcon flew onto his out-stretched arm.

An Ear To The Ground

Chapter Sixteen

M r Ramsbottom rang the final bell of the summer term. He couldn't wait to walk out of the school gates. No more would he have to put up with those ridiculous staff meetings, for a few weeks at least. CLANG – he rang the bell again and jumped out of the way as the first students shot out of their classrooms and into the playground.

'Hooligans the lot of 'em,' he grumbled to Mr Grimble as they both dodged another group of students who pushed past them.

Clara and Priscilla came hurrying out of the school building and behind them, love-struck Fitzroy Flat who was carrying Priscilla's satchel. Rodney Higgins got into a fight with Jeffrey Smidgin and Mr Grimble hauled them off to Mrs Pertwee's office.

O n the way home, Jamie noticed a van outside the old cottage. There were two men clearing away the overgrown bushes to reveal a small front garden and an old gnarled and twisted tree. The workmen stopped what they were doing and glanced over at them as they stood looking at the cottage.

'I wonder who's bought the place?' said Lucy.

'I saw Mr Drummond eyeing it the other day, perhaps he's bought it.'

'Knowing him, he was just being nosey.'

'I wonder if someone will buy the shop,' said Will looking at the derelict building that was boarded-up.

'It's been empty for so long, it's a wonder it hasn't fallen down.'

And then something black swished overhead. Hugh glanced up at the roof where a raven had landed. There was something about the way it looked down at him that made his scalp crawl, almost as if it were human. It flapped its wings, circled them and landed on the garden wall.

'I wonder who the cat belongs to?'

Jamie looked at Will as if he was nuts. 'What cat?'

'That cat, can't...? Cripes, it's vanished!'

The raven gave a loud squawk and flew away.

'How weird,' Hugh exclaimed. 'And what's happened to the workmen?'

'It's too spooky for me, c'mon, I'll race you home,' shouted Will over his shoulder as he took off up the street, his feet hardly touching the ground.

The following day, having been told that Hugh and his friends were to attend the party, the old gypsy was intent on preparing the amulets. She opened the lid of an old wooden box and took out a blue stone and a small piece of rose quartz. She passed her hand over the top of them, speaking in a strange language. She unrolled a piece of cloth, brought out an old parchment and studied the strange writings while muttering an ancient verse over and over again:

> The wings of an eagle the winds of time
> Through the eye of a needle
> Protect what is thine

She looked down at the sliver pendant now housing the blue stone. She fingered the silver chain on which it dangled and then picked up the other one. Inside was the rose quartz. She sealed the pendants with another ancient incantation, and smiled as the amulets shimmered with energy. The spell had been cast. She peered out of a window impatiently. 'Now, what's happened to Osletwistle? Demdyke should've fetched him by now.'

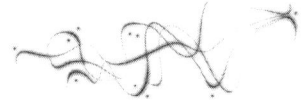

The door opened and in came the Major. 'You wanted to see me?' he asked.

'That's why I sent fer yer, obviously. What have yer got to report?'

'I've visited the Barnaby's shop a few times, and except for a ghastly woman who lives next door, a Mrs Thimble, or whatever she calls herself, all seemed very quiet.'

'No sign of Morag and her dreadful little servant?'

'None at all,' he replied.

'Yer'd better keep an eye open and an ear to the ground. Now go to the celebrations, and fer goodness sake, wear yer traditional costume.'

'I shall be honoured to escort you,' gushed the Major who had been on strict instructions from King Leo not to let her get away with her feeble excuses about why she won't be going to the party.

'I s'pose I'd better make an appearance,' she said grudgingly, 'but give me time to get ready.'

'We are here to welcome the Gorjers,' announced King Leo to the gathering. 'So join us in making these young folk feel welcomed.'

'Does that means us?' whispered Jamie to Charlie.

'Yep,' he grinned. 'Gorjer is an old Romany word for those who ain't one of us.'

Jamie was fascinated by the gypsies especially the ones wearing cloaks. A man strapped on his accordion and began to play, which didn't seem to wake an old man who had fallen asleep with his mouth open.

And old gypsy went up to him and shook his shoulder, 'Oh do wake up, Mouldheels,' said Harriet.

He opened one eye, grumbled something and promptly fell back to sleep.

'What a funny name,' whispered Hugh.

'Perhaps he has smelly feet,' Jamie whispered back.

'It could be a nickname,' offered Lucy.

'Well, you wouldn't want it to be your real name, would you?' Jamie remarked.

'Mmn, those sausages smell good.'

The sleeping wizard snorted awake and grabbed hold of a hotdog. He looked over at Hugh with his piercing ice-blue eyes and said, 'Tell me, are yer enjoying yerself, lad?'

'Don't speak with your mouth full, Mouldheels, and wipe the mustard off your chin, it's disgusting,' snapped Agatha.

'Don't nag, woman,' he shot back at her.

'Wouldn't mind a bit more mustard on mine,' said Old Chattox.

Several hours later, the distant hoot of an owl drew the party to a close. Lucy thanked King Leo and they said their goodbyes. Charlie and Rosa offered to walk with them until they reached the main road.

Meanwhile, King Leo clicked his fingers and the broomsticks appeared ready to carry the old folk home. Audra attempted to help Mouldheels onto his, but he pushed her hand away with a grouchy, 'I do wish you'd stop fussing, Audra, I'm perfectly capable of getting onto me broomstick by meself.' And with a final glare at her, he zigzagged towards the sky nearly colliding with a barn owl.

Old Chattox couldn't find his broomstick so he nabbed a lift with Nobab and with a shudder, they leap-frogged all the way home.

'Fancy that,' grumbled Harriet to Agatha. 'Those old wizards went off without as much as a bye-your-leave.' And she stood in a huff, arms folded across her chest as she watched them disappear behind a cloud.

'Huh, typical, they have absolutely no manners – no manners whatsoever! Anyway, enough of them, I want to be home before the owls go to bed.'

By the way,' said Hugh to Charlie when they reached the street, 'why did some of the Romanies wear cloaks?'

Charlie was taken aback for the minute. 'Why do you ask?'

'Well, they looked different somehow.'

'What do you mean?'

'They sort of…er… looked mysterious.'

Charlie felt his cheeks grow hot. How was he supposed to answer that? 'Well, most of them are very old and feel the cold,' he said.

'But it's very warm this evening,' Will pointed out. 'And besides, not all of them were old.'

Charlie was trying desperately to think of an answer that would make sense to them, but luckily Rosa came to the rescue.

'Gran said she'll read yer palms tomorrow.'

Thank you, Rosa, thought Charlie. 'I'll be around in the morning at ten o'clock. Is that okay?'

'Yes, do we...?'

'We'd better go,' urged Rosa and with a quick, 'See yer tomorrow,' they hurried away before they were bombarded with any more awkward questions.

Jamie had a few awkward questions of his own to ask Hugh. One being, 'Did you notice that the gypsies seemed to watch you all the time?'

'Don't talk rot.'

'They did,' he insisted.

'I don't know why, you look more like a gypsy than me.'

'What's that supposed to mean?'

'Well, for starters, you're hair is black.'

'So? Not all of them had black hair.'

'Yeah, but you still look like one – sort of.'

'I do not,' he protested.

'Oh for goodness sake,' said Pamela impatiently.

'Don't you think Charlie looked shifty-eyed when Hugh asked him about the cloaks?' asked Lucy, who was becoming really good at changing the subject.

'Yeah, but why?'

'Maybe they were too poor to buy those fancy costumes and Charlie didn't want us to know.'

'If you believe that, Pamela, you'd believe anything,' scoffed Jamie.

ZIP ZOOM WHO-O-O-SSSH.

'Jeepers, what was that?'

Lucy looked up at the sky. 'It's a shooting star.'

'I've never seen one like that before,' said Pamela.

'How many have you seen then?' asked Will.

'Not many, but…'

'So how do you know?'

'Does it matter?' she snapped. 'Anyway, it's getting late, so I think we should head for home and not waste our time arguing.'

Bossy boots, thought Will.

They made their way along the street and a sudden movement had Will glance over at the old cottage. Was that a pale face peering out of the window at them? He looked again just to be sure, but there was no sign of the face, only the reflection of a passing white cloud. The cottage stood as before, lonely and forlorn, waiting and waiting and waiting.

The following morning at ten o'clock sharp, Charlie called around for Hugh and Lucy. They went on to Pamela's house where they found her standing by the front gate waiting for them. They then called around for Will and Jamie and made their way to the Traveller's yard.

They couldn't help noticing the curious glances cast in their direction as they followed Charlie through the maze of caravans to where the old gypsy's wagon was parked under a large tree. Nearby a horse was drinking from a trough. It looked up and whinnied at their approach. The wagon was brightly painted and there were tubs with flowers and herbs placed either side of the three steps leading to a door with a round stained-glass window of a moon and stars. So with their curiosity piqued, they climbed the steps and followed Charlie inside.

A large glass cabinet faced the door. An antique table and chairs dominated the centre of the wagon and there were two armchairs and a large settee placed around a wood stove. A beaded curtain led through to the bedroom and there were oil lamps and candles throughout. To them, the wagon looked more than a little mysterious.

Charlie's grandmother gave them each a drink and they spent time talking about the party. She explained that it was a gypsy custom to honour new friends.

'We usually attend the annual Khamoro Festival but we decided to rest up instead. I'm gettin' too old fer such goings on anyway.'

'What sort of festival is that?' asked Will.

'Romanies from all over the world meet up to celebrate our culture. There is singing, flamenco, and all sorts of folk dancing. Some trade horses and such like. There can be marriages between clans. It's very colourful...'

'C'mon, Gran, they've come to have their palms read,' Charlie reminded her knowing how she could go on for hours.

'Yer all a bit young to be gettin' a proper readin' but I'll try me hardest fer yer,' she smiled. 'Well now, who wants to go first?'

Pamela was the first to sit down. The old gypsy took hold of her hand and turned her palm this way and that. Pamela sat eagerly waiting to hear her fate. What would she be told? Charlie's grandmother didn't say a word except look more closely at her palm muttering softly to herself.She traced a finger up and down the lines several times and then eventually looked up. Pamela held her breath. The old gypsy still said nothing and looked down at her palm again. After what seemed like an eternity to Pamela, she looked up again but this time with a strange expression on her face. Pamela felt her stomach clench. What had she seen? Was it something bad?

'Sorry, luv,' said Charlie's grandmother who had felt as if a door had been slammed in her face, 'but yer lines aren't tellin' me anythin'.'

Having tried to read all of their palms without success, the old gypsy was convinced that something or someone was stopping her and if that was the case, she had to act fast.

'I can't understand it; none of yer lines speak to me.' And she stood up from the table making it obvious that she wanted to be left alone.

'I'll bring them another time, Gran,' mumbled Charlie and ushered his friends out the door.

Just as Hugh was about to follow, Charlie's grandmother grabbed hold of his arm and shoved two shiny objects into his hand – the amulets.

'These are just a little somethin' to thank yer and yer sister for being such good friends to me kin,' she smiled. 'I'm afraid I haven't any fer yer friends, so yer'd best keep it to yerselves.'

'Thanks a lot,' said Hugh wondering why he and Lucy were singled out.

'It's very important that you keep them on yer person at all times.'

Hugh was amazed to hear this – what would he tell his parents?

'And in case yer wonderin' why, it's a tradition that goes back centuries. It is written in Romany law that when given a friendship pendant, yer must wear it always. Now yer don't want to break with tradition, do yer?'

Hugh left the wagon in a daze.

Jamie had a sneaky suspicion that the old gypsy was up to something, but whatever it was, he didn't have a clue.

'What did Charlie's grandmother want?' he asked when Hugh caught up with them.

'Nothing much,' he mumbled.

'Must've been something,' Jamie persisted.

Hugh avoided his friend's eyes. That made him even more suspicious. Something very strange was going on and he was more than determined to find out what it was.

'She said she was sorry that she couldn't read our palms.'

'Do you think she saw something she didn't want to tell us? I mean, it was strange she couldn't read any of our palms.'

'I don't know, Lucy,' he said impatiently.

'I just thought...oh, it doesn't matter.'

'Don't you think the wagon was weird?'

Pamela looked at Will in surprise. 'It was a bit old-fashioned, but it wasn't weird.'

'I meant the fact that it looks quite small from the outside, but it was enormous inside.'

'Come to think of it, you're right.'

Dark Delivery

Chapter Seventeen

A removal van pulled up outside the cottage and two men jumped out. They opened a door at the back of the van, let down a ramp and heaved out a large round table. An old lady dressed in a long black dress with a purple shawl pulled tightly around her shoulders, came out to greet them.

'Where do yer want this put, Missus?' asked one of the men.

It was at that moment grey clouds swept over the cottage, and a sudden squall had the men down the table and take refuge under the tree. The lady stood in the middle of the small garden as the wind howled around her and the rain poured from the skies, but she remained completely dry. A loud clap of thunder roared overhead and the wind gathered speed. The branches of the tree creaked and groaned.

'I don't think we should hang around here,' said Will wondering why it was sunny where they stood.

'C'mon, let's go.'

They decided to run until they were well away from the cottage and out of harm's way and before they knew it, they had arrived at Pamela's house.

'That old lady gave me the creeps,' said Hugh.

'Old lady?' snorted Jamie. 'She looked more like a witch to me.'

Pamela let out a sigh. 'You'll be saying she made the thunder appear next.'

'You must admit, she was spooky.'

Pamela shook her head. 'She was just an old lady.' Even so, she shot up the garden path and with a mumbled, 'See you tomorrow', she opened the front door and disappeared inside.

'Before I forget,' said Hugh when he and Lucy arrived home, 'Charlie's grandmother gave us these pendants to wear. This is obviously for you,' he said handing her a pendant that had a rose etched on it. 'And this is mine,' he said showing her the one he was wearing.

'That's so pretty. Let's have a closer look at your pendant,' she said taking hold of his. 'Oh, it has a crescent moon on it.'

'So? I wouldn't want a rose would I? Anyway, we're only to tell Mum and Dad, no one else.'

'Why?'

'She didn't have enough for all of us.'

'But why did she give them to us?'

'How should I know?' he snapped. 'She said we're never to take them off.' Why did his sister always insist on asking him questions he didn't have the answer to?

Lucy opened her mouth to speak, but Hugh jumped in with, 'And before you ask me why, she just did.'

'They must be good luck charms,' said Lucy fastening the clasp.

The following morning, Will came to call for Hugh and they decided to walk by the cottage again. On the way, they bumped into Jamie who suggested they crouch down behind the hedge in case the old lady happened to be looking out of the window.

They reached the cottage and before they had a chance to hide, a black cat jumped over the wall and ran across the road to the honk of car horns. They had just reached the end of the garden wall when the cat jumped up and arched its back at them.

'How did it land up here again?' whispered Will.

'Have a look over the road,' gasped Hugh, pointing to where the cat was sitting by the curb licking its paws.

'Cripes, it can certainly move fast.'

'Let's go to the fish and chip shop,' whispered Will. 'That way we can watch the cottage from across the street.'

'Er…what are you whispering for?' grinned Hugh.

'Was I?'

'C'mon, let's buy some chips.'

They crossed the road and entered the fish shop.

'What can I do for you, boys?' asked Mr Lure

'Can we have a threepenny bag of chips, please?'

'Been spying on the old lady, have you?'

'Sort of,' Jamie replied feeling his face grow hot.

'I suppose you'll be saying she's a witch next,' Mr Lure chuckled.

'Well, er – um…'

'Don't worry, lads, when I was your age any old lady that lived by herself had me and me mates thinking that she was a witch. And if she owned a black cat, that clinched it. We'd make up all sorts of stories to frighten ourselves with.'

I n the Realm of Shadows, the sorceress had been watching her prey in her scrying mirror and was very happy with what she saw. 'You have no idea, Mr Lure, you have no idea. And as for you, you old biddy, your pathetic attempt at palm reading failed miserably, didn't it?' But she'd had her fun, now was the time to concentrate her energies on the task at hand.

The silver broom came whizzing into the room and swept the floor clean. Morag drew a five-pointed star with her wand, muttering in an ancient language over and over again:

Cymreth Tymreth Cymreth

A clap of thunder and a lightning bolt crashed around the room with such a force that the floor shuddered and debris fell from the ceiling. The hideous creatures stepped out of the shadows, linked hands and danced around the room. The sorceress waved her wand over the cauldron and spoke in a raspy voice:

Let the broth simmer and bubble

Bring forth the spell of powerful trouble
Skin of a snake and dragon's fire
Bring to me all I desire

Morag stirred and stirred as the liquid bubbled and hissed. She sniffed at the vile odour, placed a lid on the simmering brew and clapped her hands. Her servants vanished, leaving only shadows behind and the ghosts that float through the corridors in the dead of night.

Show And Tell

Chapter Eighteen

Mr Drummond opened the door to his garage with a proud smile on his face. He tucked his new cravat into his open-necked shirt, climbed into his brand new convertible car, zoomed out of the driveway and took off up the street. He sped past Mrs Dingle's house and noticed with satisfaction, her astonished face as she peered out of her window at him.

He was driving along the road as happy as can be thinking all was wonderful with his world...and the weather was just perfect. He pulled up at the traffic lights and sat strumming his fingers on the steering wheel singing, 'Oh I do like to be beside the seaside, trrum ti tum ti ta. Oh I do...' It was then that he happened to glance right, '...like... to...be...beside...the...' his voice trailed off when he noticed massive bicycle spokes spinning to a halt beside him – what in the world? His eyes travelled upwards and he saw the most unbelievable sight ever. Perched on the top of a Pennyfarthing was the old man from the Inn wearing a deerstalker hat – earflaps were fastened under his chin with a safety pin. He was wearing a monocle on his right eye. A carrier bag was dangling on a handlebar, the floppy blue hat on the other.

The loud hooting of a horn jerked him back to reality. 'Hurry up, the lights 'ave changed,' called an irritated voice.

Mr Drummond turned in his seat and madly pointed upwards. The other driver craned his head out of his car window and called, 'What's up?'

Mr Drummond got out of his car and went over to speak to the man. 'Can't you see…? It's a Pennyfarthing – with an old ma…'

'All I can see is you, wavin' your arms around like a right nutter.'

'But you must be able to…' he looked up again – there was no sign of the Pennyfarthing or the old man.

Honk. 'What's the hold-up there?' called another voice.

'You'd better get back in your car, mate, before they haul you off to the funny farm,' the man said shaking his head at him. 'There's one born every minute,' he muttered.

Without another word, Mr Drummond scooted back to his car, panting as he jumped in. With a shaky hand, he turned on the ignition and after slamming the car into first gear; he shot up the street, smoke spurting from the exhaust, leaving a line of fist-waving irate drivers behind. He swerved into a side-street and jerked to a halt. He pulled out a handkerchief, wiped his sweaty brow and sat for a while, thinking. There was no doubt about it, chops of any kind were off the agenda and now cheese was added to his list. Satisfied with his explanation, he drove off.

Mr. Barnaby had just finished filling the shelves with new stock, when he saw something large and shiny pull up outside the shop. The door was flung open wide and Mr. Drummond entered looking decidedly smug.

'Is that your car parked outside, Mr Drummond?'

'Yes, quite something isn't she?'

'I haven't seen one like that before. What type is it?'

'It's a Hudson – an American job. Always wanted one since they brought out the Terraplane, in the thirties I think it was. Had it converted to a right-hand drive and shipped over.'

Mr Drummond then burst forth with the news he had been dying to tell him, that someone had moved into the old cottage. Besides, he'd had the satisfaction of showing his new toy to Mr Barnaby who was obviously very impressed. And when he'd driven past the Dingle's

house earlier, the expression on that old nosey-parker's face was simply priceless.

'And the boards have been taken down from the empty shop,' he said. 'It looks as if whoever's bought the place is in a hurry to get it finished.'

Mr. Barnaby handed Mr Drummond his newspaper.

'I didn't know...'

'There are workmen all over the place, never seen so many running around with hammers and things.'

'I wonder what it will be.'

'I'm sure we'll find out soon enough, Barnaby.'

'Yes, I'm sure we shall,' he replied thinking, especially if this old busybody or his next-door neighbour had anything to do with it.

'Of course, if I had known both buildings were up for sale I might've considered buying them for an investment. Well, must dash old chap things to do, cheerio.' And he was gone, leaving Mr. Barnaby to wonder where he got his money from, considering he kept quiet about his line of work.

The door opened and Mrs Dingle came scurrying in. 'Was that Mr Drummond I saw climbing into that flashy car?'

'Yes, rather grand isn't it?'

'What sort is it?'

'A Hudson, it's American, apparently.'

Mrs Dingle's eyes widened. 'An *American* car?' she squeaked. 'What's wrong with good old British?'

Hugh and Lucy had spent over an hour tidying the storeroom for their father when a rustling sound had them stop what they were doing and prick up their ears.

'Did you hear that?' asked Hugh looking about him.

'It's coming from the old trunk.'

'Perhaps it's a mouse.'

'You look, I don't like mice.'

With an irritated glance at Lucy, Hugh lifted out the clothes one by one, giving them a good shake; he couldn't find a mouse anywhere. And then he noticed the old album at the bottom of the trunk. He

brought it out and opened it. To his surprise, the pages flicked over to an old photograph. And then the strum of the piano came out of nowhere. They turned around expecting it to be their father playing one of his jokes on them – it wasn't. Lucy grabbed the album off Hugh and dropped it into the trunk, piling the clothes on top and shutting the lid tight trying to forget that it ever existed...

'What did you do that for?' Hugh frowned.

'Didn't you hear the piano?'

'Maybe Mum had the wireless on loud. Anyway, I wonder who those people were in the photo.'

'What people?'

'Don't give me that, you know who I'm talking about.'

'They're Dad's great-grandparents.'

'How do you know?'

'I showed the album to Mum, and she told me.' The door opened and Mrs Barnaby called them to dinner.

Later that night, Mr Barnaby was sitting in bed reading when Mrs Barnaby came into the room. He didn't look up, but kept his eyes focussed on his book. He knew what he was in for after listening to Lucy's story about the piano that was supposed to have played by itself. And what did Hugh say about the album? That it flicked the pages over until it came to a photograph of his great-grandparents? What hogwash!

Mrs Barnaby sat on Mr Barnaby's side of the bed and as predicted, brought up the subject of the piano. He had no intention of entering into the conversation and kept on reading his book.

'And what do you make of the album opening up to the photograph of your great-grandparents?' she asked.

Mr Barnaby turned another page hoping that she would take the hint. No chance of that. Mrs Barnaby had no intention of letting him get away with ignoring her.

'Perhaps one day you should research your family tree,' she said, looking over the book at him.

Mr Barnaby put the book down. 'It's obvious to me why you'd want me to do that,' he snorted. 'Wouldn't you be disappointed if my

ancestors turned out to be just ordinary folk?' And his face cracked into a triumphant smile.

'I suppose you're going to tell me that there is a mouse nest in the piano next.'

Mr Barnaby cocked an eyebrow at her and said, 'Exactly.'

'Don't fob me off with "exactly", Jack Barnaby. What about the time when…'

'When what, Margie?'

'When great-aunt Beatrice was visiting and she told us about...'

'It's a load of superstitious nonsense.'

Mrs Barnaby decided it was futile trying to get her husband to talk about his family, so she got into her side of the bed and slumped back in her pillow. 'I suppose we'd better try and go to sleep then.'

'That's the most sensible thing you've said for the past five minutes. Good night, Margie,' he said, flicking the light off.

'Goodnight, Jack.'

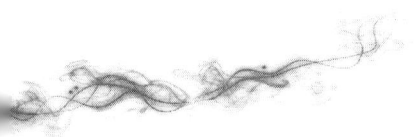

Simply Delicious

Chapter Nineteen

Three weeks later, the renovations to the shop were complete and the smell of fresh paint still lingered in the air.

The neighbourhood was busy speculating about the new shop and what it would be. There were several theories. Some thought it might be a delicatessen or perhaps a ladies hairdresser. Quite a few of the men were hoping that it would be a barber's shop. Then there were others who were convinced that it would be a butcher's shop for since the other one had closed down, they had to traipse into town for their meat. But most of the women were secretly hoping for a clothes shop or even a nice café. They didn't have long to wait to have their curiosity rewarded because a few days later a sign went up at the front door:

OPENING SOON!
Mrs. Pennywort's Olde Candy Shoppe
Homemade chocolates a speciality

Now that the mystery had been solved, the topic of conversation near and far was about the Candy Shoppe. Would the new shopkeeper fit into the neighbourhood? The mention of homemade chocolates had many wondering what they would taste like. Would they be better than Cadbury's, Nestlé's or Fry's? What would the shop be like inside?

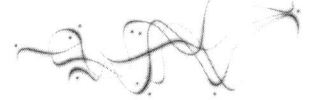

The paint had been removed from the windows but unfortunately the blinds were pulled down, ensuring that the inside of the shop remained a mystery. That made everybody even more curious. Mrs Dingle had mentioned to the Barnabys that she expected the shop to be decorated tastefully; otherwise a trip to the Council would be on the agenda.

Lucy and Pamela decided to go and check out both the shop and the cottage. The boys said they'd go along as well. They were just passing by the bakery when they bumped into Clara, Priscilla, and none other than Fitzroy Flatt. But who was the boy standing behind him? Oh no, it was toffy-nosed Bradley Percyville, who had just moved to the area: from Knightsbridge, as he kept reminding everyone. It had been his first term at school and so far he'd proved himself to be a right show-off. No one took the slightest notice of his boasts of, 'I'm descended from French aristocracy, you know.'

'We've been to have a look at the new shop,' Clara announced.

'It is très quaint,' drawled Bradley, 'but rather passé for the neighbourhood I should think.'

Gawd, there he goes again, thought Jamie, dropping French words left, right and centre.

'And the old lady who lives in the cottage came out to talk to us,' said Priscilla throwing a disgusted look at Fitzroy who had his finger up his nose.

'Don't you think she's creepy?' asked Hugh.

'No...Why do you ask?'

'No reason,' he murmured.

'She told us we could visit her any time.'

'Lucky you,' muttered Will.

Bradley made a point of looking bored and started to walk on ahead. The girls bolted after him with Fitzroy Flat in hot pursuit

'Someone must be desperate for company,' Jamie commented.

They finally arrived at the Candy Shoppe and were disappointed to find the blinds were still pulled down at the bay windows, so they

thought they'd check out the cottage instead. They were intrigued by the place especially as they never knew quite what to expect.

The old lady was sweeping the front step and looked up when she heard their approach. She put down her broom and came up to the front gate. Pamela felt the sudden urge to escape. Lucy stood behind her brother.

'Hello, m'dears,' she smiled. 'Come to have a look at the shop?'

'Do you know when it will be opening?'

'Won't be long now, by the looks of it,' she replied, and went back to sweeping the step.

'What a surprise,' said Pamela, 'she was actually quite nice.'

'So much for us thinking she was a witch.'

Two days later a large board proclaimed:

GRAND OPENING TOMORROW
Come in and sample
Mrs. Pennywort's Delicious Homemade Chocolates

The following morning, the sign on the door had been turned to "OPEN" and a crowd had already gathered outside. Mrs Pennywort beamed with pleasure, for it seemed that most of the neighbourhood had turned out for the opening.

Mrs Barnaby's first impression of the owner was of a friendly lady whose rosy cheeks shone in a round happy face. Mrs Barnaby had managed to squeeze her way through the throng of people and was about to introduce herself, when she got waylaid by one of her customers.

'Do come in and try my homemade chocolates,' smiled Mrs Pennywort stepping aside.

The crowd surged forward nearly knocking over an old lady as they pushed their way into the shop. Mrs Pennywort took hold of her elbow and guided her inside.

'Thanks m'dear,' the old lady said, 'yer very kind.'

'You're welcome,' she replied, giving her a couple of samples which she immediately shoved into her mouth.

'I like the taste of yer chocolates,' the old lady said smacking her lips together. 'By the way, I live in the cottage next door.' She then rummaged around in her oversized handbag and brought out a small package. 'Here's a little somethin' to welcome yer to the neighbourhood.'

'Why thank you, dear, how nice of you.'

'Go on, open it up.'

Mrs Pennywort took the wrapping paper off the package to find a small silver box shinning up at her. She opened the lid to a silver brooch in the shape of a crescent moon.

'It's lovely,' she said, taking it out.

'Try it on, it'll bring yer luck.'

Mrs Pennywort was in the process of pinning it onto her dress when she pricked her finger. 'Oops, how silly of me,' she winced, and immediately put her hand on the countertop to steady herself.

'What's the matter?' asked the old lady.

'I came over a little dizzy – must be all the excitement, I expect,' she replied, wiping her brow. 'But thank you for the gift, I shall wear it always.'

The brooch glowed.

'Well, m'dear, it looks proper nice on yer. I'd best be on me way, yer've got plenty o' customers waitin'.' And she hurried away just as Mrs Barnaby, who had managed to make her escape, entered the shop.

'Good morning, Mrs Pennywort. I'm from the Barnabys Newsagency just along the street.'

Mrs Pennywort shook her hand warmly. 'Very pleased to make your acquaintance, I'm sure,' she smiled. 'You must try one of my samples.' She pointed to a large basket filled with an assortment of chocolates. 'And do take some for your family to try.'

Mrs Barnaby was just about to choose one when another hand pushed hers aside. It belonged to Mrs Dotty who grabbed a handful of chocolates and immediately made a beeline for the door. She swept past a smartly dressed man who was telling his dog to sit and wait for him. He brushed dog hairs from his dark grey trousers and approached the counter.

'Good morning to you – Mrs. Pennywort, is it?'

'Welcome to…' she began.

'I just got a whiff of your chocolate as I was passing by and I said to myself, Osletwistle old chap, er…that's Major by the way, you simply must go in and have a taste.'

Mrs. Pennywort handed him the sample basket and watched as he chose a chocolate, smelt it, and popped it into his mouth.

'I hope it's to your liking, Major?'

He made a zero with his forefinger and thumb, kissed the tips, and flicked them open. 'It's simply splendid, my dear Mrs Pennywort, simply splendid. Well, must be on my merry way, tootle pip.'

He gave her a little salute, popped another of the chocolates into his mouth, and marched out the door. The dog jumped up and followed him. Moments later another man entered and sauntered up to the counter. He gazed around the shop and nodded his approval as he helped himself to a chocolate.

'Arnold Demdyke's the name, and I represent Raffity and Cavity Confectionary.'

Mrs Barnaby was wondering why the men seemed familiar.

'Good morning, Mr Demdyke, I…'

'If you would like to place an order with us, we will be only too pleased to give you prompt and satisfactory service.' He went to shake Mrs. Pennywort's hand but at that moment, Maud Underwood came hurrying in, followed by Mrs. Dingle who barged her way in front of her.

'I'm Mrs. Dingle from the rather grand house that's situated next to the Newsagency,' she sniffed, and then gave Mrs Barnaby and Maud Underwood a cursory nod. In her opinion, the publican's wife was rather rough around the edges with her bottle-blonde hair and cheap makeup plastered all over her face. And if Mrs Barnaby couldn't face up to the fact that her son wasn't the goody two shoes she deemed him to be, she didn't warrant her attention either. And where had she seen this sleazy man before, grinning at her like a Cheshire cat?

'Welcome to my…' started Mrs Pennywort.

'I would very much like to give you my custom, providing I like your chocolates of course,' Mrs Dingle announced as if she was doing Mrs Pennywort a great favour.

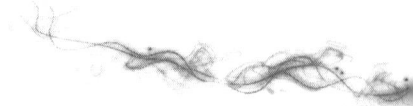

'Excuse Mrs – er, Dingle did you say? I must speak with this gentleman.' She turned to Demdyke only to find that he had already left the shop.

'How strange, that man can't be too eager for my custom.' Then, turning to back Mrs. Dingle and Maud Underwood, she smiled politely and said, 'If you'd like to take a sample home to your families you are more than welcome.'

Mrs Pennywort was wondering if she'd have any chocolates left as she watched Mrs Dingle grab hold of a large handful. Meanwhile, Maud Underwood bought a box of chocolates, and with a cheery 'Bye', rushed out the door.

'What a nice lady,' commented Mrs Pennywort.

'She and her husband are the owners of the Jolly Bodger Inn,' offered Mrs Barnaby.

Mrs Pennywort smiled, 'How nice.'

'How common, if you want my opinion,' Mrs Dingle snorted.

Major Osletwistle and Demdyke met up at the old gypsy's wagon and were busy telling her about their visit to the Candy Shoppe.

'I wonder why she called the place by that name, I mean, it's American, isn't it?' said Demdyke.

'Perhaps she prefers the name to Sweet Shop,' offered the Major.

'Well, I'm of the opinion that if one lives in England one should speak proper English,' was Demdyke's disgruntled reply. 'Still, she's a Gorjer so what can we expect?'

'You might have come to that conclusion, but I'm not so sure.'

The old gypsy looked sharply at the Major. 'Why do you say that?'

'I don't know why exactly, it's just a feeling that…'

'I want more than "just a feelin",' she snapped.

'I did happen to notice an old lady lurking around outside and....'

'And what, do spit it out Osletwistle.'

'There was something about her.'

'Who are you talking about, the shopkeeper or the old lady?'

'Both.'

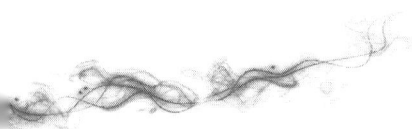

'Hmm, keep an eye on the place and wipe that chocolate off yer moustache, it looks disgusting,' she scowled. 'Anyway, I can't work wiv yer both lookin' over me shoulder. Now scram.'

Left alone, the old gypsy thought about what the Major had said about the shopkeeper and the old lady. She peered into the crystal again and an image of the shop came into view. There were people going in and out with their purchases; so far everything looked normal.

'Hmm, Osletwistle will have to keep an eye on the shop, and he must locate the whereabouts of the old lady too.'

'What did yer say, Gran?' asked Charlie, as he stepped up into the wagon.

'Ooh, don't creep up on me like that, there's a good lad, made me heart go ninety to the dozen, so yer did.' How much should she tell her grandson? She had no intention of worrying him unnecessarily. Perhaps telling him about the visit to the new shop wouldn't do any harm. She decided to keep the old lady out of it; anyway, she was most probably harmless.

'I sent Osletwistle and Demdyke to suss out the new shop.'

'What did they fink of it?'

'Demdyke said all was as it should be, but Osletwistle didn't seem too sure.' Yes, she would heed the opinion of Osletwistle; he was more clued up than old Demdyke. Thank goodness her son had made him into his personal messenger – she wouldn't have to put up with him. How he managed to bundle that simple spell she'd never know. It was about time he admitted it was entirely his fault instead of putting the blame elsewhere.

'Shall I go and check it out too?' asked Charlie.

'I don't...'

'I'll get yer some chocolate toffees; I know yer like 'em.'

'Be off wiv yer, lad,' she smiled. But her smile faded as she watched her grandson leave the wagon.

'Welcome girls,' smiled Mrs Pennywort as Clara and Priscilla came up to the counter. 'And what are your names?'

'I'm Clara Dingle and this is my friend, Priscilla Pringle.'

'Your mother was in here earlier as a matter of fact, such a nice lady,' gushed Mrs Pennywort. 'Don't you live next door to the Newsagency? '

'Yes we do, worse luck.'

'Oh? It just so happens, that Mrs Barnaby was in here as well.'

'They're a bit peculiar, the Barnaby family are,' said Clara.

'Well now, let's have no more talk of them,' said Mrs Pennywort and she looked inside the basket. 'Oh dear, I've run out of chocolates,' she apologized. 'But I have some extra special ones that I've just made. Would you like to try them?'

The girls nodded enthusiastically.

'I'll go out the back and get them, shan't be long.'

A movement by the window caught Clara's eye. The old lady from the cottage stood peering into the shop at her.

'I wonder what she finds so interesting,' Clara remarked.

'Who finds what interesting?'

'The old lady, she's outside.'

'No she's not.'

Clara spun around only to find that her friend was right.

Mrs. Pennywort returned armed with four chocolates. 'Here you are, my dears, taste the likes of these,' and she touched her brooch absentmindedly.

As soon as Clara took the first bite of chocolate, her eyes went all blurry and the shop took on a life of its own. Chocolates floated to the ceiling and Mrs Pennywort's face seemed to have changed into something hideous.

'I've got to get out of this place,' croaked Clara.

'I think I'm going to be sick,' cried Priscilla, her hand flying up to her mouth.

They staggered towards the door and managed to open it, but found themselves not in the street, but in a shimmering cave.

'Wow,' Clara exclaimed, her feeling of panic strangely forgotten.

'Where are we?' asked Priscilla who thought it was the most glorious place she'd ever seen.

'I don't know, but let's explore.'

In a small alcove, the fairies and elves appeared so lifelike that Clara was convinced they were moving. Hanging on hooks were mediaeval dresses with long pointed sleeves. Priscilla made a beeline for them and was about to try one on but Clara yanked her away to look at the broomsticks and witches' outfits.

The jangle of chains had them leap into the air with fright. A man dressed in ragged clothes and wearing chains around his ankles shuffled past them. He disappeared through a wall.

'Don't mind old Bard, he's just being nosy,' said a voice.

'C'mon, let's go,' squeaked Clara looking frantically about her.

'Where's the way out?' croaked Priscilla.

'Over there, see it?'

They rushed over to an opening but stopped short when the man in chains stepped out in front of them again barring the way. A voice in the shadows called out, 'Be gone.'

Bard bared his stained teeth at them and vanished.

The girls dashed through the opening and found themselves in another cave.

'You're not leaving so soon, are you, girls?' said the silky-smooth voice.

They caught a glimpse of a delicate hand and long dark hair. 'But you've only just got here.'

'W-who are you?' gasped Clara.

'Who am I?' the voice cooed. 'I'm the Keeper of Mysteries.'

'W-why are w-weh-here? '

'Why you are here, my dear, is because you want to be of course.'

With a swish of her cloak, the girls found themselves standing in front of a Wishing Well. The lady was right – they wanted to be there more than anything in the world.

'Here, try a lucky dip, and if you pull out a magic stone you may make a wish and cast it in the Well,' said the sorceress, jangling the bag in front of Clara. 'Now come along dear, dig deep.'

Clara took the bag and felt around inside until her hand touched a wooden box. She pulled it out and opened it. Inside was a piece of paper that read, "Better luck next time."

Clara stood and pouted.

The sorceress chuckled to herself as she handed the bag to Priscilla who pulled out a glowing silver box. Inside, shiny pink and purple powder shimmered in the darkness. Priscilla stared at the powder wondering what it was. Was it a type of sherbet?

Morag took the box from her. 'What have we here?' she said as she let the powder flow through her fingers. 'Well now, aren't you the lucky one, that's magic dust,' she beamed.

Priscilla stood and gaped – what on earth was magic dust; and what's more, what was she supposed to do with it?

The sorceress sprinkled the powder over her and said, 'This will bring you good luck.'

Clara was furious that she only got a crummy old message. Well, she wouldn't put up with that, 'I want another go,' she demanded.

She snatched the velvet bag from Priscilla who gave her an angry scowl.

The sorceress smiled in satisfaction. Jealousy and anger: how simply divine. She couldn't have wished for better energy to aid her in her quest.

'I don't want you to feel left out, Clara dear, so I'll sprinkle some over you.'

And then she poured the dust into their palms. 'Now hold it tight and concentrate on getting the magic stone for when you visit me again.'

Clara and Priscilla closed their eyes and wished hard.

'Now, how do you like the chocolates?' smiled Mrs Pennywort.

'Pardon Mrs Pennywort?'

'The chocolates – did you like them?'

'They're super,' cooed Clara.

The door opened and three children entered. Mrs Pennywort smiled at them and said, 'Welcome to my Candy Shoppe, dears.'

All That Glitters

Chapter Twenty

'Hello lads,' said Mrs Pennywort to Will and Jamie when they walked into the shop later that day. Their eyes travelled straight to the chocolate samples.

'Don't be shy, take one,' she urged handing them the basket.

Jamie went to take the basket from her but he jogged her hand and watched in horror as it fell to the floor. The chocolates spewed everywhere. Without batting an eyelid, Mrs Pennywort picked them up and threw them into a bin.

'Oh, how clumsy of me,' she apologized. 'I tell you what; I'm in the middle of trying a new exclusive recipe and would welcome your honest opinion. I'll just go and fetch the chocolates – shan't be a minute.'

Will stood peering into the cabinet, but then he had the strangest feeling that someone was watching them. He turned around just in time to see the end of a black cloak dash by the window.

Mrs Pennywort returned bringing with her a small plate. 'Sorry to have kept you waiting, here are the promised chocolates.'

In walked Mr. Drummond. 'Good day to you fair lady, Bertrand Drummond's the name,' he beamed. 'I've just come by to welcome you to the neighbourhood.'

'Nice to meet you, Mr. Drummond, welcome to my humble…'

'And while I'm about it, I wouldn't mind sampling one of your delicious home-made chocolates.' Mr Drummond eyed the plate of chocolates and picked through them until he found one he liked the look of. 'Any more to choose from?' he asked.

'I'll just pop out the back to see if they're ready.'

She took the basket with her and returned with it full to the brim. Mr Drummond rummaged around the samples and grabbed as many as he could.

'Don't think I fancy any chocolates now that Mr Drummond's sweaty hands have been all over them,' whispered Jamie.

'Well, must be on my way, things to do you understand,' and Mr Drummond marched out the door.

Mrs Pennywort turned back to the boys. 'Now, where were we?"

'Could we buy a large bag of chocolate swirls please?'

Mrs Pennywort put the swirls in a paper bag and twisted it tightly. A ghostly voice from above muttered, 'With each twist, so shall I reap.'

'Here you are, hope to see you again soon. Don't forget to tell all your friends to come by and visit me.'

A little while later, Charlie sauntered into the busy shop, giving him plenty of time to look around. Mrs Pennywort was saying goodbye to a customer and glanced over at him giving him a little smile. Charlie gulped. Had she realized he was there to spy? He hoped not, for his grandmother would have his guts-for-garters if she did. The door opened and several people walked in. Charlie had been recognized as the grandson of Cornelia Romanski. He's probably in here snooping for his troublesome grandmother, thought the sorceress.

A tall smartly dressed man came up to the counter. 'Good day to you, Mrs Pennywort, I want a large box of chocolates for my wife,' he smiled, and then added, 'it's our anniversary, you see.'

'Do choose any that your fancy from the cabinet.'

'Well,' he winked, 'I was kinda hoping that you might have some of those extra special chocolates I've heard so much about.'

'I'm afraid I haven't got any made at the moment.'

'That's a pity; Sheila will be so disappointed. Hmm, now what shall I choose?'

He moved next to Charlie who had been peering into the cabinet trying to look inconspicuous. The man smiled at him, 'Delicious looking chocolates,' he said.

'Sorry to keep you waiting, lad,' said Mrs Pennywort who was looking over the cabinet at him. 'Come over to the counter and let the gentleman choose his chocolates in peace,' she smiled.

The man gave her a sharp look, but looked into the cabinet again.

Charlie waited while she brought out a couple of chocolates from under the counter. 'Here, try these,' she said. 'They're made from my secret ingredients. Sssh, they're the last two.'

Charlie popped one into his mouth. They were the best chocolates he'd ever tasted.

'Me Gran sent me in here to buy some chocolate toffees. I fink I've got enough money,' he said, fingering his coins.

The shop door opened and Mrs Pennywort looked up just in time to see the man close the door behind him, leaving her to wonder why he left without buying anything for his wife. She shrugged her shoulders, thinking it was his loss and turned her attention back to Charlie.

'Well now, being as you are such a nice handsome young man, I've given you a few extra.'

'Gee, fanks a million, Mrs. Pennywort, I'll tell all me friends about yer shop, bye fer now.'

Hugh had made arrangements to go to town with Jamie who wanted to show him a new bike he had his eye on. On the way to Jamie's house, he spied an old tramp sitting on the ground leaning against a wall, a large carrier bag sat by his side. The man felt around in the bag and brought out a handful of flat, smooth, stones. Hugh snuck into a doorway and watched the man spread the stones out in front of him. He studied them for a while and then he looked up suddenly and called to Hugh, 'Pick up the stones fer me, lad, and put them in me bag – me fingers aren't as nimble as they used ter be.'

Hugh stayed right where he was.

'Hurry up, lad, I haven't got all day,' the old man growled.

Hugh came out from his hiding place and quickly gathered up the stones which turned out to have strange symbols etched on them.

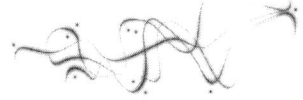

Where had he seen the symbols before? And how did the old man know he was there?

'Give 'em to me,' he said holding his wizened hand out.

The man spread the stones out in front of him again mumbling to himself. For some reason, Hugh was beginning to feel wary and was about to walk on when the old man grabbed hold of his ankle.

'Well, well, well,' he gasped, 'so yer the one. Now, yer must heed what I say, lad. Those of the dark shadows are gathering in strength. Yer must go ter the seers. That is the message of the oracle.'

Hugh stared at the old man in disbelief; hadn't somebody else said the same to him? If only he could remember who it was. And who are the seers he's talking about – but, more to the point, *what* are they? And what did "oracle" mean?

'I saw you out of my window,' said Jamie. 'Have you lost something?'

Hugh looked up in surprise at hearing his friend's voice. 'What?'

'You were staring at the ground.'

'I was talking to this old man.'

Jamie's eyebrows shot up. 'Were you? Where is he then?'

'I – um, he probably went into the chemist,' he mumbled.

Jamie eyed his friend with interest. He knew he was right, there was definitely something going on with him, something really weird. But for now, he would let the subject drop until he was absolutely sure.

Mrs Dingle stood at the front door waiting for Clara who had been sent to invite, 'the Barnaby girl and that friend of hers,' for afternoon tea she'd told Mrs Dotty earlier.

Lucy and Pamela walked up to the front door with Clara and were greeted with a cheery, 'Welcome, girls, welcome.'

The smell of over-boiled brussel sprouts greeted them as Mrs Dingle led them through to the back door. Lucy wondered whether every door in the hall had been left wide open for them to notice the expensive antique furniture in every room. It was dark and dismal, just like the house.

'Come this way, girls, I've set the table outside, as it's such a nice afternoon.' She took them into the garden where Priscilla was waiting for them.

It wasn't long before Mrs. Dingle came bustling out carrying a tray of cucumber sandwiches, a small packet of crisps between them, and four-cup cakes with thick brightly coloured icing on top. She rushed into the house again and fetched a jug of juice.

'I hope you like freshly squeezed orange juice – none of that sugary muck your mother sells in our house, thank you very much,' said Mrs Dingle making a face. 'Now, I don't want to see a scrap of food left on the plates. I don't like waste of any kind.' And off she went.

'Have you been to the new Candy Shoppe yet?' asked Clara.

'No, not yet, Hugh and I will go some time tomorrow, I expect.'

'What about you, Pamela?'

'Me neither,' she winced after she'd taken a sip of juice.

'Why do you ask?'

'No reason,' Clara shrugged. 'C'mon, we'd better polish these off before Mama comes back.

The girls munched away at their soggy cucumber sandwiches and Mrs Dingle returned carrying a large bowl of blackberry jelly. Of all the food in the world, Lucy hated jelly the most. What was she to do?

'Thank you, Mrs Dingle, but I'm full to the brim,' she said, feeling helpless when Mrs Dingle plonked some in a bowl and set it down in front of her, and what's more, with a splosh of condensed milk on the top. Yuk!

Mrs Dingle pursed her lips with determination. 'Nonsense, young lady, eat up, not a morsel to be left,' and heaped another spoonful of jelly into the bowl. 'You need fattening up anyway.'

Clara and Priscilla tucked into the jelly with gusto. Pamela gave Lucy a nudge and nodded over to the colander of fresh blackberries that Mrs Dingle had picked from the overhanging branches.

'Now that we've finished eating, I've a little surprise,' said Clara mysteriously, and produced a small bottle of nail varnish. The

girls set about painting their nails and had nearly finished when Mrs Dingle returned to take the empty bowls away.

'Would you like a second helping?' she beamed – that was until she sniffed the air. 'Can I smell nail varnish?'

Clara dropped the bottle and kicked it under the table.

'Is that Hugh and his friends I can hear over the fence?' asked Clara. Anything to take her mother's mind off the nail varnish.

'I think so, but...'

'Lucy and Pamela are over here,' Clara called. 'Do you want to come around?

'How about coming over here instead,' Hugh called back looking over at Jamie who was mouthing, 'No way!'

'Don't mind if we do,' said Clara, and stood up ready to go, but not before Mrs Dingle grabbed hold of her hand and inspected her fingernails.

'Well I never did,' she snapped. 'If you think you're going to get away with blatantly disobeying my orders, young lady, you've got another thing coming,' she warned.

'Sorry Mama, but the boys are waiting for us.' And Clara rushed the girls away before her mother had a chance to stop her.

Mrs Dingle stood with her hands on her hips glaring at their backs as they disappeared into the house. Hmm, maybe she'd made a mistake encouraging her daughter to mix with the Barnaby girl. She'd obviously brought the nail varnish with her. Anyway, why *did* she suddenly have the urge to invite those girls around? After all, the Barnaby family were not usually the type of people they would normally mix with, especially that ignoramus, Jack Barnaby.

'Could we explore your garden?' asked Priscilla who had been dying to have a good look around. Not that she'd let on to Clara.

'Oh, look at these fairy statues and gnomes, aren't they cute,' cooed Clara, and patted one of the ornaments on the head. Gosh, did it move? She snatched her hand away before she had a chance to find out.

'C'mon, let's see what's through there,' said Priscilla.

Wallynus scowled at them as he watched them go under the raspberry arch to Mr Barnaby's vegetable patch. Who did that girl think

she was, he seethed, tapping me on the head like that, *and* having the cheek to call me, what was that word – "cute?"

Their exploring finished, Clara and Priscilla climbed up into the old hall. Priscilla was suitably impressed. Clara looked around about her and felt a pang of envy. Her garden only had a lawn which was full of weeds and dandelions, an old apple tree, a few half-dead flowers dotted about, and an old wooden shed that was falling to bits. Mr Dingle had been nagged continuously by Mrs Dingle to get a gardener in, but he had no intention of doing so, that would cost him money. Besides, what was wrong with her spending time in the garden instead of wasting most of the day looking out of the window or gossiping with that awful Mavis Dotty woman!

'Well, what shall we do now?' asked Jamie who was hoping that Clara and Priscilla would go.

'Let's pretend to be witches,' suggested Clara. 'I read a book on spells when I was in the library the other day.'

Priscilla was shocked to hear her say that, especially as she'd done nothing but complain to her ever since they had gone on the ghost train, 'I'll never listen to you again, making me go on that creepy ghost train,' she'd moaned. And come to think of it, when did Clara ever visit the library?

'But you…' she started to say.

'I think I can remember a couple of the spells.'

'I thought you didn't want to have anything to do with spooky things.'

'I never said anything of the sort,' snapped Clara.

'You could've fooled me,' Priscilla mumbled.

'I think that's a good idea,' said Lucy who was now hoping that the boys would refrain from goading Clara into a slanging match.

'Are you hoping to cast a love-spell on Timmy Armstrong?'

'This pot will definitely make a good cauldron,' Clara said, purposely ignoring Jamie. 'And this stick can be my wand.'

She waved her hand over the pot and spoke in a weird voice saying, 'I call upon the moon and stars…'

Out of nowhere a raven appeared beside her. The sky darkened and thunder rumbled overhead as a strong gust of wind tipped the pot off the stove. Bats whizzed in and out and landed upside-down on the cherry tree.

'I d-don't know what h-happened,' stammered Clara.

'It looks as if your spell worked,' laughed Will, remembering his mother's words that morning. 'Mind you take a jacket with you,' she'd said, 'I think we're in for a change of weather.'

'And all the time you've accused Hugh of doing weird things to you,' tutted Jamie remembering the weather report. For once, Clara had nothing to say.

'I think it was just a coincidence,' said Lucy, who was now glaring at the boys willing them to shut up.

Meanwhile, Clara vowed to herself that she would never, ever, read spooky books again. 'I think we'd better go,' she managed to say, and the girls took off as if their lives depended on it.

'That thunder came just at the right time. Goodbye Clara, goodbye Priscilla,' laughed Hugh.

'Yeah, but where did the bats come from?' asked Will.

'What bats?'

'They whizzed through the hall and onto the tree,' he said pointing to the cheery tree where a couple of magpies had landed.

'Funny looking bats,' murmured Jamie.

The following morning, Hugh and Lucy were at last making their way to the Candy Shoppe. It seemed that every time they decided to visit it, something got in the way, but not today. Hugh was especially looking forward to trying the chocolates as he loved chocolate more than anything. They had just reached the cottage when the old lady opened the garden gate and walked out in front of them.

'Mornin,' she smiled. 'Goin' into the shop, are yer?'

'Er – yes,' said Lucy.

'I was just goin' in meself.'

Mrs Pennywort, who was cleaning the window, opened the door to greet them, 'Come in,' she smiled. 'You are my first customers of the day.'

'I see yer still wearin' me brooch,' said the old lady.

Mrs Pennywort looked down at it and smiled. 'Ooh yes,' she cooed, 'I wear it always. Why, I even think it gives me energy.'

The old lady beamed from ear to ear.

'Well, don't let me keep yer from these young folk. I'll wait.'

She shuffled over to the other side of the shop where a bubblegum machine had been installed. The bright coloured bubblegum balls jiggled about in the container as if in greeting.

'What's your name, lass?' asked Mrs Pennywort glancing over at the old lady who smiled back.

'Lucy.'

'What?'

'Er – Lucy.'

'And yours, lad?'

Hugh was wondering why he suddenly felt the hairs on the back of his neck stand up as soon as they walked into the shop. It must be because of the creepy old lady, he reasoned. The old lady looked across the shop at him and narrowed her eyes. Crikey! Could she read his mind?

Mrs Pennywort coughed politely. 'Your name is…?'

'Oh sorry, it's Hugh,' he mumbled.

'Well, I've just made these samples. Do try them.'

Two pairs of eyes watched as they popped a chocolate into their mouths.

'These are great,' said Hugh. 'Could we buy some liquorice?'

'Chocolate covered liquorice if you have any,' Lucy added.

'I've only got these,' she said pointing to long flat pieces coated in milk chocolate.

'We'll have four pieces please,' said Lucy.

Mrs Pennywort put them into a bag and said, 'Well, my dears, the next time you visit I'll have more to choose from.'

Hugh and Lucy arrived home just as Mrs Barnaby was leaving for her hairdressing appointment.

'By the way, I've had the photographs developed. I've left them on the table for you,' and she rushed out the door.

Hugh's thoughts went straight to the Candy Shoppe. He decided that there was definitely something odd about the shop, even though Mrs Pennywort was very nice to them and the chocolates were the best he'd ever tasted.

He picked up the envelope and took out the black and white photographs. The first few were of his party. It was the fifth one that made his heart lurch – what was that? He took the photograph over to the window for a better look. He turned it to the light and realized it wasn't a shadowy figure leaning against the cherry tree at all, but the sunlight filtering through the branches.

'C'mon Hugh, don't hog the photos,' said Lucy who had just fetched a glass of water from the kitchen. He handed the first few over. Meanwhile, he shuffled through the ones of the family picnic, which was fine, until the smiling faces of the children from the Hall of Mirrors looked back at him. He quickly handed the rest of them to Lucy wondering what she would make of the photograph.

'They are great of the picnic,' was all she said.

He quickly shuffled through them again, but there was absolutely no sign of the children. What was going on?

A Tangled Web

Chapter Twenty-one

'I've discovered the old lady lives in the cottage next door to the Candy Shoppe,' said Major Osletwistle expecting some sort of thanks for all the effort he'd put in to tracking her down.

'I want yer to go into Mrs. Pennywort's again. See if yer can – yer know... ruffle her feathers a bit,' was all he got in reply.

He let out a disgruntled sigh, '*Again*?'

'Yer never know she might let somethin' slip.'

'If you say so,' he grumbled.

'I *do* say so, and while you're about it, stop sulkin'.'

'I'll have you know...'

'And not a word to me son, is that clear?' she scowled, daring him to defy her.

'Completely,' he scowled back.

Should he take the sports job? Why not? He knew that it would annoy the old girl no end. And so with a click of his fingers a flash of purple whizzed around the caravans and v-vroomed to a halt in front of him. He climbed in, roared away from the yard and zoomed up the street screeching to a halt outside the Candy Shoppe. He jumped out through the billowing steam and pulled out a red poker-dotted handkerchief which he unscrewed the radiator cap with. Sssssssss – POP sssssssssss – BANG!

Mrs. Pennywort was saying her goodbyes to Maud Underwood and Mrs Dotty when in marched the Major. He gave the ladies a little bow as they walked out the door. Mrs Dotty giggled girlishly up at him, taking note of the car. Oh my, she thought, what a charming man, and his sports car isn't half bad either.

'Good day to you, Mrs Pennywort,' he smiled. 'I'd like a box of your fabulous chocolates,' and he peered into the glass cabinet.

Mrs Pennywort waited patiently while he made his choice. He smiled politely as she weighed the chocolates before launching into his spiel.

'Been busy I expect?'

'Very.'

'I should think you'd get a lot of children in here wanting free samples, eh?' he said, giving her a knowing wink.

Mrs. Pennywort was beginning to feel very uncomfortable. It wasn't so much what he said; it was the way he said it. Was he taunting her – if so, why?

'No more than any other sweet shop,' she snapped, 'and being as I'm new in town, what else would you expect?'

Ahha, he thought, he'd managed to get to her.

'Forgive me, my dear,' he said innocently, 'I had no intention of offending you. I was only asking because one likes to think that people are successful in their new ventures.' Mrs Pennywort snorted suspiciously.

The Major stroked his moustache and continued. 'I don't like to see any business fail; especially when they offer such pleasure as your establishment will no doubt give selling these dashedly delicious chocolates,' he gushed, taking the box from her.

'Do excuse my snapping at you, Major Osletwistle, I've been so busy since I opened this place and I do feel a little on edge today. Overtired, you understand.'

He nodded sympathetically. In the meantime, Mrs Pennywort took a couple of chocolates from the sample basket.

'Let me pop a couple of extra chocolates in the box for you – a goodwill gesture on my part.'

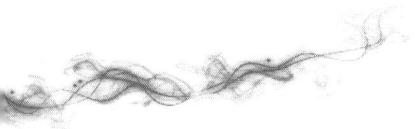

'Well, that is indeed most kind of you, Mrs Pennywort,' he cooed, 'and I shall certainly tell all my friends to frequent your wonderful establishment.' He looked at his watch. 'Well, I really must go, dear lady, be seeing you, tootle pip.'

The Major climbed into his car, turned on the engine and…was someone watching him? He glanced up and down the street and then at the old cottage half-expecting to see someone looking out at him. There wasn't. He slammed the car into gear and sped up the road whizzing past the newsagency. He had no idea that a shadow behind a net curtain knew his every move.

Morag quickly came to the conclusion that there was more to the Major than meets the eye. Was he one of the Macaba? She was convinced that he was, although she couldn't remember ever seeing him in the past. But of course, he could be a changeling like herself. So with that in mind, she vowed to be even more careful in future.

The curtain fluttered behind the window.

'Well, O honoured Mistress, I…' started the Major.

'I wish yer wouldn't call me that,' she barked. 'Me name is, Cornelia, and yer well know it, so I would appreciate it if yer would address me as such in future.'

His eyebrows shot up at that. Call the old girl "Cornelia" eh? Wonders would never cease, he must've done something right for once.

'Anyway,' he continued, 'Mrs Pennywort was not happy with our little conversation.' And then he gave her a blow-by-blow account of his visit.

She listened carefully to his every word. Yes, Osletwistle had done a good job.

'But we'll have to be very careful. She might get suspicious if yer keep turnin' up.'

'What about sending Demdyke?'

'Him?' she snorted. 'He's bound to bundle it.'

He agreed. Old Demdyke was a bit of an amateur at acting. Look at his attempt at being a travelling salesman for starters? How pathetic was that?

'We'll leave things as they are,' she paused, 'fer the time being, that is.'

'But there is one thing that I'm not altogether sure about,' he said.

'Oh? And what's that?'

'I had the distinct feeling that I was being watched.'

'Watched?'

He nodded. He was beginning to feel like a pawn in somebody's game of chess.

'Yer'll have to make sure yer not, won't yer?'

'I fail to see how I can be…'

'Well, if yer will tear about in that purple contraption of yours, what do yer expect? Anyway, afore yer go, weren't those chocolates fer me?'

Back in the Realm of Shadows, Morag was fuming at the turn of events. She had cast a strong protective spell around her, and that would usually stop an army of witches and sorcerers who would dare to interfere with her plans. Yes, she would have to be careful. Huh! It was probably her old enemy who was meddling in her affairs. Cornelia Romanski would be suspicious of a flea. Well, she would see about that. 'And if that Major what's-his-name thinks he can come snooping around for that old has-been, he's got another think coming,' she hissed. 'No one messes with me and gets away with it, NO ONE.'

'SIRAS,' she bellowed, 'where are you when I need you?'

The sorceress paced up and down muttering angrily to herself. She went over to the cauldron, lifted the lid and poured a vile smelling liquid into the bubbling brew followed by a bunch of herbs she had stolen from the herb master. Just let Marius try and interfere this time – she'd show him a thing or two. She opened her arms, palms up, and then set about casting her spell. Siras peeped around the door at her. No way was he going in there.

The Lord of Thunder appeared on a lightning flash. The snakes slithered around his feet and a deathly silence filled the air. He

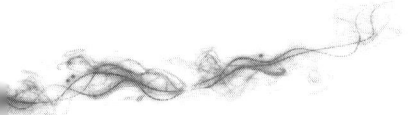

circled the room five times sparks flying around the room. He opened his arms and recited:

> I do appear this very night
> To support you in your plight
> For freedom cometh to do your will
> Events unfolding shall be a thrill

Lord Drago disappeared in a pillar of fire and smoke. Morag shook with excitement. To think that her master had appeared to her and she hadn't even asked him to.

Meanwhile, King Leo had sent Demdyke to spread the word for the Macaba to work with their scrying mirrors and crystal balls. Demdyke found many of the clan doing just that. It was with a happy heart that he called upon Old Mouldheels. He, as usual, was full of complaints. Demdyke decided that he really didn't have the time to argue with the grumpy wizard, so he set off to visit Harriet.

'Well, I can only spare half an hour a day. Anyway, I don't expect Mouldheels is pulling his weight.'

'What about your sister, Agatha?'

'What are you asking me for? Go and see her yourself. Anyway, I can't do anything while you're here wasting my time,' she grumbled.

Demdyke clicked his fingers and went in search of Agatha, hoping that she would be in a better mood than her sister. To his surprise, the old witch welcomed him with a smile. She told him that she had been very busy with her scrying mirror and had come to the conclusion that there was definitely something very odd about the shop.

Next on the list was Audra. He popped his head around the door and was more than pleased to see the other witches sitting around a table sharing a cup of tea. He explained the reason for his visit and they vowed to step up their scrying.

Demdyke then made his way to visit Elspeth who was busy trying out a new charm before she scribed it in the Book of Shadows. She went over to a bookshelf, pointed to the top shelf, and several books on spells, curses, and enchantments came floating to the ground. 'As you

can see, I'm knee-deep in work, but I suppose I can spare a few minutes a day.'

Demdyke resisted the urge to say, 'Don't bother.'

He left her and went on to visit Nobab who was busy pouring a blue liquid into a glass tube. Thank goodness Old Chattox was with him.

'If it isn't, Demdyke, come in. Sorry about the mess, I've been making a potion out of these extra special healin' herbs.' He pointed to a mound of green plants. 'Good fer the old bones, yer understand.'

'Perhaps you should give some to Mouldheels,' he commented.

'He wouldn't use it,' he scoffed. 'And it isn't as if I haven't tried.'

'I've been watching the Candy Shoppe and also an old lady who seems to be hangin' around,' said Old Chattox. And then he surprised Demdyke by saying, 'Do you think she could be – dare I say the name – Morag?'

Demdyke gasped, 'Which one do you mean, Mrs Pennywort or the old lady?'

Old Chattox shrugged. 'I couldn't say fer sure.' Great, thought Demdyke, he didn't have a clue.

'What about you, Nobab, what do you think?'

'Well,' he said rubbing his chin, 'seems to me that Morag could be anybody. After all, she's a very powerful sorceress.'

'Yes,' commented Old Chattox, 'and she was the best changeling I ever saw.'

Demdyke gasped again. 'Don't let the honoured Mistress hear you say that. Anyway, I'd best be on my way.'

'Afore yer go, I've somethin' to show yer. Bein' as me broomstick is a bit unreliable, I've managed to create somethin' a lot better.'

'That sounds interesting.'

'I can't click me fingers any more, of course,' said Old Chattox as he closed his eyes and mumbled a few incantations. A winged bike appeared before them.

'Well, goodness me, Chattox, how very clever of you. What have we here?' said Demdyke as he inspected the bike.

Chattox gave him a proud smile as he climbed on, only to find that the wings and wheels fell off under his weight.

'Oh, deary me – somethin' mighty fishy goin' on here. I mean, when I…'

The bike disappeared to be replaced by a large smelly fish. Old Chattox huffed and puffed whilst Nobab and Demdyke were finding it increasingly difficult to keep a straight face. The fish flapped its fins and grinned at the old sorcerer who was now waving his arms profusely.

'Fish, fish, I bid you farewell, to the depths of the ocean where you must dwell.' Gurgle, slurp – the fish vanished.

'Who summoned the bloomin' thing, that's what I'd like to know.'

'Don't look at me,' said Nobab.

'Perhaps your spell needs polishing up,' offered Demdyke.

Old Chattox looked a bit sheepish and said, 'I am a bit rusty, I must admit.'

Wings Of Magic

Chapter Twenty-two

Clara and Priscilla pushed open the door, not to the Candy Shoppe but somewhere dark and smelly.

'Now girls,' said a voice in the darkness, 'you will be invited to afternoon tea with the Barnabys. I want you to give them a little gift.'

A hand dangled something in front of them, and in a whirl of grey mist, they found themselves outside Priscilla's house completely oblivious to what had taken place.

'Come on, Priscilla,' called her mother from the window, 'we're supposed to be going to town.'

'I'll see you tomorrow then,' she said to Clara.

Priscilla closed the garden gate and walked up the path and just as she was about to enter the house, an enormous red butterfly dropped something shiny into the palm of her hand. It was a silver locket. She went inside and showed it to her mother.

A red-faced Mrs Dingle was waiting for Clara at the front door.

'Get inside,' she hissed and marched a flustered Clara into the kitchen where she picked up a package from the table. 'What's this?' she demanded.

'I have no idea, Mama.'

'The delivery man said you'd ordered it from the High Street Jewellers.'

'I did not,' she protested.

'Open it,' snapped Mrs Dingle.

Clara opened the package to find a silver locket inside. Where did it come from?

'I'll get to the bottom of this my girl, if it's the last thing I do.'

Mrs Dingle grabbed the phone off its hook and dialled a number. 'Is that the High Street Jeweller's? It is? Yes, well, my name is Mrs Dingle and I live at number 295 Stai...Not 255, 295...What? That's right. Your delivery man has just brought a package here for my daughter...I don't know.' She snatched the trinket from Clara's hand. 'Oh, it's a silver locket...Shape?' She rolled her eyes impatiently, 'its square with a fancy pattern on it...Oh really,' she smiled into the phone...' Ooh my...' she cooed placing her hand over the mouthpiece, 'apparently they're a new exclusive design.' She took her hand away and spoke into the mouthpiece again, 'How much is...hello...er – are you there?' No answer. Mrs Dingle was getting more irritated by the minute and was about to bellow down the phone at being kept waiting when the voice at the other end of the line returned. 'Yes, I'm still here,' she sighed. 'Good grief,' she exclaimed, throwing a stern look at Clara. 'Someone has sent it to her as a gift? Who? Oh, it doesn't say. Thank you, goodbye,' and she slammed down the telephone. 'Apparently, there's no mistake.' And seeing the puzzled look on Clara's face, she shrugged and said, 'Well, I suppose you could have an admirer.'

Clara was hoping it wasn't Bradley Perciville.

From behind his newspaper, Mr Dingle was thinking that was highly unlikely.He was certain that his daughter had bought it herself. As far as he was concerned, she was shaping up to be just like her mother and her weak excuses of, 'I bought this little number simply *ages* ago.'

The shadow peered at Lucy and Pamela as they crossed the road and waited at the bus stop. A sudden movement out of the corner of her eye had Lucy glance up at the empty flat above the bookshop. A pigeon had landed on the windowsill.

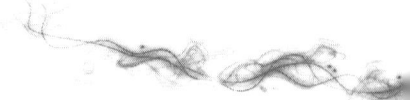

'Let's go to Mrs Pennywort's,' suggested Pamela.

'But we can buy chocolate at the cinema.'

'I know, but I haven't been to the Candy Shoppe yet. We can catch the next bus.'

Lucy suddenly had the urge to go herself. 'Okay, you win.'

They quickly crossed the road again, made their way to the shop and found Mrs Pennywort busy sweeping the floor. She looked up as they opened the door.

'How nice to see you again, Lucy isn't it? Not with your brother, then?'

'Not today, Mrs Pennywort.'

'Now who is this lovely young lady you've brought with you?'

'This is my friend, Pamela.'

'I don't believe you've tried any of my homemade chocolates have you, lass? Here you are,' said Mrs Pennywort handing Pamela the basket.

'Excuse me, Mrs Pennywort, but the basket's empty.'

Mrs Pennywort peered into the basket and frowned. 'That's funny; I've just filled it up. I'd better go and fetch some more.'

She went into her kitchen and filled the basket again. She was about to return to the shop when a grey mist swirled into the room. Mrs Pennywort stood with her hand on the door handle, staring into space.

The sorceress went over to a black pot that was bubbling away on the stove. She clicked her fingers and a small ladle appeared in her hand. She dipped the ladle into the liquid; it immediately turned purple. She poured it over the chocolates and threw two cockroaches into the brew giving it a good stir whilst reciting an incantation. A red vapour spouted from the pot. She scooped out some of the liquid; it immediately turned black. She poured it over a chocolate, 'A good helping of extra strong potion for you, Lucy Barnaby.'

Mrs Pennywort pushed open the door armed with the sample basket. 'Here you are girls.'

Lucy's hand went straight to the chocolate.

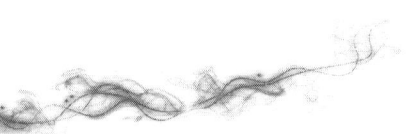

Mystery

Chapter Twenty-three

The insistent ring of the telephone broke the silence. Mr Barnaby picked it up to Jamie. He wanted to know if Hugh would be allowed to go to London for the day and that Will was coming as well. He explained that his mother was going to the Oxford Street sales and his father had a business meeting to attend.

It took over an hour to drive up to London and find a parking space. First on the agenda was lunch at the Lyon's Corner House. Jamie's father suggested the boys catch the tube to Piccadilly Circus. They made arrangements to meet him at the Eros statue by five that afternoon, which gave the boys just over three hours to see the sights.

Following the signs to Trafalgar Square they came upon it in no time at all, passing by Leicester Square on the way. They spent time feeding the pigeons and walking around the statues and fountains. On Will's suggestion, they decided to give Buckingham Palace a miss and catch the train to Tower Bridge.

They rushed out of the station and headed towards the Tower of London. The queue was so long and considering that they didn't have hours to spend, they decided to walk around the outside and came across Traitors' Gate. They tried to imagine how scary it would have

been going through the gate wondering if they would ever see the light of day again.

From there, they made their way to Covent Garden with the intention of looking around the markets. Somehow, they managed to take a wrong turn when leaving the tube station and landed up in a narrow cobbled laneway which had a few quaint houses and shops. One shop in particular caught their eye. It was much older than the others and leaning to one side. The dark green sign had: Y*e Olde Apothecary Est. 1895* written on it in gold lettering.

A strong smell of aniseed reached them as they stepped inside to find a surprisingly large store. The old-fashioned remedies and herbal cures especially fascinated Hugh and Jamie. Will picked up a bottle of brown liquid; the label promised a cure for the common cold. Did he hear someone say, 'Put it down?'

A silver-haired man stood behind the counter scooping white powder into a brown paper bag. A pair of brass scales was mysteriously moving up and down, up and down. A glass bowl with blue liquid bubbling inside it suddenly overflowed, dribbled onto the floor, and seeped its way towards their feet. A scruffy terrier came out from behind the counter and licked it up, disappearing as quickly as it came.

The chemist had a long white coat over his clothes. On the end of his nose, he wore half-glasses which he peered over continuously with his pale grey watery eyes, keeping a close eye on the boys as they explored the shop. He coughed loudly when they picked up any items of interest.

'Perhaps we'd better buy something,' whispered Will.

Hugh bought a hand-made bar of soap for his mother, Jamie, a hand lotion made from wild herbs for his, and Will bought a box of lavender pot-pourri for his mother. The old man slowly wrapped their purchases and, apart from telling them how much the items cost, he didn't smile or utter a word.

They left the Apothecary with their gifts and wandered past shops selling old and rare books, antiques, and curios. There were several fancy-dress shops, many of which sold different types of wigs, false noses and beards. They rounded a corner and came upon another shop

called "Mystery". It was painted black. The door opened and several people came out carrying books, candles, and various packages. The shopkeeper noticed them peering into the window and came out. She glanced up and down the lane as if she was looking for someone. The lady's long purple dress and the black shawl she had draped around her shoulders, made her appear much older than she was. A lace cap with shiny coins adorned her head and her glossy black hair reached her waist.

They decided to give the shop a miss, for they all agreed that the shopkeeper reminded them of the old lady from the cottage, except she was a lot younger. They hurried on by and turned round yet another corner, only to land up in another cobbled lane. The smell of coffee and freshly baked pastries drew their attention to a small café that was wedged between a shoe shop and a hat shop. The café was a quaint crooked building with a bay window and a sign advertising it as, *The Oracle*.

'I don't know about you, but I could do with a drink and a bite to eat,' said Jamie, feeling his stomach rumble.

'Me too,' said Hugh, wondering why the name sounded familiar. And then his stomach did a dive. Didn't the old tramp mention that word?

'Let's go in before we head back to Piccadilly Circus,' suggested Will.

They stepped inside the tiny café furnished with only five tables. A small counter was squeezed into a corner. They sat down and waited for someone to serve them. Jamie eyed the people who were sitting at the other tables with curiosity. They were all wearing very odd-looking clothes. He nudged Will who was busy reading the list of food on offer. Hugh was looking out of the window, and wondered why his stomach started to feel as if there were a hundred butterflies inside it. He put it down to the fact that he was hungry and thirsty.

'Did you notice that strange looking couple over there?' whispered Jamie, nodding over to a man and lady who were sitting over the other side of the room.

The man was dressed in a long dark brown coat with a cape attached. On his head sat a large-brimmed hat sporting an ostrich

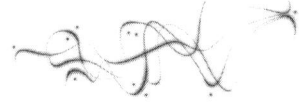

feather. He had a small mouth and a long nose with large nostrils. He kept stroking his heavy jaw whilst he glanced casually around the café, until his coal black unblinking eyes rested on Jamie.

The lady wore a long blue skirt with a bustle and a navy blue fitted jacket fastened at the neck by a cameo brooch. Her long blonde hair had been shoved carelessly under a straw hat that she wore tilted jauntily over her forehead. She was very pretty and Jamie noticed she had sparkly bright green eyes. She threw her head back and laughed heartily at something the man had said.

'Perhaps they're actors,' whispered Jamie, 'after all, this is where most of the theatres are.'

It was then that Hugh noticed the couple, for he had been busy looking at the comings and goings of the people passing by, thinking that they all appeared to be dressed in Victorian clothes.

'I think you're right,' said Hugh, glancing over at the couple.

The man leaned forward and spoke softly to the lady who looked over in Hugh's direction. For a brief moment, he thought she looked like the lady from the Hall of Mirrors, although she had different coloured hair. But when she turned around and faced him fully, he realized he was mistaken. He quickly looked away and fiddled around with the knobs of sugar in the chipped glass sugar bowl.

'What do you want?' asked a waitress dressed in a black uniform, a white apron, and a frilly cap. Where did she spring from?

'Could I have a piece of chocolate cake and an orange juice?' asked Jamie.

Hugh ordered a piece of apple pie and a glass of Tizer. Will wanted a scone with lashings of jam and cream and a glass of lemonade. The waitress hurried away.

'This place is definitely odd,' said Will.

'Well, you chose it,' Jamie replied, nodding over to two men who had just entered. They sat down by the window. The larger of the two had a scar running down the left side of his face from his forehead to his chin. He had only one eyebrow which was thick and bushy and his eyes were bright blue. His ruddy complexion, large fleshy nose, and thick lips turned down at the corners, made him look sinister; especially when he gave the waitress a smile showing pointed stained teeth. He

was wearing a ragged grey shirt under a moth-eaten jacket which he wore open over black baggy trousers. He was bare-footed.

The other man was dressed in a white open-necked shirt with puffy sleeves. The shirt was unbuttoned to the waist, showing a hairy chest and displaying a skull and crossbones hanging from a thick gold chain. He wore a black leather waistcoat, and his voluminous blue trousers were tucked into leather boots. His red scarf, tied and knotted at the back of his head, reminded them of a pirate. The black patch on his right eye completed the picture. Will noticed that he wore a large ruby ring on the middle finger of his right hand, which he kept twirling around absentmindedly.

'They're definitely actors. I mean, why else would you dress like that?' said Will. Hugh glanced over at them and caught his breath. The man with the eye patch gave him a lop-sided grin.

'Don't look now, but don't you think that man looks like the squatter?' Hugh whispered.

'Which man?'

'The man dressed like a pirate.'

'He doesn't to me,' said Jamie.

'Me neither,' said Will, just as the waitress arrived with their order.

They tucked into the food and drink hungrily. All thought of the strangely dressed people went momentarily from their minds until a hearse pulled by two black horses stopped outside. Was that a coffin inside it?

The coachman stepped down from his seat, opened the door and helped a lady onto the cobbled ground. She was wearing black from head to toe. A veil, covering her face, billowed from a large brimmed hat. The driver, who was very tall and thin, was wearing a black top hat and his dark grey coat brushed the cobbles with every step he took. The door opened and in they walked.

The couple sat down at the table next to the boys, who were trying not to stare at them. The sombre expression on the man's face caused Jamie to chuckle nervously. He brought out his handkerchief and pretended to wipe his nose. The man glared at him – his lifeless lips forming a straight line. He turned his attention back to the lady who was

dabbing her eyes with a handkerchief. To Jamie, the man looked like a skeleton, the only difference being, he had ghostly white flesh covering his face and hands.

The man beckoned to the waitress. She strolled over, pencil to the ready, took his order and hurried away. An unnerving stillness filled the air, like a graveyard waiting for its next corpse.

From the other side of the room, the man with the large brimmed hat sneezed, breaking the deathly silence which had suddenly descended upon the café. He looked over at the lady dressed in black and tipped his hat. The lady glanced nervously about the room with feverish eyes. She stood up suddenly and with a swish of her skirt, she hurried outside. Her ghostly companion was now heading in their direction. Jamie tried to warn Hugh by nudging his foot. Too late, he tapped Hugh on the shoulder. Startled, he turned around and looked up into dark lifeless eyes. The man bent down and whispered in Hugh's ear, his breath smelling of dried blood.

'Beware,' he rasped, 'there are evil forces at work,' and then he strode out the door. The two strange men, who were sitting by the window, stood up and threw a few coins onto the table. They also left but not before glancing over at the boys and smirking. The boys sat motionless, too frightened to move. What should they do?

'Let's get out of this place,' whispered Will.

They stood up to leave, but an icy hand on Hugh's shoulder forced him to sit down again. He was terrified, especially when he realized that the owner of the hand was none other than the scary man in the black top hat. Hadn't he just left?

Jamie and Will stood staring into space while a strong wind whistled against the windowpanes. The door flew open and slammed shut. That brought Will and Jamie out of their daze with a jolt. What was going on? They looked around for the waitress but she had disappeared, leaving an empty room, save for the lady dressed in black sitting alone at a table sipping from a cup. But hadn't she also left the café?

The man squeezed Hugh's shoulder with his bony hand. The lady sipped at her tea. Hugh could feel the beads of sweat forming on his forehead as the man stared down at him with his dead eyes.

'What do you want?' Hugh gasped aware that his pulse was racing.

'What do I want?' he mimicked. 'Why, absolutely nothing, boy,' and he clapped his hands.

The boys were stuffing into a piece of chocolate cake, a chunk of apple pie, and a scone with lashings of jam and cream and were totally unaware of what had taken place. A waitress with bright orange hair came sauntering over. She had a pencil tucked behind her ear and was chewing gum. She fumbled around in her pocket, brought out a notepad, ripped off a page, and waved it in Jamie's face.

'Here's yer bill and make it snappy, as yer can see, we're very busy,' and she nodded over to the other tables.

A man sat just across from them tucking into a shepherd's pie. On another table, two ladies were busy gossiping over a cup of tea, and three people occupied another table. An old man who was sitting by the window, fiddled with a few coins which had been left behind. He glanced across at Hugh, stood up, picked up his carrier bag, and shuffled out the door - or was it through it? And then it dawned on Hugh. Wasn't he the old tramp? A child pushed the door open and a family of four walked in.

'I'm hungry,' said a little girl tugging at her father's sleeve.

'I wanna sit down,' cried her sister.

'You'll just have to wait until there's a free table,' snapped the mother and bent down to wipe the little girl's runny nose.

'I'm sure those are the children we saw playing outside the nisson huts,' whispered Will to Hugh.

'But the mother looks different.'

The waitress gave the boys a meaningful look, making it obvious that she wanted the table, so they quickly finished their food, paid the bill and left. Hugh glanced up and down the lane, hoping to catch sight of the old tramp. But he was nowhere to be seen.

'Which way do you reckon we should go?' asked Jamie.

They decided to go right, hoping that would lead them to Convent Garden Square. After turning around several corners trying to find

their way out of the maze of cobbled laneways, they landed up outside the shop named "Mystery".

'We must be going around in circles,' said Will.

'And there aren't any street names, either.'

'How do we find our way out of here then?'

'Good question.'

'And where is everybody?'

'Let's go into that haberdashery over there and ask for directions.'

They tried the door but it was locked. They tried the other shops but they each displayed a "Closed for the afternoon" sign on their doors. Hugh thought it would be a good idea to return to the café and ask the waitress the way to the tube station. Will commented that they probably should've thought about that in the first place.

They retraced their steps but there was absolutely no sign of the café, only the shop called "Mystery". Jamie suggested asking the shopkeeper for directions, considering that was the only place that appeared to be open. So reluctantly they stepped inside to the strum of a guitar coming from deep within the shop. An odd scratchy voice called out – 'Welcome t' me parlour, welcome t' me parlour.' It turned out to be a Minor bird which was hopping about on a perch, bobbing its head up and down excitedly. He bobbed his head up and down again and screeched, 'Wanna cup o' tea, wanna cup o' tea?' at them.

The shop was dimly lit and there was nobody about. Should they leave and try to find their way to the Apothecary? But the thought of traipsing around the lanes again didn't seem like a very good alternative. And, besides, the sign on the door read, "OPEN".

They decided to explore the shop while waiting for the lady to show up. An enormous book bound in leather caught their eye. It had the word, "*VOODOO*", written on the cover in red and black lettering. What in the world was: Voodoo?

Gruesome masks and statues were positioned around the shop to ensure that the customers received a surprise at every turn. Pointed hats and cloaks were strewn haphazardly across a large chest. Wands in several sizes hung from large hooks. Silver goblets were displayed in the glass counter. On shelves, stood massive glass containers filled with

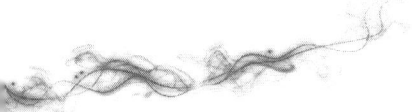

weird looking objects. Lizard tongues, fox tails, eagle claws and shark teeth, were written on the labels. On the counter were jars housing eyes in different sizes, floating about in a yellow liquid. There were garlands of garlic hanging from the ceiling along with bunches of dried herbs and lavender.

Large pots that looked distinctly like witches' cauldrons were stacked up against a wall in a corner. Books on magic charms had been tied in large bundles and placed next to the cauldrons. An old battered broomstick stood by a door.

Cobwebs and spiders were in abundance. Propped up against the cauldrons were several wooden staffs carved with grotesque faces. Ornate swords and daggers were displayed on the walls. Other books laden with dust had been stacked carelessly on shelves.

In a glass cabinet, crystal balls in various sizes were displayed on black velvet. On another shelf, an enormous leather book etched with faded gold lettering titled, *Book of Ancient Mysteries and Enchantments*, tumbled to the ground and fell open. They flicked through the fragile pages which had strange looking symbols scrawled on them. On another page, the signs of the zodiac were listed. They turned over to drawings of dried herbs and a list of tinctures and potions. On other pages, various types of wands and staffs and their usages were etched in charcoal. They turned over yet another page where the words – *Spells* and *Curses* glared back at them. Whatever the spells and curses were, were written in a foreign language; but one word stood out more than the others – BEWARE.

With a swish of a skirt and a jangle of coins, the lady came out from behind a black curtain. A sudden icy chill filled the air as frost crept over the shop like a ghostly white blanket. The lady pulled her shawl tightly around her shoulders, staring at them with her enormous dark eyes.

'Excuse me,' said Will, his voice barely a whisper,' 'but we are trying to find our way out of here.' The lady smirked at him, her eyes travelling to the open book.

'Find the book interestin' did yer?' she grinned and then…did she make the book float through the air and on to the shelf?

'Could you tell us how to get to Covent Garden?' croaked Jamie not wanting to stay in the spooky shop any longer and besides, it was freezing.

'Yer here, lad,' she said.

'I meant the tube station.'

'What's that got ter do wiv me?' she snorted. 'Don't yer wanna know what's afore yer?' She reached into her pocket and pulled out a pack of Tarot cards.

'No thanks, we haven't got time.'

The lady raised an eyebrow. 'Everyone's got time ter 'ave their fortune told.'

'Well, we haven't,' snapped Will, 'so if you'd tell us the way?'

'Please yerself,' she shrugged, and produced a pendulum on a piece of string. She walked around the shop mumbling strange words, while the pendulum swung back and forth, back and forth, until it stopped in front of Hugh.

'I'll read yer Tarot fer half price, lad.'

Hugh shook his head unable to find his voice. The lady threw back her head and laughed and laughed and laughed. What did she find so funny?

'Ah well, if yer don't, yer don't,' she shrugged and walked over to the door and opened it.

'Now turn left as yer go out. Follow the lane ter the end, and then turn right. That should take yer ter Covent Garden Square.' They thanked her and hurried out of the shop as fast as they could.

They followed her instructions, pausing only once to double check that they were heading in the right direction. They forged on until they could see an opening a little way ahead. They hurried towards the opening but landed in a small cobbled square with nothing but an old church and an empty park bench. Realizing that they must have missed a turning, they rounded another corner hoping to find someone who could help them. And then they had a stroke of luck, just ahead of them was a glimpse of sunlight.

'That must be it,' said Hugh in relief, but then he frowned. 'But come to think of it, I'm sure there wasn't a lane there before.'

'We must've missed it.'

'C'mon lets go,' said Jamie.

They hurried down the lane towards the light but skirted to a halt at the end. A horse-drawn hearse carrying a large oblong wooden box stood...waiting. They about-turned and ran as fast as they could; zipping around corners and bolting down alleyways until they arrived once again outside the shop called "Mystery".

'How did we land up here again?' asked Will, looking up and down the dark cobbled lane.

'You don't think that something is holding us here, do you?'

'What, like – a prisoner?'

Hugh nodded.

'You're bonkers if you think that. We probably got lost going around in circles.'

Jamie glanced at his watch. 'Jeepers, we've only twenty minutes until we're supposed to meet my Dad.'

The door of the shop opened and the lady came out, only this time she had a haggard face, grey wispy hair, and was bent over a walking stick. They turned ready to make a run for it but she stood in front of them, barring the way. How did she do that?

'What do you want?' squeaked Jamie who was beginning to think that just maybe, Hugh was right.

'Now why would I want somethin' from you?' she snorted. 'But would yer like yer fortune told?' She then miraculously produced a crystal ball, waving her hand over the top in a circular movement looking spookier than ever.

'We don't want our fortune told,' snapped Hugh eyeing the crystal as it hovered in mid air. 'We told the other lady that.'

'Not want yer fortune told?' the lady said, feigning surprise. 'Yer didn't think of that when yer had yer palms read,' she grinned, 'did yer?'

The boys looked from one to the other. How did she know that?

'All we want to do is find Covent Garden tube station,' croaked Will.

'Now be off wiv yer. Go ter the end of this lane, and yer'll see the station just ahead of yer.'

They bolted out of the shop and ran all the way until they reached the tube station. The train for Piccadilly Circus had just pulled in. They bounded down the steps and jumped aboard seconds before the doors closed.

'Phew!' said Hugh, 'I didn't think we'd make it.'

'Yeah,' nodded Jamie, 'but it's funny how the station just appeared in front of us.'

Will shivered. 'I don't care about that, I'm just glad to get out of there, that lady sure was creepy.'

'I know, she reminded me of that foreign squatter lady, except that the shopkeeper was ancient,' said Jamie.

'And she was English,' Hugh added.

'That's the last time I'm going to Covent Garden,' said Will.

'You wouldn't get me going there again either.'

A clown stood on the platform and laughed heartily as he watched the train disappear down the tunnel wiping away their memory of the time spent in the shop called "Mystery".

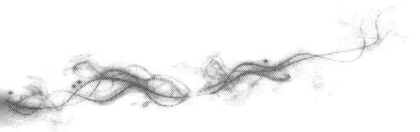

All That Glitters

Chapter Twenty-four

M rs Pennywort had that morning mislaid her brooch and had spent ages looking for it. She was busy sweeping the floor when the bell chimed. She was in no mood for idle chitchat, especially if the customer proved to be that dreadful Dingle woman or that absolute bore, Mr Drummond. Her mood changed immediately when two boys entered. Ping! A shiny object landed by her feet. It was her beautiful brooch. She picked it up and hurriedly pinned it on her dress.

'What can I do for you, boys?'

'We'd like some chocolate toffees, please,' said Jamie, glancing over to where the sample basket usually sat.

'I'm afraid you've seen the last of the samples,' she apologized, 'until I try something new, of course.'

Jamie felt his face grow hot. Did she think he was trying to get something for nothing?

Mrs Pennywort scooped the toffees out of a large jar, put them in a paper bag and weighed them. The shop door opened and in sauntered a cat.

'Not that wretched cat again,' she tutted and shot out from behind the counter shooing it away.

'I suppose it's my fault for giving it a saucer of milk,' she smiled and handed them the bag of toffees.

'Thanks Mrs Pennywort, we'll be back.'

The cat stood watching the boys as they walked along the street and licked its lips.

'Hand over the toffees, then,' said Will.

'Okay, keep your hair on,' he shot back. They both popped a toffee into their mouths.

'Blimey!' Will said of the dark cave. 'Where are we?'

'Don't ask me,' croaked Jamie looking about him.

'Let's get out of this creepy place,' whispered Will.

They felt along the walls until they came across an old battered wooden door.

'We'll try the door.'

Jamie pushed and pushed and the door creaked open to a stagecoach pulled by four black horses which came galloping towards him. He was about to yell out and warn Will, but the door slammed shut behind him. There was no escaping the stagecoach that pulled up in front of him. A little man stepped down, grabbed hold of his arm and dragged him into the carriage.

With a flick of the reigns, the stagecoach sped forward into the unknown. Petrified, Jamie looked out of the window into the empty blackness. All he could hear was the crack of a whip, the whinny of the horses and the rumble of the wheels as the stagecoach journeyed forward coming to an abrupt halt outside…'Jeez, it's a castle,' he exclaimed.

The little man dragged him through massive double doors to somewhere dark and dingy. A deer's head hung on a wall flanked either side by shiny shields and swords. An elaborate staircase dominated the centre of the large hall. A door opened and he was shoved into a room by a faceless being.

Meanwhile, Will pushed the door open to an even darker cave. A candle suddenly sprung to life and shone on a brightly coloured Persian rug.

'Jamie, where are you?' he called.

'You wanted a ride on a magic carpet, didn't you? Here's your chance,' whispered a voice in his ear. Was it Jamie having a laugh?

'Come on, Jamie, stop mucking about.'

Will felt a hand on his back and before he knew what was happening, he was pushed onto the carpet. With an almighty R-O-A-R, the carpet lifted off the ground, shot forward and he found himself standing next to – blimey...JAMIE?

Lucy had returned with Clara and Priscilla, having invited them for afternoon tea under strict instructions from Mrs Barnaby. She reckoned Hugh would probably go bananas when he found out, especially as Pamela had gone out with her family, so it would be just them.

'Will Hugh be with us this afternoon?' asked Clara.

Lucy was taken aback – why did she want to know that? After all, Clara had made it painfully obvious she didn't like her brother one bit. What gives?

In the meantime, Mrs Barnaby set about preparing the food when Mr Barnaby came into the kitchen and picked up a slice of chicken.

'Don't touch,' she said tapping his hand, 'Clara and Priscilla are here for the afternoon.'

'Good heavens! How did that come about?'

'I thought I'd better return the favour.'

'Return the favour? I'm not sure that Lucy and Hugh would see it that way.'

The bell chimed and he went into the shop leaving Mrs Barnaby to wonder why she'd had the sudden urge to invite Clara and Priscilla in the first place. The door opened and in walked Hugh.

'Do I have to, Mum?' he asked when he heard the news.

'Yes, I'm afraid you do,' Mrs Barnaby replied, 'and no buts.'

How he was going to put up with those two all afternoon, he'd never know. Perhaps he could feign a stomach ache? But before he had a chance to put his plan into action, Mrs Barnaby gave him a tray laden with food and he grudgingly took it out to the garden.

'Here you are, at last,' Clara gushed.

Hugh mumbled something in return and put the tray down on the table. Lucy was trying her hardest to make small talk, while Hugh made no bones about the fact that he was sulking.

From his post by the hydrangea bush, Wallynus had noticed a shadow hovering over Clara and Priscilla, a shadow of evil. He decided to keep a close eye on them and do something about it if needs must.

'I know you and I haven't exactly got along, Hugh,' started Clara, 'but I would like to give you a sort of peace-offering.'

She reached into her pocket – it was empty. She felt into the other one – nothing. 'I must've lost it,' she frowned. But why did she want to give Hugh Barnaby a gift in the first place – whatever it was.

'What was it, anyway?

'It doesn't matter now, does it?' she snapped.

Priscilla handed a small package to Lucy with the excuse that she had been brought up never to go empty-handed when invited anywhere for the first time. Lucy opened it to – nothing! Priscilla stared at the empty box wondering what it was she was supposed to have bought her. And come to think of it, why had she had the sudden urge to buy Lucy a gift in the first place? And what about Clara, she couldn't stand Hugh Barnaby.

'Someone must've stolen our gifts,' said Clara. If only she could remember what they were.

'It doesn't matter,' said Lucy, 'it's the thought that counts.'

A movement next to the hydrangea bush drew Clara's eyes over to it. I'm sure that weird looking garden ornament has turned to look at me, she thought. Why she had listened to her mother about mixing with the Barnabys she'd never know. There was something very peculiar about them, especially spooky, Hugh.

'That's my Mum's new garden gnome, odd, isn't it?' said Lucy who had noticed Clara staring at it.

Clara sneaked another look, but it was in its usual position, facing the other way. She made up her mind there and then that she didn't want to stay with Hugh and Lucy any longer. And as for their garden well...it wasn't normal – especially the old hall.

'Oh, look at the time,' she said glancing at her watch, 'Mama will be wondering where I've got to.'

'But you haven't finished eating,' said Lucy.

'I've got to go too,' said Priscilla who had the distinct feeling that the strange garden ornament's eyes were on her.

'What a pity...' Lucy started to say as Clara and Priscilla jumped up and hurried away.

'What's wrong with them?'

'I don't know and I don't care,' said Hugh.

'We never did find out what the gifts were supposed to be.'

'Knowing Clara, it was probably something that Mrs Dingle was throwing out.'

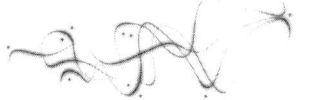

Lost

Chapter Twenty-five

'It seems yer right, Charlie, I wouldn't mind bettin' that their shadow selves have been taken,' nodded his grandmother.

Charlie gaped at her, 'I only said Will and Jamie seemed to be in a bit of a daze when I bumped into them. What do yer mean by "shadow selves"?'

'Pay attention,' she barked, 'it means a person's energy, fer the likes of those that are not in the know.'

Charlie didn't have a clue what his grandmother was talking about. And if that wasn't enough, she gave him another piece of startling news.

'Of course, Morag's probably cast them in the Place of Shadows by now.'

'She's what? Where's that?'

'It's a place where time stands still. But she's only usin' them as bait to lure Hugh into her web.' Was that supposed to make him feel better?

'And this is where the crystal comes in to play,' she winked. 'Still, me lips are sealed, can't say no more.'

'But…'

'I suggest yer go and find yer sister,' and, with a dismissive flick of her wrist, she made it obvious she had no intention of telling him anything else.

Charlie stepped down from the wagon feeling more confused than ever.

Pamela arrived at the Candy Shoppe and was just about to push the door open when she had an awful creepy feeling that someone was watching her. But before she could turn away, Mrs Pennywort came to the door and opened it.

'Hello, my dear, do come in.'

Pamela found herself following Mrs Pennywort inside but not before glancing over her shoulder.

'Now, what can I serve you with?'

'A box of chocolates for my Aunty Joyce, please. It's her birth…'

The door opened and in walked a smartly dressed lady. She also wanted to buy a box of chocolates.

'Have a look in the cabinet; I've added a few extra to my repertoire.'

'Have you any of those special ones?' asked the lady.

'I'm afraid I haven't got around to making any today.'

'What a pity.'

While Mrs Pennywort was busy weighing their purchases, the lady opened her handbag and pulled out her purse and…CLATTER! Something shiny landed at Pamela's feet. She looked down to discover that it was a small silver box. She picked it up and the lid fell open.

As her eyes adjusted to the darkness, Pamela realized she was not in the Candy Shoppe, but a large dark cave.

'H-E-L-P,' she called out. 'Will someone help me?'

Menacing laughter echoed around the walls making her hair stand on end. She looked round about her expecting something to jump out at her at any second. A feeling of sheer panic came over her and she dashed around the cave looking for a way out. In her haste, she tripped and tumbled down a black hole landing next to a pile of bones. She screamed into the darkness and scrambled to her feet, running hysterically in all directions. A candle sprang to life and she found herself in another cave.

'Never mind, my dear,' said a hypnotic voice, 'the door to freedom awaits you.'

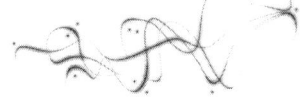

But the doorway failed to appear. Morag couldn't believe her eyes. Had it lost its power? Oh curses upon curses, she'd have to use the Genie instead.

'Help me get out of here,' called Pamela into the darkness.

'Trust me,' came the voice again...a smooth calming voice... telling her to...

Pamela found herself picking up an old bronze lamp. What should she do with it?

'Go on, dearie,' give it a rub,' urged the voice.

And Pamela gave it a rub but the Genie failed to appear. Morag could have exploded with frustration. What was wrong with Mig? Still, she couldn't expect much else, considering he wasn't of Genie blood, and if that troublesome goblin thought he was going to get away with it, he'd got another think coming. And she definitely wasn't going to let this slip of a girl escape her clutches... EITHER!If only she knew where Maestro had disappeared to, what a Genie he was, the best in the land. Marius had hinted that he had a better offer elsewhere that's why he'd left in such a hurry. Still, knowing the herb master, he was just stirring the pot. Anyway, he probably had the Genie virus, there was one going around apparently. No way would he had left her employ for good.

The Genie was lying on satin cushions enjoying a bunch of grapes and a goblet of pumpkin juice.

'Try again, dear,' said the voice, 'I'm sure if you rub the lamp in a circular movement the Genie will appear.'

Pamela tried again. The Genie didn't appear.

Morag snatched the lamp from her and gave it a good shake.

'What the…?'

Another shake of the lamp had the Genie don his hat, straighten his jacket and appear in front of a startled Pamela. The sorceress eyed her latest victim with satisfaction. Yes, her energy will add to the spell nicely. If only Mig would hurry up and get on with it.

The Genie felt Morag's eyes boring into him. Why should he always jump to her command? No, he would take his time and she'd jolly well have to wait. And so he strolled around the cave as if he

had all the time in the world polishing his fingernails on his jacket. He picked up the lamp, breathed on it and gave it a polish.

Morag seethed at his insolence, but what could she do? She needed this, this…poor excuse for a Genie, for the time being, of course.

Mig was enjoying himself immensely. He had delighted in rendering the door useless, especially now that Lord Drago had bestowed upon him the honour of becoming doorkeeper to the Place of Shadows, something his mistress had no doubt forgotten. A little reminder wouldn't go amiss.

With an elaborate display of swirling around in a column of purple vapour, he produced a wooden box, opened the lid, and tiny little creatures jumped out carrying pots of gold dust. They scurried around the cave flicking the walls until they glowed in the dark. Morag rolled her eyes. Was this little display of magic supposed to impress her? With a smug grin aimed at Morag, the Genie waved his hand and the doorway opened in readiness for its next victim. On the other side, a beautiful dress Pamela had seen a shop window was draped over a chair. She was ecstatic, how did the Genie know that she wanted it?

'Go through, dear, your wish awaits you on the other side.'

Pamela stepped through, not to the dress, but a vast room where she came face to face with – 'JAMIE and...WILL?'

'Here you are, Madam,' said Mrs Pennywort handing the lady her box of chocolates. The lady thanked her, opened the door and almost bumped into Mrs Dingle. With an, 'Excuse me,' the lady rushed past her. With a glare at the lady's back, Mrs Dingle entered the shop.

'Hello, Mrs Dingle, how are you?' Pamela asked.

'Apart from the fact that Clara had an unfortunate experience at your friend, Lucy Barnaby's house, I'm quite well,' she snapped. After all's said and done, this girl fraternized with the Barnaby girl. That made her tarred with the same brush as far as she was concerned. Her eyes flicked over to where the basket usually sat.

'I'm sorry, Mrs Dingle,' said Mrs Pennywort, 'but I haven't had time to make any more samples. What can I serve you with?'

Mrs Dingle mumbled something in reply, marched out of the shop and across the road to the bakery. She had no idea beady eyes were watching her.

Later that morning, Clara and Priscilla were walking towards the Candy Shoppe when they almost bumped into Major Osletwistle and his dog. The dog bared his teeth.

'A very good day to you, girls,' he said, giving the dog a reprimand and the lead a tug. 'Going to the Candy Shoppe are you?'

'Yes,' said Priscilla keeping an eye on the dog who was now growling ferociously at Clara.

'Well, I must be going, but be very careful won't you, tootle pip.'

'I wonder why he said that.'

'Said what?'

'You know, for us to be careful.'

'How should I know?' snapped Clara.

'And where did he vanish to?'

'Don't be silly, Priscilla, he...well, he must've...um...hopped on a bus. Yes, that's what he did.' And she pushed the door open not to the Candy Shoppe, but the small, musty, dark room.

Clara and Priscilla looked about the bleak room in fear. Where was this smelly place? How long would they be kept there? Priscilla began to feel very, very, scared.

'Have you managed to give those gifts to the Barnabys?' snarled a voice in the darkness.

'Well, you see it was like this,' blustered Clara and explained what had happened.

Morag was furious to learn that they had failed her miserably; obviously they weren't up to the task. She had plans for Clara, though; her negative energy would serve her spell well. She clicked her fingers and a door creaked open. A hideous-looking hunchbacked man entered. He grabbed hold of Clara's arm and whisked her kicking and screaming into the unknown. To her absolute horror, she found herself standing before the astonished faces of Pamela, Will, and, oh no – not Jamie Smart!

Mrs Pennywort was rushed off her feet when the girls entered the shop. They waited and waited to be served.

'Let's go to the park,' said Clara.

'Didn't you want to buy some fruit gums?'

'Not if it means having to wait forever,' she retorted.

Priscilla followed Clara out of the shop and into the street. They had nearly reached the park when Clara stopped suddenly. Did she really want to spend the rest of the afternoon with Priscilla? She could be such a bore at times and besides she was feeling very tired all of a sudden.

'I don't think I'll go to the park after all. See you tomorrow,' she said and strutted off leaving Priscilla to walk home alone. She couldn't make up her mind whether she felt more stunned or annoyed at her so-called friend's sudden departure. And what about Mrs Pennywort, she didn't even say hello.

The Place Of Shadows

Chapter Twenty-six

'What are *you* doing here?' Clara gasped.

'The same as you,' said Jamie wonderin how on earth they had landed up in a castle and a spooky one at that.

They gaped around the huge room that looked more like a dungeon except for the creepy old paintings staring out at them from the walls. A long wooden table and high-backed chairs occupied the centre of the room. Old tattered armchairs covered in cobwebs and mice droppings, were placed by a huge fireplace. An old cracked mirror seemed to be hanging in mid-air. There were a couple of dead rats in the hearth and the only light was from several candles dotted about the room.

Clara had the strangest feeling that they were not alone. 'I don't like the look of those soldiers or whatever they are,' she said pointing to the knights standing on guard either side of the massive wooden doors. Their armour was rusty and covered in a thick layer of dust.

'Don't be daft,' said Will and went straight over to them and lifted a face-shield. A mouse jumped out and disappeared down a hole.

'I don't think they're going to do much to us, do you?'

Clara pursed her lips.

'That painting gives me the creeps,' said Jamie pointing to a large painting.

'That's the Laughing Cavalier,' said Pamela. 'I've seen it in a gallery.'

'I swear its eyes are following…' his sentence was cut short when the massive doors flew open and in walked, Morag, her long blue dress swishing about her ankles.

'Ah – you've made it,' said the sorceress. 'It won't be long before you're joined by your other friend.'

'Who are y-you?' stammered Pamela.

'Me? I'm your worst nightmare,' she smirked and with a wave of her hand she was gone.

'Do you think she meant, Hugh?'

'Who else would she mean?' snapped Clara.

'Remember when we were at the gypsy gathering around the campfire?' said Jamie to Will.

'So, what's that got to do with anything?'

'We thought they were talking about Hugh, didn't we?'

'But he said we were imagining it.'

'Well, I reckon they were.'

'But why would they?'

'I don't know.'

Clara glared at them. 'Mama was right about you hanging around with those ghastly gypsies,' she spat. 'Now look where it's got us.'

No one said anything, for they had to admit that just maybe, Clara was right.

They spent the rest of the time trying to work out how they would attempt their escape. The windows were too narrow to climb through and the doors were bolted from the other side. They even looked up the chimney, but that was blocked off except for a gap that was too small for them to climb through. So far things didn't seem too promising.

'It looks like we're trapped by that lady.'

'She's not a lady,' Jamie retorted, 'she's obviously a witch.'

'She doesn't look like a witch,' said Clara.

'They don't all wear pointed hats and fly around on broomsticks, you know,' Jamie tutted.

'Huh, as if you'd know,' Clara spat.

'Well, would you?'

'For your information, when Priscilla and I were in the ghost train, a witch spoke to me.'

'Now I know you've lost the plot.'

'You've just said that the lady is a witch, so why don't you believe me?'

'Why would a witch take the trouble to enter a ghost train and speak to you?' he scoffed.

'I don't know, do I?'

'Oh stop arguing,' snapped Pamela. 'Let's clean the stuff off the chairs.'

Clara scowled over at her but said nothing. They cleaned the chairs as much as possible and sat down.

'Surely she can't keep us here for ever?'

'When our parents realize we are missing, the police will come looking for us,' said Will hoping against hope he was right.

'Being as we're stuck in this stinking rat-hole in the middle of nowhere,' hissed Clara, 'I hardly think that's likely, do you?'

The candles went out suddenly and the only light was from the moonlight which shone eerily through the narrow windows. It was then that a loud noise shattered the silence. They peered around the room wondering what to expect when a flash of metal caught their eye. One of the knights had moved from his post and was marching up and down, up and down his armour clanging with every step.

THUMP! Something heavy was trying to force the door open. BOOM! Jamie sat bolt upright straining his ears. What was on the other side of the door? Scratch, scratch, sniff, sniff – was it a dog? The sniffing gave way to a terrifying howl. The knight stopped marching and returned to his post. BANG! BOOM! BANG!

They were terrified. A gruff voice barked an order at the animal and with a whine and a whimper, it padded away. And then the clip clop of footsteps as they made their way down the staircase came closer and closer and closer. A man dressed in a white nightshirt with black stuff

oozing from his chest came bursting through the door. A lady in a white flowing dress ran after him. They disappeared through a wall.

'Jeepers, this place sure is spooky,' gasped Will.

Mrs Dingle flung open the door to the newsagency and came striding up to the counter. Her face was all red and blotchy and Mr Barnaby reckoned later that she was all but foaming at the mouth. He shot behind the card stand.

Typical of that man, thought Mrs Dingle. Still, she wouldn't waste her valuable time on him – it was Mrs Barnaby she'd come to see.

'I don't know what you gave Clara to eat,' she said accusingly. 'She has not been herself of late.'

'It was only chicken sandwiches and a strawberry trifle. I don't see why...'

'The cream could've been off.'

'Actually, Mrs Dingle, I never put cream on my trifles.'

'A trifle isn't a trifle without lashings of cream.'

Mrs Barnaby sighed. 'Is that all?'

'No, definitely not,' she snapped, 'my poor, Clara, had quite a fright in your garden.'

'Well, it was…'

'And to think that I had *your daughter* and that friend of hers, around out of the goodness of my heart,' she whined, 'I certainly didn't expect such dreadful treatment in return.' She about-turned and marched out the door slamming it shut behind her.

'Old busy-body,' muttered Mr Barnaby.

'Funnily enough,' said Mrs Barnaby, 'Hugh mentioned that his friends didn't seem themselves either.'

'Well obviously, there must be a virus going around.'

Later that night, a strange chortling noise disturbed Hugh's sleep. He tossed and turned and finally opened his eyes. He was horrified to find a raven inside his bedroom. He yelled out to his father and Mr Barnaby came running in just in time to see the bird fly out of the window.

'Now how did it do that, considering the window isn't open?' said a mystified Mr Barnaby. And if that's the case, how did it get into

the room in the first place? He set about making sure the window was tightly shut.

As he closed the door behind him he felt very uneasy, almost as if the raven signified something sinister. Good grief, he thought, I'm getting to be just like my mother-in-law; but mother-in-law or not, perhaps the feeling that something strange was going on might not be in his imagination after all. If only he knew what it was? He glanced out of the hall window half expecting to see a shadowy figure standing under a lamppost watching the shop. He checked the latch and returned to his bedroom.

A white falcon landed on the top of a street lamp, its beady eyes rested on the newsagency.

A Startling Discovery

Chapter Twenty-seven

The following day, Pamela opened the door to Lucy with the news that her parents had taken her twin brothers to town. Pamela's cousin, Angela, was staying for a few of days and had brought a board game with her which turned out to be Scrabble. Pamela had already told her cousin what had happened when they played the board game before, and Angela said she'd never had that happen to her. Lucy wasn't all that keen to play, but went along with it because she didn't want them to think she was a spoil-sport.

They were well into the game and Lucy was about to complete another word when with a click of the tiles, they rearranged themselves spelling out – HUGH-SEEK-HELP. The girls looked from one to the other in shock. What did it mean? The tiles shot around the board again and spelt – A D I E U.

'I thought you were exaggerating before, but that's creepy,' said Angela. 'And why would your brother need to seek help?'

'I haven't a clue. Perhaps we shouldn't do this anymore.'

'You'd better give your brother the message; he might know what it means.'

'He won't listen to me,' she said, 'Even though our friend, Charlie, told us that mischievous spirits roamed the earth.'

Angela threw her head back and roared with laughter. 'That's utter rot.'

'But how come the tiles moved around by themselves? Okay, so the other board game *might* have been faulty, but it's more than a coincidence that yours has done the same.'

'Perhaps the...'

A car pulled up in the driveway. The family had returned.

When Lucy arrived home, she found her father reading a letter from his brother who lived in Canada. 'You can read it if you like,' he said handing it to her.

The telephone rang and he rushed to answer it. Lucy enjoyed reading about their ski trip until she saw that her uncle had signed it off with the word, 'Adieu'.

'I didn't know uncle lived in the French part of Canada,' Lucy commented when her father returned.

'He doesn't. Why did you say that?'

Lucy pointed to the end of the letter.

Oh I see,' he said. 'Apparently, it's a family expression started by my great-grandfather.'

Lucy gulped at that.

'But you never finish your letters that way, Dad.'

'Why should I?'

Later that afternoon, Lucy told Hugh about the board game.

'Serves you right,' was all he said. He knew his sister was wondering why he didn't have a go at her, but for some reason, he felt the urge to go and see Charlie's grandmother. Lucy needn't know that. Some things were better kept to himself, at least until after he had visited Charlie's grandmother. And only then would he decide whether or not to tell her anything. After all, she had the annoying habit of wanting to know all the ins and outs of everything. Now all he had to do was find a way to see the old gypsy on his own. He decided to try the following day when they went to visit Charlie.

Lucy in the meantime, was wondering why she kept having disturbing dreams. She couldn't remember what they were when she woke up in the morning, only that she felt scared. Perhaps it was

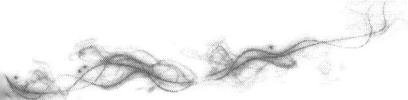

because she now knew that what she thought was a trick of light in her bedroom the other night, was in fact her great-great grandparents who for some reason, had appeared to her. Perhaps she should've told Hugh about it, but he didn't always share things with her so why should she? Besides, nothing like that had happened to her before, nor since, except for the dreams. Then again, that Scrabble game sure was spooky, but that had happened to all of them not just her. Should she mention it to Dad? Would he believe her? Maybe she should tell Mum, but on second thoughts, perhaps not.

The next day, Charlie and Rosa were waiting for them at the entrance to the yard. Four huge trucks had arrived with: Monty's Famous Circus written on the side. Men were busy unloading circus equipment. Another three trucks rumbled into the yard and a man jumped out, pulled down a door and unhooked a ramp. Another man emerged leading an elephant down the slope into the sunlight.

'That's our Uncle's circus,' Rosa explained.

A boy came up to them and Charlie introduced him as their cousin, Jethro.

'Want to have a peek at the lions?' he asked.

'Sure, providing they're in a cage,' grinned Will.

'Follow me.'

Hugh hung back and whispered something to Charlie, which Jamie was quick to notice. *Now* what was his friend up to?

'Er, we won't be long,' said Charlie and whisked Hugh away to his grandmother's wagon.

She listened very carefully to what Hugh had to say. He launched into his dream about the castle and about the raven being in his bedroom. By the time he'd finished, he was beginning to think that his story sounded a bit far-fetched, even to him. He expected Charlie's grandmother to dismiss it as rubbish and was quite surprised when she didn't.

'Charlie, I want to have a little word with Hugh. So go and join yer friends.'

'Now lad,' said the old gypsy when they were on their own, 'I want yer to come back again later. But afore yer go, I need a strand of yer hair.'

Hugh was flabbergasted. What did she need that for? But nevertheless, he sat still while she tugged at his hair, pull out a strand and place it in a paper bag.

'I'll explain why I need yer hair when yer come back,' she said. 'Not a word to be said, not even to Charlie. Is that clear? Now run along, I've work to do.'

Left alone, the old gypsy mentally told her son to gather together the council and covens for an urgent meeting of the Macaba clan.

King Leo and Queen Isabella greeted the clan at the sacred meeting place near Mendip Abbey. They explained the reason for the meeting.

'To tell the truth, I've been seeing all that in me scrying mirror,' said Old Chattox.

'Well, why didn't yer say something then?' growled Mouldheels, looking decidedly put out at being kept in the dark about such things.

'If you'd been putting a bit more effort into scrying like the rest of us,' snapped Agatha, 'you would've known. And while we're on the subject…'

'Time fer action I say,' said Nobab

'That's what we're here to discuss, *obviously*,' tutted Agatha.

'The special crystal is being prepared ready for action,' said King Leo.

'I told Cornelia that I had my suspicions about the shopkeeper right from the start,' said the Major. The clan gasped at that. Did he call the honoured mistress "Cornelia"?

'But didn't you say you had doubts about the old lady in the cottage as well?'

'Yes, but…'

'I do wish you'd make your mind up, Osletwistle,' snorted Harriet.

'As I was saying, before I was rudely interrupted,' he said giving her a sideways glance, 'it was very obvious to me that after the children had visited the Candy Shoppe their energy had been taken.'

'That's not much use. We need to be absolutely sure.'

He narrowed his eyes at the old sorceress. Harriet returned his look with defiance. She wasn't going to let the likes of: that upstart bother her one bit. After all, he was only a guardian, which was nothing more than a frivolous pastime as far as she was concerned. And he still wasn't sure about the old lady either. So what good was that? And what was the matter with Demdyke? He was looking decidedly glum. Still, he had nothing of real importance to add to the meeting. And, let's face it, he never did.

D emdyke, in the meantime, was feeling fed up being a mere messenger. Surely the mishap with the spell should've been forgotten by now? He didn't mean to blow up one of the caravans and turn everything purple within firing range of it. And wasn't he the one that was now the butt of everyone's jokes?

He had tried, unsuccessfully, to reverse the spell and return his hair to its original colour, which was black. He'd also sought the help of Elspeth and the Book of Shadows, to no avail. Why, he'd even resorted to shaving his head hoping that would cancel the spell. But alas, his hair grew back the following day, the purple streaks brighter than ever. So he decided to wear that awful hat and drape a purple cloak around his clothes. He was blowed if he was going to let Osletwistle know of his dilemma. No, better let him think that he preferred to dress as he did. Anyway, why did he insist on calling himself: Major, when he was nothing but a pompous bore? Everyone knew he'd landed in a battlefield by mistake, and somehow had managed to save an important army officer who'd nicknamed him by that ridiculous name.

'Well, he needs to be very careful, that youngster,' said Old Chattox, shaking his head, 'I think it be a cryin' shame, he'll be havin' to work wonders.'

'Wallynus tells me that Hugh has been able to make objects move and his magic abilities are quite advanced.'

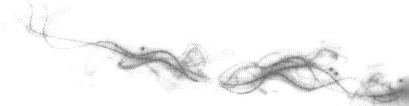

'Perhaps the boy's powers are more developed than we thought, Osletwistle,' said Audra nodding her approval.

'They need to be if he is to fulfil the legacy,' commented Dorothea.

'We'll soon find out, old girl.'

'Hey, not so much of the "old",' she exclaimed, giving the Major a nudge.

'It's just an expression my dear, Dorothea, just an expression.'

Meanwhile, having finished a game of rounders, Hugh made an excuse and returned to the wagon. The old gypsy brought out a velvet pouch and proceeded to flick a blue powder around the room talking in a language, which sounded strangely familiar to him. She placed a very old wooden box in the centre of the table. It was decorated with a five-pointed star surrounded by strange symbols etched in gold. Hugh stared at the symbols. Weren't they the same markings as on the stones belonging to the old tramp? Was he connected to Charlie's family in some way? She opened the box and very carefully lifted out a large object covered in a purple cloth, setting it down in front of him.

She removed the cloth to reveal a very large crystal ball. And all this time, she didn't say a word. Hugh felt his stomach churn as he glanced at the crystal. Was Charlie's grandmother going to tell his fortune?

'I want yer to hold this crystal ball tightly,' she said. 'That's right; now give it back to me.'

She gazed into the crystal muttering in that strange language again.

'This will help yer. Yer see, lad, it's only yer fears that makes yer have bad dreams. So have a look in the crystal and yer'll see that yer future is good.'

Hugh was beginning to regret ever telling Charlie anything. Now look where it had got him.

'Don't worry. Yer dreams will disappear.'

He looked down at the crystal and said, 'I'd never be able to see my future in that.'

The grandmother just smiled and said, 'never say "never", m'boy.'

Never Say Never

Chapter Twenty-eight

Hugh peered into the crystal again and stared into the empty void until an image began to take shape. And what he saw made him gasp in disbelief.

'That's the castle I told you about,' he exclaimed.

'Now let yer mind float and yer will…' the old gypsy's voice faded softly away.

A blue mist swirled into the crystal and it grew bigger and bigger and bigger! The mist swirled and swirled. Round and round it went until he felt it sucking him into its mysterious depths. His last conscious thought was of feeling as if he was sitting on a spinning top spinning out of control, wondering where in the world he was going to land up.

'Our other guest is about to arrive,' the sorceress announced, 'I expect you to greet him with a big smile.'

'She seems very smug if you ask me,' Jamie whispered to Will.

'Oh, more than smug,' the sorceress grinned, 'I can assure you.'

A blue mist came swirling through the open door and with the blowing of a trumpet and a drum roll…

'Glad you could make it, Hugh Barnaby,' smiled Morag. 'I'm sure you and your friends have much to talk about. I'll see you later,' and with a sweep of her hand, she left the room.

'How did you know where we were?' asked Jamie.

'I didn't,' Hugh replied. 'The last I remember was staring into a crystal ball.' He explained that he'd dreamt about the very same castle and thought it would be a good idea to ask Charlie's grandmother for her advice.

They listened intently to what he had to say. What was the connection with Charlie's grandmother?

'I knew those gypsies were nothing but trouble,' said Clara.

No one contradicted her, not even Hugh. He had to admit that strange things had happened since they had met Charlie and Rosa. And he was more than aware of the fact that his life was somehow connected to them. But why – he had no idea.

'Who was that lady?'

'Lady my foot,' snorted Jamie. 'She's a witch and a nasty one at that.'

'I don't want to alarm you, but scary things happen in this place,' said Will.

Hugh was amazed to hear their story – it was even freakier than his.

'That painting sure is peculiar,' he whispered pointing to the Laughing Cavalier. 'I swear his eyes moved.'

'Yeah I know, creepy isn't it?'

'I take offence to that,' said the Cavalier and jumped out of the painting. 'Good day to you, young folk,' he said, 'I'll have to be quick before I'm discovered.'

'How did…?' Hugh started to say.

The Cavalier snapped his fingers. 'Now pay attention. There will be a way out of the castle by way of a secret passageway. But I'm afraid it's your job to find it, lad.'

What was this crazy man going on about?

'You see if you don't, not only will you have failed the test miserably and…'

'What test?'

'Well, we need to know how strong your abilities are for a start. It's no good you carrying on the legacy if your useless.'

'I haven't a clue what you're talking about.'

'Well, my boy, you and your sister are descendants of the ancient Macaba and...'

'Who on earth are they?'

'Now don't interrupt me, there's a good lad. We are a magical clan of mystics and sorcerers, with the occasional wizard thrown in, of course.'

'*What*?'

'You should feel honoured to be one of us, and one who is so important too. Still, I don't have time to give you the rundown on all that. I'd better go before I'm discovered.' And with a little bow he returned to the painting.

'What on earth was that about?'

Meanwhile, in the Realm of Shadows, the sorceress was busy preparing a spell. She circled the cauldron five times as the flames leapt higher and higher. Morag clicked her fingers and a small drawstring bag landed in her hand. She undid the string and pulled out a bottle containing a foul smelling black liquid. She poured the contents into the cauldron; a yellow vapour spewed from it. The walls became alive with faceless beings dressed in black cloaks. The sorceress raised her arms and began to chant:

In my cauldron doth bubble and bubble
Trouble and fear I do happily sew
Double the trouble
Double the fear my prisoners to know
Let my spell grow grow grow

Morag chanted it over and over again. Pop, pop, pop, the cauldron simmered away creating its evil spell. She gave the brew another stir, grinning maliciously with every circular movement she made.

'Go forth my servants of the night.'

A horrible smell seeped its way into the castle room. Scary creatures scurried around excitedly. Their hair was long and matted. They had little ears, large bulbous noses, thick lips and protruding teeth. They

were dressed in anything they could get their hands on as long as it smelled of bogs and swamps. On their feet, they wore old bark that had been soaked in muddy water and tied with dried slime.

The prisoners stood petrified as the boggarts came closer and closer until they circled Hugh, spitting green spittle at him. At first he didn't know what to do he was so frightened, and then he felt a sudden heat flow from his hands and the creatures were zapped away on a flash of blue light. A stunned silence followed, until huge rats suddenly appeared and gathered around the walls, chattering hideously. It was then that faceless beings stepped out from a red mist.

The girls took cover behind Hugh and Jamie. Will ran around the room looking for something he could chuck at them. And then black cloaks were discarded to reveal dwarf-like men with wizened faces and long pointy ears. On their noses, tufts of hair sprouted from warts. They were dressed in old sacking gathered at the waist by pieces of twine. On their feet they wore large leaves tied at the ankles with straw.

The goblins retreated into the background when tall willowy beings with white hair, white faces and pale grey eyes stepped from the walls. They wore silver tunics made from fine cloth harvested from the far reaches of the forest. They were bare-footed. They held hands and danced around the room, changing back and forth from tall willowy beings to squat hairy creatures.

These beings were known as: the Grobs and were shrouded in mystery. There were rumours started by the goblins that they were shape-shifters, while the boggarts argued that they were changelings, like the mistress. Nobody knew for sure. However, no other being, and that included Morag, had ever seen what they really looked like. That didn't bother the sorceress one bit for, as long as they were forever at her mercy, they could be mice for all she cared.

'DO SOMETHING, HUGH,' yelled Clara. 'Throw that light at them again.'

He tried, but try as he might, nothing happened.

'I CAN'T,' he yelled back.

Meanwhile, the mysterious beings came closer and closer and closer.

Hugh grabbed hold of the nearest thing he could find – a poker, and then strange words tumbled uncontrollably from his lips:

Vantum Vantum Pergus

Within seconds, all the creatures were gone in a flash. The boys looked at their friend in amazement.

'Blimey, you really do have powers,' gasped Jamie.

'What was that language you were speaking?' asked Will.

'That's the thing, I don't know.'

'I always knew you were peculiar,' hissed Clara, 'but this is beyond a joke.'

'Who's laughing?'

Morag was absolutely furious to think that her slaves had let her down, so much so that she threw fireballs around the room in a fit of rage. 'You think you can outwit me do you, boy? I'll show you,' she fumed.

She strode over to the cauldron and snatched the lid off it. The liquid bubbled and hissed with evil power. She raised her hands to the ceiling and called to the Lord of Thunder.

She waited and waited, but Lord Drago didn't appear. She called to him again and this time a huge flash of lightning lit the room and he stepped from a wall of fire. The snake he wore as a hat uncoiled itself and slip-slided its way towards Morag, who stood rooted to the spot. She could do nothing but recoil in fear as it slithered up her body and wrapped itself tightly around her neck.

Lord Drago fixed her with a fiery glare; the snake tightened its hold.

'Well, what have we here? You dare to summon me to help you plot against a mere boy?' he spat. 'Nay, you must prove your worth to me, the Lord of Thunder,' he growled, thumping his chest. 'To honour our pact, you must work your rite alone. Do not summon me again.'

Morag felt her blood turn to ice. Would she be punished? As if reading her mind, he clicked his fingers and a sword of fire appeared in his hands. He brandished it in front of her face, taunting the sorceress

with each sweep of the fiery blade. The snake tightened its hold even more. Lord Drago threw his head back and let out a horrendous roar and with a final fiery sweep of his cloak, he vanished leaving a sickening smell of smoke behind.

Morag was trembling from head to foot. To think Lord Drago had chosen to now ignore her, the most powerful sorceress that ever lived. She was absolutely beside herself with rage that yet again, the mortal had managed to stuff up her spell. She should've thrown him and his friends into the dungeons and have done with it, except that they were full of rubble and her spell to be rid of it had failed for some reason. Still, that was the least of her worries.

Meanwhile, the boggarts sat huddled together discussing their situation.

'The cheek of it, fancy blamin' us fer failin' to scare the forkypeds.'

'Seems to me them goblins didn't do too well either,' grumbled Old Mobbins, the chief of the boggarts.

'Or them changers,' added another.

'I'm hungry,' said Griswald the second in command, 'it be a while since the Mistress fed us.'

'I bin thinkin',' said Old Mobbins, 'how about we go ahuntin' like we used to?'

'That be a great idea,' beamed Manfred, who was handsome by boggart standards.

'Aye, we shouldn't have much trouble findin' food in these parts.'

'Not like where we lived in the World of Tomorrows,' said Wartun, who was the tallest of the boggarts.

'So that's agreed then,' said Old Mobbins, slapping his knee, 'we'll set off to find somefin' to eat – be like the old days, eh?'

'Well, I mean to say, fings aren't like they used to be in the Clough at Black Lee.'

Just as they were about to set off on their adventure, Old Mobbins heard footsteps. It turned out to be Yoger who was leading his tribe of yellow boggarts towards them. Now wot did he want? If he and his

motley lot of good-fer-nuffins tried to muscle in on their territory, he'd have a fight on his hands.

'What are yer doin' here, Yoger? I haven't seen yer fer many moons past, yer must be after somefin',' he sneered, 'what is it?'

'Now, is that a way to greet an old friend?'

'Yer usually only make an appearance when yer want somethin'.'

'I just fort it would be grand ter visit wiv yer,' he smiled, showing pearly white teeth.

'What's wrong wiv yer face?' gasped Old Mobbins. 'It ain't yellow any more,' he leant closer, 'it's turned brown. And what about yer teef, they've turned white.' He gave the other boggarts a closer look. 'The lot of yer look the same,' he exclaimed.

'Ter tell the truth, me ol' friend, we've been runnin' out o' grub,' sighed Yoger.

'Wot are yer tellin' me fer?'

'Well, I was wonderin' if yer'd any ter spare.'

'Sorry to disappoint yer, but we're off to go ahuntin'. Fings are a bit tight 'round here.'

'Wot about yer Mistress – she'll be feedin' yer, surely?'

'Nay, she hasn't fed us fer a while. And she expects us to wait about here till she decides to send us any food,' he snorted. 'I tell yer; even then we only get a few crumbs to eat.'

'Why's that?'

'She gives most of the grub to the forkypeds she's keepin' as prisoners.'

'Can't yer eat the forkypeds then?' asked Yoger, licking his lips at the thought.

'Don't be sayin' such a thing.' Old Mobbins gasped. 'The Mistress would skin us alive. Nay, she needs 'em fer some mysterious quest she's on.'

'That be mighty interestin',' said Yoger, whose curiosity had now been aroused.

'We're goin' ahuntin' now, yer welcome to join us, if yer want, that is.'

'Bein' as yer've nuffin here, we might as well,' he replied, feeling the thrill of the hunt rushing through his veins.

The Calling

Chapter Twenty-nine

Alone in the Realm of Shadows, Morag was pondering on her problem when she suddenly remembered that she hadn't called upon her other comrades for quite some time. They owed her a few favours anyway.

'Siras, bring Broddle to me by the first stroke of light.'

'Broddle, Mistress?'

'The chief of the brownies, I hear tell he is somewhere in the North of England, or maybe Scotland.'

To Siras, that was a disaster. He would have to go through the veil and find the brownie. He liked the Land of Shadows and wasn't looking forward to returning to the World of Tomorrows one bit.

'But where should I look first?' he croaked.

'Do I have to do *everything* for you? Use some of your so-called powers,' she snapped.

'I'll be on me way, Mistress,' and he made for the door.

'Don't be in such a hurry,' she called, 'I haven't finished yet.'

Siras groaned. Surely she didn't want him to fetch somebody else? Unfortunately for him, his fears were founded.

'And while you're about it, you might as well fetch, Spriggle.'

Silas felt his heart sink to his boots. Wasn't he the chief of the spriggans? However he was going to visit Scotland and Cornwall in one night, he'd never know. After all, he'd probably have quite a bit

183

of persuading to do. And knowing Broddle, supposing he was able to find him of course, he could be as stubborn as a mule. And what about Spriggle, he was known to drive a hard bargain as well.

'Then, of course, there's Olger One Tooth.'

Siras gulped. Wasn't he the leader of the trolls? Things were getting worse by the minute. Now he was expected to go to Norway.

'And not forgetting Black Annis, she owes me a thing or two.'

'*Black Annis*?' he squeaked and felt the blood drain from his face.

He had been told many stories about the sorceress. One in particular, that she had made a pact with the God of the Underworld. It was rumoured that she looked like a wizened old crone with one eye and instead of teeth, she had very sharp fangs. It was said that if you were unlucky enough to lay your eyes on her you would be turned into the vilest creature imaginable. And others told of the evil deeds she had committed against the unwary. Then there were those who believed she could tear an animal as large as a pig with her bare hands in just a blink of an eye. In any event, many feared the mysterious Black Annis whatever the story, and now he was expected to find her.Oh bogs upon bogs, whatever shall I do?

'But, on second thoughts, we had a slight falling out many moons ago and she is being rather stubborn.'

What Morag conveniently failed to tell her servant, was that she and Black Annis shared far more than a slight falling out.

'I'll promise her beauty in return for her favours,' she nodded, 'that should do the trick.'

Siras listened to his mistress with a growing fear in his heart. Wasn't there some way to avoid visiting the dreaded sorceress? He suddenly came up with what he thought, was a good idea.

'Yous could always call upon Gruesome, Mistress Morag.'

'Gruesome?'

'Don't yous remember, Mistress, he's a barguest.' And then he thought of another fearsome creature, 'And then there's Grunge?'

Morag raised an eyebrow at her servant. He'd actually come up with a good suggestion!

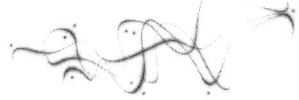

'I'd forgotten about Gruesome, he'll serve my purposes very well with what I have in mind for those snivelling mortals. I won't bother with Grunge, that griffin's far too cumbersome.'

Siras let out a huge sigh of relief, until she said, 'But not yet.'

The thought of visiting Black Annis loomed over him like a big black cloud.

'And by the way, I want to remind you to speak like those creatures,' she said. 'I don't want them getting any notion that you think you're above yourself, just because you're my personal servant. I can't have them taking offence and not be willing to give you the time of day.'

Siras stood and stared at his mistress. Talk like them? Why, he had enough trouble understanding them.

'What are you looking so glum about?'

'I find it difficult enough to follow what the goblins are saying, Mistress, let alone anybody else.'

'Why?'

'What do the goblins mean when they say, "he likes this" and "his horde that"? It makes no sense to me.'

'Oh for goodness sake, Siras, when they say "he", they really mean "I", and when they say "his", they mean "my". Got it?'

'Er – I think so,' he replied, feeling more confused than ever.

'But being as you'll be otherwise engaged, you won't have to worry about the goblins for a while – will you?'

'But I...'

'Oh, why I put up with you I'll never know,' she spat, and with a click of her fingers, a small orange stone appeared in her hand.

'Here you are, Siras, this is a translator. Although I fail to see why you can't understand them, even a bat could,' she tutted. 'Anyway, all you have to do is hold it for a few seconds and it will do the job.'

'Thank yous, Mistress, thank yous.'

'What are you hanging around here for? Be gone!'

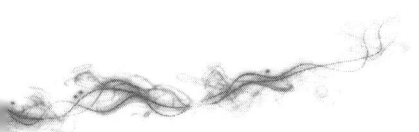

A Story To Tell

Chapter Thirty

'Don't go worryin' too much about yer friends, Charlie;' said his grandmother, 'they don't even know they're captured, much less their shadows. Anyway, I've managed to penetrate the veil of evil. But that's only the start of it I'm afraid.'

'What do you mean?'

'Well, Morag could call upon all of her sidekicks. She knows a lot of evil creatures yer see; though I happen to know she hasn't been in contact wiv 'em since way back when.'

Evil creatures, what evil creatures?

'But there's one good thing, so far her slaves have failed her miserably. Of course she could send her servant to fetch the brownies and the spriggans; not fergettin' the trolls either. Then again, there's Black Annis. Nah, I shouldn't think she'd help Morag, they had a falling out many moons ago.'

Charlie stared at his grandmother in amazement. Things were getting weirder by the minute.

'I'll tell yer about them if yer want me to.'

''Course I want yer to,' said Charlie.

'I'll start wiv, Black Annis first. Now she's *real* interstin'. She was supposed to live in a giant oak tree where it was easy to spot intruders. And then she would cast a spell on her prey, binding them to her forever. But then again, I heard tell she haunts a graveyard looking for a loved

one. Others say she is forced to live as an outcast for eternity. So you see, lad, there's so many stories, who knows what's true and what's not.'

It was then that King Leo entered the wagon.

'Rosa and Carlotta are looking for you, Charlie,' he said pointedly. 'Perhaps you'd better go and see what they want...NOW!'

'But Gran was tellin' me about...'

'Black Annis, I know,' he frowned.

Charlie left the wagon – fast.

'It's a wonder you didn't mention, Count Dracula,' he snapped and stormed out leaving the old gypsy for once, at a loss for words.

In woodland outside the castle walls, lived a horde of goblins and like the boggarts, they were also having a meeting of their own.

'Its obvious ter himself that us can't rely upon them boggarts or them grobs ter do the job properly,' their leader, Old Gordle, grumbled. 'Anyway, wot sort of a fancy name is that – grobs? They're only shape-shifters after all.'

'He was told that they were changelings,' said Dromby, a little red goblin. He was particularly good at weaving nightmares into the minds of sleeping humans.

'Whatever! Anyways, let's hope us don't have ter work ternight.'

Hoggle, one of the older goblins, was trying unsuccessfully to cover a large lump on Dromby's head with a bandage made from soggy leaves.

'Stop movin' about,' grumbled Hoggle.

'It hurts,' he winced.

'Well, yer shouldn't sit under a tree wivout makin' sure nuffin' would fall on yer head.'

The goblins thought that to be very funny indeed, much to the annoyance of Dromby. He wasn't going to tell them where his stash of food was now.

Magwart, a sprightly goblin, came stumbling out of the forest. 'He got some rabbits, he found 'em over yonder,' he said, proudly.

'Well, what are us waitin' fer, us will make a fire ter cook on,' said Old Gordle, triumphantly.

The other goblins scurried around picking up twigs and leaves.

'Does Hoggle fink Halloween will be celebrated at Blackstone Cemetery?' asked Dromby suddenly. Halloween was his favourite celebration.

'He is hopin' that it will be held some place else. Some of them witches were nowt too friendly last year.'

'What do yer expect, Hoggle, when yer tried ter poke yer nose into where it wasn't wanted,' tutted Magwart.

'Oh, oh, he finks he can hear them boggarts comin'. He don't want ter mix wiv the likes of them,' said Old Gordle, blowing out the fire and disappearing behind the bushes.

The boggarts came trudging through the woodland searching for food. Old Mobbins caught a whiff of smoke and followed the smell until he came to a smouldering fire.

'I bet it's them goblins,' he snorted disapprovingly. 'They never put their fires out properly.'

'One day they'll set the woods on fire,' nodded Twerp.

Old Mobbins snorted, 'As far as I'm concerned, the sooner the Mistress gets rid of 'em the better,' and he busied himself kicking mud over the embers. That should do the trick.

'Yeah, they only make an appearance when it suits 'em,' nodded Toddle.

'C'mon, let's go in search of them rabbits yer said yer'd hidden.'

From behind the trees, the goblins looked on. Old Gordle was furious to hear what the boggart had said about him and his horde.

'Wot a cheek,' he exclaimed, 'he finks he will have a little word wiv Old Mobbins, he can promise yer that much,' he scowled. But his scowl turned to laugher when he realized the rabbits that they had enjoyed, belonged to the boggarts.

Nearby, Old Shylog, the chief of the grobs, was not happy at all.

'All I have to say on the matter is this; it's about time the others pulled their weight around here.'

'I don't know why the Mistress wastes her time on them, Master. I mean to say, they leave most of the work to us.'

Old Shylog nodded, thinking that without the others there would be more food to eat and, more importantly, a bigger reward. Yep, he'll bide his time.

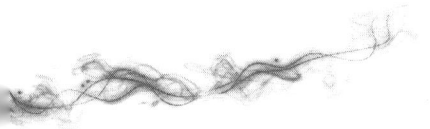

Promises

Chapter Thirty-one

The moon shone brightly in the night sky as Siras came upon a large house in the city of Glasgow. He had travelled all over the north of England and as far as the Scottish border before he came upon an old wizard who knew of Broddle's whereabouts. Siras couldn't get over the fact that he was living in such a grand place and felt a twinge of envy.

Broddle had just about finished with his household chores and had decided to go outside for some fresh air. He gave his body a good stretch and sighed contentedly. This was the life for him. He sat down on the back step and tucked into a slice of bread and honey. Aye, he was very happy with his lot. He was about to take a sip of tea, when he heard a rustling sound coming from the bushes.

'Psst, Broddle,' called a voice.

Broddle craned his neck. Who was waving to him? He stood up and took a step forward and couldn't believe his eyes. Siras is here?

'Come here and let me have a good look at yeh,' he beckoned. 'How are yeh then? I didna recognize yeh feh the minute, sit yehself doon aside me,' he said patting the step.

Siras sighed heavily. As if trying to understand the goblins wasn't enough; he now had to decipher a Scottish accent. He assumed he meant, 'I didn't recognize yous for the minute. Sit yourself down.' Ah well, here goes.

''Tis good to see yous again, Broddle,' beamed Siras at the brownie's cheery round face, 'though I didn't expect to have ter journey as far as Glasgow ter find yous. And yous have got a Glasgow accent now.' And then he suddenly remembered the translation stone. Thank goodness! Now he could talk normally as well. He put his hand in his pocket and held it tightly, crossing his fingers hoping like mad that it would work.

'I've been here for many moons past, so the accent grows on you after a while. Still, at least I didn't call you "Jimmy", eh?' he chortled. Jimmy? Who's Jimmy?

Siras launched into the reason for his visit. 'But alas, the boy is proving to be a worthy opponent.'

'What does your Mistress need my help for? What about her slaves?'

Siras went on to explain why Morag needed extra help. 'Someone with expertise,' he gushed. 'So, of course, she immediately thought of yous.'

Siras noticed that Broddle was obviously flattered by the praise. And so he pressed on, hoping the brownie would jump at the chance to serve his mistress. After all, working for Morag was an honour and most certainly far better than being a mere house-cleaner. Although why she wanted a skinny little brownie to help her in her quest he'd never know. Maybe it was because he had a long pointed nose and could sniff out trouble a mile away. Or maybe, it was the fact that those beady eyes of his could see for miles in the dark.

Broddle eyed Siras with a nagging suspicion that all was not well in the Morag camp. If he played his cards right, he'd be able to turn this situation to his advantage.

'Nay, Siras, I like it here – the folks treat me well. I haven't any interest in getting up to my old tricks.'

Siras felt a sinking in the pit of his stomach. Old Broddle wasn't interested in getting up to his old tricks? He'd have to pull something out of the hat – and quick.

'That's a pity, 'cos the Mistress has got a big reward for yous, should yous agree.' Broddle pricked his ears up at the mention of a big reward. So, he had taken the bait had he? He smiled inwardly as he

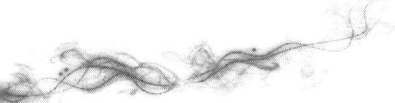

watched Siras miraculously conjure up a bag. Just as he thought, he was about to receive a little sweetener.

Siras rumbled around until he came across a cloth bundle, which he pulled out with a triumphant grin. 'Look here, Broddle, this brand new cloak and hood surely proves to yous the Mistress's good faith?'

Broddle took his time to reply. After all, he didn't want Siras thinking he was too keen. He might be able to strike an even better deal for himself. Let him sweat, aye, let him sweat.

The silence was making Siras very nervous, what would Morag do to him if Broddle refused? It didn't bear thinking about.

Broddle was well aware of the look of distress that crept into the Siras's eyes. He still wondered why the sorceress, Morag, chose a boggart to be her personal servant, although he had heard that Siras came from a Royal tribe. Perhaps that had something to do with it? Ah well, time to let him off the hook.

'Well now, that could throw a different light on the matter,' was his sly reply, taking the offered cloak.

Siras bucked up. Perhaps he would agree to work for the mistress after all? He watched with baited breath as Broddle tried on the cloak. He tugged and pulled at the material checking it for strength, and every now and then he grunted. Siras waited and waited. Was Broddle toying with him? He had the distinct feeling that he was.

'You wouldn't happen to have another cloak on you, would you?' Broddle asked.

Siras knew Broddle had him over a barrel, but nevertheless, he felt around in the bag again and produced another cloak. How many more favours would he ask of him? Broddle set about folding the cloaks into neat piles. This he did very, very, slowly. And then he looked up at Siras and smiled.

'Aye, count me in, but I can only come for a wee while mind, then it's back here for me.'

'Thankee, Broddle, yous won't be disappointed. Now we must go and find Master Spriggle.'

'Spriggle you say? It be many a moon since I laid eyes on him. Well, what are we waiting for, let's away to Cornwall.'

Siras breathed a sigh of relief, for he was already picturing being turned into a slimy toad or something equally as distasteful if he didn't turn up with the goods.

In a lonely castle ruin somewhere in Cornwall, the spriggans were enjoying the spoils from a hunting trip. The loud grunts and slurps as they tucked into their food could be heard above the sound of waves crashing onto the nearby beach. Siras and Broddle landed with a loud thump. The spriggans looked up with a start and glowered at the intruders. On closer inspection, Siras thought they looked much more fearsome than he remembered. Yes, their small hairless heads, their piercing yellow eyes, large fleshy ears, razor-sharp teeth which he noticed, were now gnashing ferociously at them, certainly looked scary, all right.

'Hey, wot do yer fink yer doin', bargin' yer way in here as if yer own the place,' grumbled a spriggan tearing at a lump of flesh.

'We're feastin', an' if yer not careful, yer'll be next,' growled another.

'Now be off wiv yer afore Oy send yer ter kingdom come,' said the fiercest looking spriggan of all.

''Tis me...Siras... yous know, the personal servant of Mistress Morag.'

Spriggle, the chief of the spriggans, peered at Siras through heavy hooded lids. He then turned his attention to Broddle who stood quivering in the shadows. Why would Siras be mixing with a brownie of all things? Still, there's no accountin' fer taste, he thought.

Siras gave Broddle a shove forward. 'Oh, an' this is Broddle, yous may remember him?'

Spriggle walked around the brownie as if inspecting a piece of merchandise. Broddle gave him a weak smile. Surely Spriggle remembered him? At least he hoped he did, for he didn't like the way he was licking his lips at him.

The spriggan snorted, pulled at the brownie's hair, gave his cheek a squeeze, and then slapped him on the back.

'Broddle,' he exclaimed, 'Oy didn't recognise yer fer the minute,' he grinned. 'Long time no see, eh?' Broddle beamed with pleasure.

Siras quickly launched into his spiel. Time was marching on, and he didn't want it to be wasted on reminiscing. And anyway, having to listen to Spriggle's Cornish accent was doing his head in. And why couldn't he just say "I" instead of "Oy"? Oh blast, I forgot the stone again.

Spriggle scowled at Siras, 'Well you needn't barge your way in here,' he grumbled, 'disturbing the peace.'

Siras was thinking that the disgusting sounds the spriggans were making as they tucked into their food were not exactly peaceful. Spriggle burped loudly into his face. Siras cringed.

'Your Mistress needs my help, eh?'

Siras nodded.

'I don't think I can give her my help just like that,' he said, clicking his fingers.

Siras knew he had some fast-talking to do, so he explained the urgency of the situation.

'So yous see, Spriggle, my Mistress admires your magic and would appreciate it if yous would show her servants how it should be done,' he gushed, knowing that a bit of good old-fashioned flattery would go down well with Spriggle, plus the fact that he was known to be greedy.

Spriggle scratched his knobbly head and rubbed his long chin. The other spriggans slurped away happily. Siras was quick to notice the fresh blood dripping from their teeth.

'What's in it for me?' asked Spriggle, who eyed Siras for any signs of skulduggery.

Siras pressed on. 'She only wants a meeting,' he explained. 'Yous can always say no to her proposition if it's not to your liking,' he said, keeping his fingers crossed behind his back.

The spriggan pretended to consider the whys and wherefores of the offer and, like Broddle, very quickly came to the conclusion that he was probably in a position to name his price, given the urgency of the situation.

'Done,' he said, 'but I can't be away from this 'ere place for long.'

Siras let out a long sigh.

Spriggle turned to another spriggan who was hovering in the background. 'Piskan, you can look after things here, and no getting any of your ideas about taking over,' he warned, 'or else.'

Piskan's face turned bright red but he gave his master a dutiful nod. He knew not to go up against Spriggle, even if that idea had crossed his mind. Still, if he played his cards right?

'Er, there's one thing I better tell yous,' said Siras.

Spriggle gave Siras a steely glare. 'And what might that be?'

'We have to go and visit with er...Black Annis.'

Spriggle's eyebrows shot up at the mere mention of the dark sorceress. 'Black Annis, you say?Oh deary me, I'll be wanting a big reward fer this.'

The not-so-merry band of three set off to find Black Annis; not a task they were looking forward to. They made their way to Leicestershire and were told that they would find the forest they were looking for in the Dane Hills. They travelled far and wide until they eventually came upon it.

A friendly band of elves came running out of the forest to greet them. When asked about the dreaded sorceress, they told Siras that they hadn't seen nor heard of her for a very long time, but that a wizard who lived in an underground cave might know of her whereabouts.

After asking around the area, they were told that the wizard had moved to a clearing not far from a stream. They came across a piskie who offered to take them to him.

They trudged behind the piskie and he left them at the entrance to the clearing, disappearing before they had a chance to thank him. They followed the sound of running water until they came upon a hut, which they approached with caution. Would the wizard be friendly?

'What are you here for?' called the wizard, from inside the hut.

''Tis the servant of, Mistress Morag,' said Siras, 'yous may have heard of her?'

'Pah! Her?' he snorted from behind them, 'of course I have.'

Siras turned around and offered his hand in greeting. The wizard pushed it away.

'What does she want of me?' he growled.

Siras explained that they had been sent to find Black Annis and were told that he knew the whereabouts of the sorceress. The wizard threw his head back and roared with laughter. Broddle and Spriggle exchanged glances. What did he find so funny?

'Black Annis, eh?' and he promptly laughed again. 'Well, I'll tell you where she is. But don't expect a welcome from her,' he grinned wickedly. He told them that the sorceress had departed to the Land of Shadows.

'Thankee, wizard, er – I didn't get your name?'

'Just call me "Wizard",' he said looking at them with his piercing black eyes, 'and afore you go, just you tell your Mistress that I send her my greetings, she'll know what I mean.' That said he disappeared along with his hut.

Siras, Spriggle, and Broddle hurried away from the forest and to their surprise, a dark cloud suddenly appeared in front of them.

'Climb aboard,' it said. Was it a trap? But who would benefit from it, the wizard?

'You wanted to visit with Black Annis didn't you? Hurry up then.'

They climbed aboard and the cloud carried them through the veil to the Land of Shadows. They found out from a goblin that the sorceress was now living in the Forest of Fear. The travellers looked from one to the other. Why was it called that?

The cloud carried them forward and onward until they reached the outskirts of the forest. It looked dark and menacing, even from a distance.

'Here we are,' said the cloud. 'Well, get off me then,' he ordered.

They gingerly climbed down and started for the forest, Spriggle glanced back at the cloud only to find that it had already disappeared.

The Forest Of Fear

Chapter Thirty-two

Siras shivered; he didn't like the feel of the forest at all. It was dark, damp, and foreboding, and what if the dark sorceress kept them as prisoners?

Broddle and Spriggle also peered about them with a feeling of dread. Black Annis was somewhere in this smelly place and she was probably watching them from one of the trees. Would she jump out and tear them from limb to limb?

The air was stifling, without as much as a whiff of a breeze, and yet the tree trunks creaked and groaned and the branches swayed back and forth. They soldiered on, convinced that every now and then they could swear that something black with scary red eyes was following them. What was it? They journeyed further into the darkness, expecting danger at every turn.

One of the trees whispered to another. 'Something's afoot. Strangers are in our midst.'

'What do you think they're here fer?'

'We'd better keep quiet and listen.'

Siras put up a warning hand and said, 'Ssssh.'

'What are you sssshing for?' asked Broddle.

'I thought I heard a voice,' he said, his eyes as big as saucers.

'Do you think it's Black Annis?'

'Nay, Spriggle, it's only a wee gust of wind,' said Broddle. At least he hoped so.

'I hear tell she talks to the trees.'

'Well, Siras, maybe the trees are telling her of our arrival,' said Broddle, with a knowing nod.

In a clearing, a group of piskies sat by a fire. They were a distant cousin of the pixies but, like the spriggans, they were very nasty indeed.

'Who goes there?' called a gravelly voice. 'Well, well, well, 'tis Siras, not seen yer fer many moons past. And if it isn't Broddle and Spriggle,' he grinned, 'Wot in the world brings yer here then?'

'We're looking for Black Annis, have yous seen anything of her at all?' asked Siras, instantly noticing the wary look on their faces.

'Yer want to meet with *the* Black Annis?' the piskie asked, his eyes widening in disbelief. 'Why would yer want ter do that?'

'I need to speak with her on a matter of great importance.'

'Yer must be barmy,' he gasped, 'I wouldn't want to be seeing the likes of her, no siree.'

Siras was beginning to feel sick. Broddle chewed nervously on his bottom lip, and Spriggle tugged at his long pointed chin.

The piskie looked from one to the other. 'Yer serious, aren't yer? Well, if yer must,' he shrugged, 'she ain't in her tree, that's been felled long ago.'

'Where does she dwell now?'

'She hangs about in that cave over yonder.' Their eyes followed his long spindly finger that was pointing to a rocky outcrop. 'See? The one with the smoke coming from it – yer can just see the light o' the fire.'

'Thankee Gorken, I'll be sure and tell the Mistress. Yous'll be well rewarded.'

'I s'pose it's not worth asking what this is about?' Then seeing the look on their faces, he said, 'Nah, I s'pose not.'

'We'll be on our way, thankee to yous once more,' said Siras, who was not sure if he was feeling thankful or not.

'Afore yer go, Siras, be careful o' the banshees.'

'What are Banshees? I've never heard of them.'

'Haven't yer? Well I'll tell yer, they're the Shadows of Death.'

''Course, there may be ghouls about as well,' nodded another. 'They like the taste of a boggart, yer know.'

'And they're a bit partial ter brownies 'n' spriggans as well,' added Gorken.

Siras looked over his shoulder nervously. That was probably a banshee that had been following them, or was it a ghoul? Hmm, better get the mission over and done with before they had a chance to find out. They bade the piskies farewell, and their look of amusement didn't go unnoticed either.

With pounding hearts, they made their way towards the flickering light. It wasn't long before they came across a clearing. Spriggle was the first to enter, followed by Siras and then Broddle. An icy mist swirled about their bodies. The eerie silence filled them with dread as the faint glimmer of the moon disappeared behind scurrying black clouds. The thought of meeting with the dark sorceress was making them feel very nervous indeed. The mist tightened its grip, leading them forward and onwards towards the entrance to the cave.

Black Annis had been watching them from afar. 'If you come any further I'll put a curse on you,' she called.

They took a step backwards.

'Who are you?' she demanded.

'Siras, the servant of Mistress Morag,' he croaked, 'she sends yous her greetings o' honoured one.'

'Morag?' she snarled spitting into the fire. A blue vapour shot into the air. 'Now, why would I want to give her servant the time of day?'

Siras felt his heart sink to his boots. The sorceress came out of the cave and stood before them with her hands on her hips.

'Cat got your tongue, eh?' she snorted. 'I suggest you go, afore I get nasty,' she growled.

Would she cast a spell on them? Would they be bound to her for all eternity?

'I beg yous to listen, o' honoured one, the Mistress wants a truce after all these years,' Siras pleaded.

Black Annis looked as if she was going to explode, but then she chuckled. 'She wants to use my powers, more likely,' she sneered, 'her own aren't strong enough, then? Must be losing her touch, that's what,' she cackled.

'No, no, she just wants to meet with yous to talk about your misunderstanding.'

In hearing that, she threw back her head and roared with laughter.

'So will yous come?' asked Siras, hopefully.

Black Annis looked at him with contempt. So, this poor excuse of a servant wanted her to visit Morag, did he? Humf, he'll be lucky!

'Just...you...go...back...to...her...ladyship...with...this message,' she hissed, poking Siras in the chest, 'that she can come here in person,' another poke in the chest, 'and not send a mere messenger as the likes of you,' she snorted.

Black Annis looked closely at Broddle and Spriggle with her one eye and grinned maliciously. They were wondering if they should make a run for it considering they had tried to click their fingers attempting an escape, but there they remained, quivering in their boots. Had their powers been taken from them forever? They shouldn't have let Siras persuade them into this harebrained mission in the first place – never again.

Black Annis strode back to her cave and stepped inside, but not before looking over her shoulder and giving them a final sneer.

'That is my answer,' she spat, 'I'm getting mighty bored with the lot of you, now get out of my sight.' With a wave of her hand, a boulder rumbled across the opening.

The terrified comrades fled from the clearing as fast as they could. They trudged their way through the forest and out into the open and thankfully, with no sign of the banshees. The black cloud miraculously re-appeared and carried them away from the Land of Shadows, through the veil, bound for Norway where they landed on a craggy cliff. With a thunderous roar, the cloud vanished. Although the snow on the mountains glowed hauntingly in the moonlight, it was nothing compared to the Forest of Fear. Which direction should they head in –

right, left, or straight ahead? Not having been to Norway before, they didn't have a clue where the trolls lived.

'Er – Siras, how are we going to understand the trolls, I mean, none of us can speak their language.' Siras took out his orange stone and grinned triumphantly.

'We'll just touch this, and it'll translate for us.'

Spriggle snatched it out of Siras's hand and held it tight.

Broddle grabbed it from him and put it in his pocket. That should fetch a tidy sum, he thought.

'Hand it over, Broddle, it don't belong to yous,' growled Siras.

They travelled far and wide asking the whereabouts of the fearsome trolls. An old witch gave them directions that unfortunately turned out to be a wild goose-chase. Spriggle reckoned it was Black Annis getting a kick out of causing them strife.

After going around in circles, they eventually came upon a goat herder who pointed them in the direction of a craggy black mountain range which loomed over the valley like a bad omen. That information also proved to be futile.

Black Annis watched as they searched in vain for the whereabouts of Olger One Tooth. Let that be a lesson to those buffoons having the nerve to visit her on behalf of Morag. But maybe it was time to return to her cave. She'd toyed with them long enough and so, with a thunderclap and a lightning flash, she vanished into the night.

Siras was beginning to feel desperate, for they were running out of time. Whatever would he do if he couldn't find the troll? Morag would skin him alive. Or, worse still, she would without a doubt, banish him from the castle in disgrace. If she let him live, of course.

Luckily, they came across an old troll who was making his way along the track. He led them through a rocky outcrop.

'Go to the end of this track and you will come to the Fjord. Ask for Zinterg, the ferryman.'

They pressed on and eventually came to the water's edge where a thick fog lay over the Fjord like a blanket of doom. There was not a

breath of air or any signs of life until a lonely figure stepped out in front of them.

'Who are yer?' he demanded.

'My name is, Siras. Are yous, Zinterg?'

''Tis me, what do yer want wiv me?'

'We were told you could take us across the Fjord.'

'Oh?'

'We need to speak with Olger One Tooth,' Siras explained.

The ferryman's eyes widened. 'Olger yer say? Come wiv me.'

He led them to a scooped-out tree trunk. 'Climb in,' he said.

Broddle and Spriggle were the first to climb aboard. Siras hung back. He didn't like boats; especially since his experience on Loch Ness proved to be such a disaster. 'Go visit Nesslewarg,' the mistress had said. 'Nesslewarg?' he'd asked. 'The Loch Ness monster, you buffoon,' she'd snapped. The boat master had assured him that: Wee Nessie, as he'd called the monster, was friendly. Well, he was wrong about that! The monster came to the surface, bared his fangs and upturned the boat. It was then that he discovered that he couldn't swim, not one stroke. Luckily, Grunge who happened to be flying overhead swooped to his rescue. He'd sworn he'd never set foot on a boat again and here he was, about to do just that.

'What's keepin' yer?'

'Nothing,' squeaked Siras and he climbed aboard.

They sailed into the silence as the fog wrapped itself around them. Siras was holding on for grim death.

'Keep yer hands inside the boat,' warned Zinterg. 'There are water dragons in these 'ere parts, and they ain't too friendly.'

Siras sat on his hands looking about him. A sudden movement in the water had him suck in his breath as he peered over the side of the boat nervously. Spriggle and Broddle grinned broadly.

''Tis only a trout,' scoffed the ferryman.

The journey seemed to take forever as far as Siras was concerned, but they eventually came to the other side and he noted, in one piece. They had just set foot on dry land when out of the bushes came an enormous dragon – steam spouting from its nostrils.

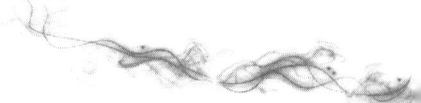

'Go, go quickly before the dragon sees yer,' urged Zinterg, 'he likes those that come from other lands,' he grinned wickedly. 'That track over yonder will lead yer to Olger One Tooth.'

The ferryman set sail and faded into the misty darkness. The dragon entered the water.

Within a cave in the mysterious mountain ranges near the Fjord, Olger One Tooth was sitting by a roaring fire chatting with his followers. The sudden sound of footsteps on the gravel had the troll-leader send one of his followers to investigate. Spartun quickly changed into a giant, hoping to scare off the intruders.

'WHO GOES THERE?' he boomed.

'Er, 'tis me, Siras, the servant of the sorceress, Morag.'

'SO?' he boomed again looking down at him with a sneer.

Siras looked up at the scaly giant whose large head sat on huge shoulders. And he didn't like the way he was flexing his bulging muscles at them either.

'I have an urgent message for your great leader, Olger One Tooth.'

Siras by now was shaking in his boots, which were beginning to feel more uncomfortable by the minute.

Broddle was also feeling decidedly wary as he craned his neck up at the giant. Their encounter with Black Annis had left him feeling a little nervous to say the least; not to mention the fact that neither he nor Spriggle had met trolls before. Spriggle, on the other hand, was convinced that he'd definitely lost his power. For when he tried to change himself into a giant so that he could look the troll in the eye, there he stood, as small as ever and feeling decidedly insignificant. He should've stayed in Cornwall where he belonged.

Spartun stood with his huge arms folded across his chest peering down at the three creatures, contemplating whether or not to let them into the cave. He had heard of Morag and knew of her reputation as a powerful sorceress and wondered whether she would bother with the likes of this sorry looking bunch. But he came to the conclusion that no one in his right mind would try and pull the wool over the master's eyes.

'Who is it, Spartun?'

''Tis, Siras, the servant of the sorceress...er...um, what did you say her name was?'

'Morag,' said Siras.

'It's the servant of the sorceress, Morag, m'lord.'

Curious, the troll master called out, 'Well, let them in, Spartun.'

The three weary messengers entered the cave to a warm welcome. Olger One Tooth had met Siras at the castle when he'd had dealings with Morag. The outcome had proved very lucrative to him and his tribe, with a little skulduggery on his part, of course. Yes, he was more than willing to give Siras the time of day.

'Welcome, Siras, long time no see,' he said, smiling broadly with his one tooth. 'What can I do for you?'

The troll listened intently to Siras's every word.

'Morag wants me to come to the Realm of Shadows with you, eh? I must admit, I'm mighty curious to know what she has to say, and what me reward will be.' And then he slapped his knee. 'All right, count me in.'

A more than happy Siras was at last going home – until he realized they were heading back to the Fjord. Not *another* boat?But this one was magnificent, a large clipper. They climbed aboard and sat down – where was everybody? A sudden blast of air had the clipper whizzing along the top of the Fjord and before they knew it, they had arrived in the Realm of Shadows.

'You're back,' spat Morag, 'about time too.' And then she greeted Broddle, Spriggle, and Olger One Tooth.

'Welcome my friends, it's been far too long,' she gushed.

'We're here teh see what help yeh be wantin', and what's in it feh us,' said Broddle, getting down to business.

'Oy would loyke ter know as quickly as possible,' said Spriggle.

'Let the woman speak, then we can make our minds up,' said Olger One Tooth. Morag was shocked to think that this, this *thing*, would dare to call her "woman". And if that ignorant troll didn't mind his manners, she would happily turn him into a slug.

But instead, she smiled at him. 'First of all, you must sup with me.' And she turned to Siras, snapping her fingers at him. 'Bring refreshments.'

'That would be well received. I have a mighty thirst on me,' said Olger One Tooth.

'I wouldn't mind a bite teh eat,' nodded Broddle.

'It be a while since Oy've eaten too,' said Spriggle.

'I expect my servant has told you of my plight?'

'We are well informed,' the troll replied.

'Good,' she smiled. 'I would like you to scare the living daylights out of those...those imbeciles.'

Spriggle raised an eyebrow. The sorceress had sent for them just to scare the mortals? How tame was that? The spriggans had better things to do with their time. 'What's wrong wiv yer helpers aren't they up ter scratch?' he asked.

'Aye, I canna understan' why yeh want our help, Mistress Morag,' said Broddle.Olger One Tooth looked on in silence.

The sorceress was fast approaching boiling point. But no, she would have to keep her cool. After all, she didn't want them thinking that she was desperate.

Siras returned with the food and drink he had just set it down when Broddle grabbed hold of his fork stabbing at the food before stuffing it into his mouth. Spriggle and Olger One Tooth tucked into theirs with their bare hands, throwing the utensils onto the floor. Spriggle slurped with each mouthful, Broddle smacked his lips together continuously, and Olger One Tooth picked bits of food from his tooth.

'You all want to know of your reward, I suppose?' Of course they do, their greed is written all over their faces, she thought.

'Oy would indeed,' Spriggle replied, and then proceeded to lick his plate.

Olger One Tooth and Broddle slurped away happily. Morag was finding it increasingly difficult to control the urge to turn them into pigs.

'Er – about the reward,' the troll reminded her.

'As soon as that boy has become my willing slave, with your help of course,' she cooed, 'you will have all that you desire.'

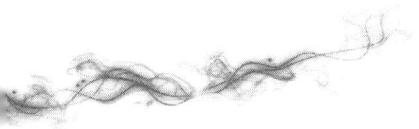

Spriggle banged his plate on the table, pushed it aside and gave a loud burp. 'That be a good feed,' he said, wiping his mouth on his sleeve.

Broddle glanced up from his plate. 'Why don't yeh just make him yer slave? That seems the easy way teh me,' he said, food flying from his mouth in all directions.

'He has to want to work for me,' said Morag, wiping away a lump of meat that had splattered her cloak. She certainly wouldn't be telling these disgusting creatures that she had to prove her worth to Lord Drago as well. 'And I have no intention of following him on his travels while he looks for the whereabouts of the crystal of Orlog.'

'That sounds excitin' to me,' said Spriggle, thinking that a bit of travel might be to his liking. Yes, he wouldn't mind in the least, providing it wasn't to the Forest of Fear.

'Depends on what you consider exciting. I, for one, would rather have a quick result,' snapped Morag.

'Bein' as yeh such a powerful sorceress, Mistress, I'm surprised yeh haven't managed teh make him yeh slave afore now.'

Morag glared at Broddle. How dare this buffoon of a brownie question her power? But then again, why had her spells bounced back at her?

'If it wasn't for that meddlesome, Cornelia Romanski, poking her nose into my business, I would have,' she hissed.

'I see yeh meanin',' nodded Broddle, 'the sorceress, Cornelia Romanski, is known to be verra powerful,' he said, noticing the look of annoyance that flashed across her face. 'Well then, hen, 'ol Broddle will help yeh.'

Siras gasped at the daring of the brownie, fancy calling the mistress "hen" – and not forgetting what he said about the old gypsy either. He was amazed when all she did was smile.

'Who will you bring to assist you?'

'There will just be Big Brairly and Wee Mulky, I'm afraid.'

'Is that all, I…'

Broddle stood up abruptly, 'I'll be awah teh fetch 'em.'

He waved his hand hoping against hope that his power had returned and was more than happy when he landed in Scotland.

Morag was so taken aback by what she considered to be his rude departure that she was speechless.

'Oy fink Oy'd better be on me way as well.'

'When will you return?'

'On the morrow,' he replied, hoping like mad that he was able to perform magic again. He squeezed his eyes shut, clicked his fingers, and with an almighty roar he vanished from the room.

'Well,' grumbled Morag, 'the manners of these creatures, I'll be teaching them a thing or two.'

Olger One Tooth ran his tongue around his tooth and grinned.

'And what about you, Olger, will you join me in my quest?'

'I think that we'll be very happy to be of help. But I'm not sure how many of me tribe I can spare, there's other things afoot.'

'I am most grateful to you, I know you are very busy,' gushed Morag.

Olger One Tooth picked up on her insincerity immediately. He'd had many a dealing with all manner of sorcerers and wizards in his time and could sniff out, without any effort whatsoever, when someone wasn't being altogether truthful. After all, you can't dupe ol' Olger. Armed with that knowledge up his sleeve, he knew that if he played the sorceress at her own game he might be able to demand more from her, no question about it. So he looked deep into her eyes and smiled. 'I'm never too busy to help a friend in need.'

'That's settled then. I won't keep you any longer. I'll see you on the morrow?'

The troll was enjoying the fact that Morag didn't want to keep company with him for any longer than she deemed necessary. And so with that in mind, he strolled around the room, picked up a jug, poured pumpkin juice into a goblet, and swallowed it in one gulp. He poured another, but this time he sipped at it very slowly before clicking his fingers and vanishing in a puff of smoke.

'I think that went well, didn't it, Mistress?' said an eager, Siras.

'You think that went well, do you?' she spat. 'WHERE IS BLACK ANNIS?'

'Sorry Mistress, I...'

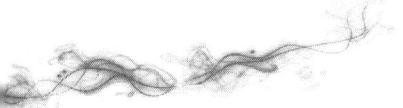

'Sorry Mistress?' she hissed, 'is that all you can say? Well, come on, OUT WITH IT,' she shrieked, 'where is that troublesome sorceress?'

'I asked her to come and visit with yous and…'

'You *ASKED* her?' she bellowed, 'I told you to TELL her,' she yelled.

'Well, yous see, it was like this, Black Annis wasn't too pleased to see us, so I thought that it would be best not to get on the wrong side of her.'

'You THOUGHT? It seems to me that you've been doing a bit too much thinking for my liking,' she screamed. 'Now tell me what she said.'

'Well, er – um, that you had to go and visit her,' he replied, feeling the beads of sweat trickle down his back.

Morag poked Siras in the chest. 'Oh she did, did she? I'll never visit that old hag,' she spat, 'NEVER!' she screeched at the top of her lungs.

Siras was now convinced that his mistress would banish him for all time. Oh bogs upon bogs, what should he do?

'Did you hear what I said, you buffoon, NEVER!'

Morag circled Siras trying to make her mind up about what to do with him. Perhaps she should change him into one of her bats? But then again she knew that complete obedience was hard to find – Siras did obey her every demand without question and besides, his ancestry was impeccable. Ah well, a kindly approach would serve her well. For the time being, that is.

'I suppose you've done well to bring the others here. You may go now, Siras, and rest up for tonight.'

Siras went away feeling very happy indeed, especially as his mistress actually thanked him for his efforts; coupled with the fact that he had got off lightly. He felt as if he was the luckiest boggart alive. Thank goodness he'd decided against telling her about the wizard. Who was he anyway? And what was the history between them?

Passage To The Unknown

Chapter Thirty-three

Broddle had arrived at the Realm of Shadows alone to be greeted by Morag who stood with her hands on her hips as she glared at him darkly. 'Where are your helpers, they should've come with you.'

'Big Brairly and Wee Mulky will be here shortly,' he replied.

'They'd better,' she spat. 'Now get out of my sight until they arrive.'

Broddle returned to the depths of the castle to join Spriggle and Olger One Tooth. He told them about his meeting with the sorceress and was already having doubts about helping Morag.

'Never mind, Broddle,' said the troll sympathetically.

Spriggle gave him a sly look and said, 'Why don't yer go instead, Olger.'

He had no intention of doing so. No, let the others work their magic first.

'Morag wouldn't be happy if we acted without her say-so.' he replied.

Broddle sat wringing his hands. 'I just hope me mates aren't too long, I mean teh say...' It was at that moment, they arrived.

Meanwhile, darkness had fallen upon the castle room.

'I'm cold, tired and hungry,' said Pamela.

Clara glared over at Hugh. 'Huh! If you've got magic powers, shouldn't you be able to conjure up a fire?'

'Belt up, Clara,' snapped Jamie. 'We don't need your snide remarks.'

'C'mon,' said Hugh impatiently narrowing his eyes at Clara. 'We should try and figure out where the secret passage is.'

'The candles have gone out so we'll have to leave it until tomorrow,' said Will.

'We'd better keep awake, just in case those creatures turn up again.'

Unfortunately for them, a sleeping spell had been cast and no matter how hard they tried, their eyelids closed and they fell into a deep sleep.

It wasn't long before the brownies crept into the room. Big Brairly felt a pang of regret at hastily agreeing to help Broddle for now that he had laid eyes on their prey, he realized he didn't want to help the sorceress at all.

'Psst, Wee Mulky,' whispered Big Brairly, 'I canna understan' why Broddle wants teh help that evil old hag.'

'Ours is not teh ask questions,' Wee Mulky replied. 'We've a job teh do, then we cin get on oower way. The sooner the better if yeh ask me.'

THUMP! A loud banging at the door followed by a bloodcurdling howl awoke the prisoners.

'What was that?' gasped Clara.

'H-e-l-p me, save me from the beast,' came a high-pitched voice.

The hideous howling rang out again.

The brownies huddled together under the table. Big Brairly vowed to have a word with Broddle, for he never mentioned anything about a wolf. They could be eaten alive!

The brownies decided to get out of there as quickly as possible. They came out from under the table unnoticed, and scrambled up the chimney, vowing never to listen to Broddle and his, 'It'll be the easiest

work yeh've ever done. An' there'll be a big reward feh me two best mates.' And to add insult to injury, the cloaks he gave them, didn't fit.

THUMP! THUMP! THUMP! With a resounding CRASH the beast broke the door down and charged into the room growling at everything in sight. However, it was not a wolf as they had feared, but a gigantic black mastiff which was now gnashing his teeth hungrily at them. Without thinking, Hugh threw a blue thunderbolt at the dog and it turned to dust in a split second.

'C'mon,' said Will, 'the doors are smashed to the ground; the knights have disappeared, so let's make a run for it while we can.'

They bolted out of the room and into the hall. They tried every door, only to discover that they were locked.

'Now what shall we do?' asked Pamela.

'Maybe the passage is somewhere behind these panels. The room we were in had solid stone walls.'

'It's worth a try anyway.'

The boys tapped at anything that looked as if it could open to a secret passage. Nothing did. And then Hugh noticed a small door underneath the staircase.

'We'll try that.'

With a little pushing and shoving the door opened. They crawled through the opening and found themselves in a dark passage.

'This must be the passage that you were supposed to find,' said Will excitedly until it led to a massive kitchen with no other way out.

The opening closed behind them sealing the entrance, and there was nobody about. A delicious smell had their stomachs rumbling. It turned out to be a pig roasting on a spit and there were several old black pots bubbling on a wood stove. In the middle of the room stood a large wooden table set for two, and on it, a loaf of bread, a lump of cheese, a basket of eggs, and a jug of milk. They broke off lumps of bread and cheese and shared the milk.

The only escape route that they could make out was a small window over a large sink. Hugh climbed up and tried the window-latch but it didn't budge. He didn't know what to do until he suddenly remembered how he made the ball roll away from the bushes at the

nisson huts. He stared long and hard at the latch and it opened. He beckoned to his friends and one by one they jumped out of the window.

As their eyes adjusted to the blackness, they realized they were in an old cemetery where the graves stood lonely and forgotten in a haunting swirling mist. An owl circled overhead and landed on a headstone. Its hoot echoed around the graveyard eerily.

'If the castle wasn't creepy enough, this place is spookier,' commented Jamie who was scared out of his wits.

'I hope we're not stuck here forever,' cried Pamela.

'We'll find our way out of here, you'll see,' said Hugh thinking: what if we don't?

'The sooner the better if you ask me,' murmured Will.

They weaved their way through the graves, but they seemed never-ending as the headstones sprouted in front of them like mushrooms.

'You've landed us in even more trouble, if that's at all possible,' spat Clara. 'We should never have followed you.'

'Shut up, Clara,' snapped Jamie. 'We're trying.'

'You shut up, Jamie,' she snapped back. 'We're never going to escape this ghastly place,' she wailed again.

'We can't give up,' said Will. 'We've got to believe we can.'

'Have a look at what's written on this,' said Hugh pointing to a large black stone covering a grave:

Here lies Lord Ethan
Keeper of the Dead

'Jeepers, this place gets spookier by the minute,' gasped Will, as the mist swirled around them bringing with it ghostly whispering voices.

'You don't think that's Lord Ethan, do you?' squeaked Clara, looking over her shoulder.

'Let's hope not,' Hugh replied just as the owl flapped its wings and landed on top of the gravestone peering at them with its huge hypnotic eyes.

'Don't look into its eyes,' warned Hugh, 'I don't like the way it's leering at us.'

The owl made a noise that sounded suspiciously like laughter. And then it turned into a raven, squawked at them, and flew off into the darkness.

'Look over there,' said Pamela, pointing to a grave that was now pulsating with an eerie purple light that on closer inspection, turned out to be like a strange-looking moss. There was something written on the headstone, but most of it was covered by a creeper. They could just make out a part of one word: Lor...oomsda...ampire.

'What do you think it says?'

'Perhaps it's Lord-something-vampire,' whispered Pamela.

'Jeepers, I hope not,' said Hugh

A loud screeching sound from behind had them swing around just in time to see a hand force its way out of a grave. And then a hideous-looking corpse sat up pointing a long bony finger at them. 'Run...run for your lives,' it rasped as another hand pulled it under the ground with a loud ZAP. Ghostly white ivy crept over the grave sealing the corpse for all time.

'Now what shall we...?'

A blood-curdling scream rang out and something dressed in a white flowing gown was making its way towards them. It had no head. The boys grabbed hold of the girls and they ran and ran until they stumbled across an old mausoleum.

'This will be a good place to hide. I'll try the door,' said Hugh.

He turned the handle and the door creaked open.

'Let's go in before that thing gets us,' cried Pamela.

They hurried inside and shut and bolted the door behind them. A large tomb covered in cobwebs awaited them.

'Who enters?' grunted a voice in the darkness. A white knight stepped out in front of them shrouded in moonlight, but there were no windows.

'What d-did you s-say?' stammered Will.

'Who enters?' grunted the knight again.

'We – er...' Hugh began.

'Who enters?' grunted the knight.

'We...' but the ghostly white knight was gone.

'Now we can't see a thing,' said Jamie.

That was until a flaming torch suddenly sprang to life lighting up the tomb. The girls huddled together in a corner. The boys stepped closer.

'Look what's written on it,' gasped Hugh. It read:

Prince Armageddon
Disturb Him at Your Peril

At that moment, huge cracks started to appear on the walls and the ground shuddered and shook beneath them. Fearing for their lives, they tried to open the door, just as the top of the tomb slid open and...

'Oh no, we're back in the castle,' cried Pamela looking round about her in despair.

Plots Upon Plots

Chapter Thirty-four

Morag was fuming that Broddle had failed her and when he came into the room expecting his reward, he was greeted with a poke in the chest and a, 'Well, what have you to say for yourself?'

Broddle raised an eyebrow at that. 'Nuthin', should I?'

'Where are your comrades?' she demanded.

Broddle was more than surprised. What did she mean?

'According to, Siras, they're nowhere to be seen,' she snapped.

'They must've gone haime efter they'd done me biddin',' Broddle replied, feeling a little niggled to say the least. After all, why should Wee Malky and Big Brairly hang around longer than was absolutely necessary?

'For your information, Broddle,' she hissed, 'your so-called helpers didn't do ANYTHING. And they soon took off when Ponzle broke down the door. If they had done their job properly, they would've taken advantage of the situation. If it wasn't for my slaves, the mortals might've escaped.'

Broddle was flabbergasted. He'd have a word with those two n'er-do-wells when he caught up with them.

'Well, yeh slaves must've butted their noses into their business afore they had a chance to put me plan into action,' was his stubborn reply.

So, thought Morag, this mild mannered brownie wasn't as mild mannered as she had thought. Should she turn him into a lump of haggis, just to remind him of her power? Or what about turning him over to the mercy of Nesslewarg? Loch Ness is particularly freezing at this time of year and there's not a lot of food floating around. Yes, the monster is rather partial to brownies. Hmm, although it would be oh-so tempting to do so, better to keep him on side, just in case.

'I do see your point, Broddle,' was all she said instead.

'Thank yeh, Morag, I'll be awah then.'

'But afore you go, here are some new brown cloaks for you and your friends. And when I have the crystal, you may never have to work again, if that is your wish.'

Broddle smiled triumphantly and with a click of his fingers, he was gone in a flash.

Meanwhile, Siras was wondering who would follow on from Broddle. He'd heard a rumour that his fellow brownies had decided against helping Morag. But then again, you could never be sure whether Yoger was just stirring the pot. He knew only too well that the mistress had not given him and his tribe the time of day when he offered to work for her. Yes, it was probably sour grapes on his part.

'Who will visit my young friends tonight?' asked Morag having summoned Olger One Tooth and Spriggle to her.

'Olger told me that he would, Mistress,' said Spriggle stealing a sideways glance at the troll.

Oh really? He and his tribe go next? No way. He would show Morag who really had the goods, after he'd tricked Spriggle into going first, of course. He'd make sure he'd stuff everything up. Still, he would keep quiet – better let the spriggan think he'd got one over on him...for now.

'I want them really scared, Olger, nice and ready for, Spriggle, here.' She gave them both one of her malicious grins.

Spriggle admired the wickedness of Morag and vowed to prove to the sorceress just how evil he could be. And he was certainly looking

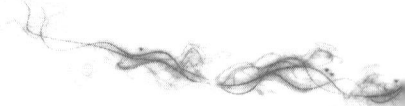

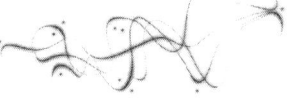

forward to proving that his powers of persuasion would show up Broddle for the simpering has-been that he was. For since returning from the Forrest of Fear, his powers had returned and miraculously, stronger than ever. Yes, Morag might even make him an offer he couldn't refuse, like ousting Siras from his position as her personal servant. He wouldn't mind whiling away his days in the castle. His mind was working overtime as he imagined all manner of riches coming his way. Let Olger work his magic first, for he was sure that he, the mighty Spriggle, could outclass the old troll – blindfolded.

'I'm talking to you, Spriggle,' snapped the sorceress.

'I'm sorry, Mistress, but I was busy making me plans.'

Spriggle felt his cheeks grow hot as Morag narrowed her eyes suspiciously at him.

'In future,' she hissed, 'when I'm speaking to you, I expect your full attention. Now go!'

Spriggle joined his four tribesmen who were eagerly awaiting their master. They had even made a fire in readiness for his return.

'Oy be havin' a thought, Master Spriggle, what if the Mistress let them kids out terwards dusk and we can dangle 'em over the cliff,' suggested Sprat, 'then yer can demand that they work fer the Mistress afore yer pull 'em ter safety.'

'Who says Oy'd save 'em?' he snorted. 'Anyways, Oy can't fink when Oy'm hungry.'

He grabbed hold of four rats and threw them into the fire. Sprat was busy tearing a fox apart with his bare hands.

Spriggle's mouth began to water. 'Hmm, the food sure smells good,' he grinned, saliva dribbling down his chin. He turned the rats over in the embers and Sprat handed them each a lump of meat. The spriggans licked their lips, in readiness of a good feed.

Olger One Tooth found his tribe already trying to come up with ideas to present to their master. He knew that he could always rely upon them to work well for him. After all, he treated them far better than some of the other troll masters, so why wouldn't they? He sat

down and stared at his feet. He knew that he would have to come up with something really clever to impress the sorceress, for he wanted to make sure that he was paid well for his efforts and, of course, make a name for himself in the Underworld. Or better still, he might gain the attention of Lord Drago. Then he would demonstrate how truly outstanding his powers were. Perhaps he would bestow upon him the honour of becoming one of his personal servants. And think how he would be the envy of the other trolls? Why, he might even oust Morag from her position as his second-in-command. He rather fancied himself in the Dark Castle. Yes, that would certainly be to his liking.

'What happened at your meeting, Master? Are we to work?'

Olger One Tooth nodded. 'After I've got Spriggle to fail miserably,' he grinned. 'That will give me time to come up with a good plan.'

'Have you got anything in mind? For Mistress Morag is a powerful sorceress so we don't want to make her angry.'

'What if we all became giants, that would scare the mortals surely?' suggested Hytterberg, a three-headed troll who had lost one of his heads in a battle against the Nejenstein dragons from across the Fjord.

Olger One Tooth looked over at Hytterberg's stump wondering how long the head would take to grow. Perhaps he'd take him to the healer, Hattenbreg. The trouble was, she lived on the other side of the mountains and, even though he could transport himself and Hytterberg to visit her, there were also the mountain Dragons of Gelortun to deal with. Ah well, the head would just have to grow back on its own.

'I don't think that's a good idea,' said one of the heads to the other.

'Well, what do you suggest then?'

'I don't know.'

'That's a fat lot of goo…'

'If you don't mind,' snapped Olger One Tooth, 'I would – what the…? HEY, LOOK OUT,' he yelled as Spartun materialized in the middle of the group causing boulders and rocks to splinter and fly in every direction. Why Spartun hadn't changed back to his normal height was beyond him. Just look at the mess he had created.

'M-master, th-there's an emergency,' he spluttered.

'An emergency, you say? What emergency?'

'Some miners are gettin' ready to blow up the caves.'

'*What*? We'll have to leave here as we speak,' he said, aghast that someone would have the nerve to enter his domain. 'We'll teach them intruders a lesson or two,' he growled. 'Spartun, go tell, Mistress Morag,' he ordered, 'we'll help her some other time.' No one messed with his caves, no one.

'We were looking forward to scaring them mortals,' grumbled Hytterberg.

'Our home is more important,' growled the troll master, 'I'll have no more said on the subject. Do you hear me?' And with a clap of his hands Olger One Tooth transported himself and his tribesmen to Norway on a lightning bolt.

S partun was petrified at having to face the sorceress. What was he going to say that wouldn't cause her to vent her wrath upon him? He knew that he was foolish to remain as a giant, especially as he didn't seem to be able to reverse the spell. After all, it had been vanity on his part. But now he had to face the consequences of his actions, like having to do his master's dirty work.

The walls shuddered and shook as if in protest when he knocked on the door.

'Enter, and you don't have to knock the door off its hinge…' Morag's voice trailed off when an awkward looking giant stood before her.

'And who might you be?' she shouted, craning her neck, 'shaking the place to bits.'

'Pardon me, Mistress Morag, my name is Spartun. I come to apologize for my Master, Olger One Tooth.'

'Oh? And why should you have to apologize for him?'

'Regrettably, he has been called away on a very urgent matter.'

Morag's eyes narrowed to slits, 'More urgent than mine?'

'Well er – um…'

'Don't stand there mumbling,' she seethed. 'I want an explanation.'

The worlds tumbled from his lips as he explained the situation as best as he could. Morag never took her glinting eyes off him.

'Oh I see,' said Morag, not really seeing at all. She considered herself so revered for her magic that no one, let alone a mere troll would take off without so much as a by-your-leave. She would see to it that Olger would feel the power of her wrath, when it suited her of course.

'But he said to tell you that he might help you another time if you still want him to. Er – um – I mean, the Master really wants to help you and is very disappointed at having to leave so soon,' spluttered Spartun.

Morag was tempted to turn this poor excuse for a Giant into a mouse. But like Broddle and his brownies, she decided she might indeed need the help of the troll at some time or other. And besides, she now had a score to settle.

'I completely understand. Do tell Olger I hope his troubles are soon over. You may leave now.'

She had hardly finished her sentence when Spartun stamped his foot, leaving behind a large crack in the floor as he vanished into the night.

The Beast

Chapter Thirty-five

'How would you like to go out for a little while before it gets dark?' smiled Morag, who had just appeared in front of her prisoners.

Hugh frowned – wasn't it dark when they were in the graveyard? And did she know about their escape?

'Well answer me, otherwise I might return you to the mercy of Lord Ethan.'

So she did know, he thought.

'That would be very nice,' gushed Clara who received a sneer from the sorceress.

Morag clicked her fingers and they found themselves outside the castle walls where the late afternoon sun had cast a golden glow on the surrounding countryside. There were alpine flowers in abundance and a bubbling stream meandered its way towards the mountains. The girls decided to sit and dangle their feet in the stream.

'Maybe we'll be able to make a run for it.'

Clara gave Will a withering look, 'Look what happened the last time you came up with an idea. What a waste of time that was.'

'We can at least try,' he snapped back at her.

'Er – I don't think so,' said Jamie nodding over to the knights who had miraculously appeared. To their astonishment, they had lifted their face shields to reveal ferocious-looking hairy faces.

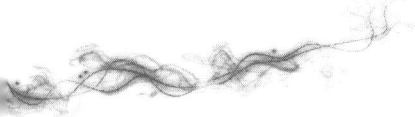

'Don't get any ideas about escaping,' growled one of them.

'We're just going for a walk,' blurted Jamie.

'Not without us yer not,' growled the other.

The girls decided to keep right where they were.

'That castle sure is weird,' said Will to Pamela when they returned.

'What happened?'

'Well, we planned to see what was around the corner so we could all make a run for it later, but we never seemed to reach the end of the castle. It sort of...grew.'

'Nothing would surprise me about this place.'

The peacefulness was shattered by an ear-splitting wail in the distance. They spun around and saw something large and dark sniffing the ground.

'Jeepers, it doesn't look like that mastiff dog. I think it might be a kind of wolf,' said Will.

'Crikey, it's standing up,' cried Pamela.

'That's not an ordinary wolf,' gasped Jamie.

'What do you think it is then?'

'It could be a werewolf.'

'Oh great, that's all we need,' said Hugh.

The barguest changed shape into an enormous bear-like creature with shaggy fur. He sniffed the air with his enormous nose, caught their scent, and came bounding towards them. The girls clung to each other in fright. Meanwhile, the boys were desperately trying to find a hiding place. The knights jangled their armour as they cowered in the doorway.

'Psst, psst, over here,' said a voice, 'come with me, I'll hide you.'

They turned around to find a shepherd beckoning to them from behind a bush.

'Come on, hurry,' he said.

Where did he appear from so suddenly? At first they hesitated, but the barguest had shortened the distance between them considerably. And so, not having much of a choice, they made a run for it. The

shepherd ushered them around a corner and led them along a gravel track and over a rough terrain until they arrived at the foothills. They travelled for some time, climbing over large rocks towards woodland and eventually came across a leafy glade. They were surprised to find a log cabin.

'C'mon young folk,' he urged, 'that's me home.'

And he hurried them inside bolting the door behind him. There were two men sitting by a roaring fire. The shepherd told them his name was Sinfred.

'These folk are my friends,' he said. 'They come to the mountains once a year to go trekking.' He introduced them as, Shorty, who was very tall, and Rumple who was short and fat and looked like a bulldog.

'Come, join us by the fire,' said Shorty.

'Whatever was that thing we saw out there?' asked Jamie.

'Thing?' said Sinfred. 'Oh, you mean, the barguest?'

'He's a phantom, yer know,' said Rumple.

'The sorceress called upon him to scare you,' said Shorty, giving them a knowing look.

CLANG – CLANG – CLUNK, the knights were clanging their way towards the hut.

'Cripes, the knights have followed us here,' said Hugh.

'Don't worry, the evening mist will come rollin' in soon enough and those lumps of tin will return to the castle.'

'But what if the witch looks into her cauldron, or whatever she uses, she's bound to see where we are.'

'We are well protected from evil here,' said Sinfred. 'I have helped many to escape her clutches.'

He told them that he had a friend who would guide them to safety, but they had to wait until it was dark. Rumple brought over steaming bowls of soup and crusty bread. The trekkers made room for them around the table.

'The thing is, a Cavalier told me I was supposed to find the entry to a secret passage,' said Hugh. 'And that means I didn't pass some sort of a test.'

'It wasn't your fault the sorceress let you out, now was it?' he grinned. 'And she had no idea that I was looking for my sheep and

happened upon you. I bet Morag will take your escape out on poor old Françoise, though,' he chuckled.

'Who's Françoise?'

'He's the Cavalier.'

'How do you know him?' asked Jamie.

'We go back many moons. In fact, I helped him out of a rather embarrassing situation once, involving an enchantress named, Shila. Still, I won't bore you with the details.'

The door opened, and a man stepped inside. He was wearing a long grey hooded cloak and he carried a lantern.

'Go with my friend, before it's too late. Go on, hurry.'

They followed the man along the mountain track that wound its way through to an open valley.

'This is where it gets dangerous, folks. There are swamps in these 'ere parts, so follow me light and don't stray from the track.'

The further they journeyed into the valley the happier they felt. At last they had escaped from the sorceress. The sun began to rise over the mountains and the man blew out the lantern. They continued on their journey, being careful to keep to the narrow track. The man suddenly stopped and inspected the ground – he walked a few paces stamping his foot as if double-checking that it was safe to walk on.

'We're through the swamps now, folk.'

They breathed a sigh of relief – until...

'A-A-A-A-R-GH,' they yelled as they landed in a swamp.

'Help us,' pleaded the girls, as the sludge slurped around them.

'Ol' Will o' the Wisp, will help yer as soon as yer mate agrees to work fer the sorceress.'

'I'LL NEVER DO THAT,' yelled Hugh. 'But I'll do THIS,' he said, and a bolt of blue light lifted Will o' the Wisp high into the air never to be seen again.

'That's very clever of you,' Clara shrieked, 'now we're going to die,' she wailed, sinking deeper into the swamp.

Hugh glanced frantically about him. Was there anything they could grab on to? And then he spied the willow trees. He didn't know why, but he could hear them talking to him. But that's crazy, trees don't

talk! But the trees called out, 'Hang on, lad, you summoned us, so we're coming to free you.'

With a loud creak and a thunderous roar, the trees appeared in front of them. They grabbed hold of the branches and managed to heave themselves out of the swamp and – WH-O-O-SH...

'Welcome back, my dear friends. Hmm, thought you had escaped, did you? WRONG!'

Excuses Galore

Chapter Thirty-six

Morag could not believe that the spriggans had also failed her. It was lucky she was looking into her scrying mirror when she did, otherwise the mortals would have escaped her clutches. And when Spriggle sauntered into the room expecting to be congratulated for his clever plan, she was astounded by his cockiness. Obviously, Siras had conveniently forgotten to tell this vile creature of his failure. She'd deal with that buffoon later.

Spriggle was so sure of himself that he hadn't noticed the speedy exit of Siras, or the look of thunder on Morag's face.

'Yer wanted to speak wiv me, Mistress?' smiled Spriggle.

'You took your time! Your so-called plan, that you assured me would not fail, has done just that,' she snapped.

Spriggle's mouth fell open. His plan had failed? 'Just 'ow in the world did that happen, Mistress?'

'YOU – TELL – ME,' she bellowed.

'But when we were in the hut, them thar children were completely taken in by me, the friendly shepherd, Sinfred.'

'Is that so?' spat Morag, tapping her foot.

'Of course,' he insisted. 'Oy called upon Will o' the Wisp, and he is someone that yer can rely on.'

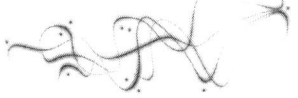

'I'd say that your so-called friend wasn't as reliable as you thought,' she sneered. 'He certainly performed like a wisp of nothing. I can certainly see why they call him by that ridiculous name.'

'But he landed them kids in the swamp,' he protested.

'Well…somehow they managed to escape,' she spat.

Morag did not want was this lowlife creature knowing what she had witnessed. Never let it be said that the mortal had performed powerful magic. After all, what would people think if they found out that he had beaten her? She would be fodder for all manner of stories. And knowing Black Annis, she would be sure to get her mileage out of it. And then there's Cornelia Romanski, how smug would she be? Oh, curses upon curses.

'Oy still carn't believe that me ol' mate let me down,' said Spriggle, shaking his head in dismay.

'Well, he has, you buffoon,' she spat.

What did she call him – a: *buffoon*?

Noticing how Spriggle's face had darkened with anger, Morag rapidly came to the conclusion that she'd better keep him on-side as well. After all, he might spread rumours about her. Oh, why she'd sent for him, she'd never know. It was all Siras's fault.

'Never mind, Spriggle, you've done your best.'

His mouth twitched into a malicious grin – he had a strong feeling that Morag would need him again. After all, it wasn't his fault that Will O' the Wisp didn't keep his end of the bargain.

'Of course, you'll help me again, should I need you?'

Gotcha, he thought. 'Yer can count on ol' Spriggle.' he replied. Yes, and then it would be *he* who would name *his* price.

'Good. You may go.'

And the last Morag saw of Spriggle was when, with a mock salute, he vanished to his crumbling ruins in Cornwall.

Down in the depths of the castle, the boggarts were preparing to eat the spoils from their hunting trip.

Old Mobbins was sitting on his favourite rock still feeling very excited after the thrill of the chase. It had been far too long since they

had gone hunting. No more would they wait to be fed by Morag. She only gave them the scraps anyway.

'Who goes there?' he called, hearing footsteps.

''Tis me, Siras,' he called back thinking that it was good talking to his own kind. Even though they reckoned that since working for the mistress, he spoke a bit strange, "like the mortals," one of them had the nerve to tell him. And Old Mobbins even accused him of trying to speak like the mistress. Now what it was he said: that I spoke posh? What did that mean?

'Did yous hear me, Mobbins, 'tis me, Siras.'

The boggart slowly turned his head and snorted, 'So it is. Huh! the Mistress wants somethin' no doubt.'

'Only to find out how yous are.'

'When has she been worried about us afore, that's what I'd like to know,' he frowned. The other boggarts looked on in silence.

'Mistress Morag wishes yous to know that she will be able to give yous a reward soon.'

'Is that so? That's very strange, because I heard tell that she asked the brownies and the spriggans fer help.'

'Yes but…'

'*And* Olger One Tooth,' he added, accusingly.

'Mistress Morag only did that because yous went missing.'

Old Mobbins sniffed. 'Anyways, wot does she want?'

'Er – um – the prisoners are lookin' for the passage.'

'So? What's that got to do wiv us?'

'Well, er…'

'Seems to me that the forkyped has power,' he nodded, knowingly.

'Sssh – not so loud, Mobbins. The Mistress might be scrying and yous don't want to make her angry,' said Siras. 'Anyway, we all know that we are workin' for the most powerful sorceress in the land who is favoured by Lord Drago himself.'

Old Mobbins shrugged his shoulders indifferently, 'If yer say so,' he sniffed again. And he turned away, making it obvious that he didn't want to discuss the matter any further.

S iras clicked his fingers, landed in woodland and began his search of the goblins. He found them just a little way ahead picking up twigs for a fire. Old Gordle turned around at his approach.

''Tis yerself, Siras, and wot would yer be wantin'?' The look on Siras's face gave him the answer, 'As if he didn't know.'

A quick touch of the translator had Siras launching into his story.

'So? What's that got to do with me and my horde?'

'Well nothin' really, except that…'

'Well, that's settled then. We are not interested.' And like Old Mobbins, the goblin turned his back on him.

Siras decided to give the grobs, or whatever they called themselves, a miss.

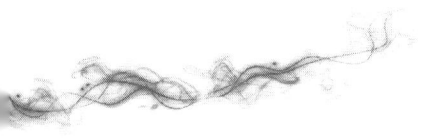

Signs

Chapter Thirty-seven

Having landed in the castle again, Hugh and his friends were frantically trying to find the opening to the secret passageway. The trouble was, there was only one way out of the room and that was through the doors, which had miraculously reappeared. But they were now bolted from the outside due to the fact that the knights seemed to have gone for good.

'The passage could be anywhere,' said Hugh.

'Perhaps it's behind the fireplace,' suggested Jamie, 'you know, like a secret hideaway.'

Hugh scratched his head, 'There again, it could be something to do with these portraits.'

'I don't think you've got a clue,' snorted Clara.

'You seem very interested in my family,' said Morag who had entered the room and was now standing behind them. Let them look as closely as they wanted, she thought, they'll never be able to escape my clutches.

Jamie and Hugh swung around, their hearts thumping in their chests. How long had she been watching them?

'You've already seen where Ethan dwells, dear Hugh' she smirked. 'If you agree to work for me your worries will be over,' and she vanished as quickly as she came.

'I'd never do that,' he said. 'She's evil.'

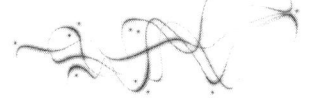

'I don't think you've any chance of getting us out of here,' sneered Clara.

'If you came up with an idea instead of being bitchy, it would help,' snapped Jamie.

'I was going to suggest asking the Cavalier,' said Will. 'But he's missing.'

They spun around only to discover that the painting was empty.

'This place gets stranger and stranger,' Jamie commented.

'But I'm supposed to figure it out myself, aren't I?'

'Oh yes, by using your powers,' murmured Clara.

'Look,' said Hugh ignoring her, 'that man in the portrait over there seems to be pointing to the floor.'

'Don't tell me we've got to dig our way out of here,' scoffed Clara. 'I...what's happened to the floor?'

They looked down at the strange symbols that had suddenly appeared on the floor. Hugh bent down to have a closer look and wondered why they looked familiar. And then the penny dropped – they were the same symbols that were on the stones belonging to the old tramp. And what about the markings on his coin, were they the same? If only he had it with him.

'I've seen these somewhere before,' he said and told Jamie about the old tramp.

He looked at him sharply, 'I knew you were up to something that day. Hmm, the symbols must mean something then.'

'That's the thing – what?'

The amulet suddenly felt hot against his chest, so much so, he pulled it out to stares from his friends, especially as it had doubled in size.

'What's that?'

'A gypsy pendant Charlie's grandmother gave me. Lucy's got one as well.'

'How come you never showed it to us before?'

'She told us to keep it a secret because she didn't have enough for everybody.'

Hugh went to undo the clasp, but it wouldn't undo. He tried to pull it over his head but it wouldn't budge.

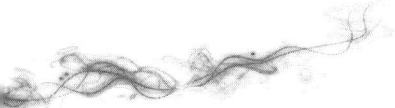

'Look,' Jamie said excitedly. 'Something's happening to the pendant. Blimey! Symbols are appearing on it as well. I'm sure they are the same as the ones on the floor.'

Hugh looked more closely at the pendant and then the floor. 'You're right; it must be some sort of a code.'

'That's all very well, but how are we going to decipher it?' said Will.

Clara had had enough by this time. 'We're never going to be able to,' she cried. 'So why don't you agree to work for the Mistress and be done with it?'

'Why did you say that?'

'Say what?'

'Call the witch or whatever she is, "the Mistress".'

'I – er, d-don't know why I said it, it j-just came out,' Clara blustered, going all red in the face.

'Hmm, we'll be thinking you're on her side if you're not careful,' Jamie remarked. Clara felt sick. Why *did* she say that?

Meanwhile, Hugh walked around the room going from one slab to another. 'Cripes! Every one of these slabs has at least one of the symbols on it,' he said. 'But none of them seem to stand out.' And then he looked over at the portrait again. 'I'm sure the finger is pointing towards the fireplace.'

'But you said it was pointing to the floor,' said Jamie.

'I know, but now it's pointing to the fireplace.'

'Perhaps there's a switch or lever hidden somewhere,' suggested Pamela.

'There's only one way to find out.'

They felt up and down the fireplace but there was nothing resembling a switch or a lever.

'So much for that idea,' said Jamie.

And then Hugh took a closer look at the mantelshelf. 'I wonder if these carvings mean something?' and he pointed to one in particular.

'As far as I can make out,' Will said, 'there is a five-pointed star, which sort of looks like a compass.'

'Really?' said Jamie stepping closer. 'I see what you mean; it has little arrows in the middle of it pointing to north, south, east and west.'

Hugh peered closer still. 'Underneath the star there is a carving of mistletoe, above, a skull. To the left there is a dragon and to the right, a sickle.'

'But does it mean anything?'

'Hmm,' said Will. 'Isn't mistletoe something to do with the Druids?'

'How do you know that?'

'Don't you remember when we had a lesson about the Druids?'

'They were supposed to have something to do with Stone Henge.'

'Oh yeah, I remember.'

'That book I read about spells mentioned them as well,' said Clara.

'But what would a skull mean?'

Hugh shrugged his shoulders, 'Haven't a clue, unless it means a dead end.'

'Is that supposed to be your idea of a joke?' hissed Clara.

'No – it could mean that.'

'But what about the sickle, what do you suppose that means?'

'Didn't they use them in olden times, when they were harvesting?'

'Yeah, but what does it mean?'

'Perhaps you should look at all the slabs to the right of the room. It could mean a reward,' said Pamela.

'Huh! I don't know how you came to that conclusion, it could mean food for all we know,' scoffed Clara.

'At least we're trying to come up with something,' said Jamie through clenched teeth.

'Sorry,' she mumbled.

Hugh looked at every single one of the slabs and he still couldn't fathom it out. And then came a stroke of luck – squeezed into a corner, there was a small oblong slab that looked out of place. He bent down and looked at the symbol and although it proved to be completely different to the ones on his pendant – it had a sprig of mistletoe carved into it. He counted five berries and he jumped up – he had found the answer!

'I know what it means,' he said rushing over to the fireplace. He walked the five slabs directly in front of the carving of the mistletoe.

'If I'm not mistaken, somewhere on this slab we'll find what we're looking for.'

Jamie and Will went over to help him look.

Will pointed to a carving that resembled a sickle with a flower etched on it. 'Isn't that symbol carved deeper than the others?'

'You're right, it's the same one that's on my pendant,' said Hugh, 'I always thought it was a crescent moon but now I realize that it's a sickle.' And then he bent down low and slotted the pendant into the carving. It was a perfect fit.

Passages Of Secrets

Chapter Thirty-eight

'Wow,' gasped Hugh, looking down at the opening. 'This is it.'

Jamie looked over his shoulder nervously. 'We'd better hurry before the witch finds out.'

And they scampered down the steps as fast as they could. As soon as they reached the bottom, the slab slid across the opening, sealing the entrance for all time.

'Now what do we do?' wailed Clara. 'We can't see a thing.'

'We'll have to feel along the walls,' said Will, 'and see where we land up.'

'But we might be in a dungeon for all we know.'

Hugh shook his head. 'I don't think so. I think I can just make out a sort of tunnel. C'mon let's go.'

'I hope we don't come across those foul-smelling creatures,' said Pamela suddenly.

'We'll just have to have our wits about us.'

They felt along the walls until they came across a cave which was lit by flaming torches. Old broomsticks were strewn about the floor. A couple of rusty cauldrons were lying on their side. A bundle of discarded wands lay in a heap, and bunches of dried herbs hung from

wooden hooks. A knight's rusty armour was propped up against a wall and lying across its legs, a broken sword.

'This place reminds me of that shop called "Mystery",' said Jamie.

A skeleton that was sitting against a wall fell at his feet. Mice spewed from its mouth and scurried down holes. The girls let out a scream.

'Jeepers,' he gasped.

Hugh picked up a torch and they followed him into the dark tunnel. They edged their way along the walls until they came to a dead end. Yellow eyes peered out of dark holes at them. They hurriedly retraced their steps but landed in an enormous cave that smelt of rotten eggs. In front of them was another tunnel and leaping excitedly from one murky puddle to another, were huge slimy black toads.

They bolted past the toads and ran as fast as they could towards the opening where a dim light was glowing. Unfortunately, the light turned out to be a fire where, too late, they realized the creatures from the castle were sitting. Old Mobbins suddenly sat up straight and pricked his ears up. Did he hear footsteps?

'Wot was that?' he said.

'I didn't hear anyfin', Master,' said Twerp.

'P'raps it be them forkypeds.'

'Don't be daft; they're still in the castle.'

'Then it must be...you know who,' said Old Mobbins.

'I don't know who yer mean, Master.'

'Siras of course,' he grunted and he stood up ready to send him packing. Siras was nowhere to be seen.

'I bet it was Old Gordle, he's always lurkin' about,' said Twerp.

'Tryin' to eavesdrop more likely,' nodded Wartun knowingly.

'Go away, Gordle,' shouted Old Mobbins.

'C'mon,' whispered Hugh, 'we don't want those creatures to see us.'

They tip-toed away and followed the passage until they saw another light in the distance.

'What do you think we should do now?' asked Jamie.

'We'll go on a little further, but if we hear voices again, we'll turn back.'

They crept very slowly towards the light until it opened on to what appeared to be, a Temple. The walls were covered with hundreds of carvings – of deer with snake-like antlers, six headed beasts with fiendish faces, and skulls with life-like eyes which glared down at them. Will accidentally touched one of the skulls and a huge boulder rumbled across the opening.

'Oh no, we're trapped again,' cried Pamela.

'WHY CAN"T YOU WATCH WHAT YOU'RE DOING,' yelled Clara.

'I didn't do it on purpose,' he protested.

'But now that old witch will find us or, worse still, we'll starve to death,' she cried.

Hugh decided he'd take no notice of Clara, and wandered about the Temple until he stumbled upon a carving of the sickle. He slotted his pendant into place and another boulder slid open. They dashed into the opening and fell helplessly down a large black hole into the unknown.

'H-E-E-E-L-P!' they yelled until they reached the bottom with a resounding THUMP. They had landed on a wide ledge on a bank of moss overlooking a vast cavern. Heavy footsteps came thumping towards them followed by an ear splitting R-R-R-R-O-A-R. A huge lizard-like head peeped out of an opening and large yellow eyes peered down at them. The dragon came further into the cavern, its tail swishing dust into the air. Fire spewed from its mouth – smoke spurted from its nostrils.

'WHAT YOU DOIN' HERE?' it boomed.

'Er – um – you see, we're trying to find our way out of here,' blurted Hugh.

The dragon lowered its head and growled, 'WHO ARE YOU?'

'My name is Hugh Barnaby,' he croaked.

That was met with another swish of its tail.

'SO-O-O,' it roared, 'YOU'RE THE ONE.'

The dragon lowered his voice, which was a relief as their ears were ringing. 'Go to the Druid and tell him that Gwynfed sent you.'

'But where do we find him?'

'That's for you to find out,' and with a final spew of fire, the dragon was gone.

Everyone was at a loss for words, especially when they looked over the ledge and saw how deep the cavern was.

'Now what do we do?' said Jamie.

'Look, over there, I see a track,' said Will.

'But how do we get to it?' asked Pamela.

'Perhaps there's a bridge somewhere,' said Hugh.

'But there's not.'

They sat down again trying to figure out how to get to the other side without falling to their deaths. And then Hugh jumped up. Just above Will's head was the sickle. He pressed his pendant into it and a wooden bridge appeared in front of them.

'Let's cross it before it disappears,' urged Will.

'You go first,' said Clara pushing him forward.

Will stepped onto the bridge grabbing hold of the rope handrails. The others followed. Far below them, molten lava bubbled and popped and the strong smell of sulphur had them gasping for breath. The bridge swung from side to side as they took tentative steps forward hoping like mad that it would hold up under their weight. They hurried across as fast as they dare and landed on solid ground. Stepping out of the shadows to meet them was a cloaked figure. Was he the Druid? Or was he Will o' the Wisp?

The Blue Stone

Chapter Thirty-nine

The Druid hurried them along many winding passages until they were out in the open. They came upon a vast expanse of barren land that was bathed in a haunting silver light. Hugh glanced over his shoulder and still the castle loomed over them, a constant reminder of its power. They trudged on and on until they came across another track, banked each side by mounds of dirt and rubble. The Druid did not utter a word but pressed on regardless, keeping his eyes focussed in front of him. They turned a corner and rising up in front of them, was a circle of huge square stone columns which looked suspiciously like Stone Henge. Inside the circle, stood an enormous amethyst cut into the shape of a pyramid. Surrounding the pyramid, the same symbols on Hugh's pendant were carved into the ground.

'Come,' said the Druid, and beckoned them into the circle. He put three objects in front of the pyramid – a piece of mistletoe, a purple flower and a blue stone. He then raised his arms to the sky and spoke in an ancient language:

Gwythr Cumthyr Iog
Samhain Arthan Belthane

A beam of light shot from the sky and onto the pyramid – thunder and lightning crashed overhead. The Druid drew a circle with his staff

as purple flames shot into the air. With a final resounding lightning flash, they found themselves in a clearing. There was absolutely no sign of the castle.

'We must journey over that mountain range before we will be well on our way to safety,' said the Druid.

He led them to a winding path that weaved its way around the foothills. They eventually came upon a grassy slope and sat down to rest their aching feet.

'Let's eat,' said the Druid and he unwound a cloth bundle to reveal almost enough food to feed an army. Jamie was thinking that there was more to him than meets the eye.

'Now eat your fill, but hurry, we are not completely out of danger.'

The track became steeper as it wound its way through the mountain passes. Eventually the ground levelled out and they made good progress. The sun began to disappear behind the snow-capped mountain peaks and there was a sudden chill in the air.

'We have only a little way to go before we can rest up for the night,' the Druid explained.

They trudged behind him along a narrow gravelly path flanked either side by vast walls of rock. They turned a corner and were confronted by a waterfall which cascaded down a high cliff into a small lake. The Druid tapped the ground with his staff and a wooden raft came hurtling across the water towards them.

'Climb aboard,' he said.

Clara opened her mouth to object, but one look from the Druid had her follow him onto the raft.

Jamie nudged Hugh and whispered, 'That shut her up.'

The raft skimmed along the surface of the lake heading straight for the waterfall. As soon as they reached it, the waters parted leading them into a large cave. They came to a halt by a little wooden jetty. They followed the Druid along a narrow tunnel until they came out to a small settlement. There were several houses made out of clay and straw. They were round in shape and had thatched roofs. Goats and chickens wandered about freely. A pig was sniffing around a basket of vegetables.

At first the settlement seemed deserted, until another Druid came out of a house followed by a lady carrying a basket of herbs. And then children came running towards them followed by a yapping dog. The man said something to the children and then the family walked towards a kind of archway that led to three huge pillars made out of clay. The man laid a sprig of mistletoe and sprinkled herbs in front of the three pillars. The family turned around, walked back to the house and disappeared inside. Jamie looked at Hugh and gulped. Didn't they look like the squatter family? What had they let themselves in for now?

'Welcome to my village,' said the Druid suddenly. 'We will stay here for the night. In the meantime, enjoy our hospitality.'

He took them to a long house where inside, Druids sat around a large table eating from wooden bowls. No one spoke, nor did they look up. Behind them were three columns crafted out of the blue stone. Jamie nudged Hugh and nodded over to the middle column. Carved into it was the very same flower he had etched on his pendant. The Druid beckoned for them to sit down and a lady who seemed to appear from nowhere, carried a large wooden tray of steaming bowls of soup over to them. All eyes were suddenly on Hugh as he nervously sipped at the soup. Would they speak to him? No one did.

The following morning, the Druid gave them each a bowl of porridge and honey.

'Where do we go from here?' asked Hugh.

'We have a way to go until we reach the forest where you will find a pathway leading to an ancient doorway. I'm afraid once there, you will have to continue the journey on your own.'

The Druid didn't tell them the name of the forest – it was the Forest of Fear.

'I hope we won't have any more trouble from the witch,' said Pamela.

'Actually, she's a sorceress and I'm afraid you still might. Don't ever forget a sorceress is much more powerful than a witch. Therefore, Morag can be anywhere at any time if she so chooses,' he warned. And then he went on to explain that once Hugh had found the passage, her

spell ceased to work against him while he was still in the castle. 'But of course, you were protected by the amulet.'

'What's an amulet?' asked Hugh.

'The pendant Mistress Cornelia gave you to wear.'

'Mistress Cornelia, who's she?' asked Jamie

'Charlie's grandmother who is an equally powerful sorceress and she gave Hugh the amulet for his protection.'

'I thought she was just a gypsy who could tell fortunes,' said Hugh, 'but she also gave one to my sister.'

The Druid had nothing to say about that. 'Anyway, we'd better be on our way.'

They were surprised when he took them under the arch to where the three columns stood. He drew three straight lines with his staff pointing towards the middle column. With a loud CRASH, a sudden squall surrounded them and they landed in the middle of a meadow. In the distance, the forest beckoned.

'I'm afraid this is where I must take my leave of you. Keep on this track and it will lead you to the forest where you will find the ancient doorway. Once through, you will be back in your own world.'

The Druid gave Hugh a small cloth bundle.

'Now I must away, I have places to go, good luck,' and with a little bow, the Druid vanished.

'Damn,' said Jamie, 'we'll never find out about Stone Henge now.'

When they eventually reached the end of the track, they decided to stop for something to eat before they went any further. There were two men dressed in shabby clothes sitting on the side of the path.

Jamie was instantly suspicious of them. 'I hope they're not here to trap us again.'

'There's only one way to find out,' said Hugh.

The men looked around at their approach. One of them stood up and raised his hand in greeting.

'Hail young folk, I am known as Griswald. We are on our way to Thwartund and have run out of food – yer wouldn't have any to spare, would yer?'

The other man stood up and introduced himself as Wartun. They were shabbily dressed in clothes made out of mouldy old sacks. Hugh was having second thoughts. Should they run for their lives?

'Is that food yer've got in that bundle?' the one called Griswald asked.

'We're mighty hungry,' said the other.

Hugh quickly undid the cloth.

'Why are you giving away our food to those old tramps?' hissed Clara, 'you don't know where they've been.'

'*Clara*,' gasped Pamela, 'don't be rude.'

'They've probably got fleas,' she snorted. 'And besides, we might run out of food ourselves and then we'll be hungry,' she insisted.

Hugh gave Clara a warning look and handed over the food. 'Here you are, help yourselves.'

'That be mighty generous of yer young man, yer kindness will be remembered, never fear.' And with a merry wave and a steely glare at Clara, the men disappeared from the track.

'Where did they go?'

'I don't know, but whoever they were, they didn't seem evil, did they?' Jamie commented.

'Just goes to show we have to be on our guard, though.'

They made their way towards the pine forest – it looked dark and creepy. Pamela clung on to Jamie for all she was worth as they stepped cautiously into the darkness. An eerie mist circled their feet. They trudged on, making their way through the thick undergrowth. Something made Hugh glance nervously up at the trees – there was something very sinister about them, as if they were watching their every move. Will shivered; he didn't like the look of the trees either. And then somewhere in the distance, they heard the howl of a wolf.

They stopped and listened. No other sound came.

They journeyed further into the forest until they came across a clearing where smoke billowed from a wood fire. The sound of muffled voices heading in their direction had them hide behind a bush. They spied a group of scary looking dwarf-like men making their way towards the fire. The men sat down and threw what appeared to be, a couple of mice into the embers.

The boys edged their way nearer so that they were within hearing range of the creatures.

'There's a rumour goin' around that now that the mortals 'ave escaped,' said one of the creatures. 'The boggarts and the other lot are refusin' ter work, or so Fingle tells me.''

'That's why them interlopers were sent fer.'

'The interlopers, wot interlopers?'

'Yer know, that motley lot who were here lookin' fer, Black Annis,' said Gorken.

'Oh them – they're workin' fer Morag as well aren't they? I wouldn't want ter work fer her, no siree

'Wot about Black Annis? That would be far worse.'

'Hmm, I'm quite happy where I am, thank yer very much.'

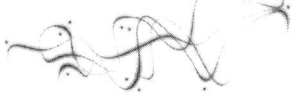

The Ancient Door

Chapter Forty

'**W**e'd better get away from those elves, or whatever they are,' whispered Will. Luckily for them, the piskies saw a rabbit and chased after it.

'I think that's a path over there,' said Hugh pointing to another narrow track.

'Let's follow it.'

They started down the track and were making good headway until they heard the sound of...thump, thump, thump which seemed to be getting louder and louder. They turned around and saw the barguest pounding towards its prey, saliva trickling down its coat. Onwards it came, bounding towards them licking its long razor-sharp fangs in readiness for that first big delicious bite.

The beast soon gained ground on them tearing through the undergrowth at an alarming speed. Realizing that it wouldn't take long before it was upon them; they took off jumping over fallen branches running as fast as they could until a wide stream stopped them in their tracks.

'Let's go across the stream,' suggested Hugh.

They waded across the freezing water and hid behind a large tree trunk. The barguest growled in disbelief. Since an old wizard had put a curse on him, he wasn't able to cross running water. 'Yer'll be turned into a tadpole,' he'd said. Huh! He wasn't going to be a feed for anyone.

Anyway, now that he could see the mortals properly, they looked a bit scrawny – there was better food to be had in the forest. Hmm, where are those elves he'd seen earlier? A few of them would go down nicely. And so, with a final ear-splitting howl, the barguest about-turned and went in search of juicier pickings.

'What shall we do now?' asked Will as they watched the barguest disappear into the forest.

'Let's cross the stream again.'

They continued on the track and came upon a fire that was still burning. They decided to sit down for a while and eat some food.

'Isn't that the mortals?' said a voice from behind a bush. 'C'mon, we'll chase 'em.'

Hugh was the first to notice the piskies. 'Look, over there, those little men are coming towards us.'

'And now they've grown in size,' gasped Jamie. 'RUN,' he yelled.

They ran and ran until the trees parted to another clearing where a silver deer was grazing peacefully. It looked up at them and said, 'Follow me.'

Should they follow the deer? Or was it another trick? And then the sound of the piskies yelling out to each other as they were scampering towards the clearing gave them no alternative. So they followed the deer towards a cave where an old lady stood at the entrance – waiting. Crikey! Did she have one eye in the middle of her forehead?

'Come with me,' she said. 'Come on, I haven't got all day.'

They followed her inside the cave to discover that she was far younger than they thought. She had two eyes, long blonde hair and a beautiful face. They decided it must have been a trick of light causing her to look grotesque.

'Come, warm yourselves by me fire. Would you like a hot drink? I'm just makin' one.'

The cave was furnished with a large table carved out of rock and seats made from wooden branches held together with twine. Over

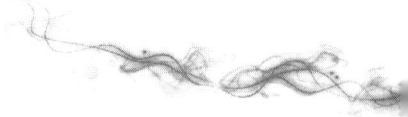

the fire, an old cooking pot was suspended in mid-air. A black curtain had been pulled across an opening to where she slept.

'You don't need to worry yourselves, I'll not harm you,' she said handing them a drink which tasted of honey, cinnamon and cloves.

Curiosity got the better of Pamela, so she plucked up courage and asked the lady why she lived in a cave.

'I like the peace and quiet and can please meself what I do.'

'Have you always lived here?'

The lady looked at Pamela for a long moment before she answered her. Pamela felt nervous all of a sudden.

'I haven't always lived here, but that's too long a story,' she said. 'How did you get to be in the forest?'

'We were captured by a sorceress called, Morag,' said Clara who had suddenly found her voice.

'Morag eh?' she snorted. 'So you're the youngsters that the Druid helped. I expect you're looking for the ancient doorway then.'

'How do you know about that?' asked Hugh. Who was she?

'I might live in a cave, lad, but I know what's afoot,' was her answer. 'But I'm afraid Morag will be on the warpath now that you've escaped from the castle.'

'I wish I knew what this was about. A Cavalier that was living in a painting, told me that I had to pass some sort of a test, but he didn't hang around long enough to tell me why,' said Hugh.

'Ah,' she grinned, 'that's typical of Françoise, likes to be mysterious, he does. C'mon, let's find the pathway to freedom.'

She obviously had no intention of telling them anything. And then she picked up her staff, tapped the ground and they found themselves in front of a large blue stone surrounded by massive boulders.

They looked round about them in panic – there didn't seem to be any way out of there. Was she Morag? Didn't the Druid tell them she could change herself into anyone or anything she wanted?

Black Annis walked around the stone three times to the left, three times to the right, and then she held her staff above her head and called out:

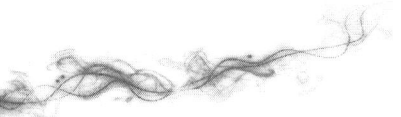

Jera Eihwaz Algiz
Berkanath Teiwaz Inguz

A purple light shot around them and the boulders parted to where the doorway covered in climbing ivy, was waiting. Black Annis had already disappeared.

'Wow,' exclaimed Will, 'we're here at last.'

The boys pulled away at the ivy until the door became clear enough for them to open.

'GET OUT OF MY WAY,' yelled Clara as she pushed against the door, but a shaft of blue light came rebounding off it.

'Ooh, my hair's singed,' she wailed.

'Too bad,' snapped Jamie.

'Come on Hugh, open me. I haven't got all day,' called the door.

A talking door – now they'd heard everything.

Hugh tried his hardest to push the door open but it wouldn't budge. So he pulled it towards him and it creaked opened. Pamela was the first to go through.

Fair Exchange

Chapter Forty-one

Hugh stood looking about him in despair. Why did the door vanish like that as soon as he went to follow his friends? Hadn't he passed the test? He decided the only chance he had was to find the sorceress who lived in the cave again. But where would he start to look? And besides, it was getting dark and what if those scary creatures found him? Or worse still, what if the beast turned up again? He felt sick at the thought.

He decided to look for the pathway – that would at least give him a fighting chance of finding the cave. He fought his way through dense bushes and trees until he had the distinct feeling that something was following him. He stopped and listened. There was nothing but the dark, damp, forest. He trudged on and on but every now and again he looked over his shoulder just to double-check that he was alone. He wasn't. Something black with red glowing eyes and blood dripping down its front was peeping around a bush at him. Hugh took off darting around trees and jumping over fallen branches hoping to get as far away as possible from whatever it was. Unfortunately, he tripped and tumbled down a ravine and landed next to something warm and soft.

'Hey, look where yer goin',' shouted a voice.

Hugh tried to make out who or what it was, but the daylight had gone and all he could make out was bright green luminous eyes peering angrily at him in the darkness.

'If it ain't the forkyped,' said another voice as a fire suddenly sprang to life.

Hugh gasped in surprise. He tried to scramble up the ravine but he fell down the wall of dirt again.

'Don't yer remember us,' said one of them helping him up. 'We're Wartun and Griswald.'

'I d-don't...'

'Yer gave us food on the track to Thwartund.'

'Yes, I remember now,' Hugh replied, relief washing over him like a warm blanket.

'Wot yer doin' here then?'

'It's a long story,' said Hugh.

'We ain't goin' anywhere while the banshee is hangin' about.'

'What's a banshee?'

'Let's just say: it's best to keep out of its way.'

''Course, it could be a ghoul,' suggested Wartun.

'Shut up,' growled Griswald, 'yer don't want to scare the lad.'

'Why are yer on yer own, I seem to remember there were others wiv yer,' said Wartun who remembered Clara – clearly.

Hugh explained that a sorceress who lived in a cave helped them to escape, but he had somehow got left behind. The boggarts looked at each other in surprise. The only sorceress they knew of who lived in a cave was the dreaded Black Annis. So she had helped the mortals had she? If that was the case, maybe she'd got rid of the banshee. Yep, that would be to their advantage. And so with that thought in mind, they cast a sleeping spell over Hugh and crept away.

Hugh woke up to something nudging at his shoulder. He was expecting it to be one of the little men – it wasn't, it was the silver deer. What happened to them? And what's more, how did he land up in the clearing again?

'Come,' said the deer, 'climb on my back.'

Hugh hauled his body onto the deer's back and held the antlers tightly. The deer snorted, spun around and took flight, landing outside the cave. Black Annis came out to greet him.

'Welcome back,' she said. 'Come, join me by me fire, you must be hungry.'

She gave him some food and he told her what had happened.

'So, the door vanished, eh? I'll help you to go through the veil to your world if you find someone for me. Let's just say it's a test to see if you're worthy of me help.'

Hugh's stomach flipped over, was she the one who had made the door disappear?

Back in the forest again, Hugh hurried along the path as fast as he could wondering if he would come across a banshee or a ghoul. He stumbled across the remains of a fire and hoped who ever had made the fire wasn't the creatures who had chased him and his friends before. He decided he wasn't going to hang around to find out, but too late, they appeared in front of him looking more ferocious than ever.

'Well, well, well, wot 'ave we here,' a mean looking piskie sneered.

'Wot's yer name, mortal?' growled another.

'Er – um – Hugh Barnaby.'

'So, yer the one who escaped from, Morag, eh?' he snorted. 'Well, yer won't escape from us.'

The piskies had now formed a circle around him, and he didn't like the hungry look in their eyes. They stepped closer and closer and all the time licking their lips menacingly. Hugh immediately tried to conjure up a blue thunderbolt, but to his dismay, nothing happened. He was shaking at the knees and beads of sweat trickled from his forehead down to the tip of his nose.

'Anyhow, wot are yer doin' here?' the mean-looking one asked.

'A sorceress who lives in a cave, sent me on a mission,' he explained.

'She lives in a cave, yer say? That must be Black Annis,' he gasped in disbelief. 'An' wot would she be sendin' the likes of you on a mission fer?' he snorted to sniggers from his followers. 'That's a likely story.'

'Let's throw him at the mercy of the banshees,' urged the evillest looking piskie of all.

'Don't do that, Gorken,' a voice rang out.

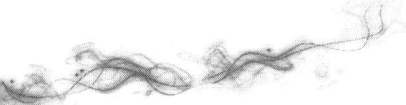

The piskies turned around at the intrusion. Hugh was relieved to see the little men who had helped him, had stepped out from behind a bush, and were now stood before them.

'Why shouldn't we?' sneered Gorken. 'Yer not gettin' soft on us are yer, Wartun?'

'Nay, 'course not, but the mortal's tellin' the truth. Black Annis might put a curse on yer if yer mess wiv the forkyped.'

'Or she could tear yer from limb to limb,' Griswald added. That was met with grunts all round.

'All right, but if he comes near me camp again wivout me say so, he'd better watch out.'

'Anyways, we bought yer these,' said Wartun offering him a couple of rabbits, 'so I fink it's time we ate.'

Gorken grabbed hold of the rabbits and sniffed disapprovingly, 'I likes rats best, fat juicy ones.'

It wasn't until he smelt the rabbits cooking, that Hugh realized how hungry he was. Griswald grabbed a couple of rabbits off the piskies and threw them into the fire until they were cooked. The creatures munched away hungrily. Wartun broke off a leg and gave it to Hugh. It tasted surprisingly good, except for a lump of fur that got stuck in his throat.

The creatures slurped and burped to their hearts content and with full bellies, they fell asleep. Hugh wondered if he should try and make his escape, but the thought of the dangers that lay in waiting for him, turned him off that idea. And besides, it was pitch black out there, and now that he had lost his magic power, things didn't look too promising. Suddenly a dreadful tiredness came over him. He lay down on a bed of leaves and listened to the snorts and grunts going on around him. His eyes closed and he drifted off to a dreamless sleep.

When Hugh woke up he was surprised to find that he was alone again. He brushed himself down and stood trying to fathom out which way he should go. There was a pathway a little way ahead and he made up his mind to see where it would lead him. He walked along the track keeping his eyes fixed firmly on the ground making sure there no

surprises, like holes to fall down or swamps to be sucked into. It wasn't until he stepped into bright sunlight that he realized he'd gone too far. He turned back again only to find that the forest had vanished. Oh no! Not only had he failed another test, but now he'd lost the forest. Was he going to be trapped in this place forever?

The sun bore down on him hotter than ever and he was beginning to feel very thirsty. He shielded his eyes against the glare looking for shade. And then something glinted at him in the distance. Was it water? He ran towards it and just as he'd hoped, he'd found a pond. He stumbled on to the ground, cupped his hands into the icy-cold liquid and drank. He felt instantly better and sat for a while wondering what to do next. Out the corner of his eye he saw movement. A man dressed in a long purple robe stepped out of a wooden hut and came striding towards him. Was the hut there before?

'Ah – you're Hugh Barnaby,' that was a statement, not a question. 'I believe you have something for me?'

'Y-yes sir, if your name is, Wizard.'

The wizard stood peering at Hugh through hooded lids. So, this boy is the one, eh?

'Don't stand there looking gormless, lad, give it to me.'

Hugh felt into his pocket and pulled out a small leaf. Whatever the wizard wanted with a leaf, he couldn't begin to imagine. But nevertheless, he handed it over and was astonished when the leaf turned into a silver cylinder.

'This,' he said, 'must not fall into my enemy's hands.'

And then he clicked his fingers and was gone in a flash of purple. Another flash of purple followed, taking the hut with it and Hugh's only way of finding out how he was to get back to Black Annis. The reality of his situation hit him hard. What on earth was he to do? He had no idea how he was going to find the forest let alone the sorceress.

'You have done well, Hugh Barnaby,' said a voice from behind. He spun around and came face-to-face with...no it can't be...Black Annis!

'Now,' she said, 'I believe Wizard gave you something for me?'

Crikey, Hugh thought, what was he supposed to give her?

'He didn't give me anything,' he mumbled.

'Feel into your right pocket.'

He did as she asked and his hand touched something small and rough. He pulled it out. It was a chunk of rock. What on earth did she want it for?

'Thank you, lad, your mission is complete.' She clicked her fingers and...

An old man stood with a smile on his face as he watched Hugh step through the ancient door and murmured, 'Welcome back.'

In her cave, Black Annis held the rock tightly murmuring an ancient incantation. The rock turned into a blue pulsating stone. 'Yes, this will free me to work my rite,' she said, throwing her head back and letting out a tremendous whoop of victory.

After

Chapter Forty-two

'I hope the Mistress doesn't turn us into bats, Master Mobbins.'

'Did yer say we might be turned into rats, Toddle?'

'Nay Master, BATS,' he bellowed.

'Yer don't have to shout, I ain't deaf yer know.'

'Sorry, but wot do yer fink she will do to us now that the mortals have escaped?'

'Don't fergets, Morag made some of her witches and wizards into bats,' Twerp reminded him.

'She needs me, so I don't finks she'll do much to get on me bad side.'

Twerp was thinking that his master should be more worried about getting on Morag's bad side. And then Old Mobbins dropped a bombshell.

'Movin' on, Master Mobbins, wherever to?'

'I don't rightly know yet aways.'

'But this is all we've known fer many moons,' protested Nobble, aghast at the thought of leaving the castle. After all, they were the envy of the other boggart tribes that dwelled in the Land of Shadows. Surely the master wasn't serious? Was he?

'Anyways, I got me a little plan formin' in me mind.'

'Humf, that's if the Mistress don't turn on us first,' said Twerp, who was not convinced that his Master's plan would come to fruition.

'Don't yer go aworryin' about the likes of, Morag, we aint wivout a few tricks of our own. Nay, leave it to me, Old Mobbins is plottin' here,' and he gave his tribe a wink as if he knew something that they didn't.

'Us have landed ourselves in a right ol' mess, Master Gordle.'

The old goblin looked very worried. 'More than a right ol' mess, Dromby, he'd say it was more like a disaster.'

Dromby grunted. 'If them boggarts had done their job properly, us would be gettin' our reward by now.'

'He don't reckon the Mistress will see it that way, yer can be sure of that much,' Old Gordle replied.

'He don't fink it be fair ter put all the blame on the boggarts,' commented Wargle.

Dromby agreed – there were others who should share the blame as well. 'Those changers didn't do much either.'

'Yer face is turnin' pink, yer must be right worried.'

'Well, goodness knows what punishment will befall us.'

'Yer needn't worry 'bout that, the Mistress will need him again, yer'll see,' said Old Gordle, confidently. Yep, especially as the brownies and the spriggans had failed so miserably and had taken off in such a hurry. Mistress Morag knows whom she can trust.

Unseen by the goblins, the grobs were hiding behind a bush and had heard every word.

'Well, what do you think about that? The goblins are blaming the likes of us along with the boggarts,' said Old Shylog, their chief.

'*And* calling us "changers",' sniffed Fig, his second-in-command.

'C'mon, let's go,' hissed Old Shylog and angrily trudged through the woodland to their camp. He was so furious with the goblins that he changed himself into his true form – a terrifying character. His knobbly body towered above his tribe. His black bushy eyebrows almost hid his

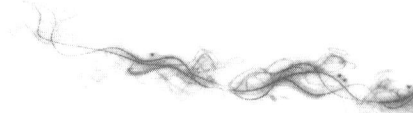

bright green eyes that were now flashing with rage. He scratched at his scaly head with long talons; folds of saggy skin wobbled about his face.

'Master, don't you think it would be best to change back? I mean, what if Siras came to visit? You don't want him to know what we really look like, do you?'

Old Shylog glared at Fynngel, one of the oldest and wisest of the grobs. 'I'll do so when I'm good an' ready,' he snapped.

'No doubt the boggarts have got a thing to say about us too.'

'Mobbins won't say anything about us, he'd know the consequences if he did,' sneered Old Shylog.

Morag was beginning to feel very nervous herself, wondering if or when Lord Drago would make an appearance and vent his wrath upon her. She was so furious at the turn of events that she transported herself to the Place of Shadows. When she opened the door to the now empty room, she made straight for her other captives – the portraits. She wrenched them from the walls and they fell in a rumpled heap on the floor, where she set about stamping on them in an almighty rage. The knights were still in hiding – they had decided they didn't want to be turned into pots and pans, or worse still, nuts and bolts! No way!

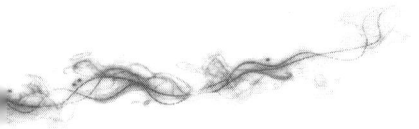

Finger-pointing

Chapter Forty-three

S iras had been sent to fetch the slaves and he wasn't at all keen to visit them again if the reception he'd received the last time was anything to go by. The first on the list were the boggarts. How was he going to approach the subject?

Old Mobbins was instantly suspicious when he saw Siras lurking in the shadows. 'Wot do yer want, Siras?' he growled.

'I – er, the Mistress wants to see yous right away, Master Mobbins.'

'Oh, she does, does she? I'll fink about it a while. In the meantime, go and tell the others.' He turned away and stoked the fire.

'I suppose the Mistress wants to see me?' asked Old Gordle when Siras landed in front of him.

'Yes, Master Gordle, I'm afraid she does.'

'AFRAID?' he bellowed. 'I'm certainly not afraid, I can assure you of that much,' and he folded his arms across his chest.

'Oh, deary me,' muttered Siras, fingering the translator nervously.

'I wish you wouldn't mumble so, Siras.'

'I was just clearing me throat. Anyway, she would like to see yous now.'

'What about them boggarts?'

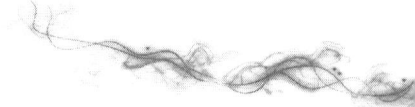

'As a matter of fact, Old Mobbins is on his way as we speak.' And he made a speedy exit before Old Gordle could ask any more awkward questions. He made his way to the grob camp to be greeted by Fynngel.

'The Master is busy, wot do you want?'

And Siras launched nervously into the reason for his visit.

'The Master won't be pleased.'

'Well, it *is* urgent,' said Siras.

'When is it not urgent that's what I'd like to know,' snarled Old Shylog from behind a rock.

In the meantime, Morag was impatiently waiting for the arrival of her slaves. So angry was she that she could barely contain herself.

'Where is that buffoon of a servant of mine…Oh there you are, Siras, and not before time,' she growled. 'And where are my good-for-nothing slaves?'

Siras shifted from one foot to the other. Just supposing they didn't turn up? But to his relief, Old Gordle appeared, followed by Old Shylog.

'You took your time,' she snapped. 'Where's Mobbins?'

As if on cue, he sauntered into the room looking decidedly put out. That didn't go down at all well with Morag; she expected them all to be shaking with fear.

'Well, what have you got to say for yourselves?' she demanded.

Old Shylog was feeling decidedly nervous. 'W-we did what you asked of us, Mistress Morag.' Would she turn them into simpering fairies? He seemed to remember another tribe of his comrades had suffered that same fate. To him, that would be infinitely worse than hanging upside down for all eternity. At least a bat got to live in the castle.

'And what excuse have you got, Gordle?'

'Well, he finks the boggarts could've done a bit more,' he grumbled.

'Humf, I don't think that's worth a reply,' Old Mobbins sneered, 'anyways, that forkyped's magic was good.'

'Huh! You think so, do you?' hissed the sorceress. 'I'll say this ONLY ONCE,' she screeched, 'if I hear you mention one more time

about how that boy made you lot fail because of his magic, I'll turn you into filthy flies.'

They looked from one to the other. Old Mobbins thought he'd best keep quiet – after all, he had plans.

'And while we're on the subject of the mortals, don't use that ridiculous name when you're talking about them – forkypeds, my foot.'

Old Mobbins sniffed. Was he expected to call them mortals? What sort of a name is that?

'I shall have to preserve my strength for a while. In the meantime, you lot have got to sharpen your wits. And by the time I have need of you, I expect better results.' She flicked her wrist dismissively and they were zapped from the castle before they had time to blink.

Morag lifted the lid of her cauldron and gave the contents a ferocious stir. She had laced it with a good lashing of her anger, a good emotion to add to the potion. And then she picked up a couple of fox's tails and threw them into the steaming brew. Snake eyes, two rats, and a dragon's tooth followed. That should do the trick.

Yes, that troublesome mortal had managed to escape her clutches this time by the skin of his teeth. How he managed to do that was beyond her, but by the time she emerged again, she would regain her power and it would be stronger than ever. She patted the cauldron lovingly, knowing that she had plenty of shadow energy left over, allowing her to enjoy her favourite guise as the lady with the long black hair and big blue eyes. She poured herself a goblet of mead, sat down, closed her eyes and let out a contented sigh.

The room suddenly grew as hot as a furnace. Morag dropped the goblet and watched in horror as it rolled towards a fuming Lord Drago. With a wave of his hand he lifted the goblet from the floor and threw it against the wall.

'Well, well, well,' he spat, 'you think your power so strong, eh? So far you have not proved anything to me,' he sneered as he circled her. 'I won't even bother to mention your slaves.'

He came right up to Morag, so close was he that she could smell his vile odour. The snakes slithered and hissed with delight. Lord Drago

directed his gaze to the ceiling and a flash of fire came spurting from his lips. Several of the bats fell onto the floor – burnt to a cinder. Morag stood very, very, still.

'Letting a slip of a boy get the better of you and you wondered why the Ancients entrusted him with their legacy?' he growled.

'B-but I…'

'It took *me* to find out why your spells have bounced back at you.'

'What?'

'Cornelia Romanski gave the boy and his sister protection amulets. Hmm, maybe I should get Morgana to work for me instead; she seems to know what's afoot.'

Morag's eyes grew wide at hearing her name. 'Morgana Gwyneth – the gossip?'

'But her gossiping got results, didn't it?' he sneered. 'And what about those pathetic girls you had working for you?' And seeing the look of surprise on her face he added, 'I know all about their failed attempt at giving the mortals the bewitchers.'

'Well I…'

'But now you will have to get the boy to give you the amulet, for that is the only way you can make him your ally.'

'How will I be able to do that now that the spell has been broken?'

'That's your problem. But it is imperative that we obtain the crystal – the key to Orlog. Our mission is to take control of Orlog from the Macaba, and that also means the power of the Sacred Scroll of Knowledge. For that is the only way the curse Lord Zelgo has cast upon me will be lifted for all time. I have no intention of being confined to the Realm of Shadows for eternity.'

'I will not fail you again, my Lord.'

Lord Drago did not reply, but instead, he waved his staff over her head and vanished as quickly as he came.

Morag was not sure whether she felt more angry or humiliated. Fancy that snitch, Morgana, knowing of her failure; no doubt she has spread the word around. And as for Cornelia Romanski – a thousand curses upon her. Now where is that servant of mine, he always disappears when I need him.

'SIRAS,' she screeched, 'come here at the double.'

He entered the room and stopped dead in his tracks.

'Whatever's the matter with you?' she said.

Siras didn't say a word.

'Hand me my scrying mirror,' she hissed, snatching it from him. And the fact that he made a hasty exit went totally unnoticed.

'I'll certainly be teaching you a lesson or two, and if…' Where has that incompetent boggart disappeared to now? Hmm, a rethinking of his position might be in order.'

She peered into the mirror still grumbling away and… 'Oh n-o-o-o,' she wailed.

Unknown to the sorceress, her servant had witnessed her change from his beautiful mistress to the old hag who was now staring back at herself in shock-horror.

Morag brought the terrified Siras back to her with a screeched incantation.

'Go visit the Bat Master for me,' she ordered. 'Tell him of my dilemma.'

Oh deary me, thought Siras, not the Bat Master.

'What's wrong with you? Didn't you hear what I said?'

Siras nodded weakly. 'B-but isn't he a v-vampire?'

'So?'

'Well, he might want to suck my blood.'

'Pah! Why would he want to suck the blood of a scrawny boggart?'

'Well, I…'

'Nay, Siras, my slaves, and that includes you, are safe from the Bat Master and his blood-sucking servants.'

'But what if…?'

'Oh for goodness sake,' she snapped. 'I do not, and I repeat, NOT, want to look like this for any longer. So I suggest you go, otherwise I might be tempted to suck your blood myself.'

The Bat Master

Chapter Forty-four

Siras transported himself to a place where nothing but desert and rolling spinifex surrounded him. He pressed on through the hot sand until he reached a solitary elm tree which guarded the opening to an underground cave – the dwelling place of the Bat Master.

'Why are you here?' asked the tree.

'I've come in search of the Bat Master.'

'What's the password?'

'It's spindleweed.'

Without another word, the tree slid aside and Siras found himself looking down at a black gaping hole. And so with pounding heart, he cautiously stepped into the emptiness. His feet thankfully landed on steps that twisted their way down and down to what, he had no idea.

He stood in the pitch-black, scared out of his wits. It was freezing. What if the bats came swooping about him, would they care whether he was protected or not? He doubted it. Several pairs of red eyes peered at him out of the darkness. Did they belong to the bats? Flapping wings overhead had him break out in a cold sweat. The smell of blood filled the air. He was convinced his would be next.

He flattened his back against the cave wall feeling his way along it, never letting the staring red eyes out of his sight. He headed towards a dim light and came out into a much larger cave where a red mist swirled around stalagmites and stalactites. A large bat swooped down

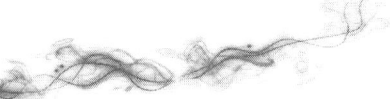

beside him; fresh blood dripped from its fangs. Was it licking its lips at him?

'What yer doin' here?' the bat sneered.

'I've been sent by, Mistress Morag, to speak to the Bat Master.'

'Mistress Morag, yer say? Wait here.'

The bat weaved its way around the stalagmites and through a large opening. Several bats swooped into the cave and hung from thick strands of spider webs which Siras knew, belonged to the mange. Those terrifying creatures were halfway between a scorpion and a flesh-eating spider. Could things get any worse? And more importantly, was he also protected against them should they show up?

The bat returned. 'Me Master will see yer,' it said. 'But first I need ter blindfold yer.'

'If you tell me where he is, I can transport myself there.'

'Wot? Wiv a blindfold on, yer'll be lucky.'

Siras grimaced, 'I see your point.'

A loud scraping sound had the bats take off in a squealing frenzy. Into the cave, came an enormous spider-like creature with yellow eyes, a large grinning mouth, and razor-sharp teeth. Its long scorpion-like tail swished from side to side as it came closer and closer, knocking a lone bat onto the ground. With one thick spider leg, it squashed the bat and scooped it up into its mouth.

'Wot do yer want, Taro?' rasped the bat.

The mange sat back on its sting munching away happily. A long black scaly tongue licked fresh blood from its lips. Yellow greedy eyes glinted at Siras before he shifted his evil gaze to the bat.

'Aren't yer goin' to share yer food, Batfang?'

'He's not fer eatin', he's come from a sorceress ter see me Master.'

'Which one, Black Annis?'

'Nay, the one they call, Morag.'

The mange made a sound that to Siras sounded very much like a snort of contempt.

'Oh *her*,' it sneered, 'I'd have been more impressed if she *had* been Black Annis.'

'If yer don't mind, Taro, I better get this boggart to the Master.'

'He's a boggart?' he said incredulously. 'He don't look like one.'
'Well, he is.'

The mange came closer; its sting swishing over the top of Siras's head menacingly.'An' he don't smell like one either,' he sniffed. 'He ain't to me likin' anyway.' And with that parting statement, the mange turned its enormous body and disappeared into the darkness.

Siras let out a quivering breath.

The bat grinned as he put his claw into an old sack, pulled something long and slimy out, and said, 'Stand still while I get this blindfold on yer.'

Siras squirmed.

'Wot's up wiv yer, Siras? Yer not frightened of a little snake are yer?' Batfang chuckled. 'It'll only kill yer if yer move suddenly,' he chuckled again.

Siras stood petrified while Batfang tied the slithering reptile around his head. The next thing he knew, he was standing alone in a gigantic cavern surrounded by vast columns of red quartz – the snake had vanished.

Candles lit the cavern and a path of red mist was flanked either side by murky water. And then the eyes of crocodiles suddenly popped up – watching and waiting. Straight ahead, an enormous bat-head carved out of red crystal gleamed at him. With a low rumble, it parted and slid open.

A huge bat stood with its wings splayed out as if ready to take flight. It twirled around in a flash of red smoke, and it changed into something resembling a man. His enormous wings wrapped around him like a cloak.

'Come,' beckoned the Bat Master.

Siras clicked his fingers, but there he stood, with shaking knees and chattering teeth. Oh, bogs upon bogs, he had to walk across that narrow misty pathway.

'Hurry up,' snapped the Bat Master.

Siras, with bated breath, stepped onto the red mist and held his breath hoping that it would hold up under his weight. To make matters

worse, the crocodiles had come to the surface and were snapping their enormous jaws at him. He gingerly made his way along the path wishing like mad he could be anywhere but there. He had almost reached the other side, when the still water became alive with man-eating fish swimming about in a wild frenzy whilst gnashing their teeth expectantly.

Siras ran the rest of the way as fast as his little legs would allow until the path stopped short. There was a wide gap from the edge of the mist to safety. Below him, the crocodiles were swishing their tails excitedly, snapping at the man-eating fish who were frantically trying to vie for a good position to sink their teeth into his flesh. The laughter of the Bat Master echoed around the cavern as Siras with heart in mouth, took the plunge and leapt into the air hoping against hope that his feet would touch solid ground. THUMP! They did.

The Bat Master was thoroughly enjoying himself. It had been a long time since he'd had so much fun. He watched as Siras gingerly made his way towards him and stood in front of him looking as if he was about to faint.

'What does the servant of the sorceress, Morag, want with me?' boomed the Bat Master.

'Firstly,' squeaked Siras, 'she sends yous her greetings.'

'And then?'

'Well, yous see, through no fault of her own, her prisoners…'

'Oh, I know all about that,' said the Bat Master dismissively. 'Get to the point.'

'Well, er, Lord Drago has punished her and now she looks like an old hag, er…not exactly an old hag, but…'

'And she wants me to reverse the spell?'

'If yous could, yous see…'

'I'll have to think about it.'

'I implore yous, Master Bat, er – Bat Master, the Mistress needs to be able to regain her changeling powers because there are other things afoot.'

The Bat Master roared with laughter. 'Aha! It wouldn't be because she wants to look young and beautiful again, would it?' he chuckled, his red eyes sparkling with amusement.

'Well, I don't know about that, but…' he blustered.

'Here,' he said, and handed Siras a small pouch. 'Tell your Mistress to mix this with snake venom and she is to take it in the twilight hours.'

'What is it?' asked Siras of the foul smelling powder.

'It's ground bat dung and mixed with snake venom, it is the most powerful antidote ever.'

'Thank yous, Bat Master, a thousand thank yous. Mistress Morag will reward yous well,' smiled Siras.

'Oh, I'm sure she will,' he grinned. 'Just you tell her that she is in my debt. Now go.' And with the swish of his bat cloak, he transported Siras back to the castle where an eager Morag awaited him.

From the shadows, stepped Lord Drago looking decidedly pleased. 'Excellent work, Zorse, excellent work,' he said.

The Bat Master smiled triumphantly, his long pointed fangs glowing in the dim light. Yes, the Lord of Thunder owed him big-time.

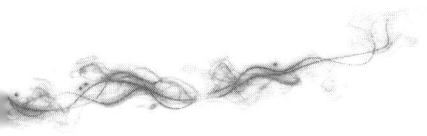

Disappearing Shadows

Chapter Forty-five

Mrs Barnaby had just finished serving a customer when Maud Underwood came into the shop to buy a magazine.

'Can't stop, Mrs Barnaby, I've a busy day ahead of me,' and she rushed out the door, just as Mrs Dingle was about to push it open. And with a, 'Sorry, Mrs D, I haven't got time for a chinwag,' she dashed up the street.

Huh! As if I'd want to give her the time of day, Mrs Dingle thought as she stepped into the newsagency. 'I don't know why that woman insists on wearing those trashy clothes,' Mrs Dingle snorted, 'she looks like mutton dressed as lamb.'

The fact that Mrs Dingle had managed to squeeze herself into a gaudy pink, candy-striped dress complete with puffy sleeves had Mrs Barnaby thinking that she had room to talk.

'Anyway, I'm glad to say that Clara's stomach problems have improved considerably. Perhaps it was a virus after all.'

'There has been one going around, apparently...'

'I must go we're off to London to see a...I must rush, bye.' And she went scurrying out the door.

'I was hoping we'd seen the last of her,' commented Mr. Barnaby.

'Don't be silly, Jack, where else would she get away with conveniently forgetting to pay for her newspaper?' laughed Mrs Barnaby, as she added yet another addition to Mrs Dingle's slate.

'I suppose she does eventually pay her bill even if it does take her six months,' and as an afterthought he added, 'maybe I should charge her interest.'

M r Dingle came hurrying home from the bank under strict instructions from his wife. The excursion to the theatre had been on the agenda for quite some time. He went to his safe and brought out the tickets which were a gift from one of his customers. And then he went into the parlour to read his newspaper in peace.

Mrs Dingle had just finished changing into her new clothes, when Clara came barging through the front door.

'It's about time you came home. Have you forgotten that we're going to London? And before you think up an excuse, have a quick bath and change into your new dress.'

Clara was about to rush off when Mrs Dingle grabbed hold of her arm and hissed, 'Hold on, young lady, what in the world has happened to your hair?' She twirled Clara around so she could inspect the back. 'It's singed! What have you been up to?'

'Nothing,' she replied wondering what her mother was on about.

'You've been using my curling tongs again, haven't you? I've told you before about leaving them on the gas stove too long.'

'I've not used them for ages, Mama...honest.'

'I haven't got time to argue with you now,' she said to Clara's back as she bolted out the door.

'But I'm not letting you get away with it, my girl,' she called from the bottom of the stairs. And what about Cedric, don't say he's still working on that ledger of his.

'Do hurry, Cedric, times marching on,' she called through the closed door.

'What did you say dear?' was his muffled answer.

Mrs Dingle flung the door open. 'I said, get ready.'

He looked down at his suit. 'I am ready.'

'What, dressed in that?'

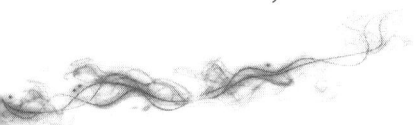

'My suit looks perfectly all right to me.'

'It's crumpled.'

Mr Dingle said a few choice words under his breath, glared at her, marched out the door and stomped up the stairs.

'Well I never,' said Mrs Dingle, 'what's wrong with him?'

I wonder how long Hugh will be. He's been talking to your grandmother for ages,' said Jamie.

'I must admit, I'm curious to know what's takin' so long meself,' said Charlie, who was getting more suspicious by the minute.

After Hugh had broken the spell and escaped from the castle, no one (and that included Charlie) had any memory of what had taken place. His father had seen to that. And as far as Charlie was aware, Hugh was just having a chat with his grandmother, who was helping him with his bad dreams.

Meanwhile, the old gypsy couldn't understand why Hugh's friends had returned and not him. She had tried to locate the door, but it was missing. It was a real mystery, she thought. She would have to find out what happened to Poz. She'd send for Wallynus, after all, the door was his responsibility. And then she heard the familiar swish of the transportation crystal and breathed a sigh of relief.

A swirling mist engulfed the room, returning Hugh to his seat as if the terrifying events had never happened.He felt as if he was coming back from a distant place.

The old gypsy was very satisfied with the outcome, and more to the point, Hugh had passed the test with flying colours. She took the crystal from him and gave him a smaller one, telling him that she wanted him to practice crystal-gazing every day. He was quite startled by this and was about to protest when he was told in no uncertain terms that she expected him to do it.

'Yer want to keep the dreams away don't yer? Besides, yer've a talent and I'd hate to see it go to waste.'

'Do I have to keep that a secret too?'

'It would be best, lad, – yer see, Gorjers just don't understand.'

'But I'm a Gorjer.'

The gypsy didn't say anything except give him a little smile. For some reason, that made him feel uneasy. What wasn't she telling him?

'Anyway, how am I to get it home without anyone seeing it?'

'Just you leave that...'

'Can I come in, Gran?' called Charlie.

'Of course yer can. Hugh and me were just havin' a little chat. Now afore I fergets, we're havin' a little goin' away party....'

The following morning, Mrs Dingle came stumbling into the Newsagency looking the worse for wear – mumbling incoherently. The Barnabys exchanged glances and could just about make out one word, "Curse."

'You've got a curse?' asked Mrs Barnaby.

Mrs Dingle nodded weakly.

'Surely you must be mistake…'

'*Mistaken*?' she squeaked. 'I most certainly am not.' And she went on to tell them that she heard footsteps in her kitchen and at first thought it was a burglar – 'But you'll never guess in a month of Sundays what I found.'

'What?'

'There were pots and pans flying about everywhere.'

The Barnabys were gobsmacked.

'And if that wasn't enough, Clara was chased down the stairs by her collection of old dolls.'

Mrs Barnaby was at a loss for words; surely it was a figment of Mrs Dingle's imagination? Mr Barnaby, however, was now convinced that they had *definitely* landed on Mars.

'Didn't I warn you?' she said, accusingly. 'It's those gypsies I tell you, but no, you wouldn't listen.'

'Don't be ridicul...'

'Up to no good, I just knew I was right,' she insisted.

'I disagree; they are decent folk and keep themselves to themselves.'

'Humf, that's a matter of opinion,' she snorted. 'In my book, they are nothing but trouble, telling fortunes and putting curses on innocent folk like me. Anyway, let's hope we'll be shot of them soon. And good

riddance, I say, never saw such goings on.' And she marched out of the shop.

'What utter rot that woman spouts,' grumbled Mr. Barnaby.

'But if she is telling the truth, do you think it could be a ghost?'

'Of course not, we all know she's a Drama Queen.'

Demdyke journeyed far and wide and managed to bring together the Macaba for the celebrations. The clan arrived dressed in their traditional attire, much to the Major and Demdyke's disgust at having to don them again. Everybody commented how very dapper they looked.

'You've lost weight, Major,' commented Agatha.

'No wonder,' he snapped, 'with all this running around like a lunatic.'

Of course, the main topic of conversation was about Hugh, 'Battling with all and sundry,' as Harriet had put it.

'I wish they'd give us a bit more notice, though,' grumbled Old Mouldheels. 'They fergets I'm gettin' too old for all these shenanigans.'

'Yer shouldn't go on so, yer'll not get any invites in future.'

'That wouldn't be a great loss,' he snorted at Old Chattox, and then proceeded to rub liniment oil on his knees.

'For goodness sake,' glared Harriet, 'why haven't you used the potion Nobab gave you? That Gorjer's stuff smells ghastly.'

'I'll use what I bloomin' well please,' he retorted.

Harriet flounced off and sat next to Audra. 'I've had it with that grouchy old wizard.'

'Well, don't argue with him, then,' tutted Audra. 'Anyway, here they come,' she said nodding over to where Hugh, Lucy, Pamela, Jamie and Will were walking towards them.

'Welcome friends,' said a beaming King Leo clapping with the clan.

Somewhat dazed, they sat down by the roaring camp fire next to Charlie and Rosa. Charlie hastily explained that it was a Romany custom to give thanks for new friends before they move on.

'C'mon Charlie,' said Rosa, 'we'd better help bring out the food.'

'Shan't be long,' he said. And they rushed off.

'Something weird about this,' muttered Hugh as he watched them disappear into a caravan.

The following evening, Clara climbed into the bath only to discover that it was empty. She turned on the taps again making sure the plug was firmly lodged in the plughole before returning to her bedroom to fetch a book.

Meanwhile, the boggarts crept back into the bathroom, emptied the warm bath water and filled it up with cold water. Clara came back, climbed into the bath and promptly screamed.

Mrs Dingle came running up the stairs as fast as her dumpy legs would allow. She opened the door, only to find Clara wrapped in a towel, pointing frantically at the bath and glaring at her mother as if it was all her fault.

'The water is freezing – you can't have fed the electric meter.' she accused. 'And look, there's a frog.'

Mrs Dingle shoved her aside and peered into the bath. 'It must've climbed up through the plug hole.'

Clara opened her mouth to speak but was stopped by a warning finger-wagging.

'And before you blame it on, Hugh Barnaby, I can't see how he would know you were in the bath.'

'You don't know what he's like, he'd know.'

'Don't be silly, Clara, you're making him sound as if he possesses some sort of magic power, which of course, is absolutely ridiculous.'

'He does,' she insisted. 'When we were in the castle…'

'Did you say you were in a *castle* of all things? What in the world are you talking about? Reading too many of those silly books of yours,' she snapped, 'that's the problem.'

'I don't know why I said that, Mama. I must have dreamt it.'

'Yes, that's what it was, Clara, a dream. No more to be said on the subject.'

'Can you get the frog out?'

'I'll go and fetch your father,' and with a final glare at her daughter, she closed the door and hurried down the stairs heading straight for the parlour. She found Mr Dingle doing a crossword.

'Clara has had such a terrible ordeal…'

Mr Dingle didn't look up, 'What has she been exaggerating about this time?' he sighed, filling in a word.

'I'd hardly call a frog in the bath an exaggeration, Cedric,' she snapped.

Mr Dingle cursed under his breath and followed his wife upstairs.

While this was going on in the Dingle household, Hugh was tucked up in bed fast asleep. His dreams were of mountains and valleys and – a castle? He woke up in the morning wondering why it was happening again. And then he remembered the crystal ball. But Charlie's grandmother had forgotten to give it to him. What should he do? It was then that the wardrobe door swung open and inside, a wooden box housing the crystal ball sat – waiting.

He brought out the box and put it on the bed. Where on earth did this come from? The lid opened and with a shaky hand, he took out the crystal. It shuddered at his touch. He sat staring into it. Nothing happened. He waited and waited, the crystal stayed as it was – a clear glass ball. He was about put it back thinking that it was useless trying, especially as he didn't have a clue what he was doing.

The bedroom suddenly turned icy cold and a frost crept over the furniture turning everything white. The crystal shook and shuddered and a black mist swirled into it. Whispering voices followed. Hugh sat in stunned silence. Why didn't Charlie's grandmother tell him this would happen? Something tapped his shoulder and he turned around to see shadows pacing the walls, back and forth they went, until a sharp voice rang out and they were gone. Hugh's eyes were drawn to the crystal again, and something dark and sinister with fiery eyes looked out at him. It was a snake, and it slithered and writhed until it seemed to reach out of the crystal at him. The snake let out a blood-curdling laugh. At that moment, a blue light surrounded it and it turned to dust. The crystal cleared and then the friendly face of Charlies' grandmother smiled out at him.

'Yer must be very careful when yer look into the crystal, lad. There are evil spirits in abundance. The next time, I'll show yer how to prepare the crystal so that it won't happen again. I'm sorry, I should've explained...'

'Hurry up, Hugh, breakfast is ready,' called Mrs Barnaby.

Lucy opened the door with a, 'Coming Hugh?'

Jeepers, had she'd seen the crystal? But the crystal was already in the wardrobe.

Later that day, Mr and Mrs Barnaby were talking to a customer when Mrs Dingle stormed into the shop. The customer made a speedy exit.

'We've had a dreadful time of it, Mrs Barnaby. What with the pots and pans episode, a frog in the bath, and other things that are too dreadful to mention, I...'

'It could be a ghost of course,' Mr Barnaby commented.

Mrs Dingle stopped her tirade. A ghost haunting her house hadn't crossed her mind.

'Oh dear, whatever shall I do?'

'Not a lot you can do about that I'm afraid,' he replied, shaking his head.

'Of course,' she snorted, 'I've never believed in ghosts. As my dear husband has mentioned on many an occasion, they're only a figment of one's imagination.'

'Hmm, I'm not so sure.'

'What makes you an authority on the subject?'

'Well,' he started, leaning closer, 'it's a well-known fact that Highwaymen haunt the Heath.' He leant closer still, 'I wouldn't be at all surprised if you've got a ghost – stands to reason, doesn't it?'

Mrs Dingle got all shifty-eyed on him. 'I'll have Mr Dingle's newspaper, if I may.' The Highwaymen, she'd completely forgotten about them. 'I must go,' she croaked and bolted out the door, nearly colliding with the postman, who was on his way in with an overseas

letter for Mr Barnaby. He was more than pleased to find that it was from his cousin, Winston, who was working in Italy, judging by the postmark.

The shadow behind the curtain grinned as the postman left the shop. Yes, Jack Barnaby, all your family will join my little game of chess – in time. One by one they'll be added.

Missing

Chapter Forty-six

Underneath the castle, the boggarts were enjoying a well-earned rest as well as regular hunting trips.

'This is the life fer me, no work,' said Old Mobbins.

'Have yer thought any more about yer plans, Master?' asked Twerp.

'Yep, but don't yer be askin' me anyfink about them now. I'll be lettin' the lot of yer know when I'm good 'n' ready.' And then he gazed into the fire thinking that if his plan worked out, he wouldn't be at Morag's beck and call for much longer. Yes, that would be to his liking. He looked over his shoulder at Siras who was now hovering in the shadows probably trying to overhear what they were saying. He was sneaky like that.

'Well, come on, Siras, out wiv it,' he snarled, and when he found out from Siras that the sorceress wanted to know if they were enjoying their rest, he was instantly suspicious. When did she ever worry about them afore?

'And the Mistress says yous should be ready when she need yous,' blurted Siras not quite looking Old Mobbins in the eye.

A frosty silence followed.

'But of course, she says she'll be restin' up for a while yet,' he quickly added.

'As we are, Siras, as we are,' and Old Mobbins turned to talk to Twerp hoping that Siras would take the hint and – buzz off!

Siras made his way to the goblin camp.

'Where did the elves go in such...who goes there?' Old Gordle frowned. He frowned even more when he saw who it was.

'Wot do yer want, Siras?'

After explaining the reason for his visit, he received absolutely no response whatsoever. Oh bogs upon bogs, he thought, perhaps the best bet would be to leave the mistress out of it. He mentioned another name instead.

'Lord Drago yer say? If that's the case, I'll fink about it.'

Siras was well aware of the looks that passed between the others, and it wasn't exactly friendly, so he clicked his fingers and vanished into the night.

'Siras is probably goin' ter sweet-talk Old Shylog as well,' one of the goblins commented.

'Yer probably right, but he don't s'pose Siras got very far wiv Old Mobbins,' said Twerp.

'Stands ter reason, that old boggart can be very stubborn – he knows that from many moons past,' nodded Old Gordle.

Old Shylog was also enjoying his freedom. Not having to work for Morag was a real treat, one he could get used to very quickly. He and his tribe had worked their fingers to the bone for her and he didn't feel at all appreciated. So the approach of Siras was not well received.

'I wonder what he wants – as if I didn't know,' grunted Old Shylog.

'He looks as if he's on a mission if you want my opinion, Master,' said Fynngel knowingly.

'Well, I won't be asking for your opinion,' was Old Shylog's grumpy reply.

Siras entered the camp with a pounding heart, but after first praising Shylog for his efforts, he launched into his spiel. The mere mention of Lord Drago had him showing interest.

'That might throw a different light on matters,' he said.

S iras returned to the Realm of Shadows with the news that her trusted slaves were ready to work again.

'Pah! I wouldn't exactly call them trustworthy,' she snorted. 'And I've just found out that Cornelia Romanski has cast a forgetting spell on the mortals, and now they have no idea that they were in the castle or anything else for that matter. I can't have that,' she fumed. 'I need them to be jumping at their own shadows.'

'But a little reminder will jog their memories, surely?'

Morag looked sharply at her servant. Well, fancy that, he'd actually come up with a good suggestion. Not that she'd tell him, he might get too big for his boots and demand more from her.

'Go and inform my slaves that I shall expect them to be ready when I call.'

S iras returned to visit the boggarts only to be told that they had no idea where Old Mobbins had gone.

'But why didn't yous ask him?'

'It's not our place to ask questions of the Master,' said Twerp, and he'd noticed, with a smirk on his face.

'Nay, yer wouldn't of the Mistress, would yer?' said another.

'Awkward lot,' mumbled Siras, and he made his way to visit the goblins. He found them tucking into the spoils from their hunting trip.

Old Gordle saw Siras creeping into the camp looking decidedly nervous. To him, that only meant one thing, either work or trouble with a capital T. Siras explained that they were needed to visit the school and stir things up.

'Just as long as you understand, I don't want to be there long. Go tell the Mistress that,' he growled.

Siras breathed a sigh of relief. Now to visit Old Shylog, whom he knew would take a lot of convincing. Yes, he was definitely harder to persuade than the others, so was his tribe, come to think of it.

S iras found them busy collecting nuts and berries. He received such a menacing glare from Old Shylog, it made his toes curl. He stood fiddling with the wooden toggle on his jacket not uttering a sound.

'Well, you'd better spit it out,' growled the grob.

And Siras told his story. Old Shylog nodded his head every now and then and very quickly came to the conclusion that he could strike a better deal if he played his cards right.

'Okay, count us in, but as long as our reward will be more generous than was promised to us afore.'

'Indeed, Master Shylog, indeed.'

'What about the others? Are they to work as well?'

'Gordle and his lot were more than happy to work, but I couldn't ask Old Mobbins because he wasn't in his camp.'

'Oh?'

'Twerp tells me he's gone somewhere, but he couldn't tell me where.'

'Oh dear, you'd better not let the Mistress know.'

'I'll be on me way then,' Siras said, noticing the grins that passed between the grob. He had a sneaky suspicion that they were enjoying themselves immensely at his expense.

The Portal That Was

Chapter Forty-seven

'Good morning one and all, I'm Alf Sparky of Sparky's Electrics. Can I leave me van outside?'

'Certainly,' said Mr Barnaby.

'I'll just get on with the job then. It shouldn't take long.' And he went to fetch his tools.

'It's about time he showed up. I bet old Mrs Dingle will be – oh oh – here she comes now.'

The door burst open and in she strode.

'I just happened to notice that van parked outside. Having some electrical work done, are you?'

'Well actually, Mrs Dingle, we are having a television aerial installed.'

'What? I hope it won't be unsightly.'

'The electrician is putting it well away from your house.'

'I should think so too...' and then the penny dropped. 'A *television*, you say?'

Mr Barnaby nodded.

'Of course, we had already decided not purchase a television – far too common for someone of our standing in the community. We enjoy going to the theatre, you know.'

'We really don't have the time to go to the theatre.'

'I suppose the likes of you wouldn't appreciate the arts anyway. Well, I must go,' and she dashed out the door.

Mr Barnaby chuckled, knowing full well that Mr Dingle would be in for a right old nagging when he arrived home from the bank.

Two children came into the shop to buy an ice lolly followed close behind by Mrs Fairweather who commented that Mr Barnaby's ice lollies were very popular.

'I must admit, they do sell well, considering they came about quite by accident,' Mrs Barnaby replied.

'You know what they say, many a good thing happens that way. Look at that bloke who discovered penicillin, now what was his name?'

'Alexander Fleming, if my memory serves me well.'

'That's the bloke, I mean – he made his discovery accidentally, didn't he?'

'I'd hardly compare Jack's ice-lollies to the discovery of penicillin.'

'A discovery is a discovery in my book, Mrs Barnaby.'

Later that day, Mr Barnaby was busy camouflaging the television set by covering it with a tablecloth and stacking a couple of boxes on top. He couldn't wait to see the look on Hugh and Lucy's face when he unveiled his surprise. He had just finished his chore when Mrs Barnaby came into the room having just locked up for the night.

Over dinner, Hugh had the distinct feeling that his parents were up to something especially as they kept looking across at each other and smiling. And when Mrs Barnaby told them to hurry up and finish their food, he was even more suspicious, considering they'd had it drummed into them from an early age to eat slowly.

'I want you both to close your eyes and no peeking, Hugh,' Mr Barnaby warned him after Mrs Barnaby had cleared away the dishes.

With the removal of the boxes and a swish of material, Mr Barnaby unveiled his surprise.

'Now you can open your eyes.'

They didn't have a clue what to expect, but when their eyes spotted the television set they jumped up and down with a whoop of

delight. Hugh rushed over to inspect it and pushed the on/off button. With a click, the black and white picture burst onto the screen.

Hugh's eyes were fixed on the television. He'd never in his wildest dreams thought that it would be so great to have one. It was even better than reading books. The news was on and the newsreader had just announced that Stirling Moss had won the Grand Prix. 'And a special report has just come in that there have been many sightings of an unusual amount of shooting stars followed by strange flashes. Our reporter has witnessed this strange phenomenon himself.'

Hugh's heart flipped over as the face of the announcer suddenly changed to a face he didn't think he'd see again. Jeepers, wasn't that the squatter man? He rubbed his eyes and looked again, it wasn't.

'And that concludes our news report for this evening,' said the announcer.

'That's funny; we saw lots of shooting stars when we were coming home from Charlie's the other day.'

'It's probably the heatwave we've been having,' suggested Mrs Barnaby. 'Oh look, Dixon of Dock Green is coming on.'

Mr Barnaby shook his head – Margie always had a simple explanation for everything. But he wasn't so sure.

Outside the castle walls, the goblins and the grob were waiting in a clearing for the boggarts.

'I hope Mobbins hurries up,' grunted Old Shylog, 'I've got better things to do with me time.'

'Well, he ain't laid eyes on him fer a while,' said Old Gordle.

'Now you come to mention it, I haven't either.'

'That be very interesting, 'cos I hear tell that Old Mobbins is up to no good,' said Fynngel.

All eyes were on Fynngel.

'Why do yer say that?' Old Gordle growled, annoyed that a snooty grob had found out before him.

'Yeah, why did you?' hissed Old Shylog.

'It seems that he has gone on some mysterious journey,' Fynngel paused for effect, 'visitin'.'

'That's very odd, even for Old Mobbins.'

'I wonder who he's gone ter visit.'

'If I knew the answer to that, Gordle, I'd be telling you,' growled Old Shylog.

I n the boggart camp they were more than surprised to see Griswald and Wartun walking towards them.

'Where yer bin?'

'We got held up visitin' a forkyped called, Clara,' said Griswald.

'Yeah, we had a score to settle wiv her,' nodded Wartun. 'Did yer know she had the cheek to look at us as if she had a bad smell under her nose?'

'Fancy that,' sniffed a boggart, 'yer smell perfectly all right to me.'

'But who are yer talkin' about?'

'Yer know – one of the forkypeds we met on the track.'

'Bein' as we weren't wiv yer, how are we s'posed to know about that?' grunted Twerp.

'Yer've been missin' fer a while...I'd say yer've bin skivin' off somewhere,' added another.

'Go on, Griswald; tell 'em 'bout the forest,' urged Wartun, who didn't want to get into an argument with Drudgery, he could be a real piece o' work when he got going.

'We're waitin',' Drudgery sneered.

'Apart from bein' trapped by a banshee...or was it a ghoul?'

'Nah, it was definitely a banshee.'

'Seems to me it was just a rabbit,' snorted Drudgery.

'A rabbit ain't all black wiv fiery eyes,' snapped Griswald. And he launched into a long exaggerated story of how they outwitted the banshee.

Drudgery snorted, 'Yer not afraid of a banshee...are yer, Griswald?' He'd heard about the banshees. Proper nasty they were and they took no prisoners. No way in the world would he go up against one, or a ghoul come to that, not that he'd let on.

'Oh yeah, I'd like to see how yer'd get on,' Griswald snorted back.

'Tell 'em 'bout the forkyped, called Hugh,' urged Wartun again.

Griswald frowned ferociously. 'Why don't yer tell him yerself,' he snapped, 'bein' as yer the one who was scared of the banshee.'

'I don't see why...'

It was then that Griswald noticed who was missing.

'Where's Master Mobbins?'

'He's gone missin'.'

'I can see that,' he sighed impatiently, 'but where?'

Twerp shrugged, but told them that they might be moving someplace else. Griswald's eyes nearly popped out of their sockets.

'What will the Mistress say?' he gasped.

Twerp shrugged his shoulders again. 'I don't think she knows yet.'

'Wouldn't Siras have told her?'

'Nay, Griswald, he wouldn't want her to know about it.'

'After all, he's s'pose to be in charge of us, makin' sure we do her biddin'.'

'I see what yer be meanin', Siras is scared of the Mistress.'

'Yeah, he's probably every right to be,' thinking that he could be turned into a bat if she were to find out.

The boggarts turned their attention to the whereabouts of Old Mobbins. But the more they tried to fathom out where their master had gone, the more they kept talking in circles.

Within a cave by a roaring fire sat Black Annis and Old Mobbins.

'Well, Mobbins, I think it won't be long afore Morag will be planning her next move against the mortal.'

Old Mobbins bushy eyebrows burrowed into a frown – mortal? There's that strange word again. She must mean the forkyped; yes that's what she means.

'The mortal's magic is strong as well, so the trees have told me.'

'Yer trees have told yer well.'

'Yep, I think it would serve us well to be of help to him. It's about time Morag got her comeuppance if you ask me,' said Black Annis.

'I can't wait to tell me tribe.'

'Welcome to the world of true magic,' said the sorceress triumphantly. Yes, this old boggart and his tribe would fit into her plans

quite nicely. And the thought that she'd got one over on Morag was even better.

Old Mobbins beamed from ear to ear – how surprised his tribe were going to be when they found out that they were about to join forces with the famed Black Annis.

'So that's settled then, we'll help the forkyped when he has to go up against the likes of Mistress Morag again.'

Black Annis and Old Mobbins leant back against a rock and contemplated their plans.

Siras landed in the clearing expecting all the creatures to be there. Alas, there were only the goblins and the grobs. Siras felt a nagging suspicion in the pit of his stomach that Old Mobbins was still missing.

'Have yous managed to find Mobbins?'

'That's your job,' snapped Old Shylog. 'Anyways, why are we here?'

'Yeah, we've been hangin' around 'ere fer ages,' growled Old Gordle. 'Wot fer, that's wot I wanna know.'

'Mistress Morag wants yous to gather yer tribes together and meet me back here when the moon appears.'

'Can't do that,' grunted Old Gordle.

'Why's that?'

'I ain't got a tribe, I got a horde.'

'Yous know what I mean,' spat Siras who'd had just about enough of them. 'I'd best get back to the Mistress,' and with a final glare, he clicked his fingers and was gone.

'Wot's up wiv him?' sniffed Old Gordle. 'Anyways, he ain't goin' ter hang around here much longer. He don't like this place, it's creepy.'

'Seems very strange us having to meet here, very strange indeed,' nodded Old Shylog. 'I can't say as I like it either.'

About time you got back,' snapped Morag to Siras. 'Luckily, I've still got plenty of the mortals' shadow energy left,' she said giving the contents a stir. 'Yes, the spell will be ready by the time the owls appear and the moon has reached its peak. Excellent! If only I could get

hold of Marius's mistletoe that would help the spell along no end. Siras, go find that old wizard and bring him to me.'

Siras didn't have a clue where to find the herb master. He had heard that he'd left his rooms in the castle and had gone goodness knows where. Still, he couldn't have gone too far, he was very, very, old. Unfortunately for Siras, he had no idea who to ask or where to start looking. Maybe he could find some mistletoe and give it to the mistress. After all, one piece of mistletoe looked the same as the other, she'd never know.

From his hiding place the herb master grinned. His plotting was coming along very nicely and when he found the mandrake, there would be no stopping him. He clicked his fingers and landed in the middle of a fairy circle. He waved his hand and an oak tree appeared. Excellent!

Meanwhile, Siras took himself off to the woods and happened upon a fairy circle where he found an old oak tree. The trunk was covered in mistletoe. He grabbed a handful and returned to the sorceress.

'Where's Marius?' she demanded narrowing her eyes at him.

'He has got an unfortunate ailment, Mistress.'

'Oh? And what ailment is that?'

'He didn't say,' said Siras looking down at his feet. 'But he sent this to yous, made a song and dance of it so he did.'

'Very well, Siras. Now go to the clearing, the portal will be waiting.'

'But why use the portal, Mistress?'

'Because, you buffoon, I don't want to waste too much shadow energy sending the creatures through the veil. Now go while I prepare the last of my spell.'

Siras landed in the clearing where the goblins and the grob were gathered. And still no sign of the boggarts.

'Well, we can't hang around for the boggarts; the portal will be here soon. And afore yous ask why yous are to use it, it's not fer me to say.'

'Who's askin'?' grunted Old Gordle.

They waited and waited and waited, but no portal. They had no idea that the herb master was watching them. With a satisfied smile, he

disappeared in a puff of smoke. Finally, the goblins and the grobs gave up waiting and returned to their camps.

Meanwhile, Lord Drago had made another visit to Morag with the news that he'd found out that the boggarts had gone to work for another sorceress.

'Morgana hasn't been able to find out who the sorceress is yet. Hmm, you'll have to have more control over your slaves if you want to remain by my side.'

Morag was spitting fire by this time. 'I wouldn't mind betting that it is none other than, Morgana, who has bewitched them. She was always jealous of me.'

'If that is so, her magic must be very powerful to snatch your slaves from right under your nose,' he snorted.

To add insult to injury, he threw his head back and roared with laughter. And with a swish of his cloak and a final look of contempt, Lord Drago vanished on a lightning flash.

Morag was beside herself with rage, so much so, that she grabbed the lid off the cauldron and chucked it at the wall. The lid rebounded off the wall with such force that it caught the rim of the cauldron and it went crashing to the ground. The contents spewed everywhere and Morag watched in horror as the liquid went sliding and squirming its way across the floor making weird grunting noises as it disappeared down a hole.

'Oh no,' she wailed, 'I'll have to start all over again.'

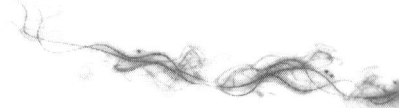

Surprising News

Chapter Forty-eight

Mrs Barnaby had just finished serving a customer when a tall well-dressed gentleman entered the shop and introduced himself as Mr Birdie. It must be the man Jack had met when they were taking refuge from the rain, she thought. Mrs Barnaby was more than surprised to see him, being as Mr Barnaby hadn't mentioned anything about it. With the intention of having it out with him later, she went to fetch Mr Barnaby leaving Mr Birdie to look around the shop. He was soon joined by Mrs Dingle who just about fell in the doorway in her hurry to see who this distinguished looking gentleman was. After all, it wasn't every day that someone so obviously well-to-do came into the newsagency.

'Good morning, lovely day,' said Mr Birdie as he turned around to see Mrs Dingle looking up at him.

Mrs Dingle puffed out her chest, touched her hair and fluttered her very short eyelashes up at him.

'Good day to you, my good man,' she smarmed. 'My name is Mrs Dingle, and I live in the rather grand house next door...You may have noticed it in passing?'

'I can't say that...'

'I only frequent this, this rather shabby establishment,' she paused looking down her nose at the shop, 'to buy my husband his daily newspaper, you understand.'

'Oh?'

'Moved to the neighbourhood, have you?'

'No I haven't er – Mrs Dingle, did you say?'

'Yes, Gertrude Dingle, but I don't think I caught your name, Mr?'

'Mr Birdie.'

'Are you visiting someone?'

'I am here on business.'

'Oh I see. You've come to buy the Financial Times I suppose. My husband...'

'Well, actually, I've come to discuss business with Mr Barnaby.'

Mrs Dingle all but had a heart attack, she was so shocked. Why in the world would such a distinguished gentleman want to do business with the likes of him?

'How interesting,' she croaked, 'and what…?'

It was then that the Barnabys came into the shop.

'Good morning, Fred,' Mr Barnaby smiled, shaking Mr Birdie's hand. 'I wasn't expecting you so soon. Would you like to come through to the living-room where we can talk, *in private*?'

Mrs Dingle stood with her mouth open, and to add insult to injury, Mr Barnaby turned and gave her a little wave as he went through the door. Ignoramus!

'Well I never did, as if I would listen to what they were talking about.' She opened the door and was about to storm out when she came face to face with Hugh.

'Hello Mrs Dingle, how are you?'

'How am I? I'll tell you how I am, I'm in a hurry,' she snapped.

Hugh was about to close the door when something made him look across the street. An old man was waiting at the bus stop. Blimey, wasn't he the old tramp? He went outside to have a closer look but the bus arrived and the man got on. However, a bus coming from the other direction pulled up at the bus stop. People piled on. The conductor called out, 'Move down the bus please.' There was nothing wrong with that, except that as the bus pulled away from the curb, it wasn't the bus conductor that pulled the bell, but a clown who gave Hugh a little wave.

Meanwhile, Mr Dingle had seen Mrs Dingle striding up the garden path, 'Oh drat, Gertrude's on her way home.'

He rushed to close the parlour door hoping that for once, she would leave him to study the minutes from a meeting he'd held at the bank – wishful thinking on his part. Mrs Dingle barged into the room and sat down in front of him, her eyes flashing with excitement.

'You'll never guess what I have to tell you, Cedric.'

He wasn't the slightest bit interested, 'What, dear?' he said his eyes focussed in front of him.

'A rather suave gentleman by the name of Mr Birdie came to visit Jack Barnaby, and what do you think for?'

'I suppose you're going to inform me,' he sighed, looking down at the mound of paperwork that was awaiting his attention.

'Some sort of business talk,' she said, incredulously. 'I ask you, and with Mr Barnaby of all people. Between you, me, and the gatepost, he's just our handwriting.'

'What on earth do you mean?' Why the wife insisted on using those ridiculous sayings his mother-in-law uses, he'd never know.

'Oh for goodness sake, Cedric, he's just our cup of tea.'

By that he assumed, she meant Mr Birdie would be just the sort of person they should mix with. He doubted it, knowing his wife's taste in people. Look at Mrs Dotty and her husband, Horace; she'd said the same about them. Not only would Horace Dotty bore the pants off anybody, he was always trying to flog him a set of Encyclopaedia Britannica of all things, and as for Mildred Dotty, well!

'I'm not quite sure why I would be in the slightest bit interested in who Mr Barnaby has been speaking to, Gertrude.'

'But…'

'Unless he chooses to use our bank of course, now that would be another kettle of fish.'

Mrs Dingle was already imagining the dinner parties that she would give for the distinguished Mr Birdie and his wife. And so, humming a happy tune, she walked out of the door closing it quietly behind her. Yes, life was about to become more in keeping with the

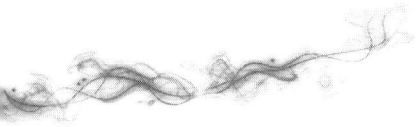

wife of a bank manager. She'd make sure that it does from now on. Should she go and make Cedric a nice cup of tea, or maybe even a cup of coffee? Why not, she might even let him have one of her chocolate biscuits.

Mr Dingle sat thinking about what his wife had told him – Mr Barnaby going into business with someone, that was a turn up for the books. What did Gertrude say his name was? Mr Birdie? Hmm, that name rings a bell. Of course! He owns that rather successful toy-making place in town. He'd been itching to get him to bring his custom to the bank for a long time. Well, well, well, fancy him knowing Jack Barnaby. Maybe he'll invite Jack to the golf club? It was about time he made the effort to get to know his neighbour properly and later, he'll invite Mr Birdie. Not that he'd got much time to visit the club, especially as Gertrude was always barging her way into the room with some nonsense or other breaking into his concentration. A lock on the parlour door might be a good idea. He was about to start on his paperwork, when something made him glance across the street at the empty flat. Did he see a movement behind the faded net curtains?

Ghosts And Things

Chapter Forty-nine

The following day, Mrs Barnaby had just turned the sign to OPEN when...'Morning, it's a lovely day. I'll have the usual if you please.'

'Good morning, Mrs Dingle how's the ghost?'

Mrs Dingle had just opened her mouth to speak when in walked Mrs Fairweather. 'Did I hear someone mention ghosts?' she asked.

'Mrs Dingle thought she might have one haunting her house, didn't you?'

'What? Oh, between you me, and the gatepost, I think it was just one of those strange phenomena that can happen from time to time, certainly not a ghost as such,' she scoffed.

'I wouldn't be so sure about that,' said Mrs Fairweather.

Mrs Dingle's eyebrows shot up at that. Trust Mrs Fairweather to butt her nose into where it didn't belong, why, she's almost as ignorant as Mr Barnaby if that was at all possible.

'How would you know anything about ghosts?'

'Well, when we went away...'

'I shouldn't think there would be any ghosts haunting Butlins Holiday Camp,' snorted Mrs Dingle.

Mrs Fairweather was taken aback for the minute. How did she know she'd been there? Probably eavesdropping, she thought, the nosey old so and so. I'll soon wipe that smug look off her face.

'It wasn't at Butlins, as a matter of fact, it was Wales.'

Mrs Dingle looked warily at Mrs Fairweather.

'Tell us what happened,' urged Mr Barnaby.

'Well, we were staying in a boarding house in a small fishing village called, Abberporth. My hubby was sitting up in bed reading a book while…'

'I don't really think I want to know about your personal life, Mrs Fairweather.'

'Do carry on with the story,' said Mr Barnaby giving his next-door neighbour a piercing look. Mrs Dingle pursed her lips.

Mrs Fairweather went on to tell them that her husband looked up from his book and saw a man dressed in old-fashioned clothes walk through the wall.

Mrs Dingle's jaw dropped. 'Well I never,' was all she could say.

Her jaw dropped even more when Mrs Fairweather told them that at breakfast the following morning they noticed an old photograph hanging on the wall.

'Guess who was in the photo?'

'We're waiting with bated breath,' sighed Mrs Dingle impatiently.

'Why, the man who walked through the wall, of course.'

Mrs Dingle stood very, very, still, her eyes darting wildly about the shop looking for...a ghost perhaps?

Mrs Fairweather leant closer. 'We asked the owner about the man in the photo and she told us he was her father.'

'Good grief,' said Mrs Barnaby.

'Apparently, the wall used to be a doorway to his room before they blocked it up.'

'There you are then, Mrs Dingle, you most probably do have a ghost,' said Mr Barnaby triumphantly.

'What rubbish,' she scoffed.

'I'd keep an open mind if I were you,' warned Mr Barnaby trying his hardest not to laugh.

Mrs Dingle chewed at her bottom lip.

'Well, I've chatted long enough,' said Mrs Fairweather. 'I'll have a Daily Mail.' And with a, 'See you later', she left the shop.

'I shan't let the likes of Mrs Fairweather worry me, Mrs Barnaby. It's too nice a day for that.'

'I must say, Mrs Dingle, you do look full of the joys of spring.'

'Everything is simply splendid,' was her gushing reply. 'Oh, and before I forget, I owe you a little something,' and she opened her purse.

Mrs Barnaby nearly dropped the money; she was so surprised – Mrs Dingle paying off her slate? However, Mr Barnaby had a strong feeling that she was up to something, especially as she was now giving him a broad smile, something she never did.

'Mr Barnaby, if I may be so bold, how are your business talks going with that fine looking gentleman, er... um – Mr Birdie isn't it?'

'Very good as a matter of fact,' Mr Barnaby replied; his radar really alert now.

'I just happened to mention your meeting to Mr Dingle, and he suggested out of the goodness of his heart, that if you should need his advice he'd be more than happy to help you.' She paused and inspected her fingernails. 'Then perhaps you might bring your business to his bank?'

'Our discussions are only in the infant stages at the moment, so you see…'

In walked Maud Underwood. Mrs Dingle grunted at the intrusion and strutted out the door.

'Morning – lovely day isn't it? How about comin' over fer a drink this evening?'

'Why thank you, Maud that will be very…'

Mrs Barnaby was interrupted by the sound of Mr Drummond's car as it screeched to a halt outside the shop. He got out, patted the bonnet lovingly, tucked in his cravat and straightened his jacket. He glanced over at Mrs Dingle who had just reached her front gate. 'Morning Mrs Dingle,' he called. Mrs Dingle turned around and gave him a curt nod. He sauntered to the shop and entered.

'Morning, everyone, just came in to buy my usual, and a Woman's Own for the wife. By the way, I was passing by that old empty cottage opposite the Heath.'

'You mean the one next to the shop that's boarded up?'

'That's right, there was a foreign looking chap walking around it with a folder tucked under his arm.'

'Perhaps it's up for sale.'

'About time if you ask me.'

Across the street, a wizened hand closed the net curtain. The shadow chuckled, 'Yes, it is about time.'

A clown stood flicking a coin into the air. He caught it, flicked it over and dropped it into his pocket. A hearse pulled up beside him and he climbed aboard. With a flick of the reigns and a whinny of the horses, the hearse vanished into the shadows.

An old man looked out of a broken window from the ruins of Mendip Abbey – a carrier bag at his feet. In his right hand he held a single flat stone. He studied the marking on the ancient rune and smiled. A white falcon appeared out of a haunting mist and landed on his outstretched arm. 'This is only the beginning, Toro,' he said.